This is a work of fiction. All of the characters, organizations, and events portrayed in this novel are products of the author's imagination or are used fictitiously.

Published by: Arbor Bay Publishing LLC
Cover design and logo by: Angela Fristoe
Editing by: Frankie Sutton

ISBN: 978-0-9984782-4-1

Debi,
Enjoy! Love you.
Lots of love,

JUST AROUND THE CURVE

BY

CHRISTINA LUND

ONE

"It's perfect!" I took my chubby finger and ran it along the lace trim above my bust. Turning toward the full-length mirror, I smiled at my reflection.

"No, this is not the one," my mother calmly said as she glided over to me, as if she was back in her glory days on the beauty pageant circuit. She extended her long, thin, perfect finger and pointed at my arms.

"Amy, dear, I really think you should get a dress that will cover your arms." I kept my gaze steady in the mirror and turned sideways so I could get a better look at my arms from another angle. I had worked hard the last few months dieting and exercising just so I could squeeze into a size sixteen dress. My mother had no idea how much work it took to lose the agonizing and miniscule few pounds that I had lost. She had always been no larger than a size six, and that was only when she was pregnant with me.

"Do you really think my arms look so chubby that I need sleeves?" I asked, as I watched her pressing her perfectly lined burgundy lips together, simultaneously raising her eyebrows.

"Well, dear, I just think a dress with sleeves would be more flattering. After all, it is your big day. You want to look your best… right?" My mother, Cathy, gave me a halfcocked smile and softened her facial expression, pretending to be more pleasant, mainly because she knew I would give in and get her ideal dress. She could smile, because we both knew I would do exactly that, because that's how our relationship was.

My mother was overbearing, controlling, and opinionated about everything, but all those qualities in particular stretched mainly to me and my life, or more accurately, my appearance. She always let me know everything I had done wrong, which according to her was quite a lot. When my father asked for a divorce and walked out almost eight years ago, I didn't need to ask him why. In general, most people even regardless of age, don't have the ability to comprehend why one parent would leave another, but I did. I was even envious of my father, secretly wishing he had taken me with him. I longed to be in a loving environment. However, taking me with him hardly seemed appropriate, considering he wanted his freedom from my mother, and his children were grown. At that time, I was a grown woman of twenty-one. Not much had changed for me in those eight years since he left. I was still living at home, even at twenty-nine years old.

I sadly took one last look at my beautiful cream-colored dress. The dress had a straight cut across the top and a gorgeous lace accent that stuck out, giving it a touch of sophistication. Even though I didn't look directly at her reflection in the mirror, I could hear my mother tapping her high-heeled shoe as she waited for a reply. I sighed for a moment before I spoke, giving myself a couple of seconds to mourn the loss of what I would always know as 'the one' dress that got away.

"Okay, could you have a few others brought out so we can try them on?" I emphasized the word 'we' since I was sure I wasn't the one picking out my dream dress. My mother gave a smug little chuckle and turned her back to walk around the corner, speaking loudly as she did so.

"Already a step ahead of you. I have a few right here that I think will be much better." The frustration was almost unbearable, and for some reason, all I could think of was cheesecake, lemon cheesecake to be exact. Lately, I had been thinking about lemon cheesecake so much in fact, that I even suggested it as an alternative to the traditional wedding cake. Of course, that suggestion was promptly laughed at by my mother. Still, that stupid cheesecake was on my mind. I was certain this was almost entirely due to the fact that I had not had a single grain of refined sugar in the last two weeks, which helped me shave off a whopping four pounds.

I took another glance at my reflection in the full length mirror and thought about how much cheesecake I would have to give up to be in the same playing field as my perfectly sized mother. A hundred? A thousand? I knew it wouldn't matter, because whatever name it was called, I had always been some form of it: chubby, fat, curvy or plump. If I had a dollar for every time that I heard, 'Oh, she's got such a pretty face and beautiful hair, if only she would lose some weight,' I could have packed up and left my controlling mother years ago. The only other saying that I heard people say to my mother on countless occasions that were more hurtful than the first one was, 'Oh, so she's your daughter?' As if it wasn't obvious enough that my mother was beautiful and still had a perfect swimsuit model's body, even at fifty-three, while I didn't even have that figure at the age of twenty-nine. I looked at my face and smiled. I did kind of have a pretty face with creamy skin, deep green eyes underneath full lashes and thick brunette hair that sometimes had a nice sheen to it.

Once, years ago, I over-stepped my place and mentioned to my mother that I might look decent enough to be a plus sized model. My mother wasted no time in squashing that idea by quickly pointing out that I was both too short, and even larger than all plus size models. It was true that I was bigger than most of those women, but even though I was portly, I still had the definition of a waist and curves in all the right places. Granted those curves wiggled, but I was still nowhere near having to be forklifted out of our house.

Sometimes, I wished I had been more like my brother, Mike. Mike was just like my mom's side of the family. All of them were super athletes: mountain climbers, bungie jumpers, hikers, surfers, and all that crazy outdoors stuff that I thought every family did together. Until I got to Jr. High, I had no idea that most families who don't live in Colorado sit around, play monopoly or cards, and watch their favorite TV shows together. Most of the time, I imagined them cooking big elaborate, high calorie Thanksgiving dinners. That's when I woke up and asked, "Why didn't the big guy upstairs place me with one of those families?" But no, I ended up with a mother that was a constant reminder that I was less than her idea of the perfect woman.

However, I was lucky to have a dad that I loved, who was always sweet and nice. When I was younger, our close relationship often caused my mother to accuse him of coddling me. My dad had been adopted, so I think he understood how sensitive I was about my weight growing up. He was just too passive when it came to the demands of my mother.

My mother was so controlling she would randomly raid the house and toss anything with sugar, carbs, fat, or taste in general, out to the trash. In those circumstances, I would go to my best friend Betsy's house.

Betsy looked just like you would imagine she would with a name like Betsy. Betsy had light strawberry blonde hair, blue eyes, freckles, and a very tiny frame, which landed her the nickname in grade school of Itsy Betsy that stuck all the way through high school. Betsy and I had been best friends since the playground days. I have no recollection of how we first met, or the spark that started it all, but according to her, it had something to do with sharing purple glitter and red ribbons during art time. I always assumed her recollection of the story to be the truth because Betsy had never seemed prone to lying or fabricating stories. However, when you thought about it, Betsy wasn't prone to much that used any sort of creativity or enthusiasm really. Betsy was predominantly quiet and reserved, and most people stopped talking to her after a few minutes because they found her dull and boring. However, I had always liked Betsy because she also had a nice, funny side to her that people only saw after she felt comfortable around them. We had always seemed a good balance for each other, even if we had completely different tastes in everything: men, clothes, music. Our balance revolved around the fact that we enjoyed each other's company.

When I started dating my fiancée, Chad Wheeler, I still spent a great deal of time with Betsy. It wasn't that I didn't like to spend time with Chad; it was just that sometimes Betsy was the only one who understood how difficult my mother made things for me. My mother had been a little nicer to me in the beginning of my relationship with him. I think mainly because she didn't believe I was ever going to get a real, serious boyfriend. However, my mother's generosity faded after she spent some time with him. Chad wasn't ugly by society's standards, but he definitely wasn't up to par with my mother's expectations. She had expected someone more like my father, who was slightly stalky, but ruggedly handsome. Chad had straight blond hair that always looked like he just got out of bed, even after he brushed it. He had ears that stuck out a tad and dark freckles on his face, but more than anything, my mother hated the fact that he wore t-shirts that were too big and shoes that he didn't tie. In other words, he didn't put any consideration into his appearance. Once I became Mrs. Chad Wheeler, I already knew what poor Chad was going to get from my mother each Christmas for the rest of his life: clothes, clothes, and more clothes.

"Sorry, dear, I had to find this lovely sales girl to help me carry a few of the dresses." My mother smiled at the young pretty girl and I felt sick to my stomach. I loathed my mother being so nice to everyone except me. I watched with a sad heart as they worked together to hang the dresses on the rack along the wall. Per the request of my mother, we had been given our own private fitting room, completely furnished with chairs and tables. I looked around and wondered how many soon-to-be brides stood in this room, their hearts racing with excitement as they put on the dress they had dreamed of and thought about the man they loved. I loved Chad and was happy to be marrying him, but in truth, what I loved most was that I would finally be moving out of my mother's house. In fact, I was so happy about that, I had started packing the day after he proposed to me. The proposal wasn't romantic in the slightest. After I thought for a moment that I might possibly be pregnant, he just shrugged his shoulders and said, "Well, we better get married then. Whatcha say?" I stared at him in confusion and just mumbled, "Sure," and the rest was history.

Chad's father owned a small trucking company that did fairly well financially. His father was also proud of the reputation he had for being honorable. Since Chad was planning on one day taking over the company from his 'honorable' father, he couldn't just knock a girl up without marrying her. Overall, I looked forward to being part of Chad's family. His father was a man's-man, but was also respectful toward women, and he constantly flattered me with compliments. Chad's mother had always been nice to me; possibly, because she had hopes someone would finally clean her disheveled son up. At times, Chad seemed so different from his parents. For starters, he would act more arrogantly than I would have liked, but I found I often brushed that off. Because his family was so nice, I found that I gave him the benefit of the doubt.

"Betsy!" I gave my first sincere smile of the day. I stepped down off the platform and walked over to her to give her a hug before my mother could beat me to it.

"Hi. How is the dress shopping so far?" She seemed quieter than usual as I gave her tiny little frame a quick hug. I let go, and my mother stepped in front of me, hugging in such a tight squeeze that she seemed to be taking in the essence of the daughter she never had. Before I could reply, my mother put her arms around Betsy's shoulders and started talking as if they were best friends.

"We haven't had any success yet, but I have a feeling that's going to change after she tries some new ones on." Betsy gave a sly smile to my mother and looked at the dress I was still in, my ideal dress.

"You don't like that one, Amy? It looks like your style." When she spoke, her voice was monotone and dim, and her mind appeared to be somewhere else. I flashed her a look that begged her not to talk about the dress I was wearing. I didn't want to hear any more remarks about it from my mother. Betsy gave a slight nod in compliance and then stared off into space for a moment.

My mother wasted no time now that Betsy was there. As she shuffled through the dresses on the rack, her shoulders slumped down. Then she spun around with a dress in her hand, a long sigh of frustration coming out of her mouth, which was the typical scene whenever she came across something that wasn't in my size. I had come to learn her sighs were more out of frustration toward me (for not being the right size) than for a particular situation.

"Betsy, honey, would you please set your things down over there on the table and come with me. I pre-ordered a dress in Amy's size from another store to be shipped here for today and it's just not here. I need you to come with me to the front so we can have them find that dress." My mother plucked out another dress and hung it on the hook next to me as she gave me instructions.

"Amy, try this one on for now, but I know the other one will be much better. I'm going to borrow your maid of honor for a moment while you change." She smiled as she practically dragged Betsy out of the room. As I was left there alone, a strange sensation swept over me at that moment, and for some odd reason I felt like crying. A cloud of depression soon followed, for whatever reason I didn't understand.

I took a deep breath, and then I struggled for a few minutes to get out of my dress since everyone had left me to fend for myself. I stared at the next dress as even more feelings of hopelessness came over me.

I heard my phone on the table beep, indicating I had a new text message. I rushed over to erase it before my mother came back in the room and got nosey, like she frequently was. I reached for my phone when I realized it was Betsy's phone and not mine that was beeping. As I began to turn, something stopped me… no. Some words stopped me. I stood, frozen for only a second, but it felt more like an eternity. I reached down and picked up Betsy's phone so I could read the complete text. Every word that glared back at me from her screen felt like a knife stabbing me in the stomach.

Chad:

Thanks for the afternoon Babe.

Can't wait to have you again.

Amy will be busy tomorrow so swing by

For the first time in two weeks, I wasn't thinking about lemon cheesecake or finding the perfect dress. I was too busy thinking about my best friend having sex with my fiancé.

TWO

"**Amy**? I'm sorry. I'm so, so, so sorry. Please call me back so we can talk? I'm sorry." I deleted the message from my cell phone after hearing Betsy's voice. I took in sharp breaths as I covered my face and began to sob again. I hadn't taken any calls from her or Chad for almost a week—not that Chad had been calling me every day. I was willing to gamble that he didn't even want to call or apologize at all, but only called a few times after he was urged to by his father.

I took the pillow off my face, sat up in my bed, and grabbed a tissue off my nightstand, wiping my eyes furiously. I heard a light tap on my bedroom door before it slowly opened.

"Hey, Sis, how ya doing?" Mike peered around the corner and then walked cautiously through the room as if my floor was covered in land mines, afraid I might explode from anger at any moment. This was the first time in almost a week I had unlocked my door and he could actually make his way into my room. The first two days I cried nonstop until I fell asleep.

"I've had better days. Don't worry; I won't go crazy on you." He nodded his head in relief and sat down in the chair next to my bed, immediately leaning forward with his arms across his knees like a seasoned basketball player. He looked at me and I could tell he was going to try and give me a pep talk. Even though he was my younger brother by two years, he always had the idea stuck in his head that he was the oldest of us two.

"I can't believe she did that, but you know what? Now we know what she's really like and him too." Even though I was jealous of my brother on frequent occasions, I still loved him and appreciated his attempt to help. I did however hate the way both he and my mom used the word 'we' all the time. My father never did that when I told him things. It was never what 'we' had to do in order to fix something, or what 'we' thought about something.

"I suppose that is one way to look at it." I wasn't really convincing with my response but he still took it and nodded some more. Then he looked at the door for a second before he lowered his voice and asked me a question.

"Did you want to punch her in the face? What did you do when you found out? Mom told me you didn't say a word to her and she didn't find out what was going on 'til she got home." Mike always referred to our mother affectionately as Mom, but I could very seldom bring myself to do that. Mainly because when I looked at her most of the time, I wasn't overcome with a feeling of loving attachment toward her, like a mom or mommy.

"It was strange, kinda like a blur. I was in my undies and just standing there, feeling sick. Next thing I knew, I had my clothes back on and then they both walked in the room. I was so shocked that I just pushed the phone in Betsy's hand and gave her a nasty look. I don't think I spoke, but I can't really remember." I tried to disconnect myself from my words or the fresh memory, but my success was short lived when my eyes slowly started to fill with tears. Mike gave me a sympathetic look as I reached for another tissue. I took a deep breath and continued.

"Then I just walked out of the room, got in the car and drove home. And yeah, for a moment, I did have the thought of punching her in the face." Mike looked somewhat surprised, but also satisfied at my last statement. I wasn't entirely what you would call a pushover, but I was known for being a relatively nice person, which was often confused as the same thing. Nevertheless, in my opinion, sometimes there are certain incidents that push even the nicest people to the edge.

"Wow, that's something, but I can't blame you. Have you told Dad yet?" In our house, how much I loved and missed my dad was no secret. Even if I was approaching the age of thirty, I still felt like a teenager who needed her dad. This was probably mainly perpetuated by the fact that I had such little admiration for my mother.

"No, I don't have the heart to tell him yet." This was true since I knew it would make him incredibly sad that I had been betrayed in such a way. I was going to wait a few days and break the news to him then, before my mom had the chance to open her big mouth and turn the whole fiasco into something that had been done to her.

"You want me to go rough him up a little bit?" This gesture made me the happiest I had been in days. I smiled at him and pretended to give serious thought to his proposal for a moment before responding.

"Thanks, but if anyone's gonna do some roughing up around here, I think it's gonna be me." We both broke out in a soft chuckle before he shook his head in amusement right before he stood up and walked towards my bedroom door.

He glanced back at me with his hand on the doorknob and asked, "What are you going to do now, Sis?" I wiped my eyes with a fresh tissue and cleared my throat before I answered without hesitation.

"I'm gonna eat lemon cheesecake." Then we smiled at each other and my brother walked out of the room and closed the door.

My whole body felt weak and I trembled, which astonished me by the amount of energy it took to be heartbroken. I pushed the grocery cart while leaning on the handle bar to help support my weak legs that were the imitation of two heavy logs. I gave up my cart support and walked over to pick up three lemons for the homemade cheesecake I was so desperately craving. My mother had been none too thrilled when I announced I was going to go to the grocery store to buy supplies for a bake-a-thon, but for one of the first times ever, she kept her mouth shut and just looked at me when I walked out of the house.

The constant faint hum of the overhead white halogen lights made me feel even more depressed, if that was even humanly possible.

"Amy?" I immediately recognized the snotty shrill voice and closed my eyes before turning around, taking every second possible before looking her in the eyes.

"Kara? Oh, hi. How are you?" I casually asked. I was more than thankful that I had taken a shower and put on fresh clothes before leaving the house, not that it helped my disheveled look and puffy eyes that much. Even though I didn't live in a typical small town, I only ever seemed to run into anyone from the past when I looked my worst, which was often. Why couldn't I for just once in my life run into someone when I looked fabulous?

"I'm great. How are *you* doing?" I could immediately tell by the feigned sympathetic look in her eyes that she had already heard the news.

Back in middle and high school, Kara was the envy of every girl. She had fire red hair, perfect almost woman-like figure and a model's face. Kara was both popular and infamous at the same time. She was popular because she was captain four years running on the cheerleading team and every girl died to be like her. She was infamous because she had a sadistic, ruthless sense of humor, with a mean soul to match. She lived in the back part of the same neighborhood as Betsy and me growing up, so we had the most unfortunate pleasure to get stuck on the same bus as Kara all through middle and high school. I had received my fair share of teasing both on the bus and in the school: fatso, Jell-O roll, plump a dump. I would have my moments of depression, but I always had Betsy to lean on.

Maybe it was the fact that Betsy and I always sat next to each other and did our own thing that had kept Kara out of our hair for the beginning of our bus riding experience. Of course, it could have been because Kara always sat in the last seat of the bus, because where you sat on the bus somehow signaled your social status in school, most popular in back, least popular in front.

Without hesitation, I could recall the exact situation that started the nightmare with Kara. While I was randomly, and a tad less then severely harassed, the same could not be said for poor Jake. Jake was the scrawniest pre-teen anyone ever saw. I wasn't sure if it was because of the massive Coke bottle glasses he wore, or if it was his almost seemingly malnourished body that magnified them. Either way, he was destined for torment from the popular kids.

It was the beginning of our freshman year of high school and within a month, Kara had become the most popular girl in high school, in part by hooking up with a senior. During that time, Betsy and I sat in our usual place, halfway between the back and the front.

On the day in my memory, we had a substitute driver and instead of picking Jake up on the way to our neighborhood, the bus stopped after we had already loaded, meaning Jake had no choice but give up his seat of seclusion in the front to one closer to the back.

Jake lived in a small, one-bedroom house two miles outside of our neighborhood and it was obvious his family struggled financially. He didn't get the latest shoes at the beginning of each year and he often wore the same shirt two days in a row. Nevertheless, he had always seemed like a genuinely nice boy with a sweet spirt. Kara never saw anything like that in anyone. She only relented after she drew emotional blood. On that day in particular, Kara quickly seized the opportunity to pounce mercilessly on Jake and rip him apart.

"Where did you get those shoes? Did you take them off a corpse? You smell like all your clothes came off a corpse too!" Her words jabbed at him as her high pitch giggle quickly followed. Her fire red hair bounced up and down with the bus. Jake had just sat there in his seat with his bottom lip starting to quiver, keeping his eyes fixed on the floor. I remember looking over at Betsy and she just gave me those pleading eyes to ignore it as if saying with her face, "We'll be at school in a few minutes, so let it go."

Then Kara really drove the knife into him.

"I bet your dad left you because you're so ugly. If I were your dad, I'd have left you too! You're so ugly and scrawny the zoo thought you got out of your cage." Her taunting was particularly hurtful because the rumor was that Jake's dad had recently walked out on him and his mom, and judging by the crushed look on his face, it was easy to guess that the rumor was accurate.

It was those remarks that flew from her lips, mixed with her screech of delight, which was quickly matched by her groupies that caused a bubbling of anger in me. In a split second, something came over me, as I stood up, spun around while gripping my hands tightly on the back of the vinyl seat as I loudly proclaimed,

"Oh yeah? Well at least he's not a red haired, senior-screwing whore!"

In that moment, I think I literally saw Kara become incarnated with Satan. Her eyes narrowed and locked onto me with a reverent venom that was incapable of humanity. She pressed her lips together so tightly I almost missed the evil hiss that slithered through them. She raised one eyebrow and then pointed her long, red polished nail toward me before she hissed her response.

"Whore? I guess better a whore than porky pig. At least guys *want* to have sex with me. Who would want to touch your fat tub of lard?" My stomach dropped when the words came out of her mouth. I had broken the one cardinal rule of our high school, and that was never, ever, cross Kara. After that day, I received almost two long years of tortuous bus rides until the end of our sophomore year, when Kara finally started getting rides from the next set of seniors.

That day Jake stopped me while we were getting off the bus. He stood there for a moment and looked at me through his thick glasses that magnified his eyes, making him look like a bug. His eyes were softly glistening with what looked like the fading of started tears. Then he quietly gave me a shy look of thanks. Back then, staring at that scrawny teen, all I could think was how his thin legs and arms were like flesh colored spaghetti noodles. I knew very little about Jake, except for the fact that he was a nice kid that couldn't help the fact that he was skin and bones, or that his dad left him.

A few times after that day, I would see him in the hall and he would give me a shy, awkward smile before nervously looking down at the ground. I had never blamed him for the hell Kara put me through. I considered what she said to him far more painful than whatever she could and did call me. Fortunately, for his high school life, Jake moved two months after that bus ride to go live with his grandparents on the other side of town.

"Um, helloooo?" Kara gave me an inquisitive look and snapped her head to one side. I guess you could take the slutty cheerleader out of high school, but you couldn't take the slutty cheerleader out of the girl. I looked down at the lemons in my hand and cracked a smile as I visualized tossing one in her face.

Six years ago, Betsy and I ran into Kara at a bar one night, and she had attempted at that time to apologize for how she had acted way back in school. We had walked into the bathroom to find her hunched over a sink with mascara smudged under her eyes, intoxicated.

"Hey, sorry for being all mean joking and stuff." She had huffed at me before she gave me a drunken smile and continued, "I was just foolish back then… Truce?" I had shrugged my shoulders and mumbled, "Sure." Then she stumbled out of the bathroom. To be honest, I didn't think about Kara, or her life or what she had said to me; well, not often anyway. It only really came back to my memory at times like this, when she was standing in front of me; looking perfect and well dressed, while I stood sleep deprived, heartbroken, and in my oversized velour exercise outfit that I usually wore to lounge around in the house.

"Sorry, I'm just a little out of it today. Things are fine," I quickly muttered as Kara looked at me and did her famous 'one eyebrow raise' to my response. I was mad that the news had even reached Kara. I was even angrier over the fact that she was pretending to be sympathetic so I would confide in her, dishing all my personal gossip to her (as if *that* would ever happen). She crossed her arms and tapped her toes against the shiny concrete floor, making it clear she expected a response. All I could think was how I wanted to call Betsy to tell her about this encounter with the evil Kara. However, the reality of the situation meant that would never be an option for me again. The realization of this fueled my fire even more. *I'm almost thirty! I'm too old for her stupid games.* I spun around and tossed my lemons into my cart as I used my voluptuous weight to maneuver the cart around her.

"Whore," I breathed as I walked past her, leaving her standing with her mouth wide open in disbelief. I was astonished how that single, tiny act of expression made me smile.

I quickly checked out and headed home. I knew I had to do something, anything. I could only imagine if Kara had already heard about what had happened, then most likely even skinny, noodle armed Jake, wherever he was, had heard.

THREE

My mother hunched over the bed of flowers that created a circle around the tree in our front lawn. She looked picturesque with her large brim hat, pale pink gloves, and matching apron that wrapped around her perfect figure. Of course, the picture was completed with white pearls draping around her neck. It would have been a lovely magazine picture for anyone else but me to view. I knew the hypocrisy behind the whole facade. My mother hated to garden. In general, she hated to do any form of physical labor, large or small, and most of all, she loathed anything that got her remotely dirty. I seemed to be the only one that ever caught her split second snarls at the ground as she pulled a weed or the flutter she made with her nostrils as they raised up and down with disgust, resembling a facial tick. Nevertheless, ever since my dad left, she was out there every year planting new flowers and wearing her beautiful apron and hat. As much as my mother hated what she was doing, she adored the image it gave off to the neighbors and people driving by. She loved the attention and praise she got; it was all about the appearance she could create.

"Oh good, come over here for a moment, Amy dear." My mother looked up at me and squinted, even though the brim of her hat cast a shade on her whole face. I stepped off the porch and slowly walked over to my mother, taking in the cool breeze and bright sun. With the exception of running to the grocery store, I had not stepped out onto the lawn in over a week. I had been a virtual hermit crab. My mother turned her attention back to her little flowerbed as she proceeded to talk in a calm, factual tone.

"I got a call this morning from the caterer and the florist. I didn't want to tell them anything because I didn't want to try to reserve them again if the wedding is still on." I crossed my arms and just stared down at her while she focused on her flowers. I took a moment to answer. When I spoke, I couldn't contain my bitterness.

"Um, why would you think the wedding is still on? Don't you know what he did? What Betsy did?" I foolishly thought for a moment that she must, for the first time in her life, be out of the loop and unaware of what had actually happened to me. No real loving mother would even suggest that *her* daughter marry a man who did such a thing. To my horror, my wide stretch of hopeful assumptions were wrong.

"Yes, I know what happened between him and Betsy." She looked up at me and tried to muster a sympathetic but mentoring voice.

"But sometimes people do make mistakes, and you are almost thirty, dear. Besides, I'm sure he feels so bad about it. He will probably spend the rest of his life making it up to you. Think how great *that* will be." She gave me a little smile and I gasped. I felt my eyebrows push together with a strength that could be felt all the way to the back of my neck. I put my hands on my hips, and for some reason, that I will never know why, I spoke in a Brooklyn accent.

"Are you freak'n kidding me?" My mother looked surprised by my response, but she continued speaking in a tone of fake concern.

"You don't have to be so crude, Amy. I'm just trying to think of you. If you don't think you can marry him, that's fine. So we will use this as motivation. We have been doing so good with our diet and exercise that we need to keep going." I couldn't believe the words that poured out of her mouth. It was as if I was another form of a flowerbed to her. She loathed all the work it took to prime and primp me, but the possibility to have a skinnier, perfect daughter to help her facade was what kept her working on me.

"Screw the diet! I'm going to eat cheesecake every freak'n day!" My mother clutched her chest and opened her mouth. Her reaction was exactly what I imagined, as if I trampled on her imaginary hopeful garden of a daughter. She stood and brushed off her apron that was already clean. She looked at me with pleading eyes that hid a little spark of insanity behind them.

"Please don't say that, Amy. You've been doing so well lately. We just have to keep at it." I could read into that tiny spark of insanity and I knew the next stage would be a random raiding of the house where all things delicious and edible were banned. I stared at her, my eyebrows still clinched tight and unmoving. I felt a huge wave of depression. I was a grown adult woman, but felt exactly like I did as a child. *Why did I let her have so much control? Why can't I just break free?*

I resented the fact that I had not been smarter, that I had not worked hard enough to break out on my own. It was as if my mother was always one little step ahead of me. She knew the little things that would keep me dependent on her and under her control. She was the one that helped me get the job as a secretary. Even though my boss was wonderful and I loved working at the real estate office, the pay wasn't that great and it became clear after six years, there was not going to be any type of advancement within the office other than if I wanted to become an actual realtor, which I did not. My mother was also the one that gladly co-signed several years ago when I leased my car, even though I was unsure about the monthly payments. Then when my grandmother became ill five years ago, I willingly helped out financially, all the way until her death.

What I couldn't blame my mother for was what I had done with the chunk of money I had saved. I had saved and saved for years to get out from my mother, but then I gladly and naively gave it to Chad as a down payment for our future house. I also paid for a non-refundable honeymoon package to Italy as a surprise for him.

"We need to keep at what? Why can't you just—" I was cut short when a piercing blade of sunlight bounced off Chad's car and hit me square in the eyes as he pulled up in front of the house. My mother glanced over her shoulder at his car and then glanced back at me with a satisfied look on her face. I could read in her expression that she believed Chad had come to apologize, and she was convinced I would run straight into his arms, but I had bad news for her.

"I'll leave you two alone so you can talk. Let me know what to tell the caterer?" I wasn't sure why she even cared so much about the caterer or the florist since Chad's family had essentially offered to pay for the entire wedding.

Just as I heard my mother close the front door, Chad moseyed his way up the driveway until he was less than five feet from me. His face was expressionless and he had his hands shoved deep in his pockets. I looked at his baggy shirt and his large sneakers. The left shoe was untied, as usual. He squeezed his lips together at first and then bit down on his bottom lip, as he always did when he was nervous. That single action released the pressure in my eyebrows and my heart was reduced to sadness while I felt tears forming and my throat tightened as it choked back sobs.

"So, I've called a couple of times to say I'm sorry and see what the deal is." His lack of emotion was a little more than troubling. I studied his face for something to hint at desperation or even true remorse.

"What do you mean, 'the deal'?" He finally looked up at me before coolly replying to my question.

"I mean, do you still want to get married or what? I already left you a message saying I'm sorry about Betsy so I'm not going to say it again." I couldn't control myself, and once again, my anger channeled a Brooklyn accent, which was extremely odd since I had never even been to Brooklyn.

"What? It's like you don't even feel sorry for what you did!" I could see that he tried to contain an eye roll, which sent a shockwave of devastation through my veins. I clinched my teeth hard to keep myself from giving him the satisfaction of seeing me cry.

"I already said on your voice mail that I was sorry and I felt bad, so stop trying to make me feel bad…" He had been too late on his slip as it hung out in the open.

"I don't expect you to feel bad… you prick! It would take an actual soul to feel something and you lack one of those." He let out a raspy arrogant sigh of annoyance, as if it was too much effort or trouble to even drive over to my house and talk to my face. I pushed more questions on him, channeling my anger to prevent any tears from coming out.

"Betsy? Really? Do you love Betsy or did you just pick the one person that would hurt me the most?" I could feel the heat radiate off my face and my heart pounded with such force I thought the adrenaline would give me the ability to pick up his car and toss it on him.

"I don't know. I care about Betsy but I don't know if it's love. She's just nice to spend time with and it just started happening one night by mistake." I could feel my heart stop in mid-beat as I was taken back in complete surprise by his statement. I had not even imagined in all my horror that it had been an ongoing act of betrayal behind my back. Nevertheless, that's what I immediately gathered by his choice of the word 'happening'. My mind frantically searched through my memory for some tiny, fraction of a clue I had missed. None could be found. Sure, there were the occasional times Betsy had acted slightly more quiet than usual, but nothing that screamed, "Hey I'm sleeping with your man."

He looked annoyed as he stood there waiting for a response. Then he spoke again to get some kind of answer and to snap me out of my shock.

"I'm asking about the wedding because of the baby. What about the baby?"

I threw my arms up in the air and couldn't contain my massive eye roll as I exclaimed, "I *already* told you! I'm not pregnant… It was a false alarm!"

Chad looked puzzled. He scratched his head like a monkey. Then he asked confused,

"But your mom said…" I cut him off mid-sentence because I couldn't care less what my mother had told him. I was bothered mainly by the fact that he believed whatever my mother had said over the truth that I presented him with.

"There's no freak'n baby!" I was almost yelling at this point. My heart ached when I saw the utter look of relief on his face. The muscles in my face relaxed for a split second and a single tear came to my eye. His shoulders dropped and his body had become obviously at ease and relaxed now that he wasn't faced with pending baby doom, now that he had been released from this horrific obligation.

"Well, it's going to take me a little while to get your money back to you from the down payment. I hope everything works out for you." The words just fell out of his mouth with no consideration toward me in the slightest. I was hit with a massive feeling of foolishness for being so blinded and ignorant all those years, ignoring his pure, spoiled arrogance.

"I hope you and Betsy are happy with your dull stupid lives and your bratty freckled faced kids!" Those words and the image they created of Betsy and Chad together was the hardest to take. I knew I would eventually pull myself together after Chad, but Betsy's betrayal was the deepest knife in my back.

Chad shrugged his shoulders and finally pulled his hand out of his pocket to check his watch. Without restraint and in pure reaction, I screamed as I reached down and picked up the hose my mother left lying next to the flowerbed. I pulled the handle and let the water hit him square in the back as he yelled, swearing at me while running to his car. It was sad that it took a water hose to get some kind of legitimate reaction from him, but I figured some reaction was better than letting him walk away to bask in his smugness. Besides, I had never imagined a water hose could give me so much satisfaction. I stood and watched him drive down the street, putting on his brakes every few seconds, probably from water running down his leg.

I walked into the house and went straight to my room. Unable to make it to my bed, I slumped down to the floor against the wall and began to sob with hot, angry tears streaming down my face.

I heard the phone ring out in the kitchen, and a few seconds later, there was a tap on my door. Mike opened the door a crack and reached his arm through handing me the phone gently. I took it from him as he softly said, "Dad," and closed the door behind him. Mike knew he didn't need to ask if I wanted to talk to our dad because the answer was always yes, especially when I was upset.

"Hi Dad," I said trying to hold back more tears, my voice cracking as I spoke sadly.

"Honey? What's wrong? You sound like you're crying." Just hearing my dad's deep, gruff, affectionate voice was enough to bring out more sobs as I spoke.

"It's just awful, Dad! I called off the wedding with Chad and you're never going to believe what happened." I didn't need to see his face to know he was sad because I could hear it in his voice.

"My baby girl, what happened?" I sniffed a little more and gathered just enough energy to tell him everything. I told him about the dress shopping and about how Mother was making it unbearable. I told him about the text, bumping into Kara at the store, and by the time I finished with the recent front lawn drama with Chad, I couldn't hold back a new wave of tears.

There was a pause, while he waited for me to finish sobbing, and then I heard the genuine sadness in his voice as he comforted me in a way only he could do, primarily because it was real.

"I am so sorry that happened to you, Amy. You don't deserve any of what they did to you. You were always a great friend to Betsy and I am angry that she did that. As for Chad, he doesn't deserve you in a million years. You are way better than he is. He was lucky to have you, not the other way around." I listened to my dad and took in all his words. He knew what to say to make me feel better.

He took another long pause before sounding a little more serious and nervous at the same time as he continued.

"There is something I have in mind, Amy. Also, there is something I haven't really told you about." His tone made me feel nauseous. I knew I wouldn't be able to handle any negative news from him, not today at least. I clutched the phone tight as he cleared his throat before speaking.

"I haven't told you this, but I've been seeing a woman for the past nine months or so. She is also in her early fifties like me. She is really sweet and nice. I think you would like her. I hope you approve of this?" I forgot all about crying as I smiled on behalf of my dad. He hadn't really dated since he left my mother, and he was always careful about talking about women with me. I guess in some sense he thought I might view him as betraying my mother, which couldn't be farther from the truth. The truth was I wanted my dad to have the happiness he never had with my mother. I had strong, old memories that stretched all the way back to diapers of my father being wholly devoted and generous to my mother and not receiving the same treatment in return.

"Dad, if you say she's nice and she treats you good, then I'm really happy for you. You don't need to be alone, Dad. I mean it's not like she's in her early twenties. She really is in her fifties, right?" I could hear him chuckle just a little bit on the other end of the phone.

"Yes, honey, she is practically the same age as me. I'm much too old to be chasing after younger women. But this does bring me to what I have in mind, an opportunity if you will." There was a short silence and then a moment later, as my heart dropped into my stomach, he continued, "She has a daughter, Nikki. She is in her late twenties and single. She's a very sweet girl. I think you two could be good friends, and she happens to be looking for a roommate." He cleared his throat when I didn't say anything, and then went on.

"I know this is scary and a big deal to pick up and move to another state. I have a little money that I saved to help with your wedding and I could help get you a job. Well, what are you thinking?" Out of all the horrible things that I imagined he might say that was not one of them. So I felt a release of tension as I leaned my head back against the wall and looked up at the ceiling. I took in a long breath, letting out an even longer sigh. He was right; it was a big risk to move to another state without a job and move in with a person I had never met before. Then I thought about college students that go off to the dorms and get random computer selected roommates.

"Do you think she would be okay with it? What if she doesn't like me or I don't like her?" I had so many questions as my brain turned all the negative fear induced possibilities around. I could hear a smile in his voice as he asked,

"Do you want to come visit me first and meet her before you decide? I really think you two would get along, but I understand your fear. It's hard to make that kind of move, plus your mom is going to be sad to lose you." I surveyed my room with all the brown boxes stacked on top of each other. All I had left to pack was the contents of a small dresser only half-full of clothes to be thrown into a box, plus my bed had to be broken down. I couldn't think of anything here holding me back. What was keeping me in this place that was causing me so much pain? I looked around the room and realized there was nothing for me anymore, besides I was coming up on thirty years old. I knew I should just do it; I *needed* to do it. With great resolve, I replied to my dad.

"No, Dad, I don't need to come out and visit first. I'm going to call the office in the morning. They won't need a two-week notice, and they'll replace me in a week. Will that be enough time for you to prepare her for a new roommate?"

"She'll be so excited! I can't wait to see you, honey. I'll call you in a couple of days so we can work out travel arrangements and what not. I won't say anything to your mom. I'll leave that discussion up to you. Don't think about Chad anymore, it's his loss. Please get some sleep. I love you, honey."

"I love you too, Dad, bye." I hit the button on the phone and tossed the cordless up on the chair as an unconstrained squeal of excitement came out of my mouth. I instantly had a newfound energy as I jumped up on the bed and put my hands behind my head, staring up at my ceiling as if I was star gazing. The thought of breaking free of my mother's mean control and leaving this city gave me pure and utter delight. It wasn't anything less than astonishing that in less than an hour I went from miserable and crying to being excited to start a new life. The overwhelming feeling of happiness I felt at that moment could not be surpassed by any other time in my short life history. I was finally doing something for me, not based off of the opinions of what others thought I should do.

I couldn't wipe the grin off my face as I rolled over and hugged my pillow tight. I was so happy I had to hug something and I knew it wouldn't be my mother. Chad and Betsy seemed to fade farther and farther to the back of my subconscious as I hugged the pillow tighter.

I closed my eyes and crossed my fingers that my future roommate, the daughter of my father's new girlfriend, wasn't a serial axe murderer or anything along the lines of crazy. However, in truth, just having the opportunity to leave my mother, rooming with an axe murderer was a risk I was willing to take.

FOUR

It was more like a movie than I had imagined. Not because it was beautiful, or music was playing, but because it always seemed to me that, when I watched a movie and the main character started on an adventure or a new part of their life, there was always a camera shot of them stepping out onto gravel. I looked down at the gravel underneath my sandals and smiled at this movie moment. I took it as a sign that good things were to come.

"Hi Sweetie!" My dad walked out of the door from his apartment and promptly wrapped his arms around me in a big bear like hug. I embraced the familiar loving smell of his Ralph Lauren cologne, which he never ran out of, ever since I could remember.

"Hi Dad. I haven't seen your new apartment. Is your girlfriend here?" My stomach was doing flips on the inside and I had a nagging feeling that I was back in grade school on the first day.

"Yes she is. I don't know if I told you on the phone, but her name is Della. She is excited to meet you. How was the drive?" He glanced over my shoulder and saw my car packed to the roof with my things. The drive was only four hours but the trip seemed a lot longer, considering I couldn't really use my mirrors.

"It was fine." This was a complete lie. It was utterly fantastic. In all my life, and with all the words I knew, I could hardly describe the euphoric feeling of joy I felt when I pulled out of my driveway and out of my neighborhood. The extreme pleasure I had as I drove past Betsy's house was almost unreal. It was truly great to leave and have the possibility to be my true self. Not the fat daughter, not the best friend who can be walked all over, and definitely not the desperate fiancé that needed to be married out of obligation. No, now I was going to be just Amy, Amy Stanton. However small it might be, I had a tiny understanding of the feeling that wrongly convicted prisoners might feel the day they are released.

I looked over at my dad as he motioned for me to follow him into his apartment.

"Are you hungry? Della figured you would be hungry and tired after the drive so she made a roast and some red potatoes." I looked over at my dad amazed. The whole time my dad was married to my mother, he never said the words, 'she made a roast and red potatoes', so it was as if he was speaking French.

"Really? She didn't need to go to all that trouble for me, Dad. I feel bad; I didn't want to put you guys out." He looked over at me and gave me faint look of disappointment.

"Don't you ever think like that, Amy. You will never be a bother to me. Besides, she makes a roast once a week anyway. She loves to cook." He grinned from ear to ear and I noticed that he had put on about ten pounds since the last time I saw him around Christmas. My dad was slightly stocky to begin with, but had a very gruff muscular stature about him. Like a boxer or retired gymnast who was now slightly past his prime, a little out of shape, but you could tell it was still there somewhere.

I quickly fixed my shirt and fluffed my hair before stepping through the doorway behind my dad, waiting to meet Della for the first time. The smell of food was also a new connection I had to register with my dad.

"Amy?" I watched in anticipation as Della walked around the corner from the kitchen. She flung the kitchen towel over her shoulder as she reached her arms out wide and gave me a quick squeeze. She stepped back and looked me over before she smiled, which revealed large dimples in her cheeks and slight crow's feet on the corner of her eyes.

"You are so lovely, Amy. Your dad said you were pretty and he showed me a picture, but you are so beautiful in person." I stared at her and blinked a few times, because I was completely out of my element. I was not used to strong words of flattery and I was surprised when it seemed to be a sincere compliment.

"Thank you, Della." I said, unable to keep my eyes from blinking.

"Oh honey! I'm just speaking the truth." Della had thick

sandy blonde hair that was cut just below her chin. She was on the shorter side and was fairly curvy for a woman in her fifties. I could tell she embraced her age and felt no shame, unlike my mother who bought every facial cream on the market and did everything she financially could afford to hold on to her youth.

"I hope you're hungry. I made all kinds of goodies and a key lime pie for dessert." *If he doesn't marry this woman, I'm going to!*

We sat at the small dinner table in the area off of the kitchen as Della brought the large glass dish to the table. I looked over and noticed a fourth place was set for another person.

"Is your daughter eating with us?" I desperately hoped her daughter was half as nice as Della seemed so far. Unfortunately, I couldn't be fully optimistic because I learned from Chad that some children were the opposite of their parents.

"I think so. Nikki said she's going to try to come tonight. She can't wait to meet you. I think you two are going to hit it off. I have a good feeling about this." Della and my dad looked at each other and smiled like they were on the ground floor of a huge plot that was about to hatch.

We ate and talked while the atmosphere never wavered from less than pleasant. After our delicious meal (and the best key lime pie bar none), Della quickly jumped up to make some tea.

"Can I help with anything?" I picked up all the plates and brought them to the kitchen. I quickly scraped them off into the garbage and rinsed them in the sink.

"If you are really tired you can go lay down in the guest room and take a little power nap. We were thinking of relaxing and watching a movie here tonight, and then tomorrow first thing take you over to the condo you'll be sharing with Nikki. Does that sound good to you, honey?" The sweet tone in her voice brought uncontrollable tears to my eyes. After Chad and Betsy, I was beginning to feel that this planet didn't have many people, other than my dad, who would be nice to me.

She handed me a tissue and gave me a little squeeze. I could tell in her face that she knew I was crying over the break up. I thanked her and wiped my nose as I nodded my head hoping she would show me the guest room. Della smiled sweetly and motioned for me to follow her to the back of the apartment.

I laid down on the guest bed in my dad's decent sized, two bedroom apartment and wiped my eyes so I wouldn't get mascara on the powder blue pillowcase. I closed my eyes and fell asleep within seconds, which was not something I had been able to do for the last two weeks.

"Ah! What? You are such a douche licker! I'm so over this… Bye." I squinted my eyes as I woke to see the figure as she flipped on the light switch.

"Oh! I'm so sorry. I was on the phone and my mom was trying to tell me something. I didn't realize she was telling me you were sleeping in here. I'm sorry, do you want me to turn them off and shut the door?" She quickly turned the lights back off as I sat up and rubbed my eyes before I realized they were probably red and swollen from two weeks of continuous crying, not quite the first impression I was going for.

"No, that's okay. You can turn them back on. It's time for

me to get up anyway." I gave her a shy smile and swung my feet over the edge of the bed, sitting up. My voice was gruff from the nap but I still managed to gather myself, as much as I could.

She took a few steps across the room and turned on a small dresser lamp that was less harsh on my eyes than the overhead light.

"I'm Amy, glad to meet you." My eyes quickly adjusted to the light and I could see the smile on her face as she leaned against the wall, speaking with such charm and grace.

"I'm Nikki… I'm glad finally to meet you too. Your dad talks about you all the time, he loves you so much." I smiled and nodded my head.

"He said good things about you too, and your mom is wonderful. I really like her. Have your parents been divorced for long?" I tried to clear my throat, as I was sure I looked and sounded like some creature that had just made out with the garbage man in the back of his truck.

"No, my dad walked out on us when I was five, so I never really had a dad." Nikki had thick, shiny golden hair that cascaded a few inches from the middle of her back. It was easy to tell she was related to her mother. Nikki had a slightly thicker hourglass figure then the average woman, complete with a thinner waist, curvy hips, and voluptuous chest area. She was also a good five inches taller than her mom was as well, so I imagined her father must have been on the taller side. I knew at least a dozen women that would kill for a shape like hers, including me.

"That's awful, I'm sorry to hear that," I replied as Nikki used her foot that was pressed up against the wall to propel her away from the wall so she could slide down on the bed next to me. She looked over at me and smiled as she leaned back on her elbows.

"I don't remember him really. According to most people, I guess he was a pretty big douche bag. But it's okay, my mom is pretty great so I didn't feel like I was missing much growing up." She looked over at me, relaxed and easy going. In my mind, I couldn't recall a time in which I found it so easy to talk to someone I had just met. It was also odd that I felt more at ease talking to her than most of the conversations I had ever had with Betsy. It felt as if Nikki and I were rekindling an old friendship from long ago. Without really thinking about it I intrusively asked,

"Was that your boyfriend on the phone with you when you walked in the room?" I shut my mouth as soon as I finished the sentence, then quickly I added, "Sorry, it's none of my business. I didn't mean to be nosey." She laughed a little and shook her head.

"Amy, I am not a secretive person. Look at me, and notice how I just started rambling all these things off to you. You can ask, besides, I'm the one that barged in the room while you were trying to get some sleep, but to answer your question, that was not my boyfriend, just some guy I went out with a couple of times. He tried giving me an ultimatum. He basically said if I didn't put out soon he was not going to have a choice but go and look for a girl that would... Sooo... I guess he better go look for her." She laughed a little and I looked at her in awe. Her demeanor and self-confidence was intoxicating. I wasn't a man or had any lesbian tendencies, but I could easily see the allure she might have around men.

"Wow, and you just dropped him like that?" I snapped my

fingers as I spoke.

"Yeah, all guys say the same things, trust me. But when it comes down to it, once you don't put out, they get out, and I don't need or want a man like that."

Nikki rolled over on her side and propped her head up on her hand, as she looked at me a little more serious.

"Can I ask you a question now, Amy?" I easily agreed, not wanting our conversation to end.

She continued with her question. "Your dad told us about what happened with your guy and your best friend. I hope you don't mind me asking, but did you suspect anything was going on? Or was it a complete shock?" I could see in her eyes that she felt really bad for the whole situation and me.

"No. I had no idea. I think I was totally dumb struck by what Betsy did more than anything else. I never in a million years thought she would do something like that. She's always been so… placid. I mean we talked and laughed and stuff, but she was always so quiet and she wasn't the kind of person who could stand on her own two feet." Nikki nodded her head, taking in my words and contemplating an opinion of Betsy. Then with such certainty she said,

"Yep, it's the quiet, boring ones that you need to watch out for. It sounds like you're way better off having her out of your life. And this guy Chad? I have a feeling you'll have him replaced with a dream of a catch within a year." I hadn't meant to, but I laughed at her confidence in me, who she didn't even really know, to land a dream guy within a year. It took a pregnancy scare to get Chad to propose, I highly doubted some male super model was going to ride up on his white horse, only to spend half an hour trying to lug my huge butt in his saddle.

"What's so funny? I'm sure you can get all kinds of guys." I rolled my eyes and shook my head quickly replying.

"Uh, no. Maybe once I lose some of this weight I'll have a better chance. I mean, no one wants a fatty." Nikki looked at me as if I had just escaped from the looney bin. She sat up and just stared at me for a moment in disbelief.

"Seriously? You are not fat. You have a great curve to you, beautiful hair, killer eyelashes… I mean I would die for your lashes… clean skin… I just met you and you got it going on. I don't believe guys aren't chasing you down." I looked back at her as if she was the crazy one. Nikki stood up, walked over to the guest bedroom closet, and started fishing through it. While she was half way in it, she stuck her head out and asked me,

"Do you have anything sexy to wear tonight or is it all packed in your boxes?" Truth be told, I didn't own very many things that could be considered sexy. Yeah, I had one top that was borderline cute, but everything was either really long, or nice and baggy to cover my chubby arms and thick thighs. I decided just to lie.

"Uh yeah, the sexy things are in boxes." She pulled out three hangers and held them up so I could see a selection. Out of curiosity, I asked, "Where are we going?" Nikki didn't reply but gave me a sly smile instead and asked about the hangers in her hands.

"I'm sure these will fit you, they're mine. Which one do you want to wear?" I was terrified. I was going to be embarrassed the minute I tried any of them on. I could just imagine a button popping off and flying across the room, or having to call the fire department because the fat girl's air supply got cut off because of the dress she was trapped in. I tried to turn her down politely.

"I'm okay. I don't think they're my size. I'm a sixteen and they look more like a ten." The sly smile remained on her face as she boldly said.

"These *are* a sixteen. I'm taking you to this cool place that I like to go to sometimes. It's on the other side of town, and at this time of day, it will be packed with lawyers, doctors, artists, all kinds of guys, whatever your type… he'll be there. But more importantly, I think we both need a drink." She opened her hands farther apart trying to give me a better perspective of the clothes. I pointed to the deep teal, wrap around dress with a deep V-neck. I didn't have anything like it. I desperately hoped it would fit, if anything, at least save me from embarrassment. Then I became more worried about ruining such an expensive looking garment.

"Thanks. You don't mind?" I got up, walked over and looked in the mirror above the small light oak dresser. Mascara was smeared all around my eyes making me look like a decomposing corpse.

"Of course not! I love clothes and I have a ton of dresses. Besides, I am an only child and I've always wanted a sister. If you like it… then you can have it." Sharing clothes was something Betsy and I had never, or could have ever done. Matter of fact, I couldn't recall sharing clothes with any female for that matter.

"I don't think I could take it. Thanks, though." She was back in the closet fishing through it when she pulled out an off the shoulder, black tunic. She glanced at me for a second as she began to pull up her thick hair into a high ponytail.

"No, I'm sure you're going to take it. I'm psychic, I foresee a future with you and that teal dress." She gave me a little devilish smile, and then added, "I also foresee a night full of martinis and chocolates."

Later that night, as we flirted with handsome men, drank and talked, I learned three very incredible, almost unbelievable things about Nikki.

First off, she was extremely open and honest when she drank, and it didn't take much alcohol either.

Second, Nikki had never been in love, not even as a teenager, except her crush on the New Kids on the Block. But the most fascinating thing that came out of her mouth after four shots was when she confided in me that she was actually still a virgin, which I couldn't hardly digest for a full ten minutes. Not because she was virgin, but because *she* was virgin. Nikki exhumed such a heighten level of sensuality and charm, so naturally, so effortlessly, her revelation of virginity destroyed all the stereotypes of why society presumes a woman past a certain age would even be a virgin.

Nikki didn't fulfill any stigma. She was a far cry from Hollywood's portrayal of some homely spinster with a dozen cats, and Nikki valued her choice to be true to herself, confident, knowing she didn't need the approval of a man to validate who she was. I found this to be a virtue that I hoped to learn from, or maybe even bravely acquire.

Thirdly, men gravitated towards Nikki in flocks and packs. She could hardly lift a glass without another being offered or the one in her hand being paid for. She was confident, but not arrogant to think she was more beautiful than the average woman.

By the end of the hazy night, I found my admiration for Nikki growing stronger by the minute, or the talking liquor, depending on how you would prefer to account for it.

FIVE

Nikki and I lay on the couches with brown boxes spread throughout the apartment. It turned out, unloading my car was much more difficult than it was to load, or perhaps it was the fact that we were living on the third floor, with no elevator. As we took a few minutes to catch our breath, I was thankful I had not rented a U-Haul, or that I brought all my heavy books and childhood knickknacks.

"So, what do you think of the place?" Nikki had her arm draped across her forehead, as she lay stretched out on the long sofa, her ankles crossed showing a shiny silver and diamond ankle bracelet.

"I really love it." I glanced around at the condo with huge modern pictures along the wall and sophisticated pieces of decor on tables and bookshelves, easily resembling updated footage from an

HGTV show. It was definitely a far cry from the college mix and matched furniture I had imagined.

"If there is anything you want to change or rearrange just let me know. I can take down some of these pictures if you have some of your own." I couldn't imagine messing up her ultra-chic vibe.

"No, everything looks just perfect." I smiled at her and she smiled back while she sat up and swung her legs around, dropping her feet to the floor.

"I'm going to get some lemonade from the kitchen, want some?" She walked past my feet with her thick blonde hair causally swaying in sync with the saucy sway of her hips.

"Sure. Did my dad say what time he and Della were coming by?" I heard the clinking of glasses from the kitchen behind me as she spoke.

"I think they said late this afternoon. I know that we're all going out to dinner this evening." I laid my head back into the light cream sofa and sighed a breath of relief as I imagined what I would be doing at this exact moment back home with my mother. Most likely, I would be sitting on the couch while she told me about a low-fat tofu stir fry she was going to make for dinner, all in the hope I would lose more weight to get Chad back.

"Should be fun. Are you going to call that guy that gave you his number last night?" I curiously asked Nikki as she handed me a tall glass of lemonade. She took a long drink and shot me a mischievous look as she replied,

"Ummm, I think the real question is whether *you are* going to call the guy that gave you *his* number last night? I wasn't the only one that got a number you know." Her mouth curled up in a sly smile as I rolled my eyes and laughed a little. I didn't want to say it out loud, but I was fairly certain the other guy only gave me his number out of default because I was with Nikki.

"No, I don't think he was really interested in me. Besides, he probably gives that number out to a different girl every night of the week." What I also couldn't say was that even though I was no supermodel, it seemed awkward that the guy was extremely lean and lanky. I just couldn't imagine myself with a man so slender. After all, I didn't want people to compare us to an apple and a toothpick. His friend however, was fairly handsome and honed in on Nikki from across the room.

"I'm pretty sure he was into you. You looked pretty hot last night, and I know there was more than one pair of eyes on you my friend. That's a fact." I rolled my eyes in response out of pure disbelief.

"What about the guy that gave you his number? He was cute."

"Fair enough, but I don't think so. Did you see how 'handsy' he was? I mean, really, he wouldn't keep to his own personal space with all the touching, and that's *always* a bad sign. In the end, men like that… don't like girls like me." I didn't know what to say to that because I didn't personally have the experience of men chasing me as they did Nikki. I didn't even have the experience of more than one guy liking me. The only guy I had ever been with was sleeping with my best friend, so all in all, I was on a totally different playing field than her. Therefore, I would just have to take her word for it.

"Yeah, I did notice he always had his hand on your arm or shoulder. Then your knee… and thigh. You're probably right, you're better off without him."

"Yep, my thoughts exactly." Nikki took another long drink of her lemonade and stood up, then turned her eyes down toward me and asked excitedly, "Do you want to take some more boxes to your room? By the way, how do like your room? Is it big enough?" I couldn't help but laugh out loud. My new bedroom was bigger than my room back at my mother's house. It had a large window with a seat built in underneath, and a major plus was that my room overlooked the luxury golf course next door, picture perfect.

"Yes, it's great. I love it. I wanted to talk about the rent because we haven't done that yet."

Nikki didn't look stressed or worried, casually she replied,

"We'll talk about it after you get a job. Honestly, I'm not hurting for money." It had occurred to me that my dad never mentioned what she did, so I was immediately curious where she worked to be so financial stress free.

"Where do you work?"

"Right now, I'm working as a waitress and every other weekend, I watch the kids of my old employer. I had a really good job in my early twenties as a loan processor when the mortgage industry was crazy hot. I was one of the first to get laid off when it all hit the fan." Nikki smiled and tapped the side of her head as she continued, "I totally saw things were going downhill, so I worked every chance I could and I saved, and saved. Yep, I put a huge down payment on this condo, so my monthly payments are crazy low, like super crazy low."

I was astonished. The more I learned about Nikki the more I liked her. I could not say the same thing about myself being financial responsible. I had made just enough as a secretary that by the time I made my car payments, cell phone payment, and helped my mother out with utilities, there wasn't much left over. Not to mention there were all the little gifts I bought Chad for birthdays and holidays that added up. I felt stupid knowing I could have saved more if I hadn't of wasted my money on him.

"That's impressive," I replied. Nikki shook her head in a slight disagreement.

"Well, not really. My mom was a single mother for most of my life. She taught me to budget and save, but I'm not always so good at that. You'll know what I mean when you see my closet." She gave me a little wink and a half-guilty smile.

She walked over to one of the many boxes by the entry door marked 'bedroom', picked one up, and walked past me toward the back of the condo. I quickly followed her lead and brought two boxes with me.

"Let me show you my sinful closet and then I can help you unpack if you want." I had no idea why, but I was beyond exuberant to see her closet. I could not refrain from sounding plain giddy.

"Sure!"

We walked through her bedroom as she took me to a large walk-in closet. Her closet itself was only a fraction smaller than my old room. Nikki flicked on the switch that illuminated a wall-to-wall, floor to ceiling, massive array of color and fabrics. The back wall was stocked from floor to ceiling with the most stylish shoes a person ever saw. I felt like I was experiencing another episode on the HGTV network yet again.

"Whoa, you have a lot of clothes. You must have made really good money being a loan processor."

"I really did. You very well might be looking at half my earnings though. Sometimes I think I might have a sickness." She walked to the middle of the closet and looked at me. She then, very seriously said, "You are welcome to borrow anything in this closet, clothes, shoes… it doesn't matter. If it needs to go to the dry cleaners, just let me know and I'll take a group of them together." I cuffed my mouth out of reaction but was still unable to contain my chuckle, because there was no way my hefty self was going to fit in her clothes. Last night had to be a one-time fluke. "What's so funny?" I shook my head and replied.

"I really appreciate the offer, truly, but I'm too big to wear any of your things." She stared at me for a moment and looked at my face. I could tell that she was trying to figure out if I was being sarcastic or honest. Then she rolled her eyes and smiled. She turned and walked through her closet and randomly plucked out a few hangers off the pole. She spun back around with an arm full of clothes. She walked over to me, extended her arms, and handed me the stack.

"Here, try these on, and if a single one doesn't fit, then I'll buy you dinner for a month. If at least one does fit, you can buy the drinks every time we go out for a month. Deal?" I was really leery, not because I didn't want them to fit, but because I was confident they wouldn't fit, and I might destroy her clothes in the process. Moreover, she would then realize what an incredible tub of lard I was, and she might feel disappointed once her perception of me was altered. Nevertheless, it would also be good for her to know I couldn't fit and she might not ask me again, and dinner for a month sounded good. She looked at me and with a little confusion said,

"You know we just went through this last night, right? Like the same exact scenario." I took a deep breath and with great reluctance, I hesitantly agreed.

"Um, okay, but please don't be disappointed." She just gave me another soft eye roll with her smile, and once again, like last night, she had a look on her face as if she knew a secret I didn't.

Then she said, "I'm sure I won't be."

I stood in front of the full-length mirror in Nikki's room and just stared in amazement. I had my fifth outfit on, and it, just like the previous others, actually fit. Granted, it was a tiny bit snug, but while trying it on, I had not heard the sounds of rips, tears, or buttons flying across the room, and her clothes actually looked good on me.

"Cute!" Nikki exclaimed as she peeked her head around the door. She crossed the room and came to stand behind me, while looking at my reflection in the mirror.

"Soooo, this is the fourth or fifth one? I'm pretty sure I win our little bet. I look forward to a month full of martinis and mimosas." I still had a feeling of disbelief that I could fit into her clothes, even if it was a bit clingy around my hips. My mind came to the conclusion she must have been heavier and these were from her fat collection. However, before my brain could finish processing the excuse, it was almost as if she could read my thoughts.

"I just wore that top last week. It looks good on you and the skirt is very flattering. I say this as a straight woman, but your caboose looks fantastic in that." I raised one eyebrow and asked,

"Caboose?" In response, Nikki shrugged her shoulders and smiled before saying,

"Yeah, what can I say? I'm a fan of saying every form of douche, so why not caboose?" I couldn't argue with that logic.

"So these are clothes that you still wear sometimes? I just thought we were totally different sizes. I mean, I just don't understand how I can wear these. I'm so much bigger than you." I looked in the mirror and twisted my hip trying to catch a glimpse of my behind to evaluate it myself. Nikki was right; the skirt did hug me in all the right places. I began to think that perhaps the real reason the clothes fit me was because I had never worn clothes that actually fit me. Most of the stuff I wore was comfortable, being a little longer and bigger to hide my chubbiness. I'd be lying if I said I wasn't a fan of sweat pants, active wear (not that I was active in them) and baggy men's t-shirts. I wore that mainly because the few occasions I did venture out in confidence to get something fitting, it was usually met with disapproving and quick reminders from my mother that tight equals rolls.

"When I met you yesterday, I knew right off the bat that we were practically the same size. You are beautiful, have all the right curves, and you are well proportioned. I'm so glad that I finally have someone to swap clothes with." The offer was nice, but I instantly felt guilty that I didn't have anything she would probably want to swap with me. I opened my mouth to say as much when there was a knock at the door.

As Nikki made her way to the door and opened it, my dad gave us both a big, wide smile and he walked in, making a beeline straight to me and giving me a big bear hug. Right behind him was Della in a light pink silk blouse and a pearl necklace.

"Hi girls, how was the move today? I wish you would have let me help you." My dad put his arm around me and glanced around the place while nodding his head in an approving manner.

"It went well. I think about half way through, we both wished we hadn't decided to be so independent," I answered and looked over at Nikki as she nodded her head in agreement. We had both decided that we didn't want to bother my dad and any of his friends with helping me move. I quickly learned why moving is among the top ten things people hate to do. Della smiled and said,

"Well, I'm proud of you girls. You both worked so hard, so now at the very least, you need to let us take you out to a restaurant since you wouldn't let us help." Della put her hands on her wide hips feigning a look of desperation. Nikki had a wide smile as she replied,

"I don't know about Amy, but I'll never say no to a good meal."

"Me either."

Nikki and I went to our separate rooms to change our clothes to go out to eat. I moved some of the boxes around, when I came across the small box that I had put my desk contents in. I was overwhelmed with an urge to open it. On the top of the papers sat the envelope that held the two non-refundable tickets that were meant to be for my honeymoon. I slipped them out of the envelope and stared at the computerized block lettering on the ticket stubs. I felt my throat stiffen as tears welled up in my eyes. I had imagined Chad and me in Italy many times, walking the streets, holding hands, and I had fooled myself into believing that Italy was going to be the place he fell in love with me. Italy was going to be the place he *truly* fell in love with me, he would finally have that 'I can't live without you, how did I never feel like this before' kind of love. I had also imagined over and over again what it was going to be like to come home and tell Betsy all about it. However, it was the realization that I had lost Betsy that was the real cause of my tears. I had always known deep down that Chad might never really love me as I wanted. Truthfully, I always knew he was a little too selfish to love anyone more than himself. Nevertheless, that thought was always softened knowing that I would have Betsy to talk to.

I heard a tap on the door and turned to see Della as she peeked around the corner.

"Hi dear, are you almost ready? Is everything okay?" She stepped in and walked over to me looking at my glistening eyes. She reached down into her large purse, plucked out a tissue, and handed it to me. I looked down at the tickets and my mind sparked immediately with the most wonderful idea.

"Della? I want to give something to you and my dad, so you guys can get away and spend some time together." I smiled and held up the tickets for her to see them. She glanced at them, as if already knowing what they were, and then gently pushed them towards me. Della then spoke in a soft and loving tone.

"No dear, those are your tickets. I know neither your father nor I would dream of taking what should be your trip. Besides, your father told me how you took care of your grandmother until her passing. Honey, you are always taking care of other people. *You* need this." I tried one last attempt to change her mind.

"I don't think I can, Della. I mean, I'll be thinking about the fact that it was supposed to be my honeymoon the whole time. I don't think I could enjoy it." She shook her head and gave me a loving squeeze on the side of my arm as she spoke,

"No, my dear, by time you get off the plane, you won't even think about that dirty dog. Take a friend and turn it into a wonderful adventure." Just then, Nikki walked through the open door. I held up the two tickets in the air and asked,

"How would you like those drinks I owe you with a side of authentic Italian pasta?

SIX

Nikki and I landed on the west coast of Genova and stepped off the plane with our large handbags and Nikki's wide brim hat. It had taken a long couple of days to convince Nikki to accept the non-refundable honeymoon ticket. She finally agreed when we made the arrangement that I would live rent free for my first three months, after I got a job, in exchange for Chad's half of the honeymoon. Even though Chad had not been a thought of mine during my flight to Italy, Betsy on the other hand had been. The other thought that hit me more directly was the realization that I was going to be turning thirty and had experienced so little compared with others of my generation.

I had never been on a plane and never had my own place until I moved in with Nikki. I had never been married, didn't have any kids and never really been in love, more importantly, had never really *been* loved. Essentially, I was like a child living by the expectations of others and had no true ambitions for myself. It wasn't that I didn't know who I was, it was that I didn't *really* know who I was, or how to get what I wanted or demand what I needed. All I had known for so long was that I was fat Amy, unlovable Amy, and Amy whose fiancé doesn't really love her so it's okay if her best friend sleeps with him. My self-exploration was cut short by the sound of Nikki's voice.

"Look at this! This weather is perfect! I'm so excited. We're gonna have so much fun." Nikki was the picture of classic Hollywood with her shiny blonde hair flowing out from under her hat. With her sunglasses and red lips that parted in a sparkly white smile was nothing less than pure nineteen fifties glamour.

"Yeah, we are." In the two weeks Nikki and I had to prepare for this trip, we were able to bond at a speed that was unparalleled in any friendship I had ever known, quickly going beyond the status of best friends and more like sisters. I believe in part it was nice for me not to continuously be around someone as thin and frail as Betsy, a visual reminder that I was big. Betsy was also the polar opposite of Nikki, like comparing a malnourished zombie with an actual live person.

"This is gonna be so great. I have a feeling you're gonna meet lots of guys. What do you think?" I shook my head and rolled my eyes as I laughed at Nikki. I knew it was in part sarcasm because she didn't worry about guys. I had a feeling that statement was directed more towards hopes to benefit me than her, because after all, she could read men better than a seasoned phycologist and predict just about every situation to an exact moment. Nevertheless, as I looked at her slightly nervous expression, it was apparent she felt out of her element.

"Meet guys? Do you really think in the short two weeks we're here, there are going to be guys?" Once again, Nikki's red lips parted as her white teeth sparked, she tilted down her glasses and winked as she spoke,

"You never know where Italy will take us." With that, she was able to place herself in a newfound element that she was confident in. I was learning that mind truly is over matter. It's not always the thinnest, tallest, sluttiest girl that gets the man she wants, but the girl who *believes* she can have the man she wants.

Within the hour, we found ourselves standing at the Trenitalia station, the Genova piazza principal, trying desperately to read the departure board to make it to Cornglia for the room I had rented as part of the honeymoon adventure I had put together. I was incredibly grateful to Nikki for researching the train systems in Italy as she took initiative and guided us to the right train.

On board, we stuffed away our luggage and found two open seats side by side among many empty seats. I leaned my head back into the chair and let out a long sigh, releasing all my built up anxiety that something catastrophic was going to prevent me from taking this trip. I heard Nikki ask,

"Are you stressed? What's with all the yoga breathing?" Nikki had taken off her glasses and large brim hat, setting them on her lap. She gave me a quick glance before she leaned forward and flipped her hair around, eliminating the small crease her hat had put throughout her hair.

"Not at all. I had been waiting for something bad to happen that was going to force me to cancel this trip. Now that I'm here, I can enjoy it and not worry." She leaned forward again, tilted her head, and looked at me as she stopped mid-stroke with her fingers still tangled in her hair.

"If you keep waiting and thinking something bad is going to happen, then something bad *will* happen. Always expect the best and the best will always be expecting you." She threw herself back and gave her hair one final shake. "Is that better?" Nikki reached her hand around and smoothed over her long side swept bang that was a new addition to her hair she had gotten just for our trip to Italy.

I had been talked into light brown highlights and a free range of her closet that included an extensive clothes fitting. I replied with the humorous and fun tone we had both become comfortable and accustomed to with each other.

"Oh stop bragging, you know your hair is perfect." She rolled her eyes and smiled, which was what I personally had already become joyfully familiar with in our friendship.

"Just so you know, I've had to put a great deal more work into my hair to compete with you. Do you know how much B-12 I've been taking? If one of us can brag, it would be you." The other thing we had in common was neither of us liked an extreme amount of hair products, and as unimportant as that preference seemed, I've known that to be an actual deal breaker for some friendships.

We heard the sounds of people slowly trickling onto the train, most of which were speaking Italian. Because of my false pregnancy scare and the speedy manner in which we had planned the wedding, our trip to Italy was happening in the off-season, which so far was more pleasant than every nook in Italy being packed with tourists like I had imagined we would see.

Two elderly Italian women sat down in the seats facing us with their large satchels and nicely tailored clothes. One lady had her gray hair pulled back in a tight bun and had adorned herself with pearls. Her companion was less extravagant with a simple gold Catholic cross around her neck. Her hair was short but well styled and given her age, it had to be dyed since a hint of gray could not be found. Both ladies sat and gave us a pleasant smile and nod. Nikki and I smiled back, and then Nikki leaned over and spoke softly,

"I bet they're sisters." I sighed in agreement with her and caught a mischievous smile as it spread across her face. Her eyes were focused off at something and her smile didn't flicker in the slightest. I asked.

"What are you looking at?" Without changing her gaze or facial expression, she replied in a very low whisper,

"I am totally not exaggerating. Two of the most gorgeous men I have ever seen in my entire life are smiling at us right now. I'm looking to see if any women come to join them."

I casually glanced around and caught a quick glimpse at the men she was talking about. It would have been hard to miss their flirtatious eye contact and charming smiles. I could see from one glance Nikki had been absolutely truthful in regards to their appearance.

"Do you hear that?" I asked Nikki.

"Huh? What?" I laughed a little as I spoke quietly, just in case the elderly women spoke English.

"I think that's the sound of your virginity flying out the window." Nikki shook her head and let out a long breathy laugh while rolling her eyes as she broke her gaze and looked over at me.

We both couldn't contain our school like laughter and eventually covered our mouths in order to contain our giggles. Our laughter must have been the final straw, because it was apparent the men could no longer contain their curiosity about us. Moments later, the two men stood in the aisle mere inches away from Nikki's knee. The taller one leaned down slightly, and then politely spoke Italian to the two elder ladies. Nikki and I glanced at each other in bewilderment as the elderly ladies smiled first at the men and then at us. Then they gladly gave up their seats. The two men, who looked to be in their late-twenties, and very well dressed, were now sitting in front of us. I instantly became intimidated and horrified, mainly in part to their level of attractiveness. I could virtually hear what little confidence I did have ooze out of me.

Nikki, on the other hand, seemed to radiate her natural sexy aura the minute they hit the seats. She crossed her legs and gave me a quick glance and a wink in such a fashion that they didn't catch our non-verbal communication. The slightly taller man, who had thick dark hair and beautiful olive skin, spoke with a heavy accent.

"Are you a Americanos?" I quickly hoped that Nikki would handle the introductions because I was terrified that two minutes talking with me might make them get up and go back to their seats. She, like always, did not disappoint me.

"Oh no, is it that obvious?" Both men looked at each other with wide beaming smiles and the taller one answered her with such sultry charm that I was afraid I might ask him to take me to a sleeper car.

"Yes it tissa. Italian woman notta smile so nicely. And youra hair issa so much beautiful." She *always* gets men with her hair! I glanced over at his friend and realized I had been given the stare down the entire time. I could feel my cheeks flush and I tried to adjust my shirt hopefully to hide some of my chub. Nikki spoke so elegantly.

"Thank you. My name is Nikki and this is my sister, Amy." I could not explain the exact science behind it, but the minute I heard Nikki call me her sister, my confidence began to fill. My legs and arms stopped fidgeting and I straightened my back, took my fingers, and ran them through my hair as I proudly smiled in agreement with her.

"Ahhh, yes. Twoa very beautifulla sisters. I am Armond and diss is my cousin Dante."

Dante, who locked eyes with me and did not advert his gaze, leaned to the edge of the seat and asked in all sincerity, with a vaguely thinner accent,

"Are you twoa meeting familia? Or boyfriendsa? Or husbands?" He watched my face expressions closely and I couldn't keep my cheeks from blushing as I answered.

"No. We just decided to take a vacation and see Italy. No boyfriends... or husbands." They looked at each other and were obviously pleased to hear this. Nikki was not only like a seasoned psychologist, she was probably more accurately a man-whisperer. She could sniff out a backstabbing, cheating, compulsive liar in a heartbeat. I was beginning to think being a virgin might have given her special powers. Perhaps sex would turn out to be kryptonite for her, but to hear the tone of sex drip from the sound of her words, no stranger could guess it.

"Soo, do you fellas have girlfriends?" Dante was immediate in his response with the shake of his head and the shake of his finger. Armond, however, glanced at the floor a split second before replying in a relaxed fashion.

"No, no girlfriends." Nikki uncrossed her knees and crossed them in the other direction. She had obviously picked up on this little glitch, and Dante and I were put in a virtual standoff for truth, whatever it might be.

"How about a wife? A fiancé?" She was so cool and collected I felt as if I should get my notebook out and jot down some notes.

Armond squirmed in his seat for a couple of seconds and then looked down at the floor before he finally admitted,

"I did have a fiancé, but she passed awaya nine months ago." The anguish was draped over his face and my heart went out to him. I so badly wanted to reach out and hug him.

"I'm sorry about that. I'm sorry I pried; it's none of my business. Please forgive me." After a long pause and a sudden shift in mood as the doors began to close, Nikki gently asked, "Do you guys live in Cinque Terre?" She was a master of making people feel both comfortable and at changing the subject.

"Yesa. We are a visiting our aunt in the town of Manarola. Where are you staying?"

"Corniglia. Then we are going to Venice for a couple of days." Dante, who had equally thick hair as Armond, but a lighter olive complexion, slid to the edge of his seat to where our knees were touching. He didn't break the lock his eyes had with mine as he asked,

"Pleasea, maybe we could show you ladies around? We would lovea to show you the most beautifula of places… would you likea?" His hazel eyes sparkled and I caught a glimpse of a shiny, expensive watch as it peeked out of his perfectly ironed dress shirt. I was exceedingly glad I had both borrowed and bought new clothes for this trip, my shabby-chic (heavier on the shabby than the chic) would not have compared to the well-tailored and high fashion clothes of Italy.

"Yes, that would be nice." As I replied to Dante, I felt a gentle nudge from Nikki's elbow and I didn't have to look over to sense the happy look on her face.

For the rest of the two-hour train ride, we never had a gap in conversation. Halfway through, Armond and I switched seats, and even through his accent, Dante and I spent what was the fastest two hours of my life, connecting in a way that had seemed impossible with Chad.

It was during that initial long conversation with Dante that I had a particular thought for the first time that actually surprised me. In a way, I owed a great deal of gratitude to Betsy. If she had not done what she did, a year from now I would be standing in my house, likely bored out of my mind while Chad played video games. However, because of the horrible thing Betsy and Chad did, I was now in Italy, having the best time of my life, bar none.

SEVEN

We set our bags down on the chairs in the room I had rented in advance. It was smaller than I had imagined from the photo, and Nikki and I would have to share a bed, but it was in a beautiful location, clean and homey. Its greatest appeal was the extremely affordable price.

We heard a tap at the door as the property owner and hostess wedged her head through the crack of the door. Her English was perfect and her accent was very soft and subtle.

"May I come in?" She glanced toward the bed where Nikki had laid her hat on the end of it. Her eyes widened and she shuffled across the room, picking up Nikki's hat as she placed it on a hook next to the door.

"Oh ladies, we never leave hats at the foot of the bed, it is bad luck."

Nikki had a curious look on her face and then nodded her

head as she stated, "Okay, good to know."

"Duly noted," I added. I knew we would have a conversation about this incident, but not until Lucia left the room. Lucia bordered on sixty but had the energy and a lightness about her of someone much younger. In addition, she gave a 'mama knows best' aura that you couldn't help but admire and obey. We watched as she bounced around the room and opened drawers, informing us about the amenities that came with the room. After a few minutes, she whisked her tiny framed self out of the room and gently closed the door behind her.

As soon as we heard the door click, Nikki and I both simultaneously ran over to the window and looked out at the ocean. To an observer, it would have seemed as if we choreographed and rehearsed that moment, but for us, it was just another sign that we had become more like sisters than anything else.

After sorting through our things and taking a quick refreshing catnap, Nikki and I went down to the edge of the beach. It was early evening and there were still a few hours until dusk, but the sun was in the perfect position to cast a glow across the sides of the buildings and apartments behind us. The ripples in the ocean sparkled like thin streaks of freshly polished silver, and it was nothing less than mesmerizing. The view would have been splendid just in itself, but the smell of the fresh earth and stone around us mixed with the cool and refreshing ocean made it, in all entirety, a moment I would relive in my mind for the remainder of my life.

"Ouch!" I heard Nikki squeal as she brushed off the bottom of her foot and attempted to put her sandal back on. She then looked at me and gave me words of warning, "FYI, beautiful beach, but not the baby soft sand you might wish for." I looked down at the sand that seemed to be a mixture of rough sand and small jagged rocks, equal parts pale brown and light gray. I shrugged my shoulders and replied,

"Yeah, but the view and weather and are so amazing I'd almost walk on glass." Nikki thought about it a second and then nodded her head in agreement. We found some empty beach chairs and dragged them closer to the edge of the water. The breeze intensified and as the sun slowly slid down the sky, you could feel the air cool ever so slightly. Nikki let out a sigh and said so casually,

"We haven't even been here a full twenty-four hours, but I'm totally in love with this place." She peered at me from underneath her white, extra-large brimmed hat. Even though we had just been on a plane, then a train, and finished with a catnap, all she needed to do was a quick touch up with her lipstick, but the rest of her make-up continued to look impeccable.

"Yes. It's, amazing, and all the people are so friendly." Not only were the people so friendly, the pace all around was relaxed, as if people had work to do, but still wanted to enjoy the day as well. I turned slightly to face Nikki in the chair next to me as I spoke.

"So what do you really think about Armond and Dante? How do you feel about meeting up with them tomorrow to go on that walk?"

"It was so obvious that Dante is smitten with you. I don't think he took his eyes off of you once they sat down. Armond is very handsome and charming, but sometimes when he was talking, I got the feeling that he wasn't being totally honest. But, it is nice to have such good-looking guys show us around a little. Have you thought about Chad since we've been here, or you don't want to talk about it?" I had found it to be a great relief to talk to Nikki about Chad and all that had happened concerning both him and Betsy, so I had no ill feelings regarding her question on the matter.

"Once or twice I thought about him, but Dante is so sweet that when he's talking to me or even just listening to me, all I can think is how glad I am that it's not Chad sitting next to me. I mean really, I'm more glad than anything else. Does that make me a bad person?" Nikki shook her heard so rapidly I was nervous that her hat might fly off her head. She had been a strong source of comfort on those nights over the last week when I hit bottom, crying over the pain of a broken heart.

"Not at all. I would be happy it wasn't him too. I think the two dull-bags belong together, but you, my sweet, deserve someone sexy and gorgeous like Dante." She chuckled, then jokingly reached out and pretended to pinch my cheek like an old woman giving her favorite granddaughter a great piece of wisdom.

"I don't know. I'm afraid he's going to look at me and realize that I'm fat. I mean let's be real. There doesn't seem to be any fat people over here." Nikki sighed in frustration and took off her hat to rub her forehead. She always appeared bothered whenever I referred to myself as fat, even though I couldn't understand why.

"Oh Amy, Amy, Amy. Maybe they like their women with a little meat on them. Besides, there is a huge difference between fat and you. You have a real nice shape to you, curvy… yes, maybe a little voluptuous, but fat? No. Stop beating yourself up. You deserve more. Please believe it, because if you don't, others won't either." The conversation was taking a turn for the deep and I was uncomfortable discussing what I deserved. Maybe I did deserve better, but I just didn't feel that way down in my core. I quickly changed the subject to our next favorite topic.

"So, do you think you might sleep with Armond?" Nikki stopped rubbing her forehead and looked over at me sternly, and then one tiny corner of her mouth curled up in a crooked smile just before she parted her red lips. Laughing a little as she spoke,

"I highly doubt it, but there is that sterotype that Italian men make great lovers."

I couldn't imagine what it would have been like to have a great first time. My first time was merely short of horrifying, though I was slightly older and out of college, the entire experience was so terrifying at the very thought of taking off my clothes. It was definitely not what you see in the movies where the music starts playing and the couple gaze into each other's eyes and are glowing under the light of the moon. Not at all, it's awkward and heads are bumping and lots of worrying that everything is good enough and then five minutes later you're lying there thinking; "Oh, that's what everyone talks about?" Well, at least that was *my* personal experience.

"You're right, Nikki, let's not even think about it. Let us enjoy this trip, enjoy their company and take away from the experience whatever that may be." Chad, no Chad, Dante, no Dante.

I needed to encourage myself more than anything to take my mind off men, as much as I could.

"I'll drink to that!" Nikki sat up and in one fluent swoop of her hand, slid her hat back on top of her head.

Dusk had now set in and a soft golden glow from the streetlights romanticized the stonework that lay all around us. The breeze from the ocean continued to make its way into the town. After we climbed what seemed like sky-high stone stairs, making our way through the city streets, we found ourselves at a small restaurant that overlooked the steep drop, sloping out over the vast night ocean. Candles had already been lit throughout the restaurant and the smells of the food was enticing enough to make an anorexic crave a meal.

"Glad this is only seven blocks from our room… too bad it's all uphill!" We were both beat with exhaustion from our travel and wanted nothing more than a great glass (or bottle) of wine accompanied by a nice long rest. We sat down at a quaint little table and soaked up the atmosphere with the soft glow of the candles and warm ocean breeze floating past us. Then we ate the best seafood that we had ever experienced and toasted to our fun adventure we were sure to have tomorrow with our newfound male companions.

EIGHT

Before I could even muster up the energy to open my eyes, I was awake. I could hear Nikki snoring and by the warmth of her breath, I estimated she was only a few inches from my face. I squinted open my eyes a fraction with struggle as a headache instantly pierced the front of my head. I could only vaguely remember the end of the evening. In addition to having graciously been given many samples, Nikki and I had shared a bottle of white wine, one of many to choose from that came from the local region. I was almost certain that neither of us had changed clothes last night or taken our shoes off.

I finally forced through my headache and opened my eyes as much as I could tolerate. I stared at Nikki who was closer to my face than I imagined. My body ached and I fought to sit up as the room came back into focus. I began to make my way to the bathroom as I turned around to make sure I had not woken her up. As I stared at Nikki in shock, my heart filled with panic.

"Nikki! Nikki! Wake up!"

Nikki reached up with her eyes still half closed and scratched her head. She opened her eyes a little further and with slurred speech asked,

"Whass going on? Heee, why are you shouting?" I didn't know what was going on or how to tell her what I was looking at. I pointed to the small oval mirror above the decorative water basin against the wall.

"I think you need to look in the mirror." With surprising speed, she was standing in front of the mirror. Nikki let out a slurred and muffled gasp, and then she reached up with her fingertips and touched her face.

Her face was red and swollen. Her top lip in particular plumped out as if she belonged on an episode of the Simpsons. The right side of her face was the worse with her eyelid so inflated she could only open it half way, making her look in desperate need of a pirate eye patch.

"Awww, I looth lithe a munsther." I couldn't console the racing of my heart and questions flooded my mind.

"Should we find you a hospital? What happened?" Nikki shook her head for a moment, and then stopped, as if she knew.

"The only thing I'm allergith thoo is pawns. Buth I tithn' hath any pawns lasth nigh, only Sarthines with the seathooth sauth and the pastha." Since the two of us combined spoke less than awful Italian, we just left it up to the server to suggest. Nikki got the sardines, but the creamy seafood sauce was a five-seafood sauce, which was now clear meaning as in five different types of seafood, not five different cheeses like we had thought, and one of the five must have been prawns.

"I think there were prawns in the sauce. I had no idea you were allergic. Do you have medication or anything? Do you need to go to the hospital? What should we do?" I couldn't hardly understand what Nikki was saying because her swollen lips made her sound like she just walked out of the dentist office.

"I only know I'm allerthith because I had a prawn at a cousin's wedding back when I was twelve. My fath swelleth up lith a balloon and my mom gave me some Benadryl. It took a couple of hours for the swelling to go down and almost a full twenty-four hours before I was somewhat normal. But I don't have any Benadryl. I didn't even think about prawns. I eath shrimth all the time." She let out a long sigh as if it took great effort even to speak, then she pulled her hands up to her eyes and I could hear her crying. I reached out and gave her a hug.

"Don't cry. I'm going to talk to Lucia. I bet she has some Benadryl. Don't worry; we'll take care of this." I opened the door, raced out to find Lucia, desperately hoping she had some Benadryl.

Ten frantic minutes later in my search, I found Lucia and she had a medicine supply that included an Italian version of Benadryl. After her constant insistence, I took her to our room. I opened the door to the sound of Nikki washing her face in the small bathroom around the corner from the door. The scene that greeted us was of Nikki splashing water on her face while tears simultaneously fell from her eyes. She turned off the water and looked up, her face still deformed and puffy.

"We have some Benadryl."

Lucia rushed over and quickly filled the glass she had been carrying with water as she put two tablets in the palm of Nikki's hand. Her perfect English was gone and she spoke Italian at a very brisk, sympathetic fashion. Lucia took Nikki by the hand and led her to the bed and in an instant, switched to speaking in English.

"Please, you must rest and drink lots of water. I will go get you some cold cloths that will help with the swelling." Nikki sighed and mumbled as she stretched out on the bed. I had never been so grateful for the help of a stranger than I was at that moment thinking of the motherly action from Lucia.

"This really suths. We're suthothe tho meeth the dighs this athernoon. I thanth go out loothing lithe this." Even though a tiny selfish part of me was so excited to see Dante I didn't want to cancel, I couldn't bail on Nikki in her hour of need, because Nikki was like a sister, and I could tell she needed me more than I needed to be with Dante.

"Don't worry about it. They gave us the number to their aunt's house, so I'll just call and reschedule for a couple of days from now."

With her one half-decent eye, she glared over at me and with a heavily muffled exclamation, she declared,

"Don't even thinth about it! You are going outh with Dante. I *wanth* you to go and have fun."

"I don't think I can. I would feel awful leaving you, just to hang with a guy. There will always be another time." Nikki took the only cloth she had and folded it, laying it across her eyes while she spoke.

"There is no sense in arguing with me. You're going outh with Dante and that is the enth of it. I can'th thinth of a gooth reason we shoulth both be cooped up in this room because of me. Justh do me one favee and call Armond and tell him noth to come." Her tone made it very clear that her sentence really was the end of the debate and I had no choice but to go out with Dante and cancel for her with Armond.

"Um, okay." I shook my head and said very reluctantly as we heard a faint tap on the door, Lucia opened it with a pitcher of water in her hand and small bowl filled with ice water and cloths tucked under her arm. She rushed to the side of Nikki and set down the bowl and the pitcher on the small table next to the bed. Any person would find it easy to picture Lucia tending to one of many kids that one could imagine she had. She had a very old-world motherly charm about her that brought a tremendous amount of comfort to this unfortunate situation Nikki was in. It was apparent Nikki felt the same. I watched as Nikki reached out her hand, grasping the hand of Lucia as she slurred a quiet and teary,

"Thanth you." Lucia in return pulled out a fresh, cold cloth and rung it, gently putting it on Nikki's face.

"Don't worry, my angela, we will have you most beautiful again, do not fret."

I had entirely forgotten that I had woken with an awful hangover. Apparently, the best cure for a hangover was an allergic reaction in your friend.

A few hours later, and one phone call in which I desperately tried to keep Armond form coming, and six outfits, I stood in front of the bed, modeling for Nikki.

"What about this one? How do I look?" The swelling on Nikki's face had gone down a great deal, but she was still a little puffy in the lips and red in the cheeks. Her eyes had gone from *Goonies* monster to auto hit and run victim within a matter of hours. The greatest change was that now I could completely understand what she was saying.

"I like this one, but I really liked that light green halter top with the mandarin collar. You should wear it with the white linen pants. That one made both your butt and your girlfriends look good."

Even though her speech was no longer slurred, she still sounded like she had a few drinks too many. I quickly changed into the suggested outfit and put the final touches on my make-up and hair. My heart was racing. There was the fear of rejection once he finally realized just how ugly I really was.

There was a tap on the door and I shouted for Lucia to come in. Close behind her followed both Dante and Armond. Nikki was initially upset about Armond insisting on coming. From my conversation with him on the phone, it seemed that he didn't entirely believe me, that maybe the story was either false or exaggerated. He could have thought that he was being stood up by Nikki.

"Good afternoon." Dante was the first to speak, walking around Armond and making a straight line to me. He placed his hands on my shoulders and kissed both of my cheeks. We smiled at each other. I glanced around his shoulder to see Armond standing still in the middle of the room, staring at Nikki in a state of shock. The wide-eyed look proved my theory correct that he believed it was all a lie so we could avoid him. Armond regained his composure and walked over to Nikki handing her some fresh flowers. Nikki smiled and thanked him as she laid them casually on the table next to her. We all stood there in an uncomfortable, awkward silence for a few seconds that dragged exceedingly long.

Finally, Nikki spoke,

"I'm sorry I won't be able to go this afternoon, and that you came out here for nothing, Armond." Armond quickly put his hands in his pocket. I presumed he thought that perhaps Nikki was contagious. He was fidgety and could hardly make eye contact with her.

"No, this no problemo, I had to be taking the train for town today. I forgot I make very big plans for this day many weeks ago. Please do not be angry." In typical Nikki fashion, which I had grown to adore, she replied calm and cool, as if already prepared for his reaction,

"Oh, that's fine. I understand." Armond hesitantly stepped forward and gave Nikki a kiss on the top of her head, his lips just barely grazing her hair. Within a blink of an eye, he expressed his apologizes and was out the door. Dante obviously seemed bothered by his cousin's reaction, but I could see he did not want it to affect our day together. He turned to Nikki and politely asked,

"Are you sure you would not like to come with us?" Nikki signaled a polite refusal as she patted the novel that lay on the bed next to her. I could sense Dante relaxing a little. He seemed both a combination of nervous and excited to be alone with me. I, on the other hand, was terrified. I had not been on a date since Chad, and we didn't really do much of the whole going on a date thing anyway when we were together. My stomach had been doing flips for hours at the thought of going it alone, with no Nikki to back me up. Nikki shook her head in a polite no.

We headed to the door as Lucia came in. Dante stopped and started speaking to her in Italian, so I rushed over to Nikki to say goodbye before I took off.

"Sorry you can't come with us. Are you going to be okay while I'm gone?" Nikki glanced over at Dante and Lucia talking and gave me a wide smile and a wink.

"Don't worry about me, I'll be fine. Lucia has been like a fairy Godmother. Besides, Dante seems so thrilled to take you out, I wouldn't want to be a third wheel. Did you see how fast Armond was out of here?" I rolled my eyes and Nikki gave me a half smirk with her slightly swollen lip that said, 'saw that coming'. Lucia finished talking and came over to the bed, setting down another pitcher of water. She had Nikki drinking water as if we were about to enter a drought.

Dante and I stepped out onto a smooth stone street. It was a beautiful afternoon and the vast array of colors on the buildings brought true life and character to the town. I could hear the soft sound of the ocean even away from the beach. The air always smelled fresh and warm, a mixture of grapes, ocean and flowers blanketed the air.

"Was everything okay with Lucia? Was she mad I left Nikki?" I didn't think Lucia was the least bit upset, but I had no idea how to ask about his conversation without seeming too nosey. He walked right next to me, his arm only a few centimeters from mine, barely grazing each other when we walked.

"No, no, no problemo. I ask her if she needs anything for Nikki… if there was anything I could help with before we leaved. She says no and that her grandson comes every two weeks to help her with repairs and maintenance, and was going to come today, so she hava plenty of help." Dante put his hands in his pockets and looked down, embarrassed as he finished speaking.

"She did say she was not a happy with Armond leaving the way he did. I could not make excuses for him, even though he is cousin. When Italian mother is displeaseda with a boy, it does not matter if he is her son or not, you will hear about it."

I stayed silent for a moment, unsure what to say in response to his remark about Armond. I then pictured Lucia and her grandson doing little projects around the rooms. I envisioned a twelve-year-old boy wearing suspenders and a cabby cap, something old world Italy, resembling *The Godfather*.

Dante looked over, took his hands out of his pockets, and

slowly slipped his hand around mine. I blushed as I quickly looked into his deep, hazel eyes. He was far too handsome for me. I could almost sense that's what the people walking past us had to be thinking. My heart fluttered. By impulse, I squeezed his hand tight, and to my surprise, he brought my hand up to his lips and gently kissed the back of it while they were still locked together. That one gesture, simple and small, made every other previous romantic moment in the entirety of my insignificant life, look like nothing, absolutely nothing. I had not realized until that gesture how much my relationship with Chad had lacked passion, love, and even the smallest touch of affection. Don't misunderstand, Chad and I had love, at least from my side I thought we did. Our relationship felt like nothing now that I stood next to a man that in such a short time seem to have genuine affection for me, and he wasn't just any rebound, bottom of the barrel kind of guy, oh no, Dante was a supremely gorgeous, sophisticated, charming, and above all, genuine.

We walked and walked, holding hands. The coastline was splendid, the view was magnificent and the weather was unbelievably perfect. Nevertheless, in truth, the view could have been awful, the weather could have been miserable, and it wouldn't have mattered because I was walking in paradise as long as Dante held my hand.

"May I tell you how beautiful you look today?" I couldn't keep my cheeks from flashing shades of scarlet. I hid my face as a little smile of shyness crept over my mouth. I was slightly uncomfortable with his charming words of flattery. It reminded me of when you see an unattractive newborn, and out of guilt, everyone is quick to tell the mother how beautiful her child is. I thought it possible he was doing the same sort of thing with me.

We had been walking for hours, and I learned that Dante was the eldest of five children, no brothers. He was going to school to be an architect, loved a great white wine, had a thing for old American westerns and country music (which I would not have guessed) and had a green thumb that he put to good use to help his uncle on his small vineyard. I, on the other hand, was unsure how much information I should give up regarding Chad. I told him about my father that I adored, my brother that I loved, and my mother who was painfully critical of me, which he misunderstood to be comparative to an Italian mother, but it was not. I tried to explain it even better, but he did not comprehend my mother in the slightest. After about thirty minutes of trying to explain why she was displeased with me, I gave up, because he just couldn't understand.

"You are so very beautiful, intelligent, and I can tell you have a great heart. What mother would not be proud?"

After hours that only seemed like minutes, we were both back at my hotel. The sun had just set and the night was in the stages of infancy with its pale gray sky. I wanted to stand there, forever.

"Would it be possible to take you somewhere in the morning? I have somewhere I would love to show you. Do you think this is alright with your sister?" I just wanted to say yes as quickly as I could, but I had a small pang of guilt for leaving Nikki in the room by herself all day while I had the best day of my life.

"Let me run in and check with her and see how she is doing. Why don't you come up?" He glanced at his watch.

"I need to catch the train back. I will wait, no problemo." I shook my head and rushed upstairs with as much speed as my heavy, tired legs could manage. I opened the door to the room to see Nikki sitting in a chair, playing cards in her hand with a much better disposition than when I left. Her face was almost back to normal with only a few red splotches here and there. She looked up as I walked in the room, a wide, beaming smile splashed on her face as she stood up. In the chair across from her was a fairly handsome man in his early twenties. He was dressed more casual than Dante or Armond, but he had a natural charm about him, like the guy you could see playing soccer in a field. What he was not, was the twelve-year-old boy I had envisioned earlier. Nikki rushed over and gave me a hug.

"I missed you Amy! Did you have a great time? How did it go?" The smile didn't fade for a single moment as she probed me with questions. I glanced at the man with my eyes and Nikki whispered in response, "That's Lucia's Grandson. He is so great; he kept me company all day. And he's coming back tomorrow to check on me."

"I'll be right back." Nikki looked confused for a moment as I dashed outside. Dante stood, patiently waiting for me. I took a pause to catch my breath before I said, "Sure, I'd love to go out with you tomorrow. I'll see you in the morning. Nikki will be busy tomorrow." Before I could bat an eyelash, he eagerly leaned forward and gave me two long kisses, one for each cheek.

"I will see you tomorrow around breakfast."

As I watched him rush off to catch the train, my heart began to flutter. I felt wary for a moment because I knew I was starting to feel something I hadn't felt before, a giddy kind of love, one that gave me confidence. I found myself falling for a virtual stranger. I was angry with myself for a moment, but then I closed my eyes and told myself to shut up and just live. After all, I was on the coast of Italy, and if you can't fall in love on the coast of Italy with a gorgeous Italian man, then there has to be something wrong with you.

NINE

If it hadn't been for the fact that I was overcome with pure exhaustion from walking, I wouldn't have been able to sleep with all the excitement bubbling out of me. Nikki and her newfound friend, Lucca, were gracious enough last night to spend an hour walking the streets and talking while I got a chance to recoup from my day. It turned out that Lucia's grandson was incredibly kind and sweet to Nikki. From the pleased look on Lucia's face that I caught a glimpse of, I suspected she was happy to see such a match. There was a strange sense inside me, as if this moment of my life was supposed to happen here with Nikki, not Chad. But the strongest feeling was as if we had always been sisters, as if I was finally living the life that I should have been living all along, and it didn't include Chad or Betsy.

I felt so free and happy among the loving and accepting

people of the Italian Riviera. No one seemed to stare at me, the chubby girl, and no one *ever* told anyone not to eat seconds. On the contrary, Nikki and I were treated as if we didn't eat enough, which was a first for me.

I was busy trying to get ready as the sun was just peeking above the ocean. The view was wonderful as the colors started to awaken. I didn't have time for the view because I was far too busy trying to find something that made me look as thin as humanly possible, or I should say thinner as humanly possible. Nikki was full of questions about my day and equally intent on giving me information about hers. After I filled her in on all the juicy and wonderful tidbits of yesterday, I asked her about her time with Lucca, and for the thirty minutes I heard his name, I don't think she took a breath. Nikki was by far more enchanted by Lucca than Armond ever had a prayer of. If you stood Lucca next to Armond, then Armond would have won hands down in the looks and style department. However, Lucca was attractive in his own right. He wasn't going to be offered a billboard ad in Times Square, but stand him next to the average American Joe at Footlocker and he would appear quite masculine and handsome. Lucca seemed to be sweet, kind, and most importantly, he was genuine, which for Nikki was a huge advantage for any man that was interested in her. Nikki was very observant with men. She could easily spot the down to earth man who genuinely liked you, from the ones who will pretend to be what you want in order to achieve their goal, sex.

"I should just shut up! Here I am going on and on about Lucca. Are you going to be okay spending the day with Dante? I feel a lot better, and don't look as if you want it to be a double date sort of thing?" I loved spending time with Nikki but my heart dropped at the idea of this. I wanted to have at least one more day alone with him, but at the same time, I didn't want to hurt her feelings. Then I thought of a truthful obstacle to the situation.

"I wouldn't mind, but I don't know how awkward that would be since Dante and Armond are cousins." Nikki nodded in agreement and to my relief she looked relieved that I made an excuse. It was apparent that she equally wanted to spend time alone with Lucca.

"That's true. I think it will be good to spend a little time with these guys. Besides, we are leaving in a couple of days for Venice." Simultaneously, sad looks crept over our faces. I had been living so entirely in the moment and absorbing all of Dante's company that it had slipped my mind temporarily that we would be leaving soon. In a few short days, I might never see Dante again, and with that thought, there was suddenly a small, but sharp pain in my heart. A sad silence lasted a few seconds but hung like a cloud, almost as if neither of us knew how to cheer ourselves up, let alone each other. Then Nikki smiled and spoke again, "We've only been here a couple of days and this trip is already the best thing I've ever done. I'm so glad I came with you."

I was reminded with her statement that we had not called our parents since we got to Italy, and I knew my dad must have been going insane with worry.

"We need to call our parents tonight." Nikki quickly nodded in agreement and then asked,

"You look really nice today. Do you know where Dante is taking you?" Truth was, I had no idea where he was taking me, and I couldn't care less, just being next to him made me feel wonderful.

"No. What are you and Lucca doing today?" Nikki smiled and walked across the room to look at her reflection in the mirror. She still had her pajamas on and her hair was sticking out all over the place. However, her skin and swelling had almost cleared up completely. I knew that with a long shower, change of clothes and a tiny dab of foundation, she would be back on her game.

"We're going to his family's vineyard today. He helps them sometimes. It's in the next town over." Her demeanor changed and she frowned as she started to comb her hair with her fingers. I was worried so I asked,

"What's wrong? Are you nervous?" She nodded and stepped back from the mirror before she answered,

"Yeah, I just realized I'm meeting most of his family today. What if they think I'm some stupid American and they don't like me?" As she spoke, it became clear to me the level in which she sincerely liked Lucca. She must have cared for him far greater than I originally assumed for this to be of any concern for her. Before I could tell her she would be adored by everyone that would meet her today, there was a tap at the door. Lucia lightly knocked once more just as I opened the door.

"Buon giorno Amy. Dante is having a cup of coffee while he waits for you." She smiled softly at me, her smile brightened even more as she saw Nikki standing behind me in the room. I said thank you and Lucia rushed off to attend to her handful of other guests. I picked up my bag and gave Nikki a quick hug before I, for once, gave her words of encouragement.

"They will all love you. Don't worry about it; just be yourself. Love ya Sis." I raced out the door and steadied my pace as I walked across the open corridor to the small breakfast area where Dante was sitting, holding a cup of coffee in his hand. He looked up with a pleased look in his eyes as the new morning sun cast a beam of light across the side of his face. Just as I reached the breakfast area, I was caught off balance by how good looking he really was. This feeling must have traveled all the way down as I tripped over my own feet.

I went flying across the room like superwoman in a non-graceful way, as if superwoman had one too many cocktails. Tripping itself is bad, but the landing determines the level of humiliation, and unfortunately for me, I ended up flat on the ground with one arm stretched out, making me look like all I needed was a stupid cape.

"Are you okay?" I quickly pulled in my knees and tried to regain what little dignity I had left by getting off my face. I laughed a little as if it was not a big deal, but my face was flaming hot from embarrassment.

Dante had his hand on my back and I couldn't bring myself to make eye contact with him. I caught a quick glance at his face and could tell he knew I felt embarrassed as his eyebrows raised in sympathy. As I tried to gain enough nerve to pull myself up while fighting the pain of having taken a flying leap into the stone floor, I felt Dante slip his arm under my knees and around my back. My heart raced with horror as I realized he was actually going to attempt to pick me up off the floor!

I couldn't conceal the panic in my voice as I quickly urged him,

"No! I'm fine, really. Just give me your hand and I can get up." He didn't say a word in response, and to my disbelief, he began to lift me off the floor. I closed my eyes so I wouldn't catch a glimpse of his expression in case he struggled to carry all size sixteen of me. A second passed and I opened one eye to see him walking out the main door with no difficulties at having me in his arms. He looked over at me and I figured that if I was going to be carried (for the first time ever in my life) I might as well play it up for the full damsel in distress mood. I draped my arms around his neck and rested my head in the crevice under his chin. I could see both locals and tourists staring at us as he sat me down on the bench just outside in the garden area. Apparently, men don't carry around women in Italy, as one might romantically imagine.

Then, he got down on one knee in front of me and gently touched his hands to the side of my thighs, which seemed to diminish both my pain and embarrassment immediately, but elevated my attraction.

"Are you alright? Are you hurt?" He asked, his voice smooth and calm, dripping with his accent. I shook my head letting him know I was fine as he reached out for my hands and turned them both facing palms up. He then leaned toward me and brought each palm to his lips, kissing them. I was completely unfamiliar with this cultural gesture, but I decided I liked it all the same.

"I will a get you somea water. I will be one mom'ent."

Dante returned with a glass of ice water in one hand and a small brown duffle bag in the other. I recognized the bag from the floor next to his chair. I was able to remember it only because I was at eye level with the bag just a few minutes earlier.

"Thank you. I really am fine. Just a little embarrassed." He slid down into the spot next to me on the stone bench and rubbed my shoulder as if saying 'no need to be embarrassed.'

Even though my body was just a little sore, it was not as bad as one might imagine after seeing my attempt at flying. We held hands and walked through the town, admiring the speckles of colored houses with lines of freshly washed clothes hanging out the windows. The stone roadways consistently slanted from one direction or another to a slight degree. There was a constant smell of fresh bread in the air, and the echoing of silverware clinking against porcelain coffee cups echoed the narrow streets early in the morning. The pace throughout town was calm and slow until we got closer to the train station, where the haste around us increased ever so slightly. I was relieved that I had thought ahead and brought my train pass with me.

Curiosity consumed me as Dante refused to tell me where he was taking me. The duffle bag made me so tense it practically took on its own persona in my mind. I would glance at it from time to time as thoughts raced to fill my mind with possible contents; rope, shovel, duct tape. Or, condoms, roofies, duct tape. Whatever twisted idea my head could spin, it always involved duct tape. I mentally scolded myself for being so negative and I attempted to console myself that there was no reason a handsome man *wouldn't* be attracted to me. However, trying to ease myself was almost pointless, because after all, I did see *Silence of the Lambs.*

Our short train ride took us to one of the other towns, where Dante's subtle enthusiasm started to rise as soon as we stepped off the train. We made our way through the streets of more narrow stone roads and multicolored buildings, which were more pastel in color than those of the previous town. We continued this way at a faster speed until we were barely outside the town.

There we came to the edge of a steep drop off that had a path that lead down toward the ocean. The path was only accessible by stone rock steps that looked manmade and centuries old. Below, I could see a small cluster of private docks that housed half a dozen boats of various sizes. This was clearly a place for the locals and not the tourists.

"Pleasea… take my hand." The jagged path was wide enough I should have had no fear of falling, but after my super woman incident earlier, I decided I better not leave anything to chance. Instinctively, I reached out and held his hand tightly. Once we finally reached the bottom, I exhaled and let out a huge sigh of relief and a sigh out of the pain I was still having in my knee that I kept hidden.

The wooden docks were misleading with the presence that they too were swaying with the waves. My eyes told me that everything was rocking with the waves, and my legs were confident in the fact that the unevenly spaced boards underneath them were solid and still. This confidence did not prevent me from becoming dizzy, so I forfeited Dante's hand in exchange for his entire arm, which pleased him a great deal.

"Are you taking me on your boat?" I asked as he looked down at me and winked before he stopped next to a beautiful royal blue boat.

"Yes. My family's boat. Do you like this?" I restrained myself as I had the sudden urge to kiss him. He held my hand and helped me on to the boat.

"What's in the bag?" I blurted out as he lifted the bag up to me.

"If you like you may look inside." For a moment, I felt idiotic for not asking this question earlier. I wasn't sure why I even tormented myself with theories of the contents. Why hadn't I just asked him back on the train? I wasn't sure, and even at that moment, I was on the fence if I should look in the bag or not. I decided to be safe and look. I prepared myself to jump ship if there was even a hint of duct tape.

Inside, were two towels wrapped in a plastic bag, also a bottle of wine, cheese, fruit and a small loaf of freshly baked bread. The smell was faint, but still good.

The waves rippled and made faint slapping sounds as tiny beads of water splashed into the boat in between misty breezes. The weather was perfect and the smell of the ocean carried by the breeze was nothing short of arousing. The coastline was full of sharp cliffs and massively jagged rocks that were sprinkled with the occasional patch of greenery. The water was so clear with nothing more than a hint of turquoise, making it visible for several feet, resembling tinted glass. The underwater reefs closest to the coast were easy to see through the ocean's transparent surface.

Dante steered the boat around close to the side of the coastline, and a big cliff rock stuck out as he slowly turned his boat toward it. On the other side of the rock an entrance to a coastline cave was hidden.

"Are you taking this boat into that cave?" My sense of adventure faltered as I looked at the cave with the low, but steady waves splashing against the side of the rocks.

"Yes, do not worry. I have been to this cave many times and the boat… she handles the waters perfectly." My feeling of ease didn't last long as I wondered how many times he had been to the cave with other women, other plump women. I shook my head as my paranoid brain decided that if he asked me to put some lotion in a basket, I would have no choice but attempt to make the swim back home.

He dropped anchor a few feet inside the cave that gave us enough light to cast a glow around us. Dante sat down next to me with our legs touching each other. My heart raced as the sounds of the rippling water echoed throughout the cave. Just sitting next to him made my skin tingle with excitement. He spoke softly but the stone around us amplified his words,

"Are you hungry?" I casually shrugged my shoulders and politely said,

"Yeah." What I was really holding back was the fact that I

was hungry all right, hungry for some good old fashion male attention. Dante reached into his duffle bag and brought the lunch out piece by piece.

As we ate, Dante broke the calm silence.

"Please tell me, why did you and your sister come to Cinque Terre?" I hesitated with the secret of Chad and my honeymoon looming over me like a dark cloud. I had refrained from telling him anything during our conversations and walks, always changing the subject when he began to ask me what brought me to Italy. I knew that with my disclosure of Chad, it could very well be the last time I saw Dante. Nevertheless, I decided that it was time to be honest, hoping I wouldn't risk as much.

"Nikki isn't really my sister, not by blood anyway. Her mom and my dad are dating; both our parents divorced a long time ago. This trip that we are on was actually supposed to be my honeymoon." While I gave him my explanation, I was amazed I had no feelings of loss or sadness when I mentioned my honeymoon without Chad. I took another bite of the sweet bread and watched his face as more questions came into his mind.

"I know you said you are not married. May I ask what happened with this… Chad husband?" It was an instinct I could not hold back and I laughed a little at the thought of Chad being my husband, even though six months earlier that's all I thought of him as.

"No, we never got married. I found out before the wedding that he was sleeping with my best friend. So now, I am here with Nikki instead of my ex, Chad. I'm fine with it now. I don't think

Chad and I were meant to be together. We never had a… spark." The ease in which the information slid off my chest cleared away the dark cloud and relaxed my conscience, but it also made me nervous as to the type of allure Dante had over me to speak so freely.

"This is a very horrible thing for one person to do to another, but I am glad that you are not married and that we found each other. I think you are a most beautiful woman." I paused in fear, not knowing what to do or how to act as my body went from tingling to vibrating. He reached out, took the wine glass out of my hand, and moved all the food away from us. He leaned in and ran his fingers through my hair as I sat there frozen, with the exception of my eyes that I couldn't keep from blinking.

"Amy, I feel you in my heart. Please kiss me." My body was screaming for me to ravish him like some nineteenth century romance novel. The warmth running throughout my veins wanted nothing less than to be with *that* man, at *that* moment, in *that* cave. However, my common sense and inner spirt urged me to be rational and cautious in regards to the fact that it was ludicrous and dangerous. Not the least of which I was with a strange man and in a cave of all places. I closed my eyes to think for a moment before realizing that doing so was perceived as a signal to Dante, because apparently, when a woman closes her eyes in Italy, it becomes permission for a kiss.

His warm soft lips met mine with such ardor and passion. His hand pressed against my back and I let go of all doubt and kissed him in return, equaling his level of intensity. I decided that a little kissing never hurt anyone, and besides, it was my honeymoon and someone should get kissed.

TEN

"Well, someone is positively glowing." I looked up from the sink as drops of water streamed down my face and off my chin. Nikki stood in the doorway with her arms crossed over her full chest, a smirky smile raised in the corner of her lip. Her face had returned to its former glory and no one would have guessed she had recently looked the part of Quasimodo.

I smiled and shook my head before I replied,

"Glowing? How can you tell I'm glowing when I have soap all over my face?" I asked playfully in my best 'figure that one out detective' voice.

"Well, you're in here humming, and this is the first time since I've met you that you have ever hummed. And there's just this… glow… around you." I was taken aback for a moment, as I had not realized I had been humming until she pointed it out. I wondered how often I did that.

I finished rinsing my face and patted my skin dry with the towel sitting on the stand next to the sink.

"Yeah, I might be glowing, just a teeny tiny bit." I pinched my fingers together and squinted my eyes half closed as Nikki's eyes widened and her mouth dropped open with a half-smile.

"Seriously? Did you two *do* something?" Her mouth was still open and the thoughts of Dante and me doing X-rated things were all over her shocked face expression. I laughed a little and walked over to the bed, knowing full well I was killing her with the suspense.

"No, we didn't do that… thing." I smiled and chocked back a laugh while she sighed and gave me a quick 'you killed me with suspense on purpose' look. Then she glared at me suspiciously and put her hands on her hips.

"I know something happened with all your glowing and humming. So, what did actually happen?"

I smiled widely and just burst with excitement as I spoke, "It was so fantastic. We just kissed. Okay, honestly it was more like a mini make-out session. We just kissed for almost two hours. I didn't even know people could do that. It was really really sexy… he's really really sexy. It was all so fantastic." The same amount of time it would take to snap a finger, we went from thirty-year-old women to teenage schoolgirls.

It was all so new. In my whole relationship with Chad, I don't think we had ever exceeded five minutes for one kissing experience. Worse of all, it wasn't until I was kissed so intensely by

Dante that I realized Chad had been only kissing me half-heartily. I guess a person doesn't realize how badly they've been kissed until they finally get kissed great.

"So you guys just kissed? Where did he take you? Did you do anything else?" Nikki had rushed over and sat next to me on the bed, soaking up every detail that came from my mouth. I was fully aware as I spoke that our whole conversation continued to resemble a teenage girl sleep over, but I didn't care. I had never truly had any of those teenage experiences, so I allowed myself to talk and sound foolish for the first time.

"He took me out on his family's boat and we went to this cave that was hidden in the side of a cliff. It was kind of dark, but very romantic. He brought some wine and lunch, and we just talked and kissed. The first time, we kissed for about half an hour, then we talked a little and after that, we kissed some more, for about another hour and a half. I could tell he wanted to do more, but something inside me just wouldn't let me do it." My heart started to flutter again and I smiled just thinking about his smooth lips on mine.

Nikki just sat on the bed staring at me, trying to read through my face expressions. Then she casually said,

"I need to ask. Can he kiss?" I looked at her and just smiled before lowering my voice in a deep sultry tone.

"Ooooh, yeah."

Nikki sat staring at me for a moment taking in all my revelation before she finally said with a sly smile,

"Good for you. I'm so glad to see you happy like this." I was swimming so much in my own joy that I almost forgot how nervous Nikki was earlier to go to Lucca's house and meet his family.

"How about you? How did it go this morning with Lucca? Did you meet any of his family?"

Nikki was surprisingly somber and mellow.

"Things went well. I met some of his family and he showed me around a little. They seemed to like me, I think. Matter of fact, his mother insisted on making a dinner for us tomorrow and Lucca even asked if you would bring Dante."

I was slightly confused because her words didn't seem to match her tone or the look on her face. She appeared almost disappointed that it went well.

"Why do you look upset? Are you no longer interested in him?" I asked before she shook her head and frowned.

"No, that's not it. I'm not upset. I'm just still nervous because I do feel something for him. I've never cared about what a guy thinks or feels about me, but this is different. I'm just scared something is going to go wrong, or we're going to leave and then that's the end of it. I know I sound like a mellow-dramatic teenager and all, but that's what's going on." She looked down at the floor and shook her head. I instinctively rubbed her back and once again found myself in an unfamiliar role as I comforted her.

"Nikki, you're a beautiful, confident woman and that's what attracts guys to you. You know who you are. Trust me, he adores you, I've seen it in his eyes." She nodded her head agreeing with me and rolled her eyes as she gave me an embarrassed smile.

"I'm acting so ridiculous. Thanks, I just need to relax and let things take their course." She flashed me a confident smile before speaking.

"Do you think Dante will make it for dinner tomorrow?" I was so glad to have a real legit reason to ask him to see me, my brain started to think of the wonderful possibility to have some more of his soft lips on mine.

"I'll give him a call. I have the perfect excuse now." My smile quickly faded and I slapped my forehead, looked over at Nikki, and said, "We need to call our parents before they freak out." It wasn't that they didn't trust us, or that we were too young to travel alone, but I had promised my dad several times that I would call. I always tried to keep my word to him. I looked at the clock next to the bed and did a quick, and probably inaccurate, calculation on the time at my dad's apartment.

"If we call now I think it should be just before midnight. I know my dad is still going to be up. How about your mom?" Nikki laughed a little and said,

"My mom will be up for a while. She usually only sleeps about six hours a night, and before you say anything, we both know I didn't get those genes." I knew that was right. If Nikki got anything less than eight hours, she was grimly relaxed and less than her sparkling self.

"I got a phone card so I think that will give us about twenty minutes." I pulled out the phone card from the front pocket of my suitcase and Nikki and I went looking for Lucia to see if she had a phone.

Lucia had a phone next to the sitting couch in the front area room for guests. A few moments later, we were lucky enough that my dad picked up on the third ring.

"Hello?" My father's voice was gruff and I could hear him clear his throat.

"Hi dad. Nikki and I just wanted to give you guys a call and tell you that we're having a wonderful time. Is Della around?" I could actually hear the smile in his voice when he spoke.

"Hi honey, I'm so glad you two are having a good time. Yes, she's right here… she's getting the other phone so she can talk too." I tilted the receiver of the phone so Nikki could listen along with me. We held the phone as it was sandwiched in between our ears. Both Nikki and I smiled simultaneously when we heard Della's voice.

"Hi, darlings, so glad you're having a good time. Tell us what you've done so far."

Our smiles faded a little and we both turned our heads toward each other saying, "Let's not bring up the guys" with our eyes. I nodded to Nikki letting her know we were on the same page, so she answered her mom first.

"We have done all sorts of things. It's so beautiful here and the people are so nice. Matter of fact, it's so nice we might be tempted not to come home." Nikki smiled and I could hear her mother whisper to my dad that she's always kidding her. Even though Nikki was smiling and appeared to be joking, I wasn't entirely sure how much of her statement was border lining on truth. I believed that I might have underestimated her feelings for Lucca.

"Oh stop teasing, Nikki. So have you tried any really good dishes there?"

Nikki let out a long sigh before replying,

"Yes, so far everything we've eaten has been fantastic with one exception, actually it was really good, but we'll just say it didn't agree with me."

"I'm sorry, dear, are you better now?"

"Yes, everything is fine now. How have you guys been, anything big happen over there since we've been gone?" I heard my father's voice chime in.

"Nope, we are just doing the same things we did when you two left. I hope everyone is treating you girls all right. If you have any problems, call me and let me know, okay? That's what I'm here for." It was statements like that from my father that really made me regret staying with my mother for as long as I did.

"Yes, Dad, everyone has been really nice to us. How are Mom and Mike doing? Have you heard from them?" I really just wanted to ask about Mike, but it felt oddly wrong somehow being in Italy and not asking about my mother.

"Oh, I almost forgot. I told Mike that I would call him and do the three-way thing when you called us. Can you hold on a sec? Mike told me how to do it… just hold on." I heard him ask Della to hang up her end, and then a second later, there was the click. We waited for only a few seconds, which felt more like an hour before he clicked back over.

"Are you still there?" I heard my dad say.

"Yeah, is Mike on the line?" I waited a moment before I heard my brother speak.

"Hey sis! How's it going over there? I bet the Italian guys

are chasing you girls like crazy. Am I right?" My brother and I always loved to kid around with each other, especially when it came to dating, or in my case, the lack of dating. Nevertheless, he always knew how to make me feel good, because even when he was joking about guys chasing me, there was that tone of belief in his voice, making his jokes more like genuine questions. Nikki leaned away letting me have the phone to talk to my brother for a moment as she relaxed on the couch.

"Don't be ridiculous, Mike. Nobody's being chased." I smiled and gave Nikki a wink as she smiled back at me.

"Sure. Right. I know you can't tell me about it because Dad's on the phone. Anyways… I do have something to remind you about." My stomach felt sick. I was just waiting for him to tell me something crazy like Betsy was pregnant or Chad ran off with Kara, but instead he said, "You didn't forget that Mom's birthday is at the end of next month, right? She has been dropping hints that she wants you to come home for her birthday dinner." The thought of my mother's birthday dinner made me feel queasy. As long as I could remember, every single year on my mother's birthday, we went through a whole charade of her pretending she didn't want anyone to make a fuss over her birthday. Then, in the end, we always took her to her favorite restaurant, which happened to be very expensive, and followed that up with the gifts we *surprised* her with, even though she always either told or severely hinted to us that she wanted, which from me was usually a small refinished piece of furniture.

The last few years, she would miraculously come home with

some piece of furniture she just happened to find by the side of the road or at the house of a friend house who was about to throw it away. Then she would drop subtle hints leading up to her birthday about how nice it would be to have it refinished so she could put it somewhere special. In all, the long tedious charade was quite exhausting. She didn't seem to understand it was just a hobby and something I did to relieve stress, not create stress.

"No, I didn't forget, but I'm not sure I can make it. You could take her out to eat, right?" I wasn't sure why, but I had such a strong feeling of guilt trying to push my mother's whole fiasco off on my brother. Mike took a long pause and I could hear my dad breathing in the phone as they both waited for me to say something else. Then as I opened my mouth, I heard my dad speak.

"Amy, would you go if Nikki came along?" I sighed and quickly made an excuse.

"Well, I'm not sure she'll be able to get the time off work since she's already taken time off for this trip and I don't even know if she'll want to do it." Nikki looked up from the couch and asked,

"Do what?" I covered the mouthpiece of the phone and whispered to her,

"Come back with me to my mother's for a weekend… for her birthday?" She smiled and nodded her head.

"Sure, that's not a problem." I uncovered the mouthpiece, hesitated for a moment and said reluctantly,

"Uh, Nikki just said that she could do that."

I heard Mike's voice first. He sounded extremely relieved as he spoke,

"Great! That will be great. Mom will be happy for you to visit. I'm not going to tell her you're coming. I'll leave it as a surprise. You know how she doesn't like us to make a big fuss over her birthday." I could detect the light sarcasm in his voice. I rolled my eyes and matched his sarcasm when I replied,

"Yeah, she's low maintenance alright." I heard Mike give a soft chuckle followed by a pause before I heard my dad's voice chime in again,

"Amy, honey, how many more minutes do we have to talk?" I had forgotten to look at the clock before I called so I wasn't sure. I motioned for Nikki to get back on the phone since I could sense Della wanted to talk to us a little more. Then I heard Mike say,

"Okay, I'm going to get off the phone now. Next time you call, have Dad three-way me again so I can check on you, too. Don't do anything crazy over there, Amy. But still have fun, sis… okay?" I was nodding my head, even though he couldn't see me.

"Okay Mike. Take care of yourself."

"Bye." Less than a second later, Della got back on the phone after I heard the click of Mike hanging up his line. The conversation lasted not more than four minutes before a recording let us know we were running out of time. Quickly, I said before the line clicked off,

"We love you guys. We'll call again in a couple…" Half way through my sentence, there were three loud beeps and then the line went dead. I looked over at Nikki and placed the receiver back on the phone. I reached in my pocket and pulled out Dante's phone number to give him a call. Nikki looked at me and smiled before she asked,

"Are you going to call Dante and invite him to come over to Lucca's house for dinner?" I nodded back as I picked the receiver back up to make my call. Nikki smiled and pointed to the other room, indicating she would be leaving me alone to let me have some privacy for my phone call. As the line on the other end began to ring, my stomach did flips. Not only for excitement to hear his voice, but also out of disappointment thinking about the conversation I just had moments earlier. The conversation and the thought of going to visit my mother for her birthday had forced me to come to the realization that this trip to Italy and my time with Dante was nothing more than just that, a trip. A trip that would end not only one day, but also soon. In a short time, both Nikki and I would be back on a plane and my time with Dante would be like dream, a really good dream that you don't want to wake from but you know you need to. I thought about all of this as I heard his voice on the other line as he answered.

"Hello?" I smiled and just hearing his voice and thinking about our dream of a boat trip made me take in every second of time.

"Hi." I could hear him smile through the phone as I added our conversation to my experience in Italy. It was all becoming so surreal, dream-like and I knew that soon I would have to wake from it all, but I wanted a few more minutes of bliss before I did so.

ELEVEN

"How about this?" I pulled a bottle of wine from the shelf that sat inside the small shop that we were in. I turned it around in my hands, noting it was from the region.

"I don't know. What if she makes something that the wine doesn't go with? What if it's tacky to bring wine? I'm not sure." Nikki looked positively distressed as she pulled off her large brimmed hat and wiped her hair from her face before neatly placing it back in position. I smiled at the frail, elderly looking woman who sat in a chair and gave us a nice smile as we walked around the tiny shop, hardly large enough for all three of us to be in. We were so close to the alley that I could hear Nikki step outside even though my back was to her. I looked at the older lady and gave her a polite nod and smile before I joined Nikki outside.

"Those are lovely." Nikki pointed in the direction of a small stand with wooden tables, adorned with white linen cloths and a thin canvas tarp, all of which was pushed against the side of a building a few feet down the alley. We walked over to the stand that held several wicker baskets of various sizes, each housing a variety of fresh flowers. Lush colors and silky pedals seemed to fit at home among the colors of the shops and houses within sight. A shorter man in his early fifties with wide shoulders and the fading of his hairline, along with his slightly protruding belly, made him instantly likeable for some unexplained reason. He had a mustache that raised high with his wide, pleasant smile. He accurately guessed we were Americans and began speaking in fluent English as we approached his stand.

"Good afternoon, ladies." We both smiled and said hi as we walked up to his table. He searched in his baskets and pulled out two flowers with long steams. Then he reached out and handed a white one to Nikki, saying,

"Here is a white flower for such an angel." Nikki blushed a little and thanked him as she smiled. He turned to me with the other flower in his hand, which had wide, deep red pedals. He smiled and said as he handed it over, "And a beautiful flower for a great beauty." I, just like Nikki, felt my cheeks blush as I thanked him. The man's smile widened even more as he put his hands behind his back, basking in his gentlemanly gesture. Nikki smiled at him and asked,

"We have been invited to a house tonight for dinner. Would it be acceptable to take flowers? Can you tell me the custom please?" Nikki's voice was basically calm, but I could catch a hint of pleading for help in her tone.

"Ah yes, flowers would be a nice thing to take. You cannot go wrong with such beautiful flowers as these. They are very fresh, cut just this morning. I will make you a beautiful bouquet that will be loved?" Nikki nodded and we both watched as he plucked a variety of flowers out of various baskets, quickly working to create a masterpiece that pleased the eyes. We looked at each other, happily relieved our short-lived dilemma was over.

"Here she is for you. A beautiful gift for any house. I charge you very little for this."

Several minutes and shops later, we sat down on a small stone bench, which sat in the shade cast by the uneven level of the brick buildings. My feet were starting to hurt, as well as my wallet as I sat the handful of shopping bags on the bench next to me. Nikki had decided to treat herself and was slowly eating cake that had a middle layer of custard of some kind, it was a 'torta' cake of something, but I couldn't remember the name of it.

I watched her and instantly got angry for turning down a piece for myself. I didn't want to put on any weight while I was on this trip. She looked over and smiled as she chewed on one of the small bits she took, the slice held in a thick napkin. She licked the corner of her mouth and said,

"You really should have gotten a piece of this cake. It's to die for. Why didn't you?" I shook my head and looked away as I heard her let out a light sigh and continue talking as I looked off in the other direction, unable to look at what I was missing. "Amy, I can go get you a piece, it's just over there, not too far. Why don't you want one? Do you not like custard or something?" I looked over at the cake, thinking about the thousands of calories swimming around in all those sweet layers of goodness before I replied.

"I do, but I don't want to get back home fatter than when I came here. Everyone says Italian food is really high in calories. Plus, I'm just thinking about when I go back to see my mother for her birthday, she'll notice if I've gained even an ounce and I don't want to listen to her go on about it. I just better not." Nikki scrunched her eyebrows together and shifted her lips to one side before she exclaimed,

"Oh ridiculous! We are on vacation. Forget calories; forget what you think your mommy dearest will say. Eat, live, love. Just stop being ridiculous!" Then she set down her half eaten slice and promptly stood up, saying one last time as she quickly walked down the street, "Freak'n ridiculous!" I sat on the bench and waited a few minutes before she returned holding a slice of cake that matched hers. She reached out and handed me a slice wrapped in a napkin and said, "Eat cake."

I gave her a little smirk and took the cake as she sat down. I took a deep breath and mumbled right before I took my first small bite.

"I just don't want everyone to think I'm so fat." I could almost hear her roll her eyes, as she didn't hesitate by giving me a sisterly lecture.

"Amy, you are not fat, but if you insist on seeing yourself that way, others might begin to think that way too. You are beautiful, nice, and smart, and *that's* how you should see yourself.

When you finally realize this, then others will see you the way you really are." I nodded in agreement, but still couldn't grasp the possibility of it. Even though I was around the corner from thirty, the girl looking back at me in the mirror was still the fat teenager with chubby thighs, not the beautiful and lean model that I wished was the reflection I saw. I also knew that Nikki would debate me on this endlessly so I quickly agreed to put the discussion to rest.

"Yeah, you're probably right." She smiled and said as she licked some custard off the side of her finger.

"Probably? You'll see one day." I kept my mouth shut and watched people as they passed by. It was hard to see myself any other way but the fat girl since I had been wishing to be thin ever since I could remember. More importantly, I had a mother who had wished the same thing for the same amount of time. I thought about Dante. He didn't make me feel fat or ugly. He was obviously attracted to me, so what if Nikki was right and I wasn't really the same obese monstrosity that I thought I viewed in the mirror. It was true I didn't have much dating experience to go on, and I didn't have a gaggle of men chasing me like Nikki.

It was easy for her to believe she was beautiful because she was constantly reminded of it. I was reminded of the opposite, and it was nearly impossible for me to forget the fact that Betsy was so much thinner than I was, and perhaps that was a big reason that Chad wanted her over me. The thin girl was more attractive to him than the fat one.

I stopped thinking for a moment and took few more bites of my cake until it seemed to vanish before my eyes. It was strange when I thought about it for a second and realized how out of place I felt not having my mother hovering over me giving me the stink eye about the cake. I thought back to when I decided to make a cheesecake after finding out about Betsy and Chad, and my mother was literally going to have a coronary when she watched me eat half of my creation. I looked down at my thick thighs and wondered just how much of a disappointment I was to her. Did she cry sometimes wishing I were a beautiful slender size two daughter that she could proudly call her own? I had noticed from early on her long pause when responding to the question, 'Is that your daughter?', and it was in those moments that I realized how not saying something can be more painful than words. The sound of Nikki's voice broke my trance.

"What are you in deep thought about? Is it Dante?" I gave her a frown and shook my head before mumbling,

"Just thinking about how I should lose a few pounds before I go back home to visit my mom for her birthday." I knew that would be the best gift she could ever get, a thin daughter. Nikki looked cross at me before giving me a half eye roll. Then she sighed and stood up, reaching out her hand.

"Come on, Amy, let's get a little more sightseeing in before we leave for dinner." I nodded in agreement and got up on my achy feet.

We strolled throughout town and visited a few more shops before heading back to the inn to prepare for dinner. The sun had begun to sink lower towards the horizon, and long wispy clouds filled with hues of purple and magenta streaked across the sky like colorful ribbons. The evening sky in all its colorful glory enhanced the tones of the brightly painted buildings overlooking the sea on the edge of the cliffs. It was as if during the fifteen minutes the sky gave off the colorful glow from the dancing ribbons, the whole village became enchanted. The sun would drift closer to the line of the sea, and dusk would fade everything to a sleepy trance. Then the spell would seem broken. It was that fifteen minutes of the day in the town of Corniglia in Cinque Terre that I immediately fell in love with.

"How about this dress?" I turned from the wide window after taking in the view to see Nikki in a flattering rose-colored dress, not that anything she owned wasn't flattering. I nodded and she took a last look in the mirror as she fluffed her already perfect hair. Then she smiled and picked up a necklace off the dresser before she spoke again.

"Is Dante going to be here soon?" I nodded again and gave her the run down on the plans for the fourth time in the last hour.

"Yes, and he already got the address from Lucca so he's going to take us right there. He knows exactly where it is." She looked nervous and fluffed her hair, again. I walked over to the window as I heard a faint whistle coming from the path to the inn. I immediately recognized it as Dante's and quickly turned to Nikki, letting her know it was time. She swallowed hard and picked up the extravagant bouquet of flowers, swaddling them in her arm like a baby.

TWELVE

By the way the small house was arranged, one could easily tell the importance of sharing a meal. The sitting room, or living room, was small and quant. However, the dining area held a long table that was not much more than a solid, wide plank of wood. You could tell it had been hand varnished and each natural curvy grain of wood looked artistic, as if the tree itself owned a paintbrush. The table, even with its large size, barely seemed to accommodate an even larger family and guests seated against it, hardly sparing more than a few inches between each person. Nevertheless, the tight fit with the brushing of elbows did not seem to bother anyone. With less than an inch to spare, the bustle and friendly talking in the atmosphere suggested that the hostess would easily accommodate anyone else who wished to join, and even a stranger would find it hard to decline because the food was not only spectacular, but plentiful.

The air was filled with a mixture of Italian and English, anything that was not immediately translated was quickly done so for me by Dante, who sat on my left. Nikki sat on my right and next to her was Lucca, attentive and affectionate. Nikki had been slightly reserved for the first twenty minutes of dinner, but now she joined in the conversation and consistently received smiles and winks from all around the table. I, on the other hand, couldn't compel myself to speak up often and gave shy smiles and polite head nods to agree with the friendly statements. Dante took great delight and pride in his role as my personal translator, as if he was aiding a damsel in distress, which in truth, at times, felt accurate.

It was clear the short time Nikki had spent at Lucca's house the day before allowed her to feel more comfortable with some of his relatives, and they seemed to have already formed a fond opinion of her. Fortunately, for both of us, the conversation was light, entertaining and sometimes humorous. Then, just when I felt like another bite might kill me, even though they acted as if we had eaten nothing, Lucca's father let out a light satisfactory sigh and leaned back saying a whole-hearted 'grazzi' to his mother.

After we finished, Nikki jumped up to promptly help clear the table. I instinctively took her lead and helped as well. In the kitchen, the women chattered in Italian, and by the smiles they were shooting each other, it was evident they really liked the both of us, but Nikki in particular. The whole evening went so smoothly that I began to wonder where Nikki and Lucca would get married. I found myself desperately hoping it would be here in Cinque Terre so we could come back. Then I thought about whether or not Nikki would live here with him or in the United States? I felt uneasy for a moment, before I smiled and thought how fabulous it would be to come and visit her, and then I could spend more time with Dante. I smiled at my little daydream as Nikki rubbed shoulders with me and whispered,

"What's that smile for?" My smile was apparently contagious as she soon had one on her face.

"Oh nothing, I was just thinking about you and Lucca and if you'll end up having a beach wedding here." She gave a little embarrassed chuckle, making me realize that she possibly was having a similar daydream of her own. Then she whispered before we followed the other women out of the room,

"Let's not get ahead of ourselves… okay?" I gave her a sarcastic smirk letting her know that I was on to her. In reply to my look, she rolled her eyes and smiled as we headed back out to our gorgeous dates.

The moon appeared particularly massive as it hung low, beginning its climb in the recently darkened sky. A cool faint breeze carried the smell of the ocean, mixed with not only the earth, but also the sweetness of the grapes around us. Tight rows of vines striped up the side of the hills. Lucca's family had taken a piece of land and maximized its full potential. The mix of the moon, breeze and luscious fragrance instinctively pulled me into the whole experience as I rested my head against Dante's arm while we strolled through the vineyard. Lucca's father had taken us on a small tour and he was caught up in telling Nikki about all the varieties of grapes when Dante and I found an opportunity to stroll off by ourselves unnoticed. I clasped his warm hand tighter in mine when he slowed to a stop, turning to face me. The large moon, which acted almost as an oversized blue nightlight, casted sharp contrasting shadows on the side of his face. His handsome bone structure and smooth olive skin put me on the edge of my toes just waiting for the thick sexy accent to come pouring out of his mouth. He ran his hand down the side of my cheek before letting it drop to his side. Reaching in his pocket, he pulled a small box out.

I looked down at the plain box, which was neither fancy nor expensive as he slowly opened it, lifting from it a beautiful pendent on a silver chain. It had a deep blue oval sapphire in the center outlined by delicate and detailed thin pieces of handcrafted silver. The design was one you would expect to see in one of the century old churches. It was beautiful. He looked at me, and without a word, his smile asked if he could place it on my neck. I shyly smiled and picked up my hair as he stretched his arms around my neck and clasped the necklace without looking at what he was doing.

"My amoria, Amy, this Necklace belonged to my grandma, I have held on to it for years waiting for a beautiful woman to give it to." I blushed out of shock as I looked down and traced my finger around the edge of the pendant. A strange thought came to me as I realized it was the first time, other than my cheap and equally tiny engagement ring, that any man had given me a piece of jewelry, let alone a family heirloom. Before I could utter any words of appreciation, Dante's lips were pressed firmly against mine. Suddenly, a wave of sadness washed over me as I pulled back and spoke to him.

"Thank you so much, Dante. It's beautiful and I will wear it always, but I don't want to start anything that probably doesn't have a chance. In a few days, Nikki and I are headed to Venice and then we're going back home right after that. We won't be coming back to Cinque Terre before we leave. Do you understand what I'm trying to say?" He looked glum for a second, nodded, and then replied,

"Yes, I do, but you can never tell what the future may hold for us. I have to return by train tomorrow, but I can meet you in Venice after that. Venice is a romantic city and I can show you many things there." A small flicker of hope sparked inside me. Could it be possible? Could we work something out and then down the road be married? Years from now, could I walk out of my own small villa carrying a child and fresh cut flowers? The thought in itself was almost too much for me to take in. Those were all thoughts of the future that I struggled to have in my mind with Chad, but they somehow seemed more natural at this moment. I replied,

"Sure, where would we meet?" He smiled wide and continued.

"There is a large bridge there connecting the two main pieces of land. It is very well known, called the Rialto. We could meet around six this Friday. I will show you many things, and with your permission, I may sleep in your room?" I nodded and then froze when I understood what he was *really* asking. He wanted permission for us to be intimate. I didn't know what to say to this indirect question, so I said nothing. Then I heard the voice of Nikki coming toward us as she called out.

"Amy? Amy?" I replied as she slid from between the row of vines.

"Here I am." I reluctantly parted from Dante and walked over to Nikki as she tried to gently free her dress that got hooked on some vine branches somehow.

I walked up to her and helped as she whispered just out of earshot of Dante,

"How are things going with Dante? I tried to ask questions about the grapes to give you guys some alone time." I smiled, partly out of foolishness for not recognizing that she had done that for me.

"I think it is pretty good, since he wants to come meet up with us in Venice. Would that be alright with you?" She rolled her eyes and replied,

"Of course it would. I don't mind one bit. I think I'm ready to head back to the hotel, are you?"

I touched my pendant and then nodded in reply.

After a few minutes arranging the plan with Dante to meet together in Venice in a few days, Nikki and I said our final good-byes and linked arms as we headed back toward the hotel. The night was still early and we passed a handful of young couples as they began to journey out on evening walks or meeting together for dates. Both of us walked for a lengthy amount of time in silence, smiling and contemplating the whole evening until Nikki finally spoke up.

"So, what did Dante say about Venice? Was he the one that asked to come see you?" I nodded and then answered.

"Yeah, he kind of in a way asked me a strange question." Nikki looked puzzled as she spoke.

"Like what?"

"Well, I'm pretty sure he asked me to sleep with him if he comes to Venice." Even in the absence of a bright sky, I could see Nikki's eyes grow wide as she exclaimed,

"Really? That's a little… bold and strange too. What did you say?" I shrugged my shoulder and answered,

"Nothing. I didn't really give an answer." If I was being completely honest with myself, I was highly flattered that not only did such a good looking guy want to sleep with my chubby fatness, but that I was the one who would be allowing, or not allowing, it to take place. If I had ever in the past run such a scenario like that in my mind, I would not have been so fortunate, because in my mind, I would have had to beg after weeks and months of dieting to get to an acceptable weight for any man to want me, really want me. It turned my viewpoint upside down a little. Nikki remained quiet for an uneasy amount of time before she spoke,

"I'm not sure what to say. I think it seems strange to ask in advance, even if he was kind of asking. Do you think you will?" It was my turn to be quiet for an uneasy amount of time as I let her question rattle around my mind and actually take a moment to think about it for the first time. Then I answered,

"I'm not sure. But, I don't think so." We both walked quietly, our elbows still locked together like schoolyard girls. I broke the silence as we rounded the corner of the street that lead down to our hotel.

"I don't think I'll ever love a place as much as I have Cinque Terre." A flood of recent thoughts swam in my mind of Dante and boat rides, tripping and flying across the air, and all the warm and friendly people that made us feel like family, not tourists.

"Yeah, me too." Nikki said as we untangled our arms and took a few final steps to the doorway. I thought again about Dante and his proposal, and if I had truly meant what I told Nikki. Just as my mind began to turn the question over again, Nikki said, "I sure hope we are half as lucky and have half as much fun in Venice as we've had here." I smiled, wondering if I would end up getting lucky in Venice.

THIRTEEN

"Watch your step. It's dark down this alley," Nikki's voice echoed as I followed her down the very narrow alley. A pang of anxiety gripped me. It felt as if any minute the stone walls would squeeze into us, causing us to pop like large grapes. We had decided to take the later train to spend as much time in Cinque Terre as we could before we headed to Venice. What I had anticipated in Venice was a bustling nightlife filled with masks and loud laughing elegant courtesans that lined the lighted streets of Venice, like one big Venice party. However, my presumption was far from reality and our attempt to venture out to find such excitement was not rewarded. The whole city was so quiet that the ripple of the canal water against the sides of the buildings echoed throughout the dark, narrow alleys.

"Do you want to head back to the hotel and just call it a night?" I asked, reluctantly touching the cool stone wall, afraid as to what might unexpectedly touch me in return.

"Yeah, sure." She shrugged her shoulders as we took a few more steps forward coming to the end of the alley. Nikki let out a little yelp and stopped dead in her tracks as she started to lose her balance. I instinctively reached forward and grabbed the back of her shirt as her toes hung from the edge.

"Do you see that? It just drops off! Thank God you caught me, or I would have walked right off the ledge!" She regained her balance and we both took a few steps back while we tried to calm our racing hearts. I peered down at a good four or five foot drop down into the water. I wondered if that might be a reason why some locals and almost all tourists didn't venture out at night.

"I'm really ready to go back to the hotel, please." I couldn't blame her and easily agreed as we turned and cautiously headed back through the alley we had just taken.

As we continued to walk toward our hotel, the feeling of defeat followed us. Evenings in Cinque Terre had been so relaxing and for a lack of description, pleasant, that I had hoped at least equally the same would be found in Venice. However, Venice had not yet shown herself to be a nighttime girl of any kind.

"Do you hear that?" Nikki asked as we made our way down a lighted street.

"You mean the water?" She shook her head just as I continued. "Is this the way to our hotel? I think we're lost, do you have the map?" Nikki did not appear to hear my question as she listened even harder before saying,

"I think I hear music, coming from over there." Surrounded

by shadows, it was hard to see her as she pointed toward another street up ahead. I strained to listen and I finally heard what sounded like violins. Then I nodded, trying to contain my hope for something to do in the ghost town.

"Yeah, I do hear it! Let's check it out." We both quickened the pace in our tired legs and turned down a long street off the canal bank to see a small cafe crammed with what I suspected to be mainly locals, as a handful of men played various instruments. The smooth sound of classical music flowed down the street as it practically engulfed us. Nikki and I looked at each and smiled as we took our steps toward the friendly atmosphere.

A group of handsomely dressed Italians were lined around the edge of the restaurant and bar in tuxedos as they played classical music on string instruments. Couples and small groups of people sat at the round tables smiling and quietly chatting as the smooth and elegant music flowed through the air. Nikki and I walked up to the host who was standing at a wooden podium just outside the door and we were politely shown to a small table outside, ten feet away from the small quartette of musical players.

Our waiter was a tall, slender man in his early twenties with thick, close-knit eyebrows. He wore a suit jacket and had his dark hair combed back on the sides. He gave a feeling of a scene out of a Thomas Hardy novel. He smiled faintly and recommended that Nikki and I try the house spritz. We were both quick to agree and he took off into the restaurant with long strides in his step. Faster than we could blink, he set the bright orange drinks in front of us. Nikki took one sip and licked her lips with a smile, while I on the other hand, didn't like the bitter orange taste that it left in my mouth.

"You don't like it?" Nikki asked when she saw the reaction on my face.

"No, you can have mine. I'm going to order a coffee or espresso or something." I slid the glass over to Nikki and the waiter magically seemed to appear next to me before I could bring my hand back to me from across the table. He smiled faintly again with his thin lips and I politely asked for a coffee.

"I'm so glad our night was not a bust like I was afraid it would be," I said to Nikki as she nodded her head in agreement.

"Me too, I could sit here forever it's so nice." We both smiled at each other and soaked in our very first night in Venice.

I can't find my rings. I had them right here. I searched through the top drawer of my dresser for what I was sure was the twentieth time. I thought they might be in the bathroom, so I walked down the extra long hallway and opened the bathroom door. I was wrong. I had opened the front door by mistake to see my mother watering her flowers.

"Amy. Amy, why don't you give me a hand with this garden?" I didn't respond to her as I walked back into the house. It was dark in the house, so I began to look for the light switch. Why wasn't anything where it normally is? I sighed a breath of relief when I finally found the switch to the bathroom and turned it on. The lights barely gave enough light to search through the cabinet doors for my rings. I didn't know when my mother had bought such ugly purple floor mats. My hand fished through the drawers and I

reached, pulling out long strands of hair. Had my mother been saving strands of my hair for some reason? I kept fishing through the door when I heard movement in the shower. I looked over and pulled back the new purple shower curtain that my mother must have bought to match the ugly floor mats. Or was it orange?

"Chad?" Chad was sitting in the bathtub, fully dressed staring up at me with sad sympathetic eyes. I stared down at him before I crouched down on the floor and asked, "What are you doing here, Chad? Why are you sitting in my bathtub?" He stood slowly and stepped out of the shower before he picked up my hand and looked me in the face.

"I've made a mistake, Amy. You know I've always loved you." My heart began to ache and a flood of different emotions began to pour to the surface. Then I meekly, and full of doubt asked,

"Really? You do?" He walked out into the hallway and I followed behind him, watching the back of his shirt, which was uncommonly wrinkle-free. We continued walking down the long hallway. I found it peculiar that my mother had replaced the wallpaper to the same one we had from my childhood. When I took my eyes off the wallpaper, Chad was gone. I walked down to my bedroom and pushed open my door.

Betsy was quickly putting on her shoes even though she had not yet put her pants back on. Her small slender frame only had on a tank top and pair of underwear, but she was worried about shoes.

"What are you doing here, Betsy?" She slowly turned her head and smiled at me. She turned back to her shoes and continued tying them.

"Betsy," I said to her in a stern voice, full of anger. She once again turned her head towards me and gave me another sly smile. I became so angry that I lunged forward to punch her in the side of her head, but my feet were stuck. They were like two concrete bricks unable to budge. Then I heard Chad's voice from the side of the door.

"What are you doing in here?" I spun around and narrowed my gaze at him before I asked in reply,

"Me? What are you doing here? And why is she in my room, half naked!" Chad shook his head slowly and then the sides of his mouth curled up in a slight smirk before his tone was so deceitful.

"You have fat ankles, Amy." I looked down at my feet because I've never had large ankles. My legs looked normal but my baggy sweat pants were dirty and torn.

"No I don't." In what was a strange combination of both slow motion and haste, Chad was pressed tightly against me, his face inches from mine. My heart raced, as I feared he would kiss me, and my heart couldn't take that. He stared at me with nothing but disgust on his face as his words hissed in my direction.

"You're a fat. Ugly. Piece of trash. I didn't love you. Ever." As the words came from his mouth, I began to cry. I heard Betsy chuckle in the background. I looked up, on her face was the biggest, happiest smile I had ever seen her give, all for the joy of my heartbreak. Chad disappeared and I lunged forward, my feet free as I smacked her hard in the back of her head.

"Amy!" I heard my mother's voice while I looked down at

my feet, the water from the hose running past my toes. She put her hand on her hips and gave me a dirty look just as I saw Chad's car back out of the driveway. He had repainted it a horrible shade of brown. I felt sad to see him leave, and then I was filled with anger as I saw Betsy sitting next to him in the passenger seat. My mother seemed to know exactly what I was thinking as she blurted out,

"Betsy is a better fit for Chad anyway. I don't know why you couldn't be more like her."

My mother turned back to her flowers and Betsy and Chad laughed in the car. The car was moving so slowly it was almost not moving at all. Then it was gone. It instantly became the middle of the night and everything was so dark. I had not moved from my spot where I was standing. I looked down into my hands and realized I was holding my favorite photo of Betsy and me, the one we took together at the mall when we were sixteen years old. However, I couldn't hardly make out the faces, everything was blurry in the picture, and then I knew I was crying. I felt a nudge on my shoulder and I jerked my arm away. I felt it again. I didn't want to see anybody else anymore. I wanted people to stop betraying me. I felt the nudge again, and again. Then I heard my name.

"Amy. Amy... Amy" The nudge wouldn't go away. I turned around to see who wouldn't leave me alone. I heard my name again.

"Amy. Amy," the voice said with the nudge. The nudge was so real. Real. Reality.

I opened my eyes slowly and saw Nikki sitting next to me on my bed. She was gently nudging me on the shoulder. I looked up at her, the sides of my cheeks wet with tears. There was a concerned look on her face as she asked,

"Are you okay, Amy? I got up to use the bathroom and I heard you crying in your sleep." My dream was still so fresh and vivid in my mind, including all the emotions that came with it. I nodded and wiped my face with my hands. It took me a few seconds to remember we were still in Venice, and I was luckily hundreds of miles away from my mother's house and everything that was in my dream.

"You must have had a really bad dream." Nikki's tone was more of a statement then a question of any kind. I nodded to her again and she looked at my face, sensing I was not yet ready to talk about it. She didn't push the subject any further, which made me grateful. She stood and walked toward the bathroom, the sun was barely shining through the window. It appeared gloomy outside. Just as Nikki reached the bathroom door, she reminded me,

"Don't forget we're meeting Lucca and Dante at the bridge today. This is our last full day in Venice. Can you believe that?" I shook my head and Nikki did as well before she closed the door and turned on the shower. I couldn't believe how fast the time went by, and soon we would be getting on a plane to head back, closer to the cause of so much of my pain.

FOURTEEN

It is amazing that in some circumstances, there is a fine line between creepy and romantic. This discovery occurred to me as Nikki and I walked down the narrow stone streets of Venice, just off the canal. Heavy, dense fog hung along the canal and slowly crept up into the city. Had any film producer been present and decided to add an eerie ambiance sound effect, it would be nothing less than creepy. However, since the city was lined with couples paired off holding hands and the faint sound of classical music combined with the ripples of the canal water, it was more romantic and calm than one might have imagined.

It was our last full day in Venice. Tomorrow we would wake early and go straight to the airport, and I would be going back to my dull, worthless reality. It was true I had a small taste of what it was like to be in Nikki's world, men smiling at me, winking at me, the feeling that perhaps I am attractive in some sense. Nevertheless, a small trickle of sadness hovered around me, much like the fog we were walking through. Soon I would go back to being plain, fat, Amy. I would no longer be the unknown, intriguing tourist with a cute smile and pleasant 'thank you'. I would be the girl who people whispered about behind her back because her fiancée would rather sleep with her best friend than her. I would go back to having people feel sorry for me because I was an unfortunate girl that men were incapable of loving for reasons that were obvious to the eye. I had not only enjoyed the friendliness of the Italian people, but I had almost become accustomed not to being judged harshly because of my curvy hips and thicker thighs. Just when I felt I might be able to view myself as nothing less than a curvy woman who was beyond her appearance, it would end.

"That looks like a cute little shop. You want to check it out?" Nikki asked as we passed the doorway of a tiny shop inside a row of stone buildings. I nodded my head and then spoke up, knowing she might not notice my head moving through the hazy fog.

"Sure."

A few moments later, Nikki opened the door and a tiny bell made the faintest rattle you could imagine. The shop was small but held many shelves of small trinkets, souvenirs and gifts. There was a slight musty smell in the shop, I suspected from the fog and the lack of a regular breeze. The light was dim but the gloomy amount of light that did slid through the window helped the little shop owner out. The owner, or so I presumed, was a short, older woman with silver gray hair that sat on a small wood stool. She smiled and lifted her wrinkled hand up to give us a slight greeting and head nod. We both smiled at her and said hello as we began to walk, or more like sway, around the shop. It was not a large lavish space, so a simple turn would take you from one section of items to another.

Two rows of Masquerade Masks hung up against the wall. I reached up and glided my fingers along the deep colored feathers that adorned the edge of the hand painted porcelain. Jewels were placed around the holes for the eyes and some sparkled with glitter while others were more artistic and subdued. Looking at them made me think of my mother and the mask she wore. I smiled with the thought that a mask would be the perfect birthday gift for her. I had no illusions of hope that she would be happy with her gift, she rarely ever was. Given her history, she would be more interested if I had been losing weight than what I had bought her, since I was the largest hindrance to her pretense. Nevertheless, if only for my own private satisfaction, I decided to get her one anyway.

As I gently fished through the masks, I heard Nikki speak to the shop owner as the older lady sat on her little stool.

"That's a beautiful necklace, do you sell that here?" I smiled and turned around to see what necklace Nikki was talking about. The shop owner had a brilliant sapphire stone that had been encased with finely intertwined silver that formed the shape of a cross with such delicate detail work it reminded me of the one that Dante had just given me. Unlike the shop owner, mine had been owned by his grandmother and probably passed through his family for decades, until he found the woman of his dreams and put it on her neck.

A warm feeling spread through my very bones as I smiled

and looked down at my blue sapphire with its detailed silver encasing the stone. I had not realized before that the pattern made the slight shape of a heart around the sapphire, which made me even happier. I heard the crackled voice of the shop owner as she spoke nearly perfect English to Nikki.

"Yes dear, that table there has a selection of necklaces like this one. They are handcrafted by a young man here in Italy. He is from Genoa, very talented." Nikki took a few steps and followed the direction that the elder lady was pointing her wrinkled finger towards. The woman smiled and started a conversation with Nikki. "They are very beautiful pieces. Are you two from America?" Nikki was cautiously picking up different necklaces and bracelets as if she was handling a Harry Winston. She turned her head and answered the woman, then asking a few questions of her own.

"Yes, we are, we are headed back early in the morning. We love it here." She took a brief pause and then asked, "How long has he been making jewelry? Is he a relative of yours?"

The woman finally stood from her stool and slowly walked over to Nikki. Her shoulders had a scarce hunch in them under her pale blue sweater. With the selected mask in my right hand, I took a few steps over to admire the pieces of jewelry beside Nikki. I slid up next to the shop owner as she stood in the middle, the three of us almost shoulder-to-shoulder with each other. I could smell the sweet, yet spicy aroma of her perfume as it floated up from the fabric of her woven shawl across her shoulders.

The woman began to select what I assumed were some of her favorite pieces and lay them along in a row across the palm of her opened hand. She answered Nikki with her faint, shaky voice.

"There is no relation. He is very good at his craft and he is also good in business. There are a few shops in some major towns that he takes a small collection of his stuff too, but I will tell you that I am the only shop in Venice that sells his jewelry." There was a significant amount of pride in her voice when she said this.

Nikki was so engaged by the craftwork in front of her that the older woman took her attention off of Nikki for a moment and turned her head in my direction, admiring the gift I had gotten from Dante that hung around my neck. Then she asked,

"Have you already purchased something from the craftsman? Is that his work?" She reached out her free hand absent by rows of jewelry for display, and gently touched the necklace on my neck. I gave her a shy grin, shook my head, and answered in return,

"No, this was given to me as a gift. It had belonged to someone's grandmother."

Nikki had broken her gaze for a moment and a sly smile came on her lips, recalling our romantic adventure in Cinque Terre. The older woman gave a pleasant smile, lifted one shoulder in a slight shrug, and turned back to Nikki explaining the price was so low, considering the value. Nikki spoke up, louder than she had thought from excitement,

"What do you think about buying one of the nicer necklaces and a bracelet together for my mom... or even your mom maybe?" I held up the mask to show Nikki.

"I've got my mom covered, but yeah, I think that's a great idea for Della. She would love that." The woman walked back over to her stool and sat next to her vintage cash register while she patiently waited. It took us almost as long to pick a necklace out as it did to choose which dress to wear to dinner.

Moments, or many moments later, we were handing over most of our reserved spending money to buy gifts for our family. The shop woman pulled out a small plain box and placed the jewelry inside before she tied it with a ribbon. Then she thanked us for our purchase and said politely,

"Those will make nice gifts. The jewelry is initialed by the artist himself. He does that with every piece he makes. S.M., Salavator Moretti. Good day ladies, have a safe flight home." We gave our goodbyes and a wave and stepped out of the small shop. Even though we had only been in there twenty minutes or so, time appeared to pause for us, as the fog had only lifted ever so slightly, and the glimpses of couples through the fog continued where it had left off.

"Do you know how long until we meet Dante and Lucca on the bridge?" I shook my head and shrugged to Nikki, indicating I had no clue. It was a lie. I had just checked the time and I knew we had exactly four hours and twenty-seven long minutes before we needed to be on that bridge.

Nikki and I locked elbows and started to weave in and out of the street traffic, looking for some nice spot to sit down and eat. We began to chatter about the shop and the older woman that was so pleasant and friendly, which was the norm in Italy thus far.

We walked all over Venice and admired the unbelievable architecture and hand carved stones around the city. I checked the time again and was relieved that nearly four hours had passed, even if it felt more like four months with my anticipation of seeing Dante. I couldn't wait, and even Nikki was starting to get fidgety and anxious when she spoke. Not long after I looked at the time, we both agreed to head to the bridge. I volunteered to carry the few small shopping bags that we had since Nikki had been holding them the rest of the time. With that, we made our way to the bridge, my stomach flipping with anxiety. I had not put a tremendous amount of thought in regards to my answer to Dante's proposal, but a little more than enough to know, I would most likely be agreeable. I had not brought up the subject again with Nikki. Mainly because I believed she might discourage me from spending the night with him. I knew that the opportunity for a chubby girl like me to land such an incredibly handsome man was a chance in a lifetime, or a one in a million shot.

"Here, this is the spot." Nikki tried hard to contain he enthusiasm as she pointed up the steps of the bridge to the wide walkway before the steps continued down on the other side. She fought to gain composure as we came to the last column on in the row at the top of the steps near the other side.

"I'm pretty sure this is the area he said they'd meet us." Nikki looked around and placed her hands on her hips, as if proclaiming we now owned a territory.

Minutes passed into what seemed like centuries as we hung over the railing, gazing down at the gondolas while they lurched out from behind the thin curtains of fog before they'd glide underneath us and out of sight, only to be followed by another. Then one would pass and fade into the fog, and the time kept moving, agonizingly slow. Even in her silence, I could tell that Nikki doubted we were at the right bridge at all, while I was beginning to doubt the men would come at all. When hope seemed to be lost, I heard Nikki speak up as she stood straight up, apparently keeping watch of the steps from the corner of her eye.

"Oh, I think they're here." I smiled when the words came out of her mouth. I quickly smoothed down my hair that had bunched up into large loose curls, thanks to the foggy weather, and told myself to calm down. The outline of a man moved closer through the fog and lifted his hand, giving us a wave. My mind flashed images of tonight and all that would come with it. The man took a few more steps, becoming clearer as he came closer to us. I could tell it was not Dante but Lucca who was approaching us. I stared intently into the fog, waiting for Dante's handsome face to break through the haze. My focus was so concentrated on the fog that I had not noticed that Nikki was no longer by my side, but a few feet in front of me, speaking with Lucca. I broke my gaze, only for a second to see the intensity of Nikki's face before she headed back toward my direction. I stared past her, still hoping Dante was right behind Lucca, coming to me at any moment.

Nikki walked up to me with Lucca a few steps behind her. A disappointed look hung on her face. Then she took a long pause, wanting to say something, but turning around in her head the best way to say it. So I just said it for her.

"He's not coming, is he?" I said as plainly, emotionlessly as I could manage. Nikki replied by shaking her head and then said sympathetically,

"No, he's not. He told Lucca he wouldn't be able to make it." Then she stopped abruptly, as if there was more to her sentence. So I asked,

"What is it, why is he not coming? Please tell." With great reluctance, she spoke after hesitation,

"Lucca said he ran into Dante at the train station and that's when he was told he wasn't coming. Then he said Dante went off with a couple of British tourists." I looked down, feeling tears starting to well up in my eyes, but I choked them back and put on a carefree face as I asked,

"Well, how did he know they were British tourists? Maybe they were college friends that needed help or something and he's going to grab the next train?" I knew after I asked the question it was not only a long shot of a theory, but it made me look desperate.

"They had British flags on their backpacks and he was very flirty with them. He even put his arm around one of the girls. Believe me, I asked all these questions too." By that time, Lucca had slowly made his way over and was now a side part of the conversation. He nodded in agreement with what Nikki was telling me, and then looked sorry to be bringing bad news.

I reached deep for any acting ability I had and shrugged the best I could before I replied,

"Well, that's okay. I'm exhausted from walking around all day. I'm going to head back to the hotel since we're leaving early." I reached up unconsciously and twirled the gift I had gotten from Dante around my fingertips. I couldn't understand it. Was I so pathetic and desperate that I was a joke to men? Was this how people saw me? Nikki asked me, a sad tone in her voice,

"Should I not have said anything? I'm sorry, Amy. I'm going to head back to the hotel with you. Lucca said he can grab the next train back." I shook my head at her offer. I honestly didn't feel like being a martyr because of Dante and I didn't want to ruin anything for Nikki. I knew it wasn't going to kill me to be back at the hotel by myself for a few hours, so I said with genuine appreciation,

"No, I'm okay. Really. Go walk around the city with Lucca and I'm going to go relax for a bit. Maybe I'll go out and walk the city on my own." Nikki scrunched the side of her lips, pondering my sincerity for not wanting her company. She decided my offer was honest and she affectionately replied,

"Okay, I won't be too long. We'll still get some dinner tonight, okay?" I nodded in agreement and she gave me a quick hug before she they both waved and headed off the bridge.

I continued to roll the sapphire charm around in between my fingertips before I looked down at it, turning it over. Looking back up at me were the very tiny, almost unnoticeable initials of S.M. Things made perfect sense in the light of those initials. Dante wasn't any more serious about me than Chad had truly been deep down. A slow trickle of sadness spread throughout my heart. It was all so depressing when I mixed this new revelation with the dream that still felt so real and new.

I felt done. Done with being walked on. Done with being pitied, but most of all, I felt done with men. I reached around behind my neck and fiddled with the hook that proved to be a near impossible feat to unlatch. Finally, I succeeded and the wrapped the charm in my hand before I poured the necklace back and forth into my hands in a mixing type motion. Then with one smooth sweep of my hand, I let the necklace and charm glide out of my fingertips to the canal below the bridge. Its lightweight body made no sound at all, as it slipped into the water and vanished.

I picked up the shopping bags and decided to tour the city on my own. After all, I was almost thirty and was not familiar with being on my own, which I finally understood would need to be a skill I would have to learn.

FIFTEEN

I stood at the kitchen counter and opened my calendar to write down the date for another interview when it hit me we had been back from Italy for exactly three weeks, and it felt so strange that three weeks had already gone by. Since then, many days I woke up in the morning still thinking in those first few sleepy moments that I was still there. However, when reality struck, a slight sadness would trigger when I came to terms with the fact that I would need to get out of bed and continue my job search for yet another day.

"Did you get an interview?" Nikki asked as she waltzed into the kitchen making her way to the fridge as she bent over, shuffling through the fridge just before fishing out a monstrous apple, inspecting it like a science project.

"Yeah, I did. It's a secretarial position, but not in a field I'm used to." Nikki had walked over to the counter and leaned against it, tilting over it against her side as we talked.

"But at least that's a good sign, right?" I agreed with her and flipped to the next page in the calendar, already knowing what was in there, not wanting to validate it by seeing it again, but I did anyway. Then I asked Nikki, desperately wishing she had changed her mind, as I was wanting to do on a daily basis,

"My mom's birthday thing is in two and a half weeks. Do you still want to come with me?" Nikki looked up from her apple and gave me the strangest look as if I had just asked her the most ridiculous question ever. Then she replied,

"Ah yeah, I told you I would when you promised your dad and brother. Besides, I'm looking forward to it." I couldn't prevent myself from rolling my eyes, even if I hadn't intended to do it so dramatically. Then I said,

"Don't be, once you meet my mom you may not want to be my friend anymore." Nikki gawked at my remark and gave me a little smirk as she shook her head.

Before Nikki could open her mouth and give me a little lecture, the phone right next to me belted out with a loud ring. I closed the calendar inside the day planner my dad had given me, and stepped to the side as Nikki pushed herself straight up and practically jumped for the phone. Neither of us had to ask who it was, we both knew it was Lucca. He had practically called her faithfully almost every day since we returned home, with the exception of the last two days.

She picked the cordless phone out of its holder and quickly answered it. Then with a bounce in her step, Nikki walked over to the living room, curling up on the sofa chair, her feet tucked underneath her. Nikki had a wide smile and an almost giddy excitement in her voice. Even though I had not really known Nikki that long I could sense her attachment to Lucca was out of character for her. By her own admissions, she was not one to fall foolishly in love and had never even been *in love* for that matter, until Lucca came along.

This whole thing between Lucca and Nikki made me begin to wonder about myself. Had I ever actually been *in love*? I could not recall, not from a lack of trying, feeling so deep with passion or love for Chad that the whole world could stand still, as they say in the movies. It was true that I had been deeply infatuated with Dante, hopeful in an unrealistic desire for a future with him, but was it love? For three weeks, these were the thoughts that floated through my mind, and I got them more often when the phone rang to start a conversation between Lucca and Nikki.

I walked into my bedroom and gently closed the door behind me, plopping down my day planner and pen on top of my long dresser. The wide rectangle mirror hung just above the dresser and I glanced up at it, taking a long look at myself while my mind continuously ran thoughts about love and what not.

I knew looking at my reflection I owed a hefty amount of gratitude to Nikki. She had not only introduced me to beautiful, well-fitting clothes, but also the perfect color palette of make-up. My hair was not only stylishly cut and healthy, but I had sensationally chic eyebrows. To top it off, I had somehow managed to drop ten pounds, which was a shock to say the least. All around, I had taken a massive step forward with my appearance. Because a little guidance and the support of a new great friend, I had essentially been reshaped into a better version of myself. Looking in the mirror hadn't been like it was before, because now, I didn't cringe a little when I walked past my reflection. In truth, I still found faults and things to change, and that fat worthless Amy was always there, even if she was hidden a little deeper behind a wonderful haircut and beautiful make-up.

I heard a light knock on my bedroom door and I reached over and pulled it open. Nikki looked at me, her eyes slightly red along with her nose as she meekly asked,

"I'm going to run out to the store, anything you need me to pick up for you?" I ignored her question, not out of meanness, but unconsciously from concern as I asked her,

"What's wrong? Did something happen?" Nikki batted her eyelashes as thick gobs of mascara got welled up in the tears she was fighting to hold back. She sniffed a few times and forced a brave smile on her face. I crossed my arms and asked her again,

"Tell me what's going on, please." She slowly strolled into the room and sat down on the edge of my bed as she took a deep breath and looked down at the floor, appearing unable to make eye contact with me.

"Lucca just ended things with me." She took another deep breath and bit the bottom part of her lip as her chin quivered in a slight vibrating motion. I sat right next to her, put my arm around her shoulders, and said,

"I'm so sorry, Nikki. I'm shocked. What happened?" Nikki

finally broke her eye contact with the floor and looked over at me with bright red lines in her eyes. She had been fighting back her tears so hard it looked like her eyeballs might explode. Then she started sobbing as bits of her words came out of her mouth at lightning speed, as if the faster she said it the less painful it would be.

"He said he really loved me and everything but his family is pushing him to marry some girl they know really well. I guess their families are really good friends with each other and he's known her since they were in diapers and all that stupid crap." Nikki could no longer hold back her tears and they streamed down her face like mini waterfalls. My heart ached for her, and I opened my mouth and tried to comfort her the best I could.

"I'm so sorry, Nikki, is there anything I can do for you?" She was looking back down at the floor and she just shook her head in reply. Taking time to compose herself, she stifled back little sobs and wiped mascara out from under her bottom lash line. I stood up and walked around the corner to the bathroom, plucking a few tissues out of the box. I returned and handed them to Nikki who gratefully took them and began to finish dabbing up the left over wet spots of diluted puddles on her face.

"Thanks," Nikki said as she sat up and straightened her back, taking one final deep breath and letting it slowly come out. Then she climbed to her feet, which I knew from my own previous experience in heartbreak had to be heavy, and she looked over at me and gave me a weak smile. The kind of smile that said, 'don't worry about me.' With a shaky, but more understandable voice, she said, "I'm going to take a long hot shower, then go shopping. Do you want to come with me to the store?" I smiled back at her and agreed with a head nod. Nikki seemed to be re-growing her confidence as she walked toward the door, then she glanced back and asked,

"I feel like either shopping or martinis. Is it too early for martinis?" I laughed a little and she smiled and shrugged before heading down toward her bathroom.

The fabric was smoother than butter, if it was even possible and it slid off my hand the moment I attempted to pick it up. The dress was a deep cranberry color that gave off a slight sheen in the light.

"That is unbelievably gorgeous. That is the dress of all dresses. Try it on." I heard Nikki say behind me, whispering in my ear like a mini shopping devil that tells you to spend money when you don't have it. I glanced over my shoulder and looked at her as if she was completely insane. I was holding a dress that girls like me adore and admire from a distance, not actually try on, and God forbid, even wear! It would take hard work and dedication and a solid sixty-pound weight loss even to pull off something so classy. It was the kind of dress that you see thin women wear, really thin women. Nikki looked back at me and purposely ignored my look and continued,

"Well, what are you waiting for? Go try it on. The color is perfect for you." I was instinctively struck with a paralyzing fear of trying the dress on. It was going to be a nightmare. It wouldn't fit me, and if it did fit by some miracle, it most definitely would not be flattering. The sheer horror of disappointment if I put on the dress overwhelmed me, but before I could begin my protest, Nikki edged her way next to me and began shuffling through the rack until she got to the very back, picking up a dress and jiggling it in front of my face as she spoke.

"Look what I have, this beauty's in your size. It's calling your name. Go try it on."

I felt my throat tighten up and my heart begin to race. I had an incredible urge to start weeping, but I didn't want to get such a beautiful dress wet with my fat tears. With a great hesitation, I turned and walked toward the fitting room, growing resentful towards Nikki for putting me in this situation. She had to know this was not going to end well. She had to know I was going to be embarrassed when I looked like a huge tub of lard. Was she doing this to me intentionally to be mean because she was miserable about Lucca?

Walking to the fitting room was like walking to the electric chair, only difference being that after the electric chair, you don't have to deal with it anymore, but after the fitting room, you have a lifetime of memory and pain. It was the next series of thoughts that scared me the most. Maybe my mother was right, maybe my life would be much better and happier if I just pushed myself and lost weight. Maybe things would be easier for me if I was no longer fat Amy but slender, can wear anything Amy. Perhaps slender Amy wouldn't have been cheated on by both her best friend and her fiancé. Slender Amy probably wouldn't even have been with Chad. Slender Amy would be with whomever she wanted because they would be lining up at her door to date her. Slender Amy would never had been made fun of in school or tortured by Kara because she stuck up for noodle arm Jake.

I paused for a moment and thought about how different my life would have been, could be, if I was skinny. It no doubt would have been different, but I was in serious doubt that slender Amy would have said anything in defense of noodle armed Jake, or I might not even have been friends with Betsy, I might have been a cheerleader and rode in the back of the bus with Kara and her cronies. Would I have been a better person if I were skinny?

Just as I finished my last thought, we arrived to the small entrance to the fitting rooms. A tall, lanky lady with bleached blonde hair that was pulled back into a tight ponytail glanced over at us, giving us a smile that looked more like a scowl while she looked us up and down. Then she asked with smirk on her face, almost taunting,

"Just the one item?" Nikki stepped around me and spoke with such command in her voice that the lanky woman immediately changed her composure.

"Yes. My friend here will be trying on this dress and we want a fitting room near the front with mirrors on all sides." I felt as if I would vomit when I heard mirrors on all sides.

The sales woman took the dress and hung it in one of the hooks before shutting the door behind her. I could hear Nikki's voice just on the other side of the door.

"Do you have it on yet?" I didn't respond to her. I piled my clothes on the bench and unzipped the dress, gently taking it off the hanger while I prayed I didn't rip it somehow with my large thighs.

I took a deep breath and looked away from the mirror as I slipped one foot in it at a time, pulling it up around my waist and gliding my arms through. I knew I wouldn't be able to zip it on my own so I cracked open the door and asked Nikki, still avoiding the mirror.

"Can you zip this real quick?" Nikki did not waste any time quickly coming in to zip me up. She took a step back, drug her eyes up and down before she exclaimed,

"You look so fantastic! You need to buy this dress. You are hot, and I mean hot in that dress."

I squinted one eye open before I opened both eyes as my reflection glanced back at me. She was right. I didn't look like fat Amy at all. I looked like sexy Amy. I had been confident that the texture of the fabric would cling and show every bump of cellulite, but I was wrong. I smiled so wide and couldn't take my eyes off myself. I told Nikki,

"This is it, this is the dress I'm wearing when I visit my mom and we go out to dinner."

Nikki agreed, and then she replied, "I'm so glad you tried this dress on. I feel so much better now. Who needs Lucca when you can have dresses to pick and choose from?" I got an idea I knew without a doubt she would love before I suggested,

"Hey, you wanna go get some makeovers? Maybe new hairstyles and what not?" Her eyes lit up and she glanced in the mirror as she smiled and replied,

"Well, we are already eights…" I interrupted her and said,

"You know what's better than eights?" She smiled back as if she already knew what I was going to say. "Being elevens." She winked and replied,

"Well… Then let's go become elevens."

SIXTEEN

I poured my coffee as slowly as possible, wanting it to delay time itself and postpone the inevitable. Today was what I had been dreading for weeks. Within hours, Nikki and I would be climbing into her car and heading to my mother's house. Nikki insisted we take turns driving her car instead of mine. I had a suspicion it was because it was newer and better than mine, which honestly I didn't mind her reason, because it was better than mine was. But driving her car didn't change the fact that soon I would be going back to a town of heartbreak, humiliation, and the reminder that I was just not good enough. I not only had to worry about the dramatic show my mother would be putting on in front of Nikki, but I had the expectation of her criticism, regarding my weight. I knew, without having to inquire, that she was wishful that I would show up after a few months on my own, a thinner, prettier daughter for her to show off. She would be sadly disappointed.

"What time are we heading out today?" Nikki blurted out in a chipper tune as she plopped down in the oversized armchair, crossing her legs with her fuzzy pink socks bouncing up and down. She often liked to stay in her pajamas and fuzzy socks when she could, which I found incredibly odd considering how much she loved to dress up, but perhaps that's why most of her nice clothes were in such good condition.

"Probably no later than eleven I'm thinking. That'll give us an hour leeway, just in case we hit traffic or want to take longer getting ready." A small smile crept on my face as I imagined getting stuck in a hideous traffic jam and having to call Mike and tell him there was no way we could make it. If only we could be so lucky. Nikki noticed my smile and said,

"I knew you really wanted to go, even if you are pretending you don't." I shook my head, disagreeing, as I replied,

"No, I really don't want to go. I was just thinking of something else." She nodded, understanding what I was trying to say and replied,

"Well, I'm coming with you so we'll have fun no matter what. Plus, I have your back." I knew she was right and I smiled at her before I took a very slow sip of my coffee, still wishing time would stop, or at least pause.

Nikki glanced over at the clock and quickly got up from her comfortable chair to head to the bathroom. The countless hours Nikki and I had spent talking about my mother and all the things I hated so much about that place didn't seem to matter. A person needed to see those things with their own eyes and experience them first hand. However, I also suspected that Nikki was trying to make the best of a situation she knew I couldn't get out of, which was the duty of being a daughter. I would have to oblige.

Nikki had done a remarkable job of recovering from Lucca, not without the occasional cry fest and entire bottle of wine however. Nevertheless, all being said, Nikki had bounced back on her feet to her confident, reliable self that naturally exuded sexiness that brought men to her. I thought if I wasn't crazy, I would have sworn even more men were attracted to her after her break up with Lucca than before. She was also raking in a sizable amount of tips at her job, and I suspected that Nikki had already replaced the money spent on our vacation. Every night when she came home, Nikki would pull a wad of money from her pocket and place it in the glass jar on her dresser. Often it consisted of twenty-dollar bills, one perk of working in a high-class restaurant.

Since our return, I on the other hand, had been politely rejected after two interviews, and I wasn't going to hold my breath for a call back from the third one. It had become clear to me when I walked into the interviews in my sharply pressed suit that when the interviewers took one look at my wide hips and chubby body it was over before it started. I was finding that not many people wanted a plump girl sitting behind the main desk to greet people when they walked in. Businesses didn't want to be preconceived with a fat image. I just crossed my fingers, put out even more applications, and sent out even more resumes. I was feeling a load of guilt about living with Nikki on the payment of a trip to Italy, even if she didn't seem to mind one bit. She never asked for or brought up the subject of money, and no awkward feeling of resentment. I knew it was all entirely put on me by my own self, but I couldn't stop it.

Each day, my anxiety increased with the thought of being near my mother, the possibility of running into Chad or Betsy, and just the overall feeling of embarrassment when I walked back into town and people whispering about what happened to me. My stomach did flips at night just thinking about it. Nikki told me that eventually I would have to face it and that I wasn't the one who should be embarrassed. She said that I was a better person than all of them combined. Always I would just agree with her, but deep down, I didn't really feel that way or believe it. Then she would say, 'you'll surprise yourself, you're stronger than you think you are.' I desperately wished she were right. I needed her to be right.

The sound of pretzels crunching caused me to look over at Nikki as she stopped chewing for a second. Flashing me a guilty look, she put her hand up as a shield to her mouth and said,

"Sorry, am I crunching too loud?" I laughed a little and she reached forward and took out the CD that was on its third cycle and put it back in the holder before she picked out another one, asking,

"Does this CD really have *Love is a Battlefield* from the eighties on it? I love that song!" I nodded and Nikki excitedly slid in the CD as we both joyfully blurted out the lyrics the minute the song played. After the second time around, she turned to me and yelled over the stereo,

"Who made this mix for you? It's fantastic." I couldn't keep from smiling as I remembered my birthday three years ago and my brother handing me a few mixed CD's that he had taken the time to put together as a gift.

"My brother." I said with affection, Nikki gave me a thumbs up just as Bon Jovi's *Living on a Prayer* came over the speaker.

Despite our delightful blast from the eighties, I had spent a majority of the drive waiting for traffic that never happened. I was equally disappointed when Nikki told me before we left that she got a girl to cover extra nights in case we wanted to stay longer, and I had to break it to her that the likelihood of that happening was very doubtful. As fun as it was to travel with Nikki, driving the four and a half hours to painful memories hovered over me like a dark cloud.

Knowing we were coming up on minutes until we reached my mother's house, I turned off the music and solemnly said to her,

"I want to say sorry in advance if you don't have a good time."

Nikki just shook her head and gave a slight sigh letting me know she thought I was crazy before she started crunching down on more pretzels. I pulled up into the drive and turned off Nikki's car, taking in a huge breath of air as Nikki exclaimed,

"This is your house, I love the flowers!"

I glanced over and noticed my mother had actually planted twice as many flowers as usual since I left months ago, which seemed pointless because we were close to fall now. Before I could say another word to Nikki, I heard a loud, "Hey" come from the front porch, just in time to see Mike standing there with his hands shoved in his pockets. I tilted my head for us to get out of the car and we made our way to the front porch as Mike took a few steps forward, relinquishing his hands from his pockets and throwing them around me, giving me a tight hug that lifted me a few inches from the ground. Then, as his smile remained plastered on his face, he said,

"Holy crap, Amy! Did you do something different to your hair or something? You look unbelievable." I smoothed over my hair and glanced down at my new, form fitting clothes before I replied,

"Just a haircut and a new shirt maybe." I had severely simplified that statement. I had gotten a minor hair trim and little makeover prior to Italy, but in comparison, what I had just had done was more like an over haul. If I were a house on an HGTV, my transformation would have been recorded to watch over and over again. It didn't matter because Mike didn't seem really to hear me as he glanced past my shoulder and looked at Nikki. I quickly stepped to the side and did a sweep of my hand toward Nikki like a model showing off a prize at a game show before I formally introduced her to Mike.

"And this is the lovely Nicolette, but you may call her Nikki." Mike did not hesitate before he stepped forward and warmly wrapped his hand around hers in a handshake as he spoke to her.

"I'm so glad to meet you. Now I can put a face with the crazy stories Amy tells me." Nikki's eyes got wide and she gave me a side glance that asked, 'what stories is he talking about', but before I could say anything in my defense, Mike chuckled a little and said,

"I'm just teasing a little, she hasn't told me anything." As they released hands, Nikki wittily replied,

"Well that's good, now we don't have to kill you." Then, to Mike's great surprise and pleasure, she gave him a little wink. The fun for me started to come to an end when I heard the shrill of my mother's voice coming out of the house as she walked through the front door.

"Amy! Well, this is a surprise. Although, I did suspect this might happen. I know you and Mike try to keep secrets from me, but I'm just too clever." Nothing like killing a mood. I wished for just once she would stop trying to one up herself in every situation.

"Well, didn't want to miss your surprise birthday." In my mind, all I could think was how much I wanted to say, *surprise, you're old, even older than last year,* which promptly brought a smile to my face. My mother mistook it for happiness to see her so she walked out, gave me a faint little hug, and staged a kiss on my cheek. Then she looked me up and down, analyzing every square inch of me before she broke her study and glanced over at Nikki.

"And who's this, Amy?" Nikki reached out her hand and my mother shook it ever so daintily. Nikki, who had put on fresh lipstick minutes earlier, smiled and tossed back her golden hair as she introduced herself.

"I'm Nikki, Amy's roommate." My mother kept her act going and touched her fingertips to the bottom of her pearl necklace before she said,

"Lovely, I am so glad you will be here with us, Nikki. Please let me know if there is anything we can do to make your stay pleasant." I had no choice but to look away since I could not prevent the massive eye roll I felt coming on. Nikki just nodded and we stood there for just moments with pleasant expressions on our faces before I finally started to head in to the house.

Without being asked, Mike brought in all our bags and took them to my old room. He was always good about stuff like that, even when he was a child. After retreating to the safety of my old room, I shut the door and sat on my old bed. I was amazed at how much I had left behind, considering how long and hard we worked to unpack the car when I moved. Nikki walked around the room and then sat next to me on the bed. Then I gave her the play by play for the upcoming evening.

"So, we're going to go to this expensive restaurant and act like it's a surprise. Mike's going to order a bottle of wine my mother likes. Then…" I was cut off mid-sentence by a tap on my door.

"Come in." Mike's head peeked around the corner of the door before he stepped into the room, wasting no time telling me a plan of his own.

"After dinner tonight when Mom passes out like she usually does, I thought the three of us could go across town to the new place. I've only been there a few times but it's nice." Mike sat down, straddling the desk chair and resting his chin on top of the back of it like I had seen him sit so many times since high school. I didn't have to look at Nikki or even ask if she was interested to know she was already on board.

"That sounds good. What place is it?" He used his long

athletic legs to wheel the desk chair closer to us as he replied,

"It's called Denver's. It's not really a club, but it's better than just a tiny little bar. They have a small floor for dancing, but they also have pool tables and the whole place is clean and mostly people our age go there." I felt Nikki sit up straight next to me as she chimed in,

"Sounds good. What time?" Mike finally looked over at her and then did a playful spin in the desk chair before he answered,

"As soon as the Eagle lands." Nikki glanced over at me, looking confused. I casually answered her inquisitive look.

"He mean's as soon as my mother passes out." She nodded and Mike clasped his hands together before rubbing them as if we just announced we were taking over the world.

SEVENTEEN

It was a record, maybe even a world record. Nevertheless, I'd be lying if I didn't admit I had a little help from the bottle of wine we brought over from Italy that lulled my mother to sleep, like a hundred and twenty pound baby. The three of us gathered around her as she lay passed out on the couch too sleepy to make it to her own bed after her birthday dinner. I gazed over at Mike and with a head nod, I let him know it was time to pick her up and put her in her bed.

With one motion, he scooped up her limp slender frame. Seconds later, he quietly closed her door and then he turned with a puzzled look on his face before he asked,

"Should I have put a blanket on her?" I shrugged my shoulders. I knew from all her birthdays before that she would sleep in until noon and there was nothing that would wake her. I suspected the wine had really done a number on her this year because at dinner in a drunken slur, she looked me up and down in my red dress and murmured,

"You actually look good in that dress." Now the real test would be wearing it out to this new place. Nikki looked down at her clothes and asked,

"Do I need to change, Mike?" The question made me giggle a little because Mike knew almost nothing about clothes, or about what would be considered appropriate and at which places. Mike was a sporty, clean jeans and t-shirt sort of guy. I threw Mike a bone and answered her question.

"You look really good. We might be a tad over dressed maybe. But better than under… right?" Nikki smiled, as she was pleased to hear me using some of her favorite mantras.

For some unexplained reason, my stomach did flips and I got chills as we pulled into the parking lot. I quivered and shook out of nervousness. Mike helped me out of the car as he asked, "Are you okay?" I nodded and took a deep breath, gathering myself. Nikki did not share the same nervous, uneasy feeling as I did. She practically leaped out of the car, enthused to be somewhere new. She even appeared to have more excitement than when were in Italy.

I, however, slid out of the passenger side as I grabbed onto Mike's hand, terrified I would catch my shoe on something and trip and fall out of the car. I felt I couldn't be too careful; especially considering the memory of flying head first onto the floor in Italy was fresh in my mind.

I pulled and tugged at my dress, scared that I had possibly been delusional in the fitting room when I put it on, or worse yet, the mirrors had been distorted somehow and I really didn't look as good as I had fooled myself into believing. Mike let go of my hand and shut the car door behind me before he said like the perfect supportive brother,

"You look really nice, sis. Don't be nervous. I have your back." I smiled up at him, feeling that he was more like my big brother than my little brother was, as I did many times before. Nikki looked over at me and in a saucy voice with a little shoulder dip, she said,

"Amy, you're hot, girl, and sexy as ever in that dress." It was not only what I wanted to hear, it was what I needed to hear. I blushed for a second, took a deep breath and relaxed myself as we walked through the entrance of Denver's Place.

The lights were dim but everything looked new and clean. The walls were a smoky gray color with mirrors and polished chrome lining the backlit bar. It was a place you might imagine in Manhattan or taken out of some movie scene. It even felt like a different state or even country, maybe even a little like a different decade, but it was most undeniably impressive.

There was a small dance floor sectioned off the main bar with a few people dancing, mainly women in their late twenties holding drinks and having fun with their friends as they swayed to the music. The music wasn't horribly loud, which made it less stressful as one didn't have to yell every drink order over the typical extreme noise.

"Hello, ladies, can I get you a drink?" A guy just at six feet asked as he flung a bar towel over his shoulder. He had sandy blond hair that reached to the bottom of his neck. He ran his fingers through his hair and quickly tucked it behind his ears. Nikki gave him a pleasant once-over before she flashed her bright white smile and replied,

"Yeah, my friend Amy and I will have whatever you recommend." He looked over at me, giving a shy, then wide smile before he turned, picking a few bottles off the shelves behind him. While his back was to us, Nikki leaned over and whispered low enough that neither the bartender nor my brother could hear. "I think this guy digs you. He is really eyeing you." In reply, I shook my head and glanced over at Mike who had wandered off to say hello to some friends he saw from work. I looked back at Nikki and said,

"I don't think so. He's not really my type anyway." Immediately, I knew that was a lie, because I clearly didn't have a type. My type was anyone who would give me the time of day and not be offended to be with a chubby girl.

"Seriously? He's got that whole all American bad-boy look going for him. It's like Captain America joined a bike gang… kinda sexy, you can't deny it." By that time, the bartender had turned around and was sliding our drinks towards us. He barely looked at Nikki as he had the same shy smile on his face when he looked in my direction. His sandy blond hair was matched with the same colored, thin goatee. His short-sleeved gray shirt had the edges of tattoos that peeked out from under the sleeve and then continued down his strong solid arms. The bartender presented himself in such a way that you might not want to get on his bad side or pick a fight with him, but his shy smile couldn't hide his softer, insecure side deep within.

"This drink is really good. By the way, what's your name?" Nikki had already finished her bright pink cocktail before I even brought mine to my lips. He finally looked over to her direction and pleasantly began to answer, just as the other bartender on the other end yelled towards him.

"Ryan!" Shouted the young guy in his early twenties from the other end, and without speaking, the bartender in front of us tilted his head, indicating that was the answer to Nikki's question. Seconds later, he headed toward the other end seeing what the young guy needed. Nikki spun her body towards me and popped the cherry in her mouth as she said,

"Okay, that bartender, Ryan, is looking at you like candy. Stop acting like you don't see it. I think I like this place."

I blushed a little because I couldn't deny that he did seem interested in me. However, I couldn't bring myself to hit on the bartender, as I'm sure many desperate women before me had done exactly that. Besides, flirting was a good part of his job. He worked mainly for tips and I'm sure that he gave the ugliest girls the most attention so he could make more money.

"Do you wanna dance?" Nikki did a little shimmy with her shoulders as she tipped her head to the dance floor, trying her best to get me interested.

"Uh… No. I haven't had enough to drink yet." Nikki stuck

out her bottom lip and gave me big sad eyes as I glanced behind her. I waved for Mike to come over and talk to us as his friends headed to the front entrance. He walked over and put his hand on the top of the bar as he sat in the open stool next to Nikki, then he asked,

"How do you like this place?" I quickly spoke up before Nikki had the chance to get Mike to talk me into dancing with her.

"It's really nice. Hey, Mike, would you please go out to the dance floor with Nikki. And don't say no."

His face started to get red as he looked out at the few people dancing. A handful more had joined them, but he was not so pleased with my request. Mike wasn't a bad dancer. He just believed he was.

"Okay," he hesitantly replied as Nikki gave me a little look that said 'don't think you're getting off so easy.' I felt more relaxed as they headed to the floor just as the bartender came back over to check on me.

"How'd you like that drink?" I smiled and nodded before I answered him,

"It was really good." I wanted to make conversation with him, but didn't feel like I was capable of it. I felt strange and awkward near him, oddly more than I did with Dante. The bartender didn't give up and kept talking to me.

"Are you from around here, Amy?" I looked up from my drink and asked out of surprise,

"How did you know my name?" He gave another shy smile and said,

"Your friend just said it when you guys sat down." I pressed my lips together, embarrassed that I had already forgotten Nikki had technically introduced me. Then as I looked down at my glass to answer, he slid another drink next to my half-empty glass.

"I'm from the next town over. I just recently moved though." I looked up and flashed him an appreciative smile for the new drink. He leaned forward and placed his elbows on the bar, clearly getting more comfortable with me. His shy smile had been replaced with a brave expression. His whole composure was more relaxed and confident. As he opened his mouth to speak, his entire expression changed when I felt someone slide on the stool next to me. I heard the shrill sound of her voice before I even saw her face.

"Um, Ryan, can you get me a long island ice tea?" With little more than a faint sarcastic smile, he turned and began making her drink. I slowly turned my head to see Kara sitting on the open stool next to me. She was digging through her purse as she looked over at me for a second, then back to her purse. Quickly, she snapped her head in my direction as her eyes widened and her mouth fell open before she practically yelled,

"Amy? Holy crap! I didn't recognize you at all! Have you lost weight?" I didn't answer her for a few seconds as I downed my drink. Then, keeping my eyes on the bartender I reluctantly replied,

"No, I just got a haircut." Kara followed my gaze and with a smirk said,

"Well that was some haircut."

I glanced over at the dance floor, now eager to take part in the fun Nikki and Mike were having, but wanting to get away from Kara more than anything else. I started getting some money from my purse to pay for my drinks as Ryan reached out and tapped the bar in front of me before saying,

"Don't worry about it. They're on the house." Kara batted her eyelashes and spoke up.

"How much do I owe you?" He glanced over at her and flatly replied,

"That'll be six fifty." She snarled and continued fishing through her purse as he walked to the other end of the crowded bar to help another customer. Without looking at me, she began speaking, almost as if she was talking to herself.

"I swear I've been trying to sleep with that guy for months now. This has never happened to me before. Guys always want me. I hate that smug guy. He's not good enough for me anyway. Creepy looking dude with tattoos if you ask me." She pulled out six dollars and continued fishing for change, clearly preparing not to give him a tip. Her nails were still bright red and she had matching lipstick that was starting to bleed just outside the crease of her lip. I finished off my drink and turned around to join my best friend and brother before I casually said,

"Maybe you're trying too hard." She looked up from her purse with a snarl on her lip before she squinted her eyes, finally remembering I had called her a whore in the grocery store months earlier. She barely parted her lips when I gave her a wide smile as I stood to join my friends, just before I said, "Have a nice night." She closed her mouth and then turned back to her drink and her purse, all by herself, completely alone. She didn't have her groupies with her anymore, or her former cheerleader friends that admired her, or anyone for that matter.

It only took about fifteen minutes for Kara to finish her drink and leave the bar. Our seats appeared to be untouched and unclaimed for some reason. The three of us sat down in the open seats as Nikki let out a huge sigh as she spoke,

"That was fun. Mike, you're a pretty good dancer." Mike shook his head and ordered a beer as Ryan put another drink in front of me. I looked up at Ryan confused and said,

"Thanks… but I didn't order this." He glanced over to the end of the bar and replied,

"The guy at the end of the bar ordered it for you. Oh, and I'm supposed to say ' a sweet drink for a sweet looking girl'… Sorry. Not my words." He cleared his throat and slid Mike's beer to him as Nikki couldn't help her childish grin.

"Well, well, well, Amy, we leave you alone for a few minutes and you already have all the guys going wild over here." Mike pretended to be angry as he said in a deep voice,

"I better get my baseball bat ready." Both Nikki and Mike chuckled a little as I rolled my eyes, then I leaned over the counter to thank the guy at the end for the drink when I instantly got nauseous.

The guy at the end of the bar was wearing a newer t-shirt and faded jeans. His shoes looked as if they had never been tied, but miraculously his hair looked lightly combed. I was looking at Chad. I immediately looked away and pushed my drink away from me as my stomach did flips and I began to shake for some unknown reason.

"What's wrong? Are you okay?" Nikki asked. Mike leaned

over the bar himself to look at what I was seeing. He got angry, his lips pressed tight together and both hands immediately became clutched into fists, then he stood up as he proclaimed,

"Okay, now I AM going to get a baseball bat. You want me to take care of this for you, sis?" I shook my head but couldn't open my mouth as a wave of emotions flooded over me. I wasn't sure what was going on. Was he taunting me, rubbing what happened in my face by sending me a drink? Was Betsy with him? Was this just a big joke to him? Did he want me back and was he trying to say he was sorry?

"Do you want to go home?" Nikki asked, realizing what the situation was without having to ask. I sat up straight and answered, feeling angry for some reason,

"No. We were here first. We're having a good time. I'm not leaving because of him." I glanced over to Ryan and made eye contact with him, motioning for him to come over.

"What can I do for you?" I slid the drink back to Ryan before I boldly said,

"Give this back to him and tell him it wasn't meant for me. Tell him… It tastes like douche-bag trash, and that's not my flavor." Ryan got a sideways smirk on his face as he replied,

"You got it." Ryan walked down to the other end of the bar with a smooth stride, confident and strong as I watched his body language while he delivered the message. Chad didn't even glance over as he nodded his head and slowly started walking towards the front, more than likely to leave after his defeat in manipulation. Both Nikki and Mike had a look of pride on their faces as Nikki and

I began to down shot after shot. In reality, it had only been three shots, but it felt more like twelve. After we had been there only two hours, Nikki's complexion had changed to almost a green color. Then she turned and asked,

"Do you feel like going home?" I shook my head as Ryan walked up to the bar, catching the conversation. Then he politely suggested without hesitation,

"If Amy feels like staying longer I can always order her a cab. I don't mind." Mike had an uneasy look on his face with the thought of leaving me behind at the bar. I spoke up before he could refuse the suggestion.

"Yeah, that sounds good. If you feel like taking Nikki home that would be great." Nikki was looking more ill by the moment so she nodded in agreement with the plan and Mike began to protest.

"I don't know if I like that idea. Are you going to be okay by yourself?" I gave Mike the 'I'm really the big sister' look and said,

"I'm almost thirty. People my age actually go to places by themselves." Mike still looked uneasy but reluctantly agreed. Nikki gave me a little hug and looked around the bar before she said,

"I think that little creep is gone. We haven't seen him for a while so he must have left. Are you sure this is okay?" I nodded and said good-bye as they headed to the entrance. I sat at the bar and watched Ryan for a few minutes as he was toweling off some glasses with a smile on his face.

I was lost in my own world as several minutes passed by as I saw people come and go before I felt someone glide their hand across my shoulder followed by Chad's voice.

"Hey, Amy, you look really good." Just like the snake he was, Chad slithered into the stool that Nikki had left vacant. I started to feel sick and tremble again. I couldn't stand the thought of looking at him so I stared down at the granite bar in front of me. Chad took his hand and slid it down the side of my dress as he said,

"I can't believe how sexy you look in this dress. I don't remember you looking like this when we were together." My chin started to quiver as emotions raised up from within. I couldn't help but think I was being mocked and ridiculed. Why didn't I see how manipulative and callous he was from the very beginning? I was angry and sad at the same time. I wondered if he touched Betsy in the same way he was touching me at that moment. It was unfamiliar to me, even odd coming from him.

"Just go away, Chad." He was leaning against the bar on his elbow, facing me as I kept my eyes straight down on the bar. He slid his hand from the side of my dress and rested his hand on top of my thigh as he continued,

"I'm not with Betsy anymore. So I'm thinking if you want to start things back up again we can see what happens." I didn't know if it was the alcohol or lapse in time since the day I found out about them, but I didn't have the stamina to say anything. I was a disappointment to myself because of that.

"Hey, I think you're bothering the lady." Chad looked over at Ryan who stood with his arms crossed with his jaw line tense and a stern look on his face.

"She's fine. We're just talking." I dragged my eyes up to Ryan and said,

"No I'm not. Please ask him to leave." Ryan went from stern to angry as he glared down at Chad. Then he said very seriously,

"You heard her, right?"

Chad nodded and lifted his hands gesturing that he was leaving before he leaned in and kissed me next to my ear as he whispered,

"I'll wait for you outside." Ryan stepped forward and Chad shot him a dirty look before he headed out the main entrance.

"Are you okay, Amy?" Ryan asked, softening his expression as my chin began to quiver and warm tears came up to my eyes. I held them back and cleared my throat as I nodded in reply. Then I asked,

"Can I have two more shots please?" He shook his head and gently replied,

"I think maybe you should slow down, or stop even. You're not going to feel so good." I glared at him with tears in my eyes and quietly asked.

"Can I just have one then? It'll be my last one I promise." He nodded and took another breath, all my emotions feeling so raw and powerful. My thoughts were running rampant and the idea of Chad waiting for me outside, him wanting me, those thoughts had me torn between a revengeful satisfaction and disgust. My mind flooded with scenarios and situations, none of them that involved Chad ended with any resolution, but I still couldn't keep myself from thinking them.

I started to drink my shot slowly until the room became hazy, trying desperately to put the knowledge of Chad waiting for me outside out of my mind. At least now I wasn't met with the hopeless feeling of worthlessness that had been there so many times before.

EIGHTEEN

Before I even opened my eyes, I could feel the cool cotton sheets against my bare skin. *Bare skin? Naked?* I was naked and pretty sure I was in a bed that wasn't mine. I couldn't open my eyes. I was too terrified to see what I had gotten into. I gathered all my courage when I smelled the faint aroma of coffee. I definitely wasn't in my own bed. I cracked open my lids as the sound of a man faintly whistling floated past the bed.

"Morning, how do you feel? Do you need some aspirin?" I slid down into the covers and pulled them up to my chin, terrified I had already showed too much of my pudgy bust-line. I thought it was quite possible that both of my sets of cheeks were flaming red with embarrassment. My lower half wasn't even properly covered with panties. *Panties? Oh no, where are my panties!*

I reached up and touched my head. The pain from the bright

morning light was beginning to travel around in circles. He glanced at the window and then quickly rushed over to the opposite side of the bed to adjust the blinds.

"Sorry, I forgot to turn them the other way to keep out the light. I'll get you some water and aspirin. Maybe coffee too?" I nodded and watched him walk out of the bedroom door and turn a corner to what I assumed was the kitchen, although I couldn't remember. I couldn't remember anything at all honestly. I hastily scanned the room for my dress and panties and caught sight of them piled on the top of his dresser. This was humiliating. I was going to have to rush over and put them on as fast as possible before he came back.

I slid off the side of the bed and wrapped the sheet around me as I stood and took a few steps toward my clothes. I was snapped back toward the bed, as the sheet wouldn't budge. It was tightly tucked under the mattress. Apparently, I was trying to use the sheets of a man who actually made his bed. I gave the sheet a couple more strong tugs before it put up the better fight and won. I didn't waste time and threw down the sheet before I sprinted to the safe haven of my clothes across the room. I did this while desperately trying to hold all my fleshly assets in place. Unfortunately, I was at least four hands short in order to accomplish this.

"Oh, sorry." As if hypnotized by a train wreck, his eyes were wide as he stood in the doorway with a glass of water in one hand and a bottle of aspirin in the other. Snapping out of it, he quickly turned around, as I stood frozen with terror, my face beet red. I was most certain that even my entire body was red. I was mortified; all size sixteen of me was standing there, naked, with only what seemed like freakishly small hands unable to cover what needed to be kept hidden. I felt positively sick and nauseous with humiliation. Even more so that I was standing in front of the hot bartender, Ryan.

He shyly turned his head and looked toward the other wall. He might have only caught a brief glimpse, but I knew the image would be one that he would have on his brain for an eternity. Then I became even more mortified wondering if he had already seen the image before. I struggled to breathe and felt like I was going to have a panic attack. I was so embarrassed, then I heard him clear his throat, timidly speaking,

"I'm sorry, I didn't realize you were going to get dressed right now. I'm going to shut the door. Just let me know when you're done." He walked backwards a few steps and then leaned to the side and set the water and the bottle down on the side table, still averting his eyes from my massive nakedness.

This was so awful. This was beyond awful. It was humiliating, mortifying, and the worst part was I didn't even know what level of mortification I should feel. I could hardly remember a thing. I vaguely remember walking into his house or the ride over, but I absolutely could not remember a thing about the sex. Did we have sex? How much sex? Did I say something stupid or crazy… did I *do* something stupid or crazy? This was bad, so very, very bad. I never, ever thought I was going to be in a situation where I would have sex and not remember it. I was consumed with an unbelievable amount of regret about staying at the bar last night or even going for that matter.

I swallowed my pride, not that I had any left at that point, and quickly put my dress back on. I winced when I saw the nude high waist control panties. As if last night couldn't be any more embarrassing, I had to go out with a granny panty fizzle.

Just when I thought I was at my lowest point of humiliation, I caught a glimpse of my reflection in the mirror. My hair was ratted and tangled; my mascara and eyeliner were smudged so far down my bottom eyelid I looked like a zombie. Not only did I look hideous, but also the desire to wash off the smell of alcohol and possible sex was so strong that I had to fight the urge to beg him to use his shower. Not that I would have been at all worried that he might make a move on my less than hot self in the shower. I let out a fitting cave-woman sounding grunt and fished through my purse in order to find some Kleenex and a rubber band. A few seconds later, I was barely presentable, a notch above hideous, but just below awful.

I cracked the bedroom door open and peeped outside. I wasn't sure how I was going to make it home, but I thought if I could just get outside and use my phone I could avoid any further humiliation and the walk of shame. I took one-step out of the bedroom when I heard his voice from the kitchen.

"I forgot to tell you if you like to use the shower or anything in the bathroom I put all new towels in there for you." I knew he must have smelled something disgusting that stretched to the kitchen for him to offer his bathroom so openly. I took a long pause and tried to keep from sounding thrilled, as if he just told me I won the lottery. With all of my effort to be casual, I said,

"Are you sure it's okay?" I heard clinking in the kitchen. Suddenly, he looked around the corner, replying with a smile,

"Yeah, not a problem. I'm just cooking some breakfast. It won't be done for a few minutes so go for it." Pointing at the door across the hall, I asked,

"Is this the bathroom right there?" He shook his head and said,

"Nope, third door on the right." I glanced down the hall and wondered why I hadn't realized how large the place was. Then again, I didn't even know if we had been intimate at night so I couldn't really be that hard on myself.

The bathroom was almost the size of Nikki's closet. Okay, realistically it was only a little more than half the size of Nikki's closet, but it still was spacious. It sparkled like a five star hotel bathroom, completely polished and spotless. This place was definitely not the type I would have pictured him in. This place was the kind you would imagine some super rich spoiled bachelor with the advantage of a full-time cleaning crew would live.

I took the best shower of my life, not that it could wash off the guilt, but at least it could wash of the vodka. After I dried off with an oversized burnt orange towel, I cringed at the thought of putting my dirty clothes back on. I decided to forfeit my panties all together. I stared at them for a moment and then the shiny stainless steel trashcan before coming to the conclusion that I must roll them up and put them in my purse.

The moment I stepped out into the hall, I was greeted with the smell of coffee and toast. I fluffed my hair a little with the towel and walked around the corner to his kitchen. He had a dishtowel over his shoulder and a skillet in his hand. Then he set down the skillet, took toast out of the toaster, and stacked it on a plate. The white tank undershirt exposing his muscular arms showed a black and gray Marine Corps tattoo just below his left shoulder. His right arm was covered in tattoos that reached just a few inches above his elbow, all of which seemed strategically placed to flatter his muscles. Now that we were sitting in full light, I could see that every square inch of him was in prime shape and chiseled. I had not really taken notice of any of that while in the bar. However, staring at him in the kitchen, I realized it was no wonder I came home with him while I was intoxicated. I wanted to stare at him when I was sober too. I found it odd how drawn to him I was. He was a far cry from the dark haired Italian men that I so easily found attractive. He looked nothing like Dante, which only proved that I truly wasn't attracted to any particular type of man.

He turned and smiled at me as he took the towel off his shoulder and laid it on the countertop. I broke my trance and felt my face blush as I smiled back. He said,

"I hope omelets are okay. I made them with sautéed mushrooms, red onions, red peppers, fresh basil and some gorgonzola cheese. Is that okay?" I bashfully nodded my reply and began to slide into one of the chairs as he grabbed the back of it and helped me scoot up to the table in an old-fashioned kind of way.

"Wow, this looks really good. Thank you." He gave me a wide, pleased smile in reply and sat in the seat across from mine. He appeared to be nervous for some reason and cleared his throat as he tucked his rugged yet sexy blond hair behind his ears. I took a sip of coffee as he cleared his throat again, glancing over at my plate. I took a bite of the omelet when a few seconds later he asked,

"How is it?" He asked while my mouth was crammed full of the hot breakfast. I was surprised by his ability to cook and swallowed my bite replying,

"Great! Where did you learn to cook like this, Ryan? I can call you Ryan… right?" A look of relief came over his face and he let out a slow sigh as he replied,

"I'm glad you like it. A lot of it is self-taught. I did a lot of cooking growing up. My grandma got sick when I was in high school, so I would cook to help out. Then I ended up doing most of the cooking in the Marines just because I was so good at it." He stopped for a second then answered my last question.

"Yeah, you forgot my name already?" He chuckled a little and I looked down at my plate to avoid eye contact for a moment while questions about our late night activities swirled around in my head. I really wanted to ask what had happened because I knew his memory of last night had to be better than mine, because there was no way it could have been worse. I took a deep breath and swallowed hard before I attempted to ask as casually as I could,

"Um, so… about last night…" I paused intentionally, hoping he would just fill in the blanks or at the very least give some major clue about what we did and why I was completely naked. Instead, he just said,

"Yeah?" I took yet another long breath and continued,

"Did we…" Once again, I hoped he would just say

something. Finally, he understood what I was trying to ask, then he said,

"Did we have relations last night? Is that what you're asking?" I could feel that my face was bright red as heat steamed off my cheeks. He had a playful smile on his face as he asked curiously, "You don't remember?" My stomach turned over with nausea and I bit my bottom lip as I shook my head in reply. His smile became a combination of curious and more playful as he continued, "Really? Wow, I don't know how you could *not* remember last night. It was pretty… intense… I think that's the word I'm looking for." His smirk widened slowly across his face as he took a long sip of coffee, trying hard not to smile as he did so. The feeling of humiliation swept back over me and I felt positively sick as I glanced out the window, trying not to cry out of shame. He stopped smiling and an apologetic look came across his face. Then he said in all honesty, "Amy, I'm only kidding you. We didn't do anything last night. That's the truth." I looked over at him in shock and asked,

"We didn't? Why didn't I have any clothes on this morning?" He chuckled a little to my question and answered,

"No we didn't do anything, and as far as your clothes being off, I didn't have anything to do with that. You were pretty drunk last night, so I carried you to the bedroom and set you on the bed and I went to get some extra pillowcases. When I got back, your dress was just piled on the floor and you were passed out in the bed." I could tell by his tone that he was telling me the truth, which eased my anxiety a great deal, but also made me a little surprised. I would never have thought I would take all my clothes off at some strange man's house. I never would have done that six months ago.

Ryan cleared his throat again out of nervousness before he asked, "If you're not busy today, I thought we could hang out. If that's cool?" I found it incredibly flattering that such a rugged and sexy guy felt nervous around me in a teenage sort of way.

"Well, I need to go home and check on Nikki and ask if she minds. She did me a favor by coming with me here so I can't just leave her in the lurch. If she doesn't mind, then sure I'd like that." He nodded his head in response and my eyes slid down his body. I couldn't stop looking at his arms. I was torn between staring at his muscles and staring at his tattoos. He caught my gaze and looked down at his shirt, which made me blush out of embarrassment for getting caught. I quickly asked a question to prevent him from saying anything.

"So, how long have you worked at the bar?" There was a momentarily look of confusion on his face before he answered,

"Actually forever… it's my bar." He said it so casually I was taken aback. When I was engaged to Chad, he would gladly throw around who his dad was and what he owned to give himself any perk he felt owed to him, but Ryan was different. I forgot myself and put a bite in my mouth before I replied, as if I was eating with a friend and not some possible romance.

"Oh, that's nice. Who's Denver?" Once again, he had a puzzled look on his face as he answered my question.

"I am. Denver is my first name, but I don't go by that. I got used to answering to my last name from being in the service. So, not really sure why I named my bar after my first name… but I did." I nodded and finished off my plate, just as you would expect the chubby girl to do. I put down my fork and looked away, unable to believe I scarfed down the entire plate of food as if a worldwide famine was about to happen. Ryan stood, picked up the plates, and wasted no time washing and drying them. His action led me to ask,

"Are you one of those people that have OCD?" I shut my mouth and slightly shook my head at myself. What was wrong with me? Why was I asking stupid questions and letting just about anything fall out of my mouth. He must be more than sorry he brought me home last night. Instead of giving me a 'boy you're a strange girl look', he just smiled and replied,

"Nope. I was a total slob before I was in the service. Now I keep up with the cleaning because I'm mainly bored, and because I don't want you to think less of me." It seemed I wasn't the only one saying strange things in this conversation. How could I think less of someone I just met? I wasn't really thinking much about him yet anyway, but I suppose he did have a point.

"Oh, I see. I'm going to get my cell phone and call my brother and let him know I'm okay. They're probably freaking out right now." He nodded in agreement, as I walked across the room, reached down into my purse, and pulled out my cell phone. I dialed Mike and before I even brought it to my ear, he was already on.

"Where are you?" I heard him ask just as the phone reached the side of my face.

"Oh, don't freak out. I went home with the bartender last night, but we didn't do anything." I wasn't sure why I felt the overwhelming need to throw that last statement in there so quickly, but I did anyway. I glanced over to see if Ryan heard my proclamation to my brother but he had left the room and shut the bedroom door behind him. Then I heard Mike say,

"Okay. I was worried when we got up this morning. Mom hasn't even woken up yet. Why don't you bring him over? He seems like a cool guy." I could see where this was going with Mike. He didn't want to be outnumbered by women and was hoping for relief, even if it was in the form a stranger we just met at the bar last night. I didn't give any answer to his question and said instead,

"Can you put Nikki on the phone?" I heard a little shuffling then a few seconds later, I heard Nikki's pre-coffee gruff morning voice.

"Amy? Where are you?" I went through the whole spiel again with Nikki before she said with a slight chuckle in her tone, "Sure you didn't do anything with that hot bartender. I can't leave you alone for two minutes, can I? I agree with your brother, bring him over." I knew there was no way out of arguing with both Nikki and my brother. I quickly said my good byes just as Ryan walked out of the bedroom in clean clothes and wet hair, how it was possible for him to shower and dress that quickly I could not even comprehend.

"Do you want to go over to my mom's house today?" I asked as a sharp pain hit my stomach. The thought of asking him over like a teenage crush, and watching him being scrutinized by my mother was beyond stressful. I would have to keep his ownership of the bar a secret. If my mother sensed he had any money of any kind, she would be very hard on me in front of him.

"Yeah, that's great." He reached up next to the counter and picked up a set of car keys.

I had not anticipated going home with a bartender, correction, bar owner, when I went to visit my mother, but since it had happened, I might as well give in and let things run their course.

NINETEEN

With Ryan right behind me, I cautiously tiptoed through the front door as I heard chatter coming from the kitchen. It was the voice of my mother that caught my ear. I put my finger up to my lips signaling to Ryan to be quiet for a moment. Then I quickly ducked into my old room, frantically changed out of my smoke and liquor smelling dress and threw on a pair of tight jeans and a long sleeve t-shirt, leaving the door cracked an inch or two while I did so. I was too busy worrying about my mother giving me the third degree over my day old dress even to consider Ryan might easily have another glimpse of me in the buff.

I quietly opened the bedroom door and stepped out into the hallway as I found Ryan looking at the old family photos that were hanging along the wall. Each frame was slightly different from the last. The older the photo, the more worn the frame holding it was.

He held his hands behind his back as he leaned forward and stared at one of the very few pictures of me on the wall. The majority of the photos were older ones of the days that my mother had been in pageants and competitions. Some were in black and white. Ryan had found the only school picture of me nestled among the others. I always cringed every time I saw it. My hair was pulled into a side ponytail and my cheeks looked pink for some reason as I grinned while wearing my black and white polka dot shirt.

However, it was not the embarrassment of looking so goofy that made the photo cringe worthy. It was the memory of the morning of that photo as my mother carefully picked out my shirt, woke me up extra early to do my hair and refused to let me eat breakfast just in case something might bloat my face. The only thing that day I had to smile about was the silver butterfly necklace around my neck that my mother did not want me to wear because it didn't match, but I snuck in my backpack. Looking at my photo, I knew the grin on my face was due to my small victory that day as my little necklace hung around my neck. Even still, I remembered when I had brought the packet of school pictures home, my mother had been hardly satisfied with how it turned out given her extreme efforts to make me camera ready. In the end, she just sighed and threw it in a frame, hanging it just a few inches from Mike's picture.

"I really like this picture of you," he said, still keeping his eyes on it. I wasn't sure if he was teasing me or being sincere. I began to reply when I heard the light footsteps of Nikki come around the corner as she said in a surprised voice,

"Amy! When did you get here?" Then she glanced behind

her and lowered her voice determining that my mother had not heard her say my name as she continued, "Your mother is showing me her old pictures… when she was in pageants. I'm not going to lie… I don't know how much more of this I can take." She looked over at Ryan before she said to him, "Well, well, well… Mr. Bartender, I hope you treated my best friend real good last night." Nikki threw her arm around my shoulder and gave him a pretend stern look as if she was my guardian angel. I shot her a look instantly to let her know I was already embarrassed as it was and I didn't really want to talk about it. Then I just blurted out,

"We didn't do anything." Once again, I felt the overwhelming need to clarify that. I began to wonder what I would be blurting out if we had actually done something. Ryan smiled at Nikki and said gracefully,

"Don't worry… Amy was a perfect lady." I started to feel more comfortable with the conversation and banter going on between them when I asked Ryan under the protection of Nikki's arm,

"What are you saying? You were the perfect gentleman?" The side of his mouth curled up into a little smirk as he shrugged one shoulder and replied coyly, "I don't know about that." Nikki dropped her arm and turned as she stared at me, an amused look sweeping across her face like a teacher watching a student finally figuring out a difficult math problem. I knew we couldn't delay it much longer as I heard my mother's pretentious tone call out.

"Amy? Is that you?" I shot Nikki an apologetic look before I turned to Ryan and whispered,

"Sorry."

My mother sat at the kitchen table as if she was ready for her presentation all the way from her neatly pressed clothes to her full make-up and pearl necklace. Mike was at the counter pouring some strange greenish brown liquid out of the blender into a glass that he handed my mother.

"What's that?" I inquired unable to hide the look of disgust on my face. My mother lifted her glass and then elegantly proclaimed,

"It's a complete detox and nutrition breakfast supplement. It will make you feel great, Amy, plus it will help with skin aging and it's wonderful for losing weight." I received a minor headache from the eye roll I was forcing myself to hold back. I instantly became thankful for eating breakfast at Ryan's house that was neither liquid nor the color of food-poisoned diarrhea. My mother set her glass down and finally realized there was an extra person in the room as she addressed him.

"Oh, who are you?" She didn't hide the fact that she was looking him up and down as I started to become fidgety. I mentally told myself to keep my mouth shut so I didn't blurt out something stupid that my mother might ask me about.

"I'm Ryan. I'm a friend of Amy's." He reached out and my mother placed her hand daintily in his for a faint, weak handshake. She kept her eyes on him for a few moments too long, attempting to assess the situation. She gave up and continued as she glanced in my direction from the corners of her eyes.

"Were you planning on refinishing that end table I found,

maybe for my birthday, Amy?" She quickly said to Ryan as a little side note, "Yesterday was my birthday." She was trying to get any praise she could for herself. Ryan cleared his throat then said,

"Oh, well then, happy birthday." My mother gave him a little pretend shy look and swept her hand across the air as if she didn't want anyone to make a big fuss about her. The room felt uncomfortable and awkward, possibly only to me, but I spoke up nonetheless.

"Maybe. I need to run to the store and get some things to finish it though." Nikki snapped her head up in delight that I might be leaving and taking Ryan with me. Then Nikki said,

"You should take Ryan and I'll stay here with your brother." I had to give Nikki major credit for sticking it out with my family the way that she did. As I nodded, I didn't waste time and headed to the front of the house, yelling back at Ryan,

"Just give me a sec… I'm going to grab a few things out of my room." I went into the bedroom and quickly put on my make-up and brushed out my hair. It was amazing what a good haircut and the right amount of make-up could do for a girl.

I switched over the contents of my purse to another one when I heard the doorbell ring. I didn't think much about it as I had answered the door a million times before. I opened the door to see Chad standing on the front porch, his shirt wrinkled and his eyes tired and heavy.

"Hey Amy. I waited for you outside the bar last night but I never saw you come out." He pulled his hand out of his pocket and checked his watch in his typical manner, which I never really understood since he didn't have pressing business to attend. He waited for me to respond, but when I didn't, he just continued, "You looked really good last night, so that got me thinking. What do you say we put the wedding back on?" I just stood there, angry and frozen, expressionless with the only exception of my blinking eyelids. It really was as if I was nothing more than a plaything to him, some toy he could discard whenever he felt the need to, only to pick back up again. I narrowed my eyes at him and replied with nothing less than disgust,

"You have got to be kidding me. There is no way I would ever consider getting back with you, ever." He bit down on his bottom lip, which I had finally come to recognize was his way of manipulating me, and it no longer worked. I clinched my teeth together before I blurted out, "Just go away. I don't ever want to see your ugly face again." He stopped biting his lip and looked at me not only as if I was less than he was, but as if I was nothing.

"That's fine, Amy, I was just giving you another chance. You're the one who's going to miss out. No one is ever going to want to be with your fat, dumb, ugliness anyway." He shrugged his shoulders as if his words were mere conversation and not the hateful things they really were. My mind paused, turning his hateful words around in my thoughts, wondering if he was right, and sadly believing he might be.

"What are you doing here?" I heard Ryan's voice just over my shoulder as Chad lifted his eyes to look at Ryan behind me. Then Chad asked arrogantly, as if he were standing on his front porch and not mine,

"What are *you* doing here?" Ryan had made his way next to my side as I stood my ground, watching Chad's face, desperately trying to hold back the tears I felt coming. A combination of so many things were forced on me to deal with, but most of all the thought that Chad might be right and he would once again get the satisfaction of hurting me.

"I'm here with Amy. So I'll ask you again… What are you doing here?" Ryan's tone became more intense and demanding as he crossed his arms. Chad put a smug look on his face and let out a chuckle before he replied,

"I just came to give Amy a chance to come back, but I see some stupid guy is trying out the fat girl experience." He laughed a little and a tear came to my eye. Ryan glanced down at me and then looked back at Chad and took a step out onto the porch as he stretched out his arm and tightly grabbed a wad of Chad's wrinkled t-shirt collar up in his fist, putting his face inches from Chad's.

"I don't ever want to see your face again. You got that. That's my fiancée you're talking about." He opened his fist and Chad stumbled back a few steps, a completely honest look of terror in his eyes.

"Alright… whatever man." He glanced quickly over at me, the terrified look still lingering as he started to take a few steps to his car. Then I wiped my eyes and yelled out before he reached his car.

"Chad! Wait." Ryan looked at me with shock as I leaped off the front porch and ran up to him. Chad had a baffled expression on his face as I said,

"I forgot something." He gazed at Ryan behind me as he

quietly said,

"What?" Then I stretched out my fingers and pinched them tightly together as I brought my hand sharply against the side of his face. A twinge of pain radiated throughout my hand and up my arm at the moment of impact. Chad grabbed the side of his face and snarled at me as he yelled, "You—" He stopped as he glanced over at Ryan behind me. Then he shot me a dirty look as he climbed in his car and took off down the road. I turned and headed back up the front lawn, feeling more than lighter. I was not only relieved, but also satisfied.

Ryan just looked down at me and nodded with a smile on his face as he spoke,

"Okay, rightfully so… rightfully so." Then he cleared his throat and threw in there, "Sorry about the whole fiancée thing. He was pissing me off. I'm not crazy or delusional or anything."

"It's okay… So far you're the best fiancée I've had." We laughed a little as we went into the house to get some ice for my hand.

TWENTY

"Why is your hand pink?" Nikki asked peering over my shoulder as I reached into the freezer to grab an ice pack.

"I was just saying bye to someone in a way that made sense, that's all." Nikki looked confused and then I whispered low so my mother wouldn't over hear me from the kitchen table, not that she would because she was busy talking out loud about stupid things that happened when she lived the pageant life, not that anyone was really listening though.

"I'll tell you later… But I'm totally gonna marry that bartender." I spoke only half in a whisper and the other half I just mouthed the words for Nikki to read my lips. Nikki looked even more bewildered and just shook her head in acknowledgment that she would just wait to hear the story. I smiled wide, not because I was giddy about what I just said, because I sure wasn't. I smiled because my words, even though a joke, felt factual to me. I was going to have something real with Ryan. I could sense it deep down. Unlike everyone else, Ryan liked me. He really liked me, not the fat me, the sad lonely me, or the put on a nice dress and look a tad better me. He liked just plain Amy and I could tell.

I interrupted my mother who was mid-sentence in a story that I had heard a million times before about the time she beat out another girl that lacked grace when the girl tripped over her dress, basically ensuring the crown to my mother.

"I'm not gonna be able to finish that piece of furniture in the garage for you, sorry Mom. I just don't have the time it will take." My mother had not yet closed her mouth and slowly brought her lips together as the corners drooped down in a frown. She stuck out her bottom lip in a slight pout before she asked,

"But you always got stuff done before when it was my birthday." I took a deep breath and let it out along with my reply in one breath.

"True, but not this year." Then I finished with, "I've got things I want to do before Nikki and I head back in two days." Still holding the sad pouty face, she turned her eyes over to Ryan who was leaning against the counter with his arms crossed, pretending to have been listening to my mother's story just minutes earlier. She looked him up and down, taking in his tattoos and long hair before she replied to me while her eyes were still on him.

"I see." I could tell her mind was turning over the thought that this guy might be the replacement for Chad. Her pout turned back into a small frown as she took in all the ink and chin length hair on his head. I already knew my mother didn't approve of tattoos because to her they made the skin look permanently dirty as she had said on more than one occasion when I was growing up. Regardless of his tattoos, not a soul could deny the fact that Ryan's clothes where clean, fit him well and his shoes were tied and his hair brushed. A feat Chad, even with his family's money, seemed unobtainable for him.

"Ryan? Correct? Tell me what you do for a living." She brought her glass of greenish brown sludge to her lips and sipped on it, trying to pretend it tasted good. Ryan uncrossed his arms and slid his hands in his jean pockets. He cleared his throat and looked nervous before he answered,

"I own a bar in the next town over. Denver's Place." He took his hand out of his pocket and ran his fingers through his hair before putting it back in his pocket. My mother just cleared her throat and casually said,

"That's nice." As if it really meant nothing to her.

I remembered I had yet to give her birthday present from Venice when I exclaimed,

"Oh, Mom, I have something for you!" Ryan looked relieved the attention was off of him just as my mother looked equally relieved it was back on her. Her eyes grew bright and a pleasant smile crossed her lips as she spoke.

"Oh really?"

I quickly walked down the hall to my bedroom, reached into my bag, and pulled out the box that I had professionally wrapped in Venice with shiny purple and gold paper. It looked beautiful and I knew I was raising the bar for future birthdays with my mother. I quickly walked back down the hall and handed her the gift as she brought the tips of her fingers to her lips and gasped.

"Oh, it's lovely wrapping." She carefully opened the paper, as not to tear it. Then she lifted the intricately detailed masked and sighed with a smile. "This is beautiful, Amy, did you get this in Italy for me?" I nodded my head in reply as a slight smirk came upon my face. It was the perfect gift after all for my mother. "I feel like I should try it on."

My smirk turned into a full-blown smile now, as I said,

"It's your mask, you can wear it, hang it on the wall… Whatever you like." She kept her eyes on the mask for what seemed like forever as she turned it around in her hands several times while she ran her thin fingers along the detail of it. I took that moment to run down to my old room again, put something on better than just my jeans, and long sleeve t-shirt. A few moments later, I heard the door close behind me as Nikki entered the room, talking in a low voice.

"I'm not gonna lie, your mom does not shut up about herself. Seriously. Like nonstop." We both chuckled a little bit as Nikki sat on the edge of my old desk chair that was against the wall. Then she asked, "What's going on with the bartender?" I shrugged my shoulders as if it wasn't a big deal and took a breath just as I draped my new shirt on over my head before I said,

"He asked if we can hang out today so I told him yeah." Then I quickly added, "As long as that's okay with you?" She looked equally as relaxed and said,

"Sure, your brother said we should all go to see that new movie that just came out yesterday, so I'm okay with whatever. We could go as a group or I can just go along with your brother if you want to hang out with Ryan. I'm okay either way. He did say your mom had a spa appointment this afternoon though." I chuckled a little and replied,

"Yeah, she goes every year on her birthday. She will be there almost all day. Usually, I have her piece of furniture finished and waiting in the middle of the kitchen when she gets back, but not this year." We both looked at each other and then busted out laughing. Then Nikki said,

"Why don't you go out with Ryan now and then Mike and I will meet you guys at the movies later?" I nodded. This sounded like a solid plan. Now all we had to do was convince the guys it was good. I opened my mouth to confirm this plan with Nikki, as there was a soft tap on the door, which had to belong to Mike.

"Come in, Mike." As he had been doing since we were kids he peered his head around the cracked open door.

"Hey sis. Did you want to go to a movie and bring that guy Ryan with us? He seems like a good guy. I like him. He already told me he's cool with going to the movies." Nikki and I smiled at each other and then looked back at Mike. Then I said,

"Sure, but I'm gonna hang out with him first, maybe go get lunch if you and Nikki want to do something while mom is at the spa." Mike titled his head for a second and looked up towards the ceiling as he said,

"Sure. I was just gonna hang out here at the house, but if

Nikki wants to go somewhere I can take her." Nikki shook her head as she said,

"No, not really. We can just hang out here. I'm good with that." All three of us looked at each other in confirmation that the plan was set. Just as Mike was closing the door, I pulled out my thigh high boots and skintight pants. Nikki and I had searched for over a week to find thigh high boots that actually fit my thick thighs because she was determined to prove me wrong when I told her finding a pair to fit would never happen. I started to rush, as I knew I had to change quickly before my mom scared off Ryan for good. Nikki smiled at my boots and looked really pleased as she commented on my choice,

"Now that's what I'm talking about, sexy diva."

TWENTY-ONE

"Wow." That's all Ryan said when he stopped in his tracks in the hallway, just as I was stepping out of the bedroom. I shook my head at him letting him know I knew he was being silly. Then he continued, "Those sure are some pair of boots you got on there." He brought his hand up, ran his fingers through his hair, and tucked it around his ears. Then he cleared his throat again, which had become apparent it was a nervous tick for him, and said, "hey, do you want to hang out for a few minutes at Bayview Park before lunch?" I lit up because I loved Bayview Park. Betsy and I would ride our bikes down there and just hang out all the time in high school. It was never crowded because the cool kids didn't think it was cool enough for them. Betsy and I would often be the only ones there. I quickly answered,

"Yeah, that's cool."

I barely said bye to my mom as we hurried out of the house and jumped in Ryan's car, which was both nicer and newer than Chad's. He leaned over and turned down the radio as he asked,

"What happened with you and that little creepy guy?" I smiled at first because I realized compared to Ryan, Chad was nothing more than a little creepy guy. Then I frowned knowing I might change in his eyes to sad Amy and get only pity from him moving forward. I took my chances and just answered,

"We were engaged but I found out right before the wedding that he had been sleeping with my best friend. My best friend since grade school."

He didn't say anything for a minute and just shook his head in amazement. Then I continued with a question, "I'm surprised you didn't hear about it in the next town over. I've heard that bartenders know everything." I chuckled out of nervousness. He reached up and combed through his hair before he replied,

"I had heard something about your situation, but I hadn't made the connection yet that it was *your* situation that people were talking about in the bar. Believe me; neither your ex nor your best friend did themselves any favors by doing that to you. It doesn't matter if people know you or not, a situation that happens to someone like that… makes anyone mad to hear." I looked over at him and scrunched my eyebrows together in puzzlement. I had been under the assumption the whole time that I looked like a loser, which I had been made a fool through my humiliation. If what he was saying was true, none of what I put myself down for was accurate. I asked,

"Really?" He nodded his head and recounted,

"Oh yeah, I have some bikers come in about once a week and they overheard your story and were ready to find out who this Chad was and rough him up a little." I let out a breath I had been holding and scratched the back of my head. I was right assuming that since Chad's dad was fairly popular, it only seemed normal that gossip would spread the way it did. I turned to him and said,

"That surprises me." He shook his head in disagreement and said,

"It shouldn't, but to be completely honest, now that I know the story was about you and that little jerk, you really dodged a bullet on that one." He chuckled a little, looked over at me, and smiled. My heart actually felt warm because I knew he was saying more than he really was.

The small narrow lake had ducks swimming along the edge. There had never been ducks in the lake during my high school years so those few ducks gave the park a different feeling. There was a huge, flat top bolder a few yards from the water. Perfect for climbing up on and watching the lake. Ryan headed straight for the bolder, and with one quick swoop leaped up on the large rock and sat down. Before I could even get my boot hooked in the indent on the side of the rock, he reached out his arm and grabbed my hand, swooping me up as well and sitting me next to him.

"Comfortable? I mean comfortable enough for sitting on a rock?" He asked, with a boyish grin on his face.

"Yeah. They used to call this the kissing rock, although I don't know why. People never came out here to kiss on it… At least as far as I know." He laughed a little and said,

"You're funny, Amy." I smiled over at him. The afternoon sun was hitting his hair and I could see thin specks of gold streaked in it. I scooted towards the edge of the rock so my feet could dangle off more easily. He reached out and put his hand against my stomach as protection, unaware I had moved to the edge on purpose.

"I'm good. Just wanted to sit on the edge." I looked over at him and asked out of curiosity, "How old are you, Ryan?" He looked back over a little confused and said,

"I just turned thirty, four months ago. You?" I sighed a little out of relief and replied,

"Yeah, me too. I'm about to be thirty soon."

The ducks started talking with each other as the loud quacks along the edge of the riverbank were followed by softer quacks further off in the distance. Ryan and I talked and he told me about his time in the service and all the places he had been. He also told me he could afford to buy his bar and his place because he was a computer programmer who had programmed training software for the military that they paid him very well for. He jokingly called himself "G.I. Nerd" as he told me about his time in the service. It was also clear he had seen active duty as well. He had been places and done things I couldn't even begin to imagine. We had easily been talking for over an hour. He asked so many questions I started to give more vague answers as I began to realize I had accomplished nothing compared to everyone else my age. I stopped talking and looked off at the ducks down the riverbank as he asked,

"What was your mom talking about with the furniture in the garage?" I shrugged my shoulders and casually replied,

"It's just a little hobby I have. I take old furniture, usually small things like coffee tables and nightstands, and I refinish them. I actually like doing it. The last few years I've refinished something for my mom. The largest piece I did was my first one with my dad when I was eighteen. It's the dresser in my old bedroom at the house." He glanced over and a wide smile crossed his face as he said,

"Wow. That's pretty cool." I shook my head and glanced at the water. I didn't think it was anything special. I was quiet for a few minutes before he said, "I'm sorry, am I hounding you with too many stupid questions?" I shook my head and with all sincerity, I surprised myself by confessing,

"No, I just haven't done anything with my life and I don't have much to talk about. I'm not an interesting person, not like other people, like Kara." I turned my gaze back towards the ducks thinking about how my attempts had been unsuccessful trying to get a job near Nikki and start paying her rent. I felt that in reality, all my attempts had been unsuccessful for that matter, my attempt to become skinny, my attempt to get married and getting my own house. I took a big sigh just as he said sternly,

"That's ridiculous for you to say that. You *are* interesting. There's a million girls like Kara. She comes in the bar all the time trying to get me to take her home. Girls want to be like her and I don't know why. But you? There's no one else like you. I knew that the first minute I saw you. Don't be so hard on yourself." His tone let me know his words were not negotiable and he was most definitely being sincere. I nodded and gave a faint smile as I agreed.

"You're right." Then he cleared his throat and changed the subject.

"Are you getting hungry? I know a good burger place close to the movie theater, and then we will have plenty of time to meet your brother and Nikki there." I signaled with a nod that I agreed.

We sat on the rock for only a few more minutes of silence when suddenly I blurted out like a teenager,

"I like you a lot, Ryan." He looked amused and replied,

"I like you too, Amy." He then slid off the large boulder with a smile still on his face, turned around and reached his arms up to me signaling he wanted me to slide down to him so he could help me. I really felt I couldn't refuse him as I slid down the rock into his grasp. His strength was apparent as he gently and effortlessly wrapped his solid arms around me and helped me down to safety. Then, as his smile softened to a playful smirk, he asked, "Didn't you say this is the kissing rock?" My heart immediately began to race as I held my breath for a split second before I replied,

"Yeah… I did." He smiled down at me, his hair falling loose from behind one of his ears and touching his face. My heart went even faster than a few seconds earlier, and my knees felt weak.

"Amy?" I heard a faint timid voice as both Ryan and I turned our heads to see Betsy standing just a few yards away from us. My adrenaline started to pump even harder, but not because I thought I was going to get kissed.

I pressed my eyebrows together as I demanded from her,

"What are you doing here?" She looked like she had lost some weight and in all honesty, her already tiny frame couldn't afford to lose any weight. In addition to that, her hair was stringy and oily, practically uncombed. Her face was paler than normal with a ghostly white color. She spoke up just a fraction louder and said,

"I saw cars at your house so I thought maybe you came home for your mom's birthday. I stopped by to speak with you and your mom said you went out. I thought you might be at our park… so I came here." My mind started turning over what she had said. I didn't completely understand why, but her use of the word 'our' made me angry. Did she think she lived in a world where everything of mine was also part of hers? Was Chad not my fiancée but 'our' fiancée? I took a long time to respond. She continued nervously so she could fill the awkward silence. "So how have you been?" What came out of her mouth was nothing more than air to me. She had little to no emotion behind them.

"You tell me," I said to her as I narrowed my eyes. For some reason, the same sad and angry feeling I had during my dream a few weeks earlier, along with the lingering memory of that dream, flooded back to me. She took a small step forward, pulling one arm across her chest and grabbing her elbow tight, something she always did when she was scared. Then she said softly,

"Amy… I am really sorry. I didn't mean for it to happen or for you to find out. I was going to end it before your wedding, I swear… please forgive me." A million questions I had pushed to the back of my mind for weeks, even months, filled me, filled me with anger, filled me with resentment, but most of all, filled me with fear of the unknown. I asked, cold and callously,

"Tell me, how long had you been sleeping with him when I found out?" Betsy grabbed her elbow tighter and swallowed hard. Then she replied,

"Only a few months." Her words were quiet as they passed through her thin lips and even thinner frame. I took a quick deep breath, and with anger, I exhaled right before I asked,

"What's a few months?" I could see her start to shake, and because she was so thin and frail I imagined she might pass out. Then she said,

"About eight, maybe nine." The rage boiled up in me so strong that my chest got tight and I could hardly breathe. The thought of betrayal not from Chad, but from Betsy was almost unbearable. My eyes slowly filled with ragingly hot tears, but I choked them back as I said,

"I don't care about Chad. You actually did me a favor with that, but I might not ever be able to get over how you stabbed me in the back. How you betrayed me, killed our friendship. You went against the friend code." For a brief moment, a sad expression flickered across her face, then as quickly as it came it left, leaving her face plan and dull once again. I felt Ryan's arm wrap around me as he leaned down right behind my ear and lowered his voice just out of Betsy's earshot,

"Do you want to leave?"

I wanted to do a great many things. I wanted to go and slap her in the face. I wanted to cry. I wanted to run. I wanted to crawl in a hole and wake up and none of this happened. I wanted to be free. I looked up and quietly replied to him so she couldn't hear me,

"Yeah, it's time for us to leave." Then I turned my gaze back to her and said, "No. I am not at a point where I can forgive you. I may never be at that point. Just leave me alone." I took Ryan's hand and walked past Betsy, unable to make eye contact with her. It occurred to me that not only had she ruined my wedding, but she ruined the mood and first kiss I was going to have with Ryan. I was fearful after he watched that I might never have another chance with him.

TWENTY-TWO

Our car ride over to the hamburger place was relatively quiet and docile. So many questions about Betsy and Chad filled my mind and I couldn't keep them from coming. I had a feeling Ryan could sense I was preoccupied in my thoughts and was being courteous and letting me have some time to think. However, at the same time, I wished he would just say something, anything at all to take me from my awful thoughts. I felt a huge wave of relief when I heard him clear his throat as if he was about to say something. He looked over at me for moment before he returned his focus on the road. Then he asked,

"Seriously, are you okay?"

"Yeah, I think so, but I guess I'm still trying to process it. I'm sorry." He took his eyes off the road to ask.

"Sorry for what?"

"I'm sorry for all this drama you've seen in such a short time. I'm sure this is not what you had in mind when you asked to hang out with me today." He smiled and took his hand off the wheel for a moment and tucked his hair around his ear before he said playfully,

"Seeing a beautiful girl slap a guy that cheated on her so hard her hand imprinted on his face… is exactly the sort of thing that makes my day." I shot him a quick look and sarcastic smile before I blurted out without thinking,

"Are you referring to me as *beautiful*?" He shook his head almost in the same exact fashion that Nikki does before she gives me some empowering lecture about loving myself.

"Of course I am… because you are." I couldn't keep from smiling and blushing as I looked away from him and out of the car window. Then in a more serious tone, he said, "Betsy looked horrible, like she hasn't eaten or slept for months. I'm not sure she's showered either. If that creepy guy cheated on you, he for sure cheated on her too. Guys like that don't change. I know guys like that."

I nodded my head while still gazing out of the window. I knew Ryan was right, and oddly, on some level, I got comfort from that. Not from her clear distress that had taken over her life, but comfort that I didn't walk down that aisle. When would I have found out about them? Would we had been married for weeks, months, or years before it came out? What if Betsy had gotten pregnant? What if we both had gotten pregnant? What if he had multiple affairs after I married him? What if Betsy wasn't the only one he cheated on me with. I turned my gaze over to Ryan and asked as he focused on the road,

"Do you think Betsy was the only one he cheated on me with?" Ryan tilted his head slightly to the side as he was still looking at the road while he pondered for a moment, then he replied,

"Given that he had no morals to cheat on you with your best friend, odds are good she wasn't the first one… and I'd say she wouldn't have been the last either." He quickly frowned and glanced over to me with an apologetic look on his face before he said, "I'm sorry to say that, and you need to know that guys like that don't care about women at all. They only care about getting what they want. It had nothing to do with you… at all."

I smiled at him because for probably the first time, I felt like what he was saying was more than likely right. I knew it wasn't because of me that Chad cheated. It wasn't because I was fat-Amy, desperate-Amy, or lonely-Amy. No, Chad cheated because he was just selfish and arrogant. I was still looking at Ryan as he glanced over and saw my smile and then he smiled back in return before he took his hand off the wheel and wrapped it around mine just as I heard *Love is a Battlefield* coming out of my purse. He released my hand as I leaned forward and picked up my purse from between my legs to fish out my cell phone. I had forgotten that I changed my ring tone for Nikki to that song on our drive out to my mom's house because we both loved that song.

"Hey Lady," I said cheerfully in the phone. Nikki replied back almost equally as cheerful.

"Hey, there's a showing to that movie in about twenty-five minutes. I know it's a little earlier than we originally planned, but would you guys be able to make it to that one?" I was beginning to wonder if maybe Mike was getting on her nerves but I pulled the phone away from my ear and quickly asked Ryan.

"Would you be okay if we went to an earlier showing that played in twenty-five minutes?" He nodded his head and replied,

"Yeah, no problem. We're only a few minutes away from the theater." I pushed the phone back to my ear.

"Yeah that's no problem. So we will just meet you guys there, okay?" Nikki's voice was apologetic as she spoke.

"One more thing. That girl from work that was supposed to cover my shift called me because her aunt passed away… and she needs to go out of state for the funeral. I can't find anyone else to cover for me so we need to leave by tomorrow afternoon. I'm sorry, Amy."

I didn't completely understand why, but I felt like crying. On the drive here, I wanted nothing more than to turn around or leave after my mom's birthday dinner as quick as possible. Given the drama of seeing Chad, Kara, and Betsy, I should have exclaimed with joy that I couldn't wait to go back home. I glanced back over to Ryan and realized I was in the car with the only reason I didn't want to leave. As odd as it was, I was more sad to take a car ride home and leave Ryan, than I was to take a plane ride across an ocean and never see Dante again. I cleared my throat and replied,

"Hey don't worry about it. I completely understand. No big deal." Unaware of what we were talking about, Ryan once again wrapped his hand around my unoccupied hand as it lay on top of my thigh. Nikki and I said bye and hung up the phone. Ryan casually asked,

"Is everything okay? Are they still meeting us there?"

"Oh yeah, they are. Everything's fine." I glanced back out the window and couldn't bear telling him I was leaving tomorrow. I didn't want to put a cloud over the rest of the evening. He already knew I was going back home in a few days but it just now seemed so abrupt. I knew this feeling was overwhelmingly foolish because it wasn't as if we lived an ocean away, and in the scheme of things, a four and half hour car drive was nothing really. Yet it felt like this was the end for us, the end of our possibilities.I was still looking out the window when Ryan asked,

"Are you still hungry? We can grab something quick if you are." I glanced over and shook my head before saying.

"No, actually I'm not hungry. If you are, we can get something before the movie."

"How do you feel about grabbing that burger after the movie instead?" Ryan suggested.

I couldn't help smiling, because he seemed genuinely concerned that I not go hungry, which at the same time was amusing to me for some reason.

"Sure." I turned my gaze back to the window as I let my smile fade. I would tell him I was leaving tomorrow when we went out to eat, not before the movie. My smile returned to my face as we pulled up to the movies. I immediately saw Nikki's car near the front of the theater and was surprised they were there already. Ryan also saw Nikki's car and pulled into a parking spot only a few cars away. He quickly got out, ran around to my door, and opened it for me, reaching out to take my hand. It was so odd and storybook, but it was almost as if this was natural for him to do. I could tell he wasn't just trying to impress me. I sensed this is how he would be to me as long as I knew him. I was confident in that feeling. I reached out and took his warm hand. He didn't let go of my hand while we walked into the movies.

Nikki was a huge fan of popcorn. She ate it frequently as a snack back home so it was no surprise when we sat down that she had a huge tub of the white fluffy clouds sitting on her lap. Nikki and I sat next to each other while the guys capped off the ends. She leaned over with her hand hovering over the tub and whispered,

"Sorry about the time change. Your mom called and said she was going to get out of the spa early, so we just told her we were leaving for the movies before she made plans for all of us." She gave me an apologetic look before she started plucking a few pieces out and setting them on her tongue. I nodded and opened my mouth to whisper back just as the light began to dim. I felt the warmth of Ryan's hand wrap around mine and saw Nikki glance down briefly as our hands interlocked before she turned her eyes back to the screen in front of her. The widest smile crossed her lips that lasted for minutes, which I could see from the corner of my eye.

I couldn't pass a quiz on the movie or even recall most of the dialogue. However, I would probably be able to tell anyone about the temperature of Ryan's hand or the faint smell of his crisp cologne and leather. There was an overwhelming comfort and feeling of protection just sitting next to him, my arm rubbing against his, our hands locked tight. I thought nothing about Chad and Betsy during the movie. All my questions now were thoughts and wonders on the possibility of a relationship with Ryan given we lived so far from each other. I had seen how difficult things had been for Nikki trying to have a long distance relationship with Lucca, and how devastated she had been when it ended. I wondered if the same thing would happen to me even though we weren't separated by an ocean. I wondered if he would get tired of driving and phone conversations, or if he would meet someone else entirely. Perhaps some pretty girl would walk into his bar one night and then our phone calls would just stop. One thing I did know, I had no intention of moving back to my hometown. I didn't want to revert to what I had finally escaped from.

Shortly after the movie and everyone saying how much they loved it, Ryan and I headed to the restaurant to get something to eat. I was going to need to let him know I was leaving tomorrow and just deal with where things went. I was entirely aware he might just decide to stop anything before it even started to avoid a future hassle, but it was better to let him know now instead of saying good-bye as we drove away tomorrow. I tried to convince myself it was probably a hidden blessing we were going back tomorrow, since I already had another interview set up for the next week. Italy had been a learning experience for me, for both Nikki and me actually. I no longer wanted to prolong the end of something if that's what was going to happen, but I knew I had to take that risk.

TWENTY-THREE

We pulled into the drive while Ryan's hand stayed wrapped around mine. He had hardly relinquished my hand all evening but for the rare occasion. The act of having my hand held was not something I was at all familiar with, but I knew I wanted to be. I also knew I wanted to be familiar with this comforting feeling of protection and acceptance. Ryan made me feel beautiful, even the look in his eyes said he found me amazing. I was unfamiliar with that also. Dante had looked at me in a very similar way, but it wasn't the same, not as organic and sincere as the look in Ryan's eyes.

Nikki and Mike had probably been home a good forty minutes before us. I felt an uneasy sick feeling as the car rolled to a stop and Ryan turned the key and the engine died off. I could see a ladder at the corner of the garage where my mother stood picking a few weeds out of the gutter along with some debris from the storm she said blew through last week. I watched as she let it fall lightly to the grass next to the driveway. She had on her favorite large brim hat and I could even tell she was wearing pearls from the angle she was standing. The only thing she was missing was her pink gardening gloves, the ones that matched her pink gardening apron. She had substituted them for her thicker light gray pair. Her hair had even been freshly cut and styled, most likely at the salon and spa. She was a perfect picturesque version of herself thirty years earlier.

I got an uneasy feeling in my stomach as we got out of the car. I was quick to climb out of my door before Ryan could run around and get it for me. I wanted to spare him and me of any disparaging looks that might fly in our direction from the lady on top of the ladder.

"Hello, Amy dear, how was the movie?" I never understood why she had to give off such a pretentious tone with every question she asked me. I also couldn't understand why she just didn't love me or accept me, all fat size sixteen of me. Most of all, I didn't comprehend why she just didn't want the best for me as all the other mothers I saw do for their daughters. Every conversation with her was painful and agonizing, and it always had no point or resolution to anything. It felt like I had spent a lifetime wondering all this. I gave her a faint smile and replied,

"It was pretty good."

She batted her eyelashes before she stopped, her mouth momentarily dropping as she looked down at Ryan and his tattoos, and his hair that fell around his face. She quickly took a breath and returned her smile as she strived to be polite asking him.

"How did you like the movie, young man?" He replied with a charm I didn't recognize.

"It was good, ma'am, you should really go see it. I think you would like it." My mother beamed, as she basked in the attention she was getting. I motioned for Ryan to follow me into the house.

"Why is Mom on a ladder?" I asked out loud, as I walked down the hallway and into the kitchen. It was obvious she was cleaning out the gutter. My real question was actually why was she on a ladder at this particular moment considering I was only visiting for few days and she just got home from the spa.

"She said she just wanted to clear a few things out of the gutter real quick. I put the ladder up, but told her to hang on for a second and I would do it for her," Mike answered loudly from the living room next to the kitchen. I turned to see him tying his boots that he always wore to do anything outside.

"Mom never listens. I told her to hold on I was coming right out."

"I know, but she's on that ladder. Hey, where's Nikki?" Mike motioned toward the bedroom as he grumbled about a rock in the bottom of his boot, pulling it off to dig it out. Then he glanced over at Ryan and said with a smile,

"Hey, Ryan, you taking off soon or are you good on a ladder?" Mike's smile widened because being the only male in the house for a long time, he never had male companionship or help with anything. Chad never helped with anything remotely physical or labor intensive. Ryan stepped forward with a long stride toward

Mike while tucking his hair behind his ear.

"Yeah, man, I got you. I can get up on a ladder no problem and give you a hand." I smiled towards them as I felt I was getting a small glimpse into what Ryan was like with his military comrades. I quickly indicated I was going to the bedroom to talk to Nikki and headed down the hall while I left Ryan and Mike to chat for a minute.

"Hey, Nikki, you putting your clothes together?" I asked walking in the bedroom as Nikki sat on her knees next to her suitcase folding clothes and neatly placing them in rows and stacks.

"Yeah, I'm really sorry we have to head back tomorrow. That girl couldn't find anyone else to take the shift. I feel bad 'cause I can see things are going smooth with the bartender." Nikki had a guilty expression on her face as she looked down and took out and refolded a shirt she had not even worn. I walked over and sat on the bed putting my hand on her shoulder before I said,

"Really it's not a big deal. I promise. I mean, it would be cool to spend a little more time with Ryan, but it's not a problem for us to head back in the morning." She nodded and draped a scarf alongside some silk shirts. Then she said,

"Do you want to do anything tonight before we leave tomorrow? Your mom is doing something with the gutters so I don't know if she had anything she wanted to do tonight." I shook my head and replied,

"I feel like I should probably try to finish that stupid corner table, but I just don't want to and it will take too long. I'm not in the mood after seeing Betsy when I was at the park with Ryan this morning."

Nikki snapped her head in my direction with her eyes wide and exclaimed,

"Wait! What? You saw Betsy? What happened? What did she say to you? What did you say to her? Why didn't you tell me about it at the movies?" Her eyes went from wide to narrow for a look that said. 'I can't believe you didn't immediately tell me about it.'

"I'll tell you all about it on the car ride back. I'm going to go outside and get the mail for my mother because I'm sure she forgot about it."

Nikki went back to organizing her clothes in a fashion so they wouldn't wrinkle just as I closed the bedroom door behind me. I was not fully intending to go outside only to get the mail, but to confront my mother as to why she didn't even give me a heads up about Betsy stopping by to look for me.

As I headed to the front door, I could hear Mike's boots as he was shuffling around the kitchen, most likely getting a bottle of water before heading outside. I stepped outside and I was immediately caught off guard by the glare of the early evening sun setting. I walked over to the driveway while shielding my eyes from the low setting glare with the sides of my fingers pressed against my forehead.

"Mom, come down from there… both Mike and Ryan are on their way out to do that." She took a deep breath and let out a long sigh, which I heard more than I saw.

"Well, there were just a few things I wanted to get done.

There are weeds actually growing out of this gutter and a bunch of nasty junk from the storm." I rolled my eyes, which I was sure she couldn't see before I continued,

"Fine, I get that, but Mike and Ryan are on their way out." She completely ignored my statement as she went on.

"You know, Amy dear, there might be some furniture supplies in the shed, if you want to try and finish that corner table. I have the perfect spot for it that I have been saving for months." It was now my turn to take a deep breath as I replied,

"Actually, not really, Nikki and I have to leave in the morning. I have a question for you." She glanced in my direction but not completely at me. I went on before she cut me off. "Why in the world didn't you tell me Betsy was looking for me? You have my cell phone number. Why didn't you warn me?" She leaned a little to the side and draped her hand across the air in a floating motion as she spoke with annoyance.

"Well, I figured you might avoid her and that wouldn't be the best thing for you to do. People make mistakes, Amy, and that's just how life is." She turned back towards the gutter as I took my hand away from my forehead and placed both of them on my hips.

"That's kinda true, but I might not be in a place where I can both forgive *and* forget." She paused again twisting her body further in my direction.

"I was also nervous you might be mean to her like you have been with Chad. You never know what the future holds, Amy, and he might want you back one day… and you might want him back. And you don't want to live a life with no friends and no husband, do you?" Her words cut me deep down to my core. I was torn between utter rage and a sense of deep sadness, but mostly an uncontrollable urge to cry.

"I do have friends! I will never, as long as I live, ever have anything to do with Chad, ever again, as in never ever. I just met Ryan and I can tell he is already ten times the man Chad ever was. Why can't you see that people really do like me, mother?" She gave me an eye roll as if I was being too dramatic and reverted her gaze back to the gutter as she calmly said,

"I didn't say you didn't have any friends. I was just trying to open your eyes to the negative possibilities of your life when you are mean to people, that's all. Since you brought up your newfound friend, we both know how we feel about tattoos. They make your skin look permanently dirty."

I looked up at my mother and began to yell. I knew full well how she disapproved of any dramatic show for the neighbors to witness.

"Who are you to talk to me about being mean? I can't remember the last time you were even nice to me! You act as if you hate me. As if you're embarrassed that I'm your daughter! And how you feel about tattoos is not how I feel about tattoos." Tears pooled in my eyes and I could feel the stress and years of frustration boil to the top. I couldn't hold it back anymore. I was exhausted.

She turned her body even farther and raised her voice ever so slightly as she looked angry. An expression she tried hard to never show.

"Don't be ridiculous… and stop yelling for Pete's sake." Her lips were now pressed tightly together and curled down in a frown as her eyebrows scrunched slightly together. My tears kept coming and one thin trickle fell down my face in a hot stream. I looked at her realizing she wasn't registering anything I was saying to her. I glanced over noticing the guys had just stepped off the front porch as I looked up at the ladder and yelled,

"By the way… I hate refinishing furniture for you!" My mother spun even further and kept her voice just a notch below a yell as she snarled,

"Stop yelling, Amy, I already told you. You know I hate that." I started walking toward the house to pack my suitcase as I yelled, for the neighbors to hear.

"Oh yeah, well I hate you." She got frustrated, not with my words but with my loud tone and my public display that might alter her illusion. She grabbed a hand full of weeds and debris and she angrily yelled my name,

"Amy! I told…" I stepped on the front porch just as I heard her scream followed by a deep thump. I spun around and in seconds, both Mike and Ryan were on their knees next to her side.

"Mom! Are you okay?" Mike was yelling as he lifted her head out of the dirt. I took a step off the porch and froze in terror. The only part of my body able to move was my heart, which was pounding at an alarming rate. I took a breath, when seconds later, I heard my mother moan. Then she moved her legs as she tried to sit up. Ryan put his hand under her head as he spoke to her softly,

"Don't move. Tell me what hurts." She began to cry and whimper like a lost child as she mumbled,

"My back… and my head. I hurt so much." Ryan nodded and spoke to her calmly trying to comfort her.

"Okay, just hold still. We're going to call some help." She weakly nodded her head and Mike slipped his hand under her head as Ryan took his away. Ryan glanced towards me, stood up and walked over as I stood there, both afraid and relieved. Afraid that I almost killed my mother, but relieved she hadn't died. I felt an unbelievable amount of guilt. Ryan walked up and calmly said,

"We need to call an ambulance for your mom. I'm not sure what she broke or how hard she hit her head. I think it's lucky she landed half in the dirt but she needs to go to the emergency room." I nodded and quickly looked down feeling like a horrible daughter, a horrible person. Ryan reached out and held my hand and we quickly walked into the house together. I reached for the phone and dialed 911 as Nikki ran into the kitchen.

"What's going on? What was all the yelling about?" I shook my head in embarrassment as I told the dispatcher what had happened and asked for an ambulance. "Your mom fell off the ladder?" Nikki asked as she heard my conversation with the dispatcher.

"Yeah, I don't know how hurt she is. I'm going to go to the hospital tonight to make sure she's okay. I don't know if I can travel back in the morning with you. I'm not sure what to do." Before I even had any ideas, Ryan took a step away from the counter he was leaning on and spoke up.

"If you need me to drive you back home I can do that. It's no problem for me, really." His offer was more than generous as I wasn't sure he understood it was a four and half hour car ride. So I declined politely.

"It's a four and half hour drive, Ryan, I couldn't ask you to take that time out of your schedule to do that. I really appreciate it though."

"I wasn't actually offering, I'm saying I'm going to. I own my own business and I make my own schedule. I decide what I do on my calendar and what I don't."

Nikki stood unsure how or if she should interject and I opened my mouth to reply as Mike swung open the front door.

"The ambulance is here! They are putting mom on the stretcher right now." We raced to the front door and I ran over to my mom as they lifted the stretcher and carried her to the ambulance while she lay strapped down, with her neck in a brace. Her head was locked firm against the hard gray stretcher as a strap across her forehead pressed tight against her skin.

"I'm sorry, Mom. Mike and I are going to be right behind you in the car." She swallowed hard and a single tear streamed down the side of her face from the corner of her eye.

"I'm scared, Amy. Do you think I'm going to die?" I reached out and touched her cold hand, which all of a sudden seemed so thin and frail.

"No, I'm sure you're not going to die. You'll be fine and back on your feet in no time." She could barely move her head as she just blinked her eyes and pressed her lips together in a tight sad frown. As they effortlessly carried my tiny mother on the stretcher to the back of the ambulance and glided her in, a short young guy in an EMT shirt and dark rimmed glasses said something to Mike before he jumped in the back of the ambulance and shut the doors.

"He told me the best emergency entrance to take and park in at the hospital. Let's go." Mike had seen the inquisitive look on my face and answered my question before I even could ask it. Mike jumped behind the wheel and all four of us loaded into Mike's car and pulled out of the driveway just minutes shy of the ambulance.

TWENTY-FOUR

The sun seemed unusually bright as it poured in through the windows and I fought to open my eyes. My body ached and I was beyond exhausted as I moaned and rolled over, feeling nauseous from sleep deprivation. The whole house was motionless and silent with the exception of Nikki breathing with faint breathy snores every so often. I slid out of the bed and cracked open the door. As I stepped out into the hallway, the floor felt like little cold wood planks as I skated my bare feet along the top. I walked into the kitchen and immediately went to the cabinet next to the fridge to grab a bottle of Aspirin for the massive headache I felt coming on. I slowly and quietly opened the fridge, poured some water, and took the medicine before I glanced over to the living room. Ryan was stretched out on the couch on his back; one foot barely touching the end of the couch with the other leg was bent at the knee, while both his arms were up near his face with his forearms crossed over his eyes. His body was in a position I would expect to see from someone taking a nap on a lazy afternoon, not what I expected from someone in a deep slumber. Unintentionally, I coughed. He let one arm fall from his face and repositioned it on top of his stomach as he cleared his throat. I turned to tiptoe out of the room when I heard his gruff morning voice.

"Amy?" I turned back around, I didn't know why but I acted surprised to see him on the couch, even though I was the one that gave him a pillow. It had been a long night at the hospital and it didn't seem right to make him drive home after being there with me all those hours.

He squinted his eyes opened and struggled to look in my direction from the early morning sun that came in by way of the kitchen window.

"Oh, hi, how are you?" I looked down and shook my head realizing what a complete idiot I looked like acting surprised and nonchalant that he was in my living room.

"I'm okay. How about you? How are you holding up?" I wanted to complain about feeling exhausted but it hardly felt fair to complain at all to him after he had dealt with a lot the day before, solely because of me. I knew he could not have predicted spending time with a girl who was facing so many current issues, like a jerk ex-fiancée, betraying ex-best friend, and being a girl that yelled so loud at her mother that her mother fell off a ladder and ended up in the emergency room. That honestly was a lot to take in on a first date for anyone I believe. So I mustered a tiny bit of pretend energy and replied,

"Oh me? I'm not too bad." He stayed on his back and glanced at the ceiling and I saw a wide smile spread across his face as he dropped his other hand down on top of his stomach. It was obvious that he knew I was lying. With the smile still on his face, he continued to stare at the ceiling as he replied,

"That's good. What time are you planning on going back up to the hospital today?" I glanced over at the clock and replied,

"Well, the doctors said they are going to schedule her CAT scan later this morning, but it will take a few hours to get test results. I was thinking about getting stuff to make her a cheesecake and take it up there, but she told me last night she didn't want anything to eat today." I glanced back at the clock realizing I had not answered his question in all my babbling so I quickly added, "I'll probably head up there in two or three hours. I was thinking of just closing my eyes for another hour maybe." He stretched out his knee and sat up while he swung his legs around, dropping them off the couch. Facing me, he straightened up his back, then arched his shoulders back before he rotated them forward, reaching his hands out in one long stretch. I stood and watched him, and I was amazed how well toned and muscular he was. He looked like he was in perfect health, even more so than Mike, and Mike was an avid tennis and softball player. I glanced down at my bright pink tank top and my black and pink sleeping shorts and cringed at my curvy thick thighs that stuck out from the bottom of my shorts. Then he looked at me and said,

"I was gonna go to my place and grab a shower and take you up to see your mom if that's okay with you?" I didn't know what to say, and I didn't know why on earth he was being so nice to me, especially all the time. I replied,

"Oh, I was just going to go up there by myself or with Mike after Nikki jumped on the road. It's okay. You have done a lot for me already, like a whole lot. I really am thankful, if I hadn't told you that yet." He chuckled a little and gave me another sly smile.

"Yeah, you told me a million times last night. It's no problem, Amy." He reached up and smoothed his hair behind his ears, the way he did when he got nervous. It was interesting that even though he just woke up, his hair was still neater then Chad's, even when Chad had just brushed it. "Listen, Amy, you can't blame yourself about your mom. I know you were really upset last night, but it's not your fault that she fell off the ladder. We all say things sometimes, especially to family. You can't beat yourself up over it." I frowned and looked away before I said,

"I know I shouldn't, but I still feel like it's my fault."

"Well, it's not. Accidents happen."

I nodded, not because I completely agreed with him, but because I didn't want to keep talking about how it wasn't my fault when I still felt it might have been. Even after last night, I still couldn't understand why she hated me so much. I didn't understand why she couldn't love me like all other mothers loved their daughters.

"Come here," he said softly as he patted the spot on the couch next to him. I smiled and blushed, and then I walked over and sat on the spot he had patted. I could feel the warmth as it radiated off his body. He said gently, "If you change your mind just call me and let me know. I can take you up there. It's not a big deal. You're a great person, Amy, no matter how you feel about it right now." I nodded and looked down at my hands as he wrapped his arm around me and pulled me in for a side hug. My heart started to flutter as I let him hold me tight against his side. "Amy? Can I ask you a question?" I turned towards him at the same time he turned towards me; his hands now had dropped down to my hips. I was scared for some reason but answered him anyways.

"Yeah, sure." My stomach flipped and my heart raced. He reached up, and instead of tucking his hair behind his ears, he stretched out his hand and gently smoothed my hair behind my ears and stoked it off my shoulder. Then he smiled and said,

"Remember the kissing rock?" I could feel heat coming off my cheeks, as I was positive I was blushing. I surprised myself with a sly smile, as I was bold enough to reply,

"Kinda, but you'll have to remind me."

"Hey, what's up?" I glanced over just as Mike came shuffling through the kitchen while he dragged his feet, as if they weighed a hundred pounds. He sounded rough and his hair was a mess. I wasn't even sure his eyes were open as I shot him a dirty look, which he didn't even notice as he opened the fridge and pulled out the orange juice, taking a huge swig out of the jug. I wanted to yell at him for ruining what would have been my first kiss with Ryan. However, he was unaware how his intrusion just affected me. I chuckled softly thinking about how it never seemed to happen with Ryan. How someone always seemed to interrupt at the right moment. I heard Ryan answer Mike as I just sat and watched my brother shuffle around the kitchen like an old man. Mike had never been a morning person.

"Hey… how are you?"

Mike gave a thumbs up, reached into the cabinet, and pulled out a bowl before shuffling over to the other side of the kitchen, pulling out a box of cereal from the pantry. He turned his head and looked at us before he said,

"Hey, did you guys eat already? Want some cereal?" Mike shook the box of cereal. In return, I shook my head. I wasn't a big fan of cereal, or usually a fan of breakfast for that matter. Mike, on the other hand, never skipped breakfast.

"Do you want me to whip up some eggs? It's easy for me to do," Ryan offered.

Mike's face lit up and I cleared my throat, thinking of yesterday morning where I thought I had slept with Ryan in my drunken stupor and how embarrassed I felt.

"No, Ryan was gonna go back to his place to grab a shower. Don't ask him for any more favors."

"You're right. Ryan's done a lot already. You need to go get some rest, man." Ryan stood and started to speak to offer help again when Mike lifted his hand and stopped him, saying, "Seriously, man, you've done so much for us and had Amy's back. We all only got maybe four hours of sleep. You need to go relax, unwind, and maybe get some more sleep. But seriously… thank you, man." Mike was unusually assertive and Ryan didn't try to overstep the boundaries. Ryan walked over to Mike and patted him on the shoulder as he said,

"Anytime." Then he looked back at me and winked. I walked across the chilly floor and headed for the front door as Ryan followed behind me.

As we walked down the hall, I could hear the faint breathy snores coming through the thin crack from the bedroom door as Nikki lay sleeping. I felt it best to let her get as much sleep as possible before she started driving home.

We reached the front door and opened it as a fresh, sweet smelling breeze swept past my bare knees. I reached next to the door and picked up his keys from the bowl that had been delicately placed on the tall stool that I had refinished and that my mother always kept in the corner by the door. I handed him his keys and said,

"Thank you, Ryan. I can't tell you what it means to me that you were there for me yesterday, all day yesterday even." He smiled as he took the keys out of my hand replying,

"Anytime Amy." Then he leaned within inches of my face, his hair falling from the safety of his ears and touching my cheeks.

I jumped back just as the phone rang, startling me. Ryan smiled and I could tell he was holding back a laugh as I exclaimed,

"Are you kidding me right now?" Then he gave me a wave and shut the door behind him. I was beginning to feel this was the longest delay in history to be kissed.

TWENTY-FIVE

I walked down a wide, cold and eerily quiet hallway in the main hospital. My mother was no longer in the emergency wing. They had moved her to a short stay wing while they ran tests. She had called, interrupting a kiss, to let us know they got her in for testing earlier than they thought. She was now able to have visitors as she waited for her results. I woke Nikki up until right before I left, which was a few hours after the phone call. Mike was going to help load her car and then come up to the hospital after she left. I wasn't sure if that was a good idea since neither Nikki nor Mike were good functioning morning people. Nevertheless, I agreed to come up to the hospital first since I still felt mostly at fault.

I walked into the room where my mother was and noticed how cold it felt. She had a small table tray that hovered over her hospital bed. A white Styrofoam cup sat on the edge of the tray with a straw bent towards her lips. The smell of rubbing alcohol and hand sanitizer lingered in the air as I stepped into the room.

My mother was almost unrecognizable. She had no make-up on and no jewelry. Her hair looked tangled and oily, and her skin was pale and splotchy. The bags under her eyes seemed more apparent than I had ever seen them before, and her lips were dry and cracked. She looked sick and frail, nothing she would ever want anyone to see. It was amazing how she could take such a significant turn in her appearance just overnight. I was struck with the realization that it must take her a tremendous amount of time every morning to look the way she did on a daily basis.

I cleared my throat to catch my mother's attention as she was staring out of the window. She heard me and slowly turned her head in my direction, a faint weak smile spread on her dry lips. She spoke softly,

"Hello Amy, want to come sit on the edge of the bed?" She slowly raised her arm and pointed to the empty edge of the bed as she looked at me with tired glistening eyes. The whole experience was strange and unreal for me. I looked over at the I.V. drip and realized she must have been heavily medicated. I took a few steps and slowly sat on the edge of the bed next to my mother. I felt her frail icy hands as they reached out and touched my arm. I glanced over at her with her faint smile still on her face and her eyes still glistening. Then she asked, almost unbelievably sincere, "How are you doing, Amy? Are you okay?" I stared at her, confused before I replied,

"Uh, yeah. I'm good. How are *you* doing?"

She shrugged her shoulders a little and glanced out of the window before she glanced back at me. I became extremely uncomfortable because I was completely baffled as to what was going on between us. This was out of the ordinary. Heck, it was out of this universe. I became worried that she already got her results and it was horrible news. She was now on her deathbed or something. Then she said faintly,

"I'm not too bad. The medicine has really helped with the pain, so I'm better today than I was last night." I asked,

"Did you already get your test results?" She shook her head 'no' then continued talking,

"Not yet, dear, but I want to tell you how glad I am that you came to visit me on my birthday. It really meant the world to me." My throat immediately became dry. I was worried she was going to try to manipulate me into moving back in with her. I couldn't do it. I had finally gone out on my own like I should have done years ago and now I was concerned she was trying to suck me back in. I gently said,

"You will get better one day at a time, but I can't move back. I'm sorry." She patted my arm before she smiled and replied,

"Oh I know that, Amy dear. I wasn't asking you to. You have your life now and you spent over two years taking care of your grandma like a trooper years ago when she got really sick before she passed away. I know you could have moved out then when she had to move in with us. You really helped so much." Her eyes started to fill with tears as she smiled sincerely while continuing to pat my arm. I didn't know what to say. I sat there next to her unable to move, just staring at her.

For the first time since I could remember, I was having a real conversation, a deep conversation, with my mom. We weren't talking about how I needed to lose weight or what I needed to do to change myself. We were having communication that I imagined any average mother to have with their daughter that they loved. Did my mom love me? I cleared my dry throat and could only get out,

"Sure… You're welcome." I had no idea how to respond in this conversation. Then I said, "I'm sorry I couldn't finish that table for you this year. Do you want me to try and finish it for you before I leave?" She shook her weak head with a faint smile on her lips before she replied,

"No, Amy, don't worry about it. I know it takes time and it's not going anywhere." I nodded and glanced out of the window, unsure what else to say. Then she stopped patting my arm and loosely wrapped her cold fingers around it as she said,

"Amy? Can I ask you something?" I nodded and stared at her as she continued, "Am I that difficult to live with?" I cleared my throat again and softly replied,

"Yeah, sometimes. Can I ask you a question now?" She had a look of understanding on her face as if she had known all along the answer to her question, but had just never been told. She looked at my face as I asked, "Why do you hate me? It's like you're embarrassed that I'm your daughter." She didn't try to dispute my words as she squeezed my arm tighter, her hands still icy cold.

"I don't hate you, Amy. Yes, I have tried to get you to lose weight, to be thin, but I'm not embarrassed by you." I looked at her while tears slowly formed in my eyes. Then I wiped my few tears away and asked,

"But why do you try so hard to make me thin? Why can't you be okay if I'm not a size four? I will never be a size four or beautiful. Why can't you just love me because I'm your daughter?" She took a slow breath in and let it out twice as slow, as she took her hand off my arm and placed both of them on her lap.

"Amy, I have been beautiful my whole life. When I was in pageants and I was modeling, I had every man you could imagine trying to get my attention. I didn't want for anything. Men bought me expensive dinners and jewelry and treated me like I was something." She took another long deep breath and then slowly leaned forward and took a little sip out of her straw with her dry lips. Then she continued, "Your father was the only one who didn't do silly things to try to buy my affection. I knew he wasn't the most good looking or most charming man I could have, but he had the biggest heart. Unlike the others, he sincerely wanted to give me a good life." I looked at her, somewhat confused before I asked,

"I don't understand what this had to do with me." She nodded weakly, then continued,

"There is a certain level of power a woman possesses when she is beautiful. The more beautiful, the more power, and men fall at her feet. From the moment you were born, I wanted you to have that power, have that life. I wanted that for you. Your life is so much easier than you can imagine. The world is not the same for beautiful people as it is for the plain people, or even the average" My eyes filled with tears because I looked at my mother in her frail state and realized she had not lived life to the fullest. She had lived an entire life with illusions and appearances. I said,

"I couldn't have had that unless I was a size four?" She got a frown on her face and a look of deep regret before she replied,

"I see now you can, and you could have. I shouldn't have pushed you so hard. I regret pushing your father away too. I was horribly mean to him and I don't blame him for divorcing me." I reached up to her table tray and grabbed a tissue out of the box before I patted the tears away from my eyes. Then she continued,

"I want to tell you something Amy that you may not forgive me for." I looked at her blinking, afraid. I felt I couldn't take any more of this deep conversation. I very reluctantly asked,

"What is it?" She reached out and placed her hands on my arm once again before she started speaking softly,

"I had an affair on your father years ago, before he left and divorced me. He didn't find out about it until after he had already left though. I didn't feel bad for doing it to your father at the time, but I've come to realize that I was wrong for doing that to him." I stared at my mom barely blinking. A very slow anger started to rise inside of me. Even though it was not personally done to me, it felt that way. I had so much love for my Dad that I couldn't believe she would do to him what Chad had done to me.

I pulled my arm back, away from under her cold hand and crossed them around my chest before I asked,

"With who? Is it someone I know?" My mind began to turn around anything from the past that might have seemed suspicious, but there was nothing in my memory that stuck out. She took a breath and then weakly said,

"It was a very short fling. It happened less than two months with Rick Wheeler." I felt sick hearing the last name Wheeler. I glared angrily at her and demanded,

"Wheeler as in someone related to Chad?" She nodded weakly and very quietly responded,

"Yes, it was Chad's uncle. It was long before you ever even met Chad. None of Chad's family knew with the exception of Chad's father, who I'm sure would never mention it." In reply, I exclaimed,

"You almost let me become Mrs. Wheeler! How would dad feel about that? This is awful, that whole family is awful, well, except for Chad's dad. He's actually pretty nice, but still, they're awful!"

She looked down at her hands and then slowly leaned forward to take another sip out of her white Styrofoam cup. She looked beyond exhausted. I just stared at her, unable to say anything else, not because I had nothing to say, but because I had so much to say, I didn't even know where to start. I was so disappointed that this whole conversation had turned into a confessional for my mother. I opened my mouth and said the only word I could at the moment,

"Why?" She shrugged her shoulders as she replied,

"I don't have a good reason. I think I was just being selfish, missed the attention from men. Rick came along and he was the opposite of your father."

I felt sick listening to her words. Tears started to fill my eyes. I never felt loved by my mother, and I never felt close to her either, but this was the first time I had a deep feeling of disappointment in her. I put my hands up to my face and softly cried. My breaths were soft and quiet as gentle tears came to my eyes. I uncovered my eyes and pulled another tissue out of the box as I patted my eyes. Then I heard her voice.

"Amy, I know it's going to be hard for you to forgive me. I am sorry, I shouldn't have hurt your father and I shouldn't have been so hard on you growing up about your weight. I just wanted you to know what it was like to have the type of power I did." I looked at her exhausted and weak frame. I also was both exhausted and weak from being sleep deprivation as I spoke.

"You look really tired; I should let you get some rest. I'm going to go down to the cafeteria and come check on you in about an hour." To my surprise, she didn't make a single recommendation on what I should eat in the cafeteria. I got up and left the room, hoping it wasn't too late to catch Nikki before she headed back home, I wanted to jump in her car with her and leave this place once and for all, whether or not Ryan was here.

TWENTY-SIX

"Mom, grab on to my arm, I'll push the walker up to you. Go slow." Mike's voice was a combination of instructional and soft, as if he was giving lessons to a kindergartener.

"I know, Michael. I'm taking my time. Push that walker closer to me." Her personality had almost returned to its former self, but with some subtle differences. At first, I thought her change in temperament and our heart to heart had been a direct result of her high dose of medication. I didn't have any explanation for her confessional however, which I had not told Mike about. However, to my surprise, she had not nagged me about food or even criticized me once for the last three days she stayed in the hospital. She hadn't even given me the eye over what I was wearing or how I looked. I had expected that to change when she heard from the doctors that she had slipped a disc in her lower back as well as pulling a hamstring, but most importantly, she was not going to die. After her results, I was sure she was going to let me know I needed to try to shed a few pounds before my interview next week, but she never did.

Three days ago, I had missed Nikki by only fifteen minutes and I sucked it up and got my mom's room ready for her to come home. When she first fell off the ladder, I had originally thought about cancelling my interview to stay longer to help Mike out until my mother got better. However, I just couldn't be around her after her confessional, even though I was aware that sounded selfish. I had already dealt with so much infidelity that had been done to me behind my back, I wasn't in a place I could deal with my mother's infidelity to my dad, even if it was years ago.

"I don't know if I can make it to the front door." She winced her face in pain with each tiny motion she made. Mike walked slowly with her as she inched like a snail in pain towards the front porch.

"Just a few more feet. Amy ordered a wheelchair to be delivered to the store and Ryan is picking it up with his truck. He should be here shortly. Don't worry, Mom, we arranged stuff so you don't have to walk a long distance in the house." She continued to wince in pain as she nodded her head letting Mike know she had heard him. Over five minutes later, my mother finally made it to the front porch. I heard the sound of an engine running, made my way to the window, and peered out as a silver pickup truck rolled to a stop at the end of the driveway. Ryan jumped out and quickly went to the bed of the truck pulling a large box from the back. He stretched his arms out and was barely able to wrap his fingers around the edge of the wide box as he carried it up to the porch. My mother had stopped to take a breather, as she looked exhausted from her short journey from the car to the edge of the porch.

Without saying a word, Ryan set the box on the front porch and then walked down the steps and stood next to my mother. Looking at Mike he asked,

"Do you mind if I help you?"

"No man, not at all. We just need to get her up these steps, but it's going to be hard for her to walk up with her pulled hamstring." Ryan turned around and glanced at the porch, assessing the situation and then he politely said to my mother,

"Ma'am, I'm going to slowly pick you up. If anything begins to hurt let me know immediately."

My mother, too weak to protest, nodded in agreement, as Ryan very carefully picked her up as if she was as light as a small toddler was. He slowly moved up the front steps and through the front door that I had just unlocked and opened. I ran inside the house behind him as he gently set her down on the couch. She winced lightly for a second and then exhaled as if she had just finished a marathon. I went into her room, picked up a throw blanket, brought it out, and placed it across her lap.

"Are you hungry? I made some soup last night if you want any." My mother shook her head and sat in silence for a few minutes. I pointed to the table next to the couch and told her, "I got you a whistle in case we are too far away for us to hear you." She glanced over and looked at the whistle, then closed her eyes as if she needed a few moments of quick rest. I took a chance to go to the front porch where Ryan and Mike had retreated. They were both pulling the plastic wrapped wheelchair out of the box, as bubble wrap floated from the box onto the wood planks.

"Did you have any issues picking it up since I paid with my credit card over the phone?" Ryan looked over at me and smiled as he tucked his hair behind his ear.

"Nope. None at all. They pretty much had it waiting in the front to be picked up."

I had an unbelievable urge to walk across the porch, wrap my arms around him, and ask him where he had been my whole life. Instead, I said,

"Thanks. I really appreciate you doing that. Actually, I really appreciate everything you've done." He looked up from the blue wheel chair that Mike was now looking over to make sure it was all attached and safe, and then he said,

"Anytime." As Mike was hunched down, he glanced up at Ryan and said,

"Seriously, man, you have been a huge help. You're a standup guy, Ryan. I hope Amy doesn't scare you off, but even if she does, you can come hang with me." Mike shot me a joking brother like smirk and then chuckled as I rolled my eyes and laughed. Ryan had a sly smile as he tucked his hair behind his ear, locking eyes with me he replied to Mike,

"I don't see that happening. Besides, I'm not easily scared." I laughed lightly and said,

"That's good to know, Ryan. I get tired of having to hide my axe and rope that I keep in my trunk. It's just a lot of work to be honest." We both looked at each other and laughed a little just as we heard the slight sound of the whistle coming from the house. I signaled to both guys that I would go check on my mother as I quickly walked into the living room where she lay on the couch.

Even though she looked a fraction better than she had when I first saw her in the hospital, she was still weak and frail, far from her former appearance. Her eyes looked tired and the light gray bags under them were more visible than I had ever remembered before. The fine wrinkles around her lips and side of her eyes seemed to have aged her twenty years in less than a week. It felt as if I was looking at the physical essence of her inner self.

"Amy, dear, is it time for me to take more pain medication? I'm feeling pretty sore." I glanced at the silver art deco clock on the wall before I replied,

"You can in one more hour. I'll grab you a few more pillows from the bedroom. That might help." She turned her thin feathered lips down into a frown as she nodded her head and sighed. I ran to her room and grabbed her another wool throw and three feather pillows. She always insisted on using only feather pillows for some reason.

I gently placed the pillows around her body then draped the throw around her shoulders. She barely moved and just sighed as I stepped away from the couch. I grabbed a book off the counter that I had just picked up for her and slid it next to the whistle.

"What's that?" She asked glancing at the book.

"I picked up a book for you. I know you always say you wish you had more time to read so I got you something to read. It's called *Her Side of the Fence*. I hear it's pretty good. Anyway, I have to bring something in for you, so I'll be back in a few minutes." I heard her mumble as I was walking away,

"Thank you, Amy."

A few moments later, I was back on the front porch as Ryan and Mike were tightening a loose screw they had found.

"Ryan, would you be able to carry something in the house for me? It's not really heavy, but more like awkward."

"Sure, Amy."

We both stepped into the dark garage as I pressed the white rectangle button next to the door. The heavy garage door screeched and creaked as light slowly flooded in from the bottom and worked its way up the gray cement until it landed at our feet. I motioned for him to come toward the side of the garage, which had not been used for housing cars for several years, but had instead been turned into one big storage and junk container.

"What are we looking for?" I pointed over at the used and almost discarded piece of craftsmanship. The different types of wood were intricately placed in almost a diamond kaleidoscope effect.

"It's a side table my mother picked up several months ago that I didn't have time to work on before the wedding. Someone was just going to throw it away, but it is really well made and has several types of wood in the design of it."

He looked it over and then looked at newspaper spread out under the table with drops of both varnish and lacquer speckled across the news articles. Then he asked,

"Did you refinish this?" I shrugged my shoulders and then casually said,

"Yeah, it had a really dark tinted varnish on the top so you could hardly see the different wood designs. I think someone else messed with how it originally looked. I sanded it, put a clear coat on, and then I put a shiny polyurethane lacquer over it."

"That's amazing, Amy. It looks really good." He bent down and examined it even closer, slowly taking his fingertips and running it along the top as if he was handling fine china. Then he crouched down to his knees and looked at the legs of the table before standing back up and once again tucking his hair behind his ears, he continued, "I'm really impressed. How long did that take you?"

"A few hours. I did it the first day my mom was in the hospital after I got home. The sanding took the most work. Everything else is easy after that."

"Okay, Amy, so where do you want me to take this?" He gently placed his hand on top of the table. I stared at him with the sun pouring in and reflecting off the natural gold streaks of blond in his hair. His eyes had a soft familiar sparkle to them and a warmth that flooded my heart. I felt foolish thinking about how much I felt about him in such a short time. It didn't make any logical sense, but also at the same time, I thought about how quickly I developed feelings for Dante. I knew the main difference between Dante and Ryan was that Dante was a master of illusions and the appearance of sincerity, while Ryan had been the genuine deal since day one. I smiled thinking about what type of husband and father Ryan would be one day. Then I shook off the thoughts and came back to the present moment.

"Could you carry it in and set it on the other side of the couch next to my mother?" He nodded and I followed him inside as he was careful not to accidently bang the piece of furniture when he was walking through the doorway. He gradually set the table down next to the couch as my mother peered over and a long smile slowly grazed across her lips. My mother said,

"You finished it, Amy. It looks so nice. Could you put it over there in that corner please?" She raised her thin arm as the wool throw hung over it and she gracefully pointed to the corner between the kitchen and living room. Ryan nodded and picked up the piece and moved it to where she asked. He was repositioning the piece of furniture, as I was shocked when I heard my mother say, "Thank you, Ryan." With a confused look still on my face, I glanced over at Mike who was sitting in the high back chair. He just shrugged his shoulders at me and shook his head as if he had no explanation either.

My mother had never made it a habit or practice to refer to people using their names, especially people she didn't consider on her level. It had taken her almost a year to refer to Chad by name instead of 'that boy'. She had also left me with the impression that Ryan's longer hair and body art automatically put him way below her level. To hear her not only thank him but also use his name was shocking to me. Ryan, unaware of what had just happened, casually smiled and glanced over at her.

"You're welcome." I cleared my throat and motioned for Ryan to follow me as I headed to my old room. We walked in and I shut the door behind him before I let out a breath and sat on the edge of my old bed. He pulled up the chair Mike typically used.

"Amy, do you want to stay longer or are you still planning on heading back tomorrow?"

I glanced around my old room and old wood desk I had sat at for many years all through high school and into my adulthood. Then I glanced over at Ryan, thinking about my mother and about her having an affair with Chad's uncle. I had a sadness and wanted to be away from this place and near my dad and Nikki again.

"Ryan, I have decided that I still want to go back tomorrow. Are you still willing to drive me?" A small feeling of fear rose in my stomach as I became concerned that he had possibly changed his mind. He looked down and a sad look crossed over his eyes, as he said,

"Yeah, of course I am. What time do you want me to pick you up?" His voice cracked for a moment as if we were saying goodbye. I surprised myself as I reached out and put my hand on his arm.

"Early in the morning, around seven thirty if that's okay? That way you won't get back late." He reached forward and tucked some of my hair behind my ear as he leaned forward, inches in front of my face. I looked in his soft blue eyes and with his thick light brown lashes and smiled. I leaned in closer to him, my heart fluttering.

"Amy, I'm worried about Mom!" For one of the few times I could remember, Mike came right into my room without knocking.

"Why, what has happened?" He let out a breath, and in all

seriousness said,

"She asked me to order Chinese, fried chicken and shrimp!" Mike quickly walked across the room and plopped down next to me on my bed letting out a huge breath of air, completely unaware he had killed another moment for Ryan and me. I laughed a little, not because it was funny, but because I guess everyone needs Chinese food every couple of decades.

"It's okay, Mike, just order her what she wants. She probably won't even eat it when she sees what it looks like." He nodded and let out another breath as we all stood up and walked to the hallway.

I handed Mike the phone as Ryan waved and walked out of the front door, saying just as he was closing it,

"See you in the morning, Amazing Amy."

TWENTY-SEVEN

Crisp smelling air floated in the house as I opened the front door. The sun had just begun to rise in the early morning sky and there was a faded yellow glow against the dewy grass as the birds were wide-awake and whistling loudly to each other. I stepped out on the wood boards of the porch as my unprotected toes in my flip-flops chilled with the soft breeze of cool morning air that kissed the tips of them. I decided to venture out and across the street to collect the mail.

"Good morning, Amy. Is your mother doing better?" The chipper yet weathered voice of Mrs. Murray carried to me. I glanced away from the mailbox at the shorter woman in her late sixties. Her light brown hair had streaked with so much gray that in the early yellow sunlight for a split moment, she might be considered a blonde. Mrs. Murray had lived in the neighborhood for decades and often power walked at dawn in the same purple windbreaker since I could remember. I smiled at her just as I pulled a few flyers from the mailbox, and she slowed as she approached me a few feet from the box. Typically, I never saw her stop. She always seemed to be moving. Any waves 'hello' or quick inquiries were usually exchanged in the amount of time it took her to walk past our mailbox. She had just so happened to catch me at the end of the driveway the day after my mother had gone to the hospital. I had given her a brief explanation for the ambulance the other neighbors had started to inquire about. Now she was thirsty for the latest update of the situation.

"She got home from the hospital yesterday afternoon. Now she's recovering, but overall, she is doing okay. She just needs her rest and to relax and not over do things." The older lady paused for a brief moment just a few feet from me as she slowly walked in place and lightly swung her little pink dumbbells that couldn't weigh more than a pound each.

"Is there anything I can do for your family, honey?" I shook my head because I couldn't think of anything an older woman who was widowed and retired could do for my mother.

"No thank you, Mrs. Murray, but I appreciate you asking." She started to propel herself forward slowly before she switched subjects.

"Amy, honey, I was so sorry to hear about your wedding. I'm going to let you know that none of us retired folk really liked that boy anyways." Then she smiled and stepped close to me as if she was telling me a deep secret as she continued, "You're going to find yourself a real nice boy, honey. You're far too pretty to stay single. Some boy is bound to snatch you up." She winked her little old wrinkly eye and since she had no hands free, she pointed out her elbow and tapped me on the arm as she walked by, her purple windbreaker swishing as she bustled away. I smiled and then waved as I lightly called out,

"Thanks, Mrs. Murray." I wasn't at all surprised about the older people in the neighborhood knowing about my marriage to Chad not going through. All the elder neighbors that lived at the end of the street or in the cul-de-sacs had a tendency to talk about the neighborhood news as they got their mail, walked their little dogs, or came home from the pharmacy after picking up all of their prescription medications. Overall, the neighborhood was aged, with its rows of modest size ranch houses, and a few two story houses speckled here and there that were built fifty years ago. It wasn't uncommon to find well-maintained lawns with little patches of gnomes around the flowerbeds.

I briskly walked up the driveway and held the mail in my arms as I crossed them tight across my chest. I glanced up at the early sun that slowly inched its way up and smiled. A wave of peace and happiness came over me as the thought of getting in the car with Ryan and going back to what I now considered my home came to my mind. I was sad to be far from Ryan, but I couldn't wait to be back where I felt so independent and safe. I had only twenty more minutes to finish getting ready before Ryan got here. That would be just enough time to finish my make-up and hair, and ensure Mike was situated with our mother and her pain meds. I decided I wouldn't tell Mike about mother's short affair with Chad's uncle years ago. I probably never would be able to either.

I heard Mike shuffling around the kitchen and pulling a carton of orange juice out of the fridge as I walked in and slid the mail on the counter top by the stove.

"Hey sis, how did you sleep last night?" He spoke softly even though my mother's door just down the short hall from the living room was closed. It had been a tight squeeze to get her wheelchair down the hallway to take her to her room last night, but Mike easily managed.

"Not bad. You think you'll be okay taking care of Mom after I leave?" He took a long swig of Orange juice then he set down the glass.

"Yeah I'll be fine. You've already rationed out all her pain meds and the times she's supposed to take them for the next two weeks. I have a lot of vacation time saved up that I haven't even used yet, so I took a few days off work. I'm sure everything is going to be fine. This is not like when grandma got sick a few years ago and came and stayed with us." I nodded my head knowing he was completely right. Unlike Grandma, Mom would recover and she was not fighting a losing battle with stage three cancer.

"Yeah, you're right."

Mike picked up the glass and took another big gulp before he set it down and wiped his already clean lips with the back of his hand. Then as I turned to walk to my room to finish getting ready, he said,

"You know what, sis, you did so much for Grandma when

she was here. I didn't see it back then but I realize it now. You're a great sister; I want you to know that." I looked at him and raised one brow as I joked with him replying,

"You growing soft on me, little Mikey."

He laughed, stepped forward, wrapped his arms around me, and squeezed me tight. Then letting go, he said,

"No sis, just wanted to tell you that. I'm always here to have your back, little sis." I rolled my eyes and spun around before I raised my hand and exclaimed,

"I am the oldest child!" I heard Mike chuckling as I walked down the hall and into my room to change and finishing getting ready before Ryan arrived in less than fifteen minutes.

I pulled the curling iron away from my hair as the last piece of hair to curl swirled down my neck like a silky ribbon. Just as I unplugged the curling iron, I heard my cell phone go off as Nikki's picture lit up my screen. I thought it was early for her to be calling so I snatched up the phone and answered a little alarmed.

"Nikki? You okay?" There was a long pause before sounding confused, she answered.

"Yeah, why wouldn't I be? How 'bout you? You okay?" I let out the breath I had been holding and said,

"I'm good, it's just a little early for you, isn't it?" I heard her laugh a little as she responded,

"This is true. I wanted to get hold of you before you got on the road." I glanced over at my old clock on the side of my desk noting Ryan was supposed to be here in less than two minutes. I checked my make-up and moved some hair from my forehead before

I said,

"Ryan's gonna be here any minute. We haven't talked yet about what's gonna happen after he takes me home."

"You mean if you'll be in a relationship or keep talking?" Even though she couldn't see me, I shook my head as I replied,

"No, I meant like how long he was staying before he headed back, but we haven't talked about any of that either." Nikki responded with amusement,

"Well, you'll have a few hours to do that. I also called cause you got a call on the voicemail for your interview and they want to move it up to tomorrow morning. They just said to call and confirm that this would work for you before tomorrow. I didn't check the message till late last night. And… you have something at the apartment that was delivered here. I wanted to tell you before you got on the road next to Ryan."

I wasn't worried about moving my interview, but I was pondering in my head what in the world could be delivered to me at the apartment. I hadn't ordered anything or wasn't expecting anything.

"Well, what was delivered?" Nikki replied,

"Okay, so I got a call on…"

Just then, the doorbell rang and I cut Nikki off.

"Hang on a sec, because Ryan's here. Can you tell me after I get the door? It's not something bad, is it?"

"No, it's not, I don't think. I feel like it's gonna get a lot of questions, so try to call me if you guys stop anywhere on the way here, so I can tell you. Then you tell me what you want me to do about it."

I quickly responded as my mother blew her whistle just as I heard the squeak of the front door and Mike opened it.

"Okay, I'll call you if I can when we stop somewhere. Sorry, gotta go, Ryan's here. Love ya."

"Be safe. Love ya too."

I clicked off the phone and dashed out into the hallway just as Ryan was walking past the bedroom door. I could smell the leather of his rider's jacket and fresh shampoo as his semi damp hair made it clear he had just taken a shower right before he left his house.

"Well hello, Amazing Amy, all bright eyed and bushy tailed."

As I stepped out into the hallway, I stopped in front of Ryan, which put us almost toe to toe with each other. Mike was swinging around the corner, apparently to check on our mother, as I glanced up at Ryan and gave him a sly smile. Then I replied,

"What makes you think you can see my tail?" He equally gave me a sly smile and leaned forward, a few inches from my face he said,

"You forget… I already have." Then he gave me a little wink as my stomach dropped along with my smile. I could feel my cheeks blush red with the embarrassing memory as he softened his face before he continued, "I'm sorry, Amy, I was just teasing you. I didn't see your bushy tail. Well, not for that long anyways." He blushed, then continued, "But jokes aside, you look really nice today."

I thought of the way I had heard Nikki respond to a compliment once, so because at that moment I was at a loss for anything better to say, I decided to use it.

"Thanks, I was just cursed this way." Just then, I heard Mike's voice coming from the living room.

"Amy, Mom wants to say bye before you leave." I let out a breath and looked up at Ryan again.

"I'll just be a second. If you want something to drink before we go, I can grab it for you." Before he could answer, Mike was at the end of the hallway by the kitchen waving us to the back part of the house.

"Hey, Ryan, come on in. We got some bottles of water in the fridge if you want one." Ryan nodded then said,

"Yeah that'd be great actually." As I walked through the hallway and into the kitchen, I was surprised when I glanced over to the living room to see my mother already sitting there with her wool throw draped over her lap.

"Amy dear, come say bye to me." She reached out her thin fingers and pulled them towards her motioning for me to come over in a way a small child might do. I walked over and gave her a gentle kiss on her cheek before I stood up and said,

"I'll call when I get there. Mike's got all the information and already scheduled doctor appointments on the fridge. Rest up mother, and you'll be fine." She smiled and nodded her head, then shifted her eyes to look behind me at Ryan who was standing by the kitchen with a bottle of water in his hand.

"Drive safe, young man," Mom directed to Ryan.

"Yes ma'am."

I walked to the kitchen and grabbed Ryan's hand as I led him out of the kitchen, not caring if I held his hand in front of my mother. I was overwhelmed with this undeniable desire to leave, and I wasn't entirely sure why. I had a small bag in my hand while Ryan walked a few feet in front of me holding my full size suitcase. My suitcase still carried the airline baggage tag from Italy, which I couldn't get myself to remove, primarily for sentimental reasons.

He popped his trunk and slid my luggage in before shutting the door and stepping around to the side opening the back door. He reached forward and gently took my smaller bag out of my hand, sliding it in the back seat of the car. I looked at his car, and then a little curious asked,

"So, you have a car, a motorcycle, and a truck. Do you have anything else, maybe a helicopter, or do you feel three is enough?" I laughed a little and he smiled shyly, looking embarrassed.

"I actually have one more car, but I rarely drive it, so it doesn't really count." I let out a laugh as he opened the passenger door for me to get in. As I slid onto the leather seat, I looked up at him and I said,

"Even if you don't drive it, you have it, so it still counts." After he closed my door, I immediately rolled down my window. I glanced up at the front porch with Mike leaning in the doorway, stuck my hand out of the window, and gave him a soft wave as I shouted,

"Bye, little bro!" He took his hands out of his pockets and raised his hand as he shouted back in our direction speaking to both of us.

"Bye sis. Take care of her, okay man?"

"Yes sir." He slid into his seat and put the already running car in drive as we began to pull off down the street.

Just as we turned the corner, my phone lit up with a text:

Nikki:

Don't forget to call me and let me know what you want me to do with these things that came for you before you guys get here.

See ya soon!

"Everything okay?" Ryan asked as he noticed my puzzled face while I stared down at my phone pondering what could possibly be at the apartment for me. For a reason I wasn't sure why, I replied,

"Yeah, great." Then I leaned forward, slid my cell phone in my purse, picked up my purse off my lap, and turned my body setting it on the floor behind Ryan's seat. I looked out the window for a few moments wondering and running all different type of scenarios through my head of what could be at the apartment. Had my dad bought something for me and had it delivered? Maybe Della left something at the apartment. We had given them a spare key when we went to Italy and told them to hold on to it just in case something happened. I heard Ryan's voice cut through my deep thoughts.

"If you don't mind, there's somewhere I'd like to take you. It's about an hour from here and it's on the way. Would you be interested?"

"Yeah that's good. Just don't tell me you have rope and an axe in the trunk." He looked over and gave me sly smile as he replied,

"Oh no, Amy, you were right. It's a lot of work to hide all those, plus my axe isn't sharp, just to be honest." He glanced over, gave me a wink and looked back to the road. I laughed a little as the early morning sun had made its way higher into the sky above the horizon. It was already turning into a perfect day.

TWENTY-EIGHT

With the wind unusually breezy, it felt as if the car ride was more like a boat ride as we sailed down the open road. It was early enough that the road was practically empty with only a few cars. I had flooded Ryan with a series of questions as I tried my best to keep his attention off the fact that I was an underachiever that had accomplished virtually nothing in my life. He had shown a great level of interest in my trip to Italy and I was surprised to learn he had been deployed there several times himself, even though he had not been on the Riviera coast. Conversation with him was superior to anything I had experienced with Chad or Betsy because almost everything that came out of his mouth had substance. Ryan was extremely intelligent and seemed to have a firm grasp on people and the psychology behind what made them tick, which I assumed helped him in owning a bar. I was surprised after my assumption that he loved owning a bar, to learn that in truth he actually didn't like owning a bar, or being around intoxicated people all the time.

The first hour seemed to fly by just as he started to pull his car off an exit.

"Do you need gas already, Ryan?"

"I should probably get some while we're here, but that's not why I'm getting off. There's a place I want to take you, then we'll grab something to eat and I'll get some gas too, if that's cool with you?"

We drove through the seemingly ordinary, yet small town. A few minutes later, sounding confused, he said, "I swear my friend told me it was in this town off this exit. We should have seen it by now. This is odd. I hope I didn't get off the wrong exit." I glanced over at Ryan, more confused than he was, as I asked,

"What are we looking for?" His smile widened, as he said,

"Never mind… found it."

Confused, I looked out of the window and didn't seem to see anything spectacular. It looked like nothing more than a big storage building or warehouse just at the edge of town, just a few blocks across the railroad tracks next to an open field. I looked over at him while the wide smile never left his face before I asked,

"What is it?"

"You'll see. If I know you, even a little… you'll really like this place."

Unsure how to respond, my heart started to beat faster for some unknown reason. My mind kept picturing a massive pastry shop and I began to wonder if he saw me as just 'fat-Amy' like everyone else. We walked into the large open space through the glass double doors as Ryan reached over and grabbed my hand, squeezing it with excitement. I looked around and held my breath before I let out a squeal of delight.

There were rows and rows of wood furniture. Some used, some looked decades, if not centuries old, others looked newer but unfinished. There were all kinds of furniture: bedroom furniture, armoires, desks, tables, and so on.

I released his hand for a second and clasped mine together as I exclaimed,

"I'm so excited! This place is amazing." I looked over at Ryan who was still grinning from ear to ear, as I impulsively jumped toward him, wrapped my arms around him, and gave him a big hug as I said, "Thank you. This is great." He looked down at me and said,

"I thought you would love it, Amy." I immediately thought of my dad and all the projects we could do together with some of these pieces. How much it might cost to transport some of the furniture and if we could get a space to store it. I let all those worrisome thoughts fade as Ryan once again reached over and grabbed my hand as he walked, while I skipped down the first row.

I let my free hand glide along the top of many of the items. Some were smooth as if they had several coats of polyurethane put on them over the years that desperately needed refinished. Others were rough or not finished at all. I was completely surprised when I looked at the price tags of a few pieces to see how little they cost.

I held my breath again as I stopped and stared straight ahead at a beautifully crafted French style antique vanity that sat at the end of the aisle. I let go of Ryan's hand and quickly walked up to it as I put my fingertips on the brass curled handles before I slowly opened the drawer. A few seconds later, Ryan was at my side as I bent down and got a closer look at the detail on the side and front of the vanity.

"You like it?" He asked as I continued running my fingers along the edge of the curves and ridges the swirled around the edges.

"I love it. I've never seen anything like it before, in person I mean. I think I could refinish this and make it look really good. I'd have to use a soda blaster though." I continued to examine all the small details of the piece as I noticed a few small scratches in the white paint job as I continued speaking to Ryan. "See how these small scratches show almost a red colored wood. I think this is actually red cedar, but the paint has covered up the scent of the cedar though. At first I thought it might be cypress, but it's far too heavy to be cypress." I was still looking at it as I realized Ryan was staring at me with an amused look on his face. Embarrassed, I continued, "Well, I could be wrong. Just a guess." My smile faded as I realized that it was impossible to transport it in the car that Ryan had. I also wasn't sure where I'd do the refinishing even if I got it back home. I casually said to Ryan to alleviate any thoughts he might have that I even wanted it.

"Yeah, actually it's just okay. Not really interested though." I shrugged my shoulders and gave him a soft warm smile as I stood back up and grabbed his hand before I continued, "You wanna look around for a few more minutes before we get back on the road?" He looked a little confused for a second, then smiled at me as he replied,

"Sure. Just let me know when you're ready to leave. We can be here as long as you like."

I nodded and smiled as I started to stroll around the vast sea of wood furniture, my heart aching a little inside like a small girl at the pound who wanted to take all the cute puppies home. I turned back to look at Ryan and asked,

"How did your friend know about this place and why did he suggest it?"

"Well, I told my buddy last night about the end table you refinished and how you liked to do that. I think he had an ex-brother-in-law that lived out this way and told him about this place, but to be honest, I'm not completely sure." I turned and continued to walk up and down the rows before my heart couldn't handle any longer not taking home any of the orphaned furniture. I quickly said,

"Did you still want to go get something to eat?" He reached over, and for some reason, he gently slid my hair off my shoulders, letting it cascade down my back, before answering with,

"Yeah, there's supposed to be a diner in this town. Let's go check it out."

The wind had died down to a slight breeze as we climbed back in the car after having lunch at the diner. We each had hamburgers and chocolate shakes and my body was now ready for a quick nap. I kept telling Ryan at lunch how much I loved the place and appreciated him for taking me, but I was careful not to let him see or know I was sad I wasn't taking anything back with me. He appeared to be unaware how it was killing me to leave all those pieces behind. Nevertheless, I told myself it was the thought and all the effort of Ryan that really meant something. I resolved that even though I had not bought anything, the whole experience really showed me what kind of man he was deep to his core. I could feel a warm glow in my heart starting for him. Not an infatuation, but something genuine, something I had never felt before, not even for Chad or Dante, it was an honest affection.

The car started to coast down the highway again and I was watching the scenery passing out of the window when my eyelids became heavy. I heard Ryan's voice telling me softly,

"If you're tired, go ahead and close your eyes. I put your address in the GPS, so it's not a big deal if you need some shuteye."

"No. I'm okay, just looking out the window." The sun now had a soft golden glow around and big cloud shadows were patched along the open field as we drove along. The hum of the engine lulled me until I started watching the white line in the road, and then everything went black as I fell into a deep sleep.

"Amy… Amy, I think we're here."

I slowly opened my eyes as I blinked a few times. The car was parked in front of the building of condos. I yawned and stretched my arms. Then I looked over and said,

"Yep, we're in the right place."

Ryan unlocked the doors as he leapt out and walked around the side of the car, opening my door for me. I reached out, taking his hand as he helped me out of the car. After three agonizing flights up the stairs, we finally stood in front of the door. I tried not to give away how stiff my legs were from being in the car for so long, but I assumed my efforts were in vain, since I took each step with the motion of a ninety-year-old lady.

I twisted my silver key in the lock and pushed open the door, with Ryan standing right behind me. The door slowly swung open revealing Nikki sitting on the couch in her server's uniform as she flipped through a magazine. She glanced up, looking surprised as we both stepped in. Then she said with an uncomfortable laugh in her tone,

"Oh, you didn't text me back." Ryan raised his hand and gave Nikki a little one motion wave as she gave him a smile, then he asked,

"How are you?"

"Hi, Ryan, really good."

My shoulders dropped, feeling bad that I had forgotten to text her back. I looked at her oddly and then put my hand to my forehead as I replied,

"I'm sorry, Nikki. Ryan took me to this amazing place and I passed out on the rest of the way back. I still have to call that office for my interview tomorrow before they close." I opened my mouth to ask if everything was okay when I caught the scent of flowers as a slight draft carried it across my nose. I looked over to see multiple bouquets in a variety of colors and vases. None was smaller than a tiny baby was and I didn't doubt they cost a fortune. I looked over at Nikki trying to figure out who sent her the flowers. Wide-eyed, I exclaimed, "Who sent you all those flowers?"

Nikki cleared her throat just as Ryan, who was standing next to one of the vases, half spun the vase to me with a card positioned right on top, nestled on a little stick. Then he said, plainly answering my question,

"I think these are for you, Amy." It was obvious my name was on the front of the card and my heart dropped with the calm, yet slightly curiously jealous look on Ryan's face. Nikki spoke up quickly.

"Yeah, those came yesterday and I didn't get them inside until late after work, and I wasn't sure if I should put them in your room or not. I didn't know if you were allergic… That's when I checked the voicemail and heard about your interview with Vanessa Winters. She wants to do it tomorrow." My mind raced with questions of who sent those flowers. Was it Chad? I would imagine not, since Chad was a tightwad. However, I knew better than to open that card in front of Ryan. I already felt awkward and uncomfortable with him standing next to them. I glanced over at Nikki and silently motioned with my eyes that I needed to have a private conversation with her in another room. She quickly caught on and spoke up,

"By the way, I had an issue with that suit you wanted to wear to your interview. I have to show you, I need you to look at it please, and I wrote the number down to the office and left it in your room. Ryan, we'll only be a moment. Can I get you something to drink?"

Ryan shook his head politely, as he walked closer to the couch, before he said,

"No, I'm good. Can I sit here?" Nikki nodded and jumped up as she walked over to me and took my arm, pulling me to the back part of the condo she said to Ryan.

"Go right ahead, we'll be right back." Moments later, we were in the back part of the bedroom as she let out a breath before she said,

"You were supposed to text me back. I didn't know if he was coming inside or if I should hide them, or what I should do with them. I'm sorry to give you the message late about the interview, but I didn't hear the voice mail 'til this morning." I put my palm on my forehead and replied,

"It's my fault. I forgot to text you back and then I fell asleep… so sorry. Do you know who they're from? I'm afraid to look. Did you see Ryan's face?" Nikki put her hands on her curvy hips as she clinched her thin waist before she said,

"Well, I had gotten a call on the voice mail here from Lucca the first day I got back from your mom's saying he ran into Dante. I called him back and Lucca said when he ran into Dante that Dante asked for your address because he said you forgot something important and he needed to return it to you. Then I guess he told Lucca he was planning on coming to visit America in a few months. I think he's trying to butter you up and work his way back into your good graces. I'm gonna be honest, I think Dante wants an easy way to get a green card. In fact, Lucca even suggested that. Yeah, I saw Ryan's face. This could be good or bad for you. He could get jealous and try to get more serious, OR, he could think you lied about being single and disappear. I don't know."

My stomach felt sick thinking of the second possibility. I didn't want Dante or even have a desire to see him ever again after he played with me, and I wanted him even less so thinking that this might all just be a ploy to get a green card. It made me ill to think he might come to visit America in a few months. My heart also dropped with the thought that Ryan might think I was lying to him about being single and he might never talk to me again. I didn't reply for a long time before I asked Nikki in desperation,

"What should I do?" She took her hands off her hips, reached forward, and put them on my shoulders as she advised,

"Just be straight forward and tell him the truth, minus the kissing on the boat of course." I nodded and said,

"Of course." Then it was my turn to put my hands on my hips as I narrowed my eyebrows and quizzed her. "Wait a minute, are you talking with Lucca again? How long has this been going on?" She calmly shook her head and replied,

"Nope. He basically called just to tell me about running into Dante. I think just giving us a head's up. I can't talk to him romantically ever again. He devastated my heart. I won't go through that again… ever." I put my hand on her shoulder as a sad look came across her face from the memory of Lucca. I gave her a little shake and said as if our roles had switched,

"I don't think any of these Italian men are what we thought they were. We're both better off without them." She nodded her head in agreement, as she smiled and replied,

"Couldn't agree more. Hey, you never told me your interview was with Vanessa Winters. I kinda know her. Well, I mean she comes and eats at the restaurant sometimes. She's one of my regulars actually." My face lit up and I dropped my hand as I asked Nikki,

"Really? What is she like? Do you think I'll get the job?" Nikki tilted her head a little to the side as if she was throwing around different ideas and scenarios before she said,

"Well, she tips really great, like really, really well. She comes in about twice, maybe three times a month by herself to eat lunch, and every once in a while, she meets another woman there that I'm pretty sure is her best friend. But Vanessa Winters is hot, like unbelievably hot. She's very professional though. She kinda comes off as a shark, but still nice, if that makes sense. I tried to search her name on the internet after I noticed it on her credit card. She seems low key about herself." I stared at Nikki blinking for a few seconds before I said,

"Okay, but do you think I will get the job?" Nikki shrugged her shoulders before she replied,

"I honestly don't know, but the suit you want to borrow will get you some job somewhere, that's for sure. I didn't make that up about the number to the office being in your room. I put it on your bed. The office is still open I'm sure." I thought about it and then I replied,

"Okay, I'll call real quickly and confirm that I'm okay to do an interview tomorrow, get it out of the way I think." I let out a sigh and shrugged my shoulders as I decided to push away the thoughts of my upcoming interview, since there was nothing I could really do about it. I decided the flowers and Ryan misunderstanding was more pressing. We walked back out into the living room. Ryan sat on the couch, flipping through the same magazine Nikki had been looking at earlier. I cleared my throat and started to ask Ryan if he wanted to go for a walk just as the phone on the counter rang. Nikki leaned over and grabbed the phone.

"Hi Mr. Stanton, no, Amy just walked in the door. I'd love to but I have to leave for work in an hour. I close the restaurant tonight. Sure, I'm thinking she'd love to. Let me put her on for you. One second." She quickly placed the phone in my hand and I put the phone to my ear as I heard my dad's warm voice on the other end.

"Amy, my pumpkin! I'm glad you're home safe. Della and I want you to come over for dinner tonight and bring that young man that your brother told me drove you back. I won't take no for an answer." I nervously whispered to Ryan as I put my hand over the receiver,

"My dad and his girlfriend want both of us to come over for dinner tonight. Do you need to head back soon or is that okay with you?" Ryan closed the magazine and tucked his hair behind his ear, then said casually,

"Sure, dinner sounds good."

I quickly told my dad we'd be there in an hour then hung up the phone. I picked the receiver back up as I said to Ryan,

"I need to confirm my interview for tomorrow, just take me a second."

He nodded his head and walked over to look out of the window that was next to the largest vase of flowers as I confirmed my interview, watching him at the same time with an uneasy feeling in my stomach. After I spoke with the receptionist of human resources who confirmed my time on Ms. Winters schedule, I hung the receiver back up. Still staring at Ryan's back, I meekly asked him,

"Do you want to go for a walk or freshen up or anything right now?" He looked down at the table next to him and politely replied,

"Yeah, we can go for a walk. That's a good idea, I think we should talk." I swallowed hard and out of Ryan's view, I shot Nikki a look of fear, as she calmly mouthed, "Don't worry," which did little to alleviate the fear in the pit of my stomach. I knew I wasn't prepared for the possibility of losing Ryan this soon. Every minute I spent with him made me want even more of him in my life. I was fearful some stupid flowers might put a rain cloud over that.

"I'm going to go change my clothes to something more comfortable, then we can walk around the pond if you like." He turned around, facing me as I walked to the bedroom, full of worry that he wouldn't believe me and be out of my life forever.

TWENTY-NINE

"So, you're not seeing anyone right now?" Ryan had asked me more than once as we had circled the pond. I had been truthful with him about Dante, having left out any kissing that happened, obviously. As we talked, it became apparent that Ryan seemed worried I was secretly with someone but afraid to tell him. He had been quiet for a long period of time, for blocks of time, as I tried not to ramble out of desperation for him to believe me, which Nikki advised I be careful not to do. I heeded her advice and by the third turn around the pond, he reached over and wrapped his hand around mine, as he had done several times before. Then he simply looked at me while we stood next to the pond and said,

"If you say you're unattached, then you're unattached. I trust you, Amy." I nodded and smiled, but even though he said exactly what I had hoped, I couldn't seem to get rid of the sick feeling in my stomach.

Hours later, we drove down the road towards my dad's apartment while silence filled the car. I realized I must have appeared guilty or dishonest with my behavior towards him. I pushed a wide smile on my face, reached over, and touched his hand as I said,

"Thank you for coming to eat at my dad's place. Della is a great cook. Della is Nikki's mom, so that practically makes us sisters."

"How do you get along with you dad, Amy?" I answered in all sincerity,

"I love my dad. He is a rock for me, and he's nothing like my mother. I guess you could say I'm a daddy's girl." Ryan squeezed my hand tightly and smiled as he looked over at me saying,

"That's great." I pointed to the road up ahead and instructed him to turn right as we pulled into the apartment complex of townhome styled apartments. Ryan pulled his car into a spot and unlocked his door, leaping out and walking around to help me out of the car. I instinctively took his hand as usual and smiled as he looked down at me, his hair falling from behind the comfort of his ears. He leaned down towards my face and my heart fluttered, harder this time than ever before. Then he casually asked,

"If this Italian cat comes to visit here, are you planning on seeing him at all? I'm just curious." I swallowed hard and honestly replied,

"Absolutely not. I'm not interested in him at all."

Ryan nodded his head and glanced to the side, appearing to

think over my answer. After he appeared satisfied with my reply, he leaned even closer to my face and said,

"Okay, good to know. I'd hate to throw down with an Italian guy for my lady's hand. They throw a pretty mean punch, you know." I let out a sigh of relief and smiled as I slowly rose to the tips of my toes, putting me closer to his.

"Amy! Hello, my darling… Your dad said you'd be here any minute."

I glanced up as Della stood on the balcony with a little green watering can in one hand while she waved at us with the other. The hanging plants that lined the balcony drooped over, fighting for their last week or two of life as the autumn season lurked around the corner. She continued to wave as I lifted my hand and waved back. Then she exclaimed,

"Bring that young man up here so your dad can take a look at him. We've heard all about him." Even though she was up on the second level, I could faintly see the wink she gave me as she turned around and walked back into the apartment with her sandy blonde hair swooshing just below her ear as she closed the sliding door behind her. I instantly got nervous, as I was worried that it might be too much pressure for Ryan, even though he had handled my mom like a champ. I knew we had just cleared the air about Dante but that issue was still fresh. I shrugged my shoulders and glanced up at him as I said,

"Well, if you can tolerate my mom, you should love my dad." He tucked the hair behind his ears yet again and gave me a little shy smile as he replied.

"No worries, Amy, if you love your dad, I'm sure I will too."

The food was nothing less than excellent. Della had prepared a delicious five cheese manicotti with fresh basil mixed in the cheese filling and small diced red and yellow peppers. It was a very close second to the authentic Italian food I had experienced. I had no complaints for Della. After I giggled a few times when I heard the word 'five' in five cheese, I finally gave in and retold the story about Nikki's face swelling up. Nikki had even told the story herself last week, as she was finally able to laugh about it.

After we finished laughing about the swelling of Nikki's face and my flying nosedive into the floor, my dad casually asked me,

"I'm not trying to pry, Amy, because you're a grown woman, but has Chad paid you back the money that you had saved to buy a house?" I cleared my throat as I could see out of the corner of my eye Ryan tilt his head out of curiosity.

"Not yet, Dad, but he will, I think."

My dad nodded, not looking fully satisfied with my answer, but he let it go. Della stood up and announced she needed to get something from the kitchen.

As our plates lay empty in front of us, my dad sat for several long seconds just staring at Ryan. Analyzing him in his mind, turning over in his thoughts which questions he should bombard him with. I had never actually seen my dad like this towards a love interest, not even Chad, but to be fair, I hadn't had that many prospects in my life for him to analyze at all. Then my dad leaned forward and said with a wide smile on his face,

"I heard from my son, Mike, that you helped quite a bit when Amy's mother fell… Is that true?" Ryan shifted in his seat and seemed unusually nervous as he replied,

"I just did what I could, Sir." My dad nodded and then continued,

"And you were willing to drive Amy all the way back home, a drive that's several hours long?" Ryan shifted a little more in his seat and once again politely replied,

"Yes Sir." Then my dad tilted his head and asked,

"Do you have a job?" Ryan sat up straight in his chair as I heard Della bustling around in the kitchen, presumably putting the dessert together. I heard Ryan say,

"Yes Sir, I work at a bar." I quickly blurted out in addition to his reply,

"He actually owns a bar, Dad." My dad nodded his head then asked,

"How you like that?" Then Ryan replied,

"It makes money, Sir."

I let out a breath as Della walked over to the table, a small pan of peach cobbler in one hand that she held with an oven mitt, and a few plates in the other. She set it down as she spoke,

"Oh, I forgot the ice cream, I'll be right back." She started to turn to the kitchen just as my dad asked Ryan,

"Does it make enough to provide for a wife, or a family?" Ryan cleared his throat just as Della snapped around and lightly smacked my dad on the arm.

"For heaven's sake, Gene! Leave the poor boy alone. He's a very polite young man. You're gonna scare him off, now cut it out."

My dad glanced up at Della and they smiled at each other as if they were sharing a special joke with each other. Then he said to her,

"You're right, my love." I smiled and found it interesting that he called her that because he never called my mother a pet name. Then he turned to Ryan and said,

"You seem like a swell guy, Ryan, just make sure your intentions with my daughter are honorable. Can't have her fall for another guy like that Chad fellow." My dad gave him a serious look that let him know he meant business.

"Absolutely Sir. I agree, Sir." My dad cleared his throat and then leaned forward and glared at Ryan before he very seriously asked in a deep tone,

"I have one question for you, Ryan." Ryan stared back at him, nervous, and asked,

"Yes, Sir?" My dad scrunched his eyebrows together and asked,

"Do you like peach cobbler?" Ryan let out a slow sigh through his nose, gave a half sly smile and said,

"Yes Sir."

"Okay, you're cleared, Ryan. Welcome to the family." Then he chuckled a little bit and scooped some cobbler on to a plate that he handed across the table to Ryan.

"I'm so very sorry. I've never seen my dad be like that to anyone. I didn't know it was going to be an interrogation. I'm sorry about that." Ryan took his hand off the wheel and placed it over mine as he said,

"It's okay. Your dad just loves you and he is looking out for you. If I had a beautiful daughter, I would do the same exact thing. It's not a problem. I had a really good time and your dad's cool." I glanced over and stared at him, smiling as I noticed he used the word 'beautiful' again. Then I asked,

"Really? You weren't nervous or uncomfortable? I know I was."

"A little bit at first, but I could see he was just looking out for you. Amy, what was your dad talking about that Chad owes you money? I know it's not really my business so you don't have to answer."

"It's okay. You can ask. I had just been saving for a long time to move out and get a house, so when Chad and I were gonna get married, we combined the money I had saved with a little bit he had saved for a nice down payment. I also saved some back for that trip to Italy." Ryan appeared annoyed as he said,

"He needs to pay you back. I didn't realize your ex was Chad Wheeler, as in the family that owns the logistics trucking company. He should never have taken anything at all from you for a house. His family has plenty of money. That makes me mad, and he cheated on you… he makes me mad all around." I wasn't sure what to say for a minute as Ryan looked really angry at Chad.

"Yeah, Ryan, that's true. His parents have a lot of money but his dad doesn't spoil him with money like you would think. Not that it makes it okay. I'm sure his dad is gonna make sure Chad pays me back." I glanced over and could see Ryan's jaw clinching tight, which I had never seen before.

In a very serious tone, while his eyes focused straight on the road he said,

"He will pay you back. I'm sure of it, and soon." Unsure of where my courage came from, I asked,

"Ryan, where is this going with us? I mean, what do you see happening down the road with whatever this is?" He looked over at me, a little confused, and then contemplated for a second before he responded.

"I like you a whole lot, Amy… a *whole* lot. I can see you being my girl, but I don't want to rush you on anything because I know you've been through a lot lately. I want to become your best friend first and be there for you. And yes, I want us to become serious, eventually. If that's how things progress. I will say I am very attracted to you, but I'm not about just that with you. I respect you."

I was half satisfied and half uneasy about his reply. It was a rollercoaster of build-ups and let downs. I wasn't sure what I was hoping or even expecting him to say. I knew as soon as I asked the question that it was a ridiculous question, especially to ask a guy I met roughly a week ago. It did seem like everything was moving fast, and there was still the issue of the distance between us.

We pulled around into a parking spot in front of my condo as the sun made its way closer to the ground. Dusk had passed us by twenty minutes and soon it would be dark. I realized I had not asked Ryan about when he was heading back and now I faced the issue of my interview late tomorrow morning.

Ryan turned off the car and walked around my side to open the door. I reached out my hand as he gently helped me out of the car. As we began to walk toward the stairs, I asked,

"I didn't ask when you needed to head back. Would you like to stay the night?" With a playful tone in his voice, he said,

"Well, I'm not sure if that would be appropriate since I'm pretty sure your dad has your place bugged or under surveillance." I slapped his arm as we reached the door and I put the silver key in the door unlocking it.

"Ohhhh… You're so funny, Ryan." I laughed a little.

With a smile still on his face, he reached forward and gently brushed my hair back off my shoulders and smoothed it down my back with his fingertips, almost doing it unconsciously. Then he said,

"Yeah, I can sleep on the couch, and head out tomorrow if that's not a problem for you?"

"Not a problem at all. You did me a big favor driving me back home. So you can stay or leave whenever you want."

"That's good, because I was so afraid you were gonna kidnap me and take advantage of me. I'm glad I'm at liberty to leave at my own free will. Thank you for that." I laughed a little and rolled my eyes before I sarcastically replied,

"Not a problem. It's the least I can do." He reached forward and smoothed my hair once again as I opened the front door.

The smell of flowers seemed to loom over the whole atmosphere as I glanced over at the beautiful bouquet, my stomach dropping as I did so. Then I got an idea as I spun around, and with a very serious and pleading look in my eyes, I asked him,

"Could you please help me with one more huge thing? I really need your help big time." Ryan looked at me, slightly curious before he asked, "Sure. What is it?"

I reached forward and took his hand as I asked more serious than I needed to,

"Can you please help me carry some of these flowers downstairs and to the trash dumpsters around the corner? They are probably too heavy for me."

"Absolutely."

THIRTY

Hazy, soft yellow morning sun billowed from the bottom of my bedroom curtain as it settled on the beige carpet beneath it. I coughed and rolled over, hugging my pillow with the smile I could feel on my face as I thought about Ryan. Ryan? I sat up instinctively as I remembered he was still sleeping on the living room couch. I quickly glanced at the clock and let out a sigh of relief as the clock said only a few minutes past eight a.m. I wasn't sure why I had woken up at that time, but I was sure Nikki was still fast asleep, as she typically didn't wake until ten or eleven in the morning after she closed the restaurant the night before.

I froze after I heard the latch on the front door quietly close. I didn't know if I should be worried about an intruder or if Ryan had sneaked out to leave without saying good-bye. I threw my feet over the edge of the bed and slid off putting my toes on the soft carpet as I slowly walked out into the hallway heading to the kitchen area.

"Good morning, Amy. How'd you sleep?" Ryan was walking from the front door towards my kitchen with a brown bag in one hand and a carrier with three drinks in the other. I looked at him curiously, as he was wearing sweat pants and a t-shirt. The shirt was wet around the collarbone and neck area from what I assumed was sweat. I asked,

"Did you go for a run this morning? Where did the clothes come from?" He cleared his throat as he slid the bag and drinks on the kitchen counter and glanced over at me, fully awake and energetic.

"I sure did. I didn't want to wake you ladies, so I went out to my car and got my duffle bag I keep in my trunk. I always have two changes of workout clothes and one change of daily clothes in my bag. Then I went for run at dawn. It always helps me clear my mind. Do you have a plate?" I walked around to the other side of him as I reached up and pulled down a large platter plate from the cabinet and set it next to the bag on the counter. I stared at him as he started to pull bagels and muffins out of the bag and put them on the platter.

Then I remembered I just got of bed and hadn't even looked in the mirror yet. I was sure my hair was a crazy mess and my breath could do battle with the fiercest dragon.

"Be right back." I yelled as I turned the corner and walked down the hall to the bathroom. I looked in the mirror and was horrified to discover I was right. I quickly combed through my hair and even more quickly scrubbed my teeth as I practically used half a bottle of mouthwash to take off the remaining stench. I glanced around and found Nikki's mascara she had in a decorative mug that she always kept stick and tubed cosmetics. I put on two fast layers of mascara before I headed back to the kitchen. I walked up next to Ryan.

"Coffee black for me and a mocha raspberry latte for you," he said as he handed me one of the cups. I was surprised as I asked him,

"How did you know this is one of my favorite drinks?"

"Remember? You told me at the restaurant before we went to the movie how you always used to get a latte every morning before work. I'm a bartender, so I remember drinks people like really well." He chuckled a little and took a drink of his coffee. Then setting down his Styrofoam cup on the counter he said with energy, "This is a pretty nice area. All the shops and stuff seemed really cool. I was surprised to see some store fronts for sale."

"Yeah, I really like this area. Nikki makes good money at the restaurant, so I guess some people in this area have money. According to her, the real estate market is big right now." He thought for a moment and then asked seriously,

"Do you think you'll ever move back home?"

My heart immediately took a dive and my stomach flipped as I felt the sudden urge to vomit. I felt this was the question I had been dreading for the last week and we were now in the moment where we would go our separate ways. I stayed quiet for a few moments as I thought about how to reply. I didn't want to be unfair, lead him on, and make him think it was a possibility even though it wasn't. However, I also didn't want to tell him I never would move back, and then we decide the distance was too far and we should just end things before they even really start. My heart was racing so fast as I sadly answered him.

"No. I can't see myself going back. I like being away from there and living here in this area."

He leaned against the counter and looked down at the floor as he rubbed the back of his neck. I felt my eyes slowly start to get damp with tears as I felt the end coming near. Then he smiled and said,

"I can't blame you. This is a nice area. I think I'd like to come see you here if that's okay." I didn't speak but just nodded my head in reply. He took a long sip of his coffee as he slowly pushed the platter towards me and smiled. Then he said, "Help yourself to one of these bagels, or muffins. I'm told the cranberry orange one is 'to die for' as the young girl said." He raised his eyebrows trying to entice me. I leaned over and opened the fridge, bringing out a container of cream cheese.

"I'll take the brown sugar cinnamon one." He winked and said,

"Okay, that's in my memory bank now. Do you mind if I take a quick shower before I head out?" I glanced at the clock and answered him,

"Sure. There are plenty of towels in there. If you need anything let me know, okay?"

He set down his cup and reached around the edge of the counter towards the floor to grab his duffle bag. Then he disappeared down the hall and into the bathroom. Moments later, I heard the shower running as I enjoyed the last few bites of my bagel. I knew I had only a few hours before I had to leave for my interview so I slowly made my way to my room to put on the suit that I had hung on the back of my door for the interview.

A few long tummy-sucking minutes later, I finally squeezed into the skirt as I heard the shower come to a halt. I left the expensive looking pencil skirt unzipped in the back as I took a few deep breaths after all the effort I had put in to getting dressed. To be fair, Nikki had warned me that she hadn't worn this particular suit for a few years and it might be smaller than either of us was used to. It was so gorgeous with its deep charcoal color and rich fabric with double stitching, I decided it was worth the try. She had advised me to get dressed several hours before I left the house to make sure I wanted to wear it and I was glad I did.

"Unbelievable." I glanced over as Ryan stood in the doorway with wet hair and fully dressed. I looked confused for a moment as he said, "Sorry the door was cracked open, I didn't realize you were changing in here. You look beautiful in that suit. I mean amazing." His gaze started at my toes and slowly worked their way up to my eyes. I looked at him and saw something in his eyes that almost looked like adoration. I blushed and said,

"Thanks." He cleared his throat and walked out to the kitchen as I walked out behind him asking. "Are you taking off now?"

He nodded and turned around, reaching out, he moved my hair off my shoulder as he had done several times in the last two days. Then he took a step forward and looked down at me and replied,

"Yeah, I need to get on the road and you have an interview to ace." His hand was still stroking my hair as my knees started to feel weak and my heart began to race. I said quietly,

"Please drive safe and I can't begin to tell you how much I appreciate everything you've done for me."

"Of course, Amy. You're amazing." I blushed a little, and turned my head just as I heard a loud yawn.

"Hey, lady, you ready for your interview? Wow, that suit on you is killer. I mean like really hot. You need to wear those black pumps with it." Ryan took his hands off my hair as he took a few steps back and smiled at Nikki, who hadn't even fully realized Ryan was near my face or in the kitchen for that matter. Ryan politely said to Nikki,

"Thank you for letting me stay at your place last night. I have to take off. You ladies have a wonderful day."

Nikki finally took her gaze off the suit and smiled wide at Ryan.

"Yeah, of course. Drive safe, Ryan, and don't forget to call Amy when you get home tonight." She gave me a wink.

"Yes, ma'am." Ryan reached out and touched my hair one more time. He scooped up his duffle back and walked to the front door. I followed quickly behind him, reached forward and opened it, stepped out into the hallway, and watched him walk down the hall. I waved as he waved back with a large warm expression on his face and a soft spark in his eyes. I stepped back in the condo and sadly closed the door, instinctively flipping the lock. I heard Nikki's voice behind me as she softly asked,

"Are you okay?" I leaned my back against the front door. With a long sigh, I said,

"Yeah. I'm just really, really sad to see him leave."

Nikki slowly walked over to the couch dressed in her black fuzzy pajama pants that had red lipsticks patterned all over them. She plopped down on the couch pulling her knees up and crossing her legs Indian style as she yawned one more time before saying,

"You know what I think it is?" I shrugged my shoulders and asked,

"What?" Very factually, she answered,

"I think you have feelings for him. Like real feelings… And I think he seems like a legit guy. A genuine guy. I can tell he cares about you, a lot." I shrugged my shoulders again and said,

"What if you're wrong? Even if you're right, he's hours away. Long distance never works." Nikki softly said,

"I don't think I'm wrong, and he's only a few hours away, not across an ocean. You can't say long distance never works. Just take things slow with him. But I think he's the real deal." She gave me a knowing smile as she stood up and yawned again before she said, "I'm headed back to bed for another hour or two. Knock them dead at your interview and I'll see you when you get home tonight." Then she shuffled her feet as she walked back to the hallway. She slowly turned around as she said, "Amy, you're the best sister any girl could ask for. I'm really glad we're friends."

"Same." I heard her close her bedroom door as I made my

way to the closet to hunt for those black kitten heels I knew would complete this whole outfit.

THIRTY-ONE

"Good afternoon, I'm here for an eleven thirty appointment with Ms. Winters." The petite girl in her mid-twenties peered up at me from behind a large half circle reception desk while she put a pleasant but professional expression on her face. Her dark hair was cut in a short pixie cut, and black rimmed glasses housed her deep brown eyes.

"Yes… you must be Ms. Stanton, correct?" I nodded and held the stylish black leather briefcase that I had borrowed from Nikki close to me as I said,

"Yes, that is correct."

My heart was racing and my stomach fluttering as I was overtaken with nervousness. The building had wall to wall windows and floods of natural light that poured in, reflecting off of the highly polished marble floors and glass around the lobby. With her pleasant smile never faltering, the petite girl stood and walked around the desk with a little brisk walk, her heels clinking on the floor. Her skin was a freshly tanned olive hue and her cream blouse was far too tight, leaving a gap in the middle giving the illusion she had something to create a gap with.

"Please have a seat in the waiting area and I will let Ms. Winters know you are here. She's been expecting you." I glanced at my watch, glad I was fifteen minutes early since she was expecting me. I smiled and nodded at the girl as I unsuccessfully attempted to walk over to the waiting area without my shoes clinking on the floor as loudly as they did.

Several minutes later, I heard the bell sound from the elevator as the dark haired young woman briskly walked back to her desk. I glanced back over to the elevator as nothing short of a super model in an expensive noir skirt suit walked out behind her. The Icelandic blonde glanced over, and with a wide smile slowly spreading across her deep red lips, she began to walk in my direction. Her figure was perfect, not exhibiting a single flaw. Her legs were long and lean and the curve in her waist was enough to show off a shape that well paid models would die for. Her skin was a pale ivory and her hair was a straight platinum blonde. Her eyes were a deep, piercing dark blue and my legs began to shake as I stood while she reached out her hand, her red lips parting to show a flawless set of white teeth, of course.

"Hi, Ms. Stanton, I'm Vanessa Winters." She reached out to shake my hand and I smiled as professionally as I could as I took her hand in mine and shook it.

"Thank you so much for this opportunity, Ms. Winters." She released my hand and continued smiling as she said,

"Please, call me Vanessa. Follow me to my office if you don't mind." My stomach continued to do flips as I realized I was by far the fattest person within eyesight, and probably the whole building for that matter. As both of our shoes clinked against the floor, she glanced back and gave me a soft smile, sounding sincere she commented, "That is a beautiful suit, Ms. Stanton." I relaxed a little as I replied,

"Thank you."

After she politely asked me to take a seat, I slowly sat on the fragile looking chair in front of her desk, afraid I might break it. As she walked around to the other side of the glass desk, she had a sway in her hips as she moved, that was sensual but not in a provocative way. Then she smoothly slid down into her chair. Her office, which also housed an entire wall of windows, was decorated in modern art deco and was almost completely white, with the exception of a few silver or chrome pieces and glass everywhere just like the lobby. I casually glanced around and only noticed one single picture of a young woman in a silver picture frame, who I guessed to be in her early twenties. I wanted to ask who she was because I noticed a slight resemblance but not quite enough to know if it was family. She crossed her legs and sat up straight in her chair, reaching over and pulling my resume off of the stack of papers in a short pile on her desk.

"Tell me a little about yourself. Are you married, have kids?"

I swallowed hard as I felt that I was in another situation unsure how much of my cancelled wedding I should share with someone, especially a possible employer. I coughed a little and replied,

"No. Not married or have kids." She glanced down at my resume in front of her and asked,

"I see that you've recently moved to this area. Was there a reason for the move?" I took another breath and then as casually as I could muster I said,

"I felt a change was needed. To be honest, I called off my wedding with my fiancée. I really needed a change in my life." Her facial expression flickered with a look of understanding as she continued to glance over my resume.

"Is it accurate to assume that's what made you quit your former employer?"

"Yes ma'am." She leaned back in her chair and the atmosphere morphed to casual, friendly.

"Do you have any family in this area?"

"Yes, my dad has lived here for several years, but I live with a roommate. You might know her actually." I gave a sincere smile, glad I was given the perfect opportunity to drop Nikki's name as she told me I could maybe to help get the job. Vanessa had a look of curiosity as she asked,

"I do? Who is she?" I made another assumption from the look on her face that she must not have very many female friends, or possibly friends in general.

"Her name is Nikki and she works at the restaurant down the

street from here. She's a blonde server." Vanessa smiled wide and said,

"Oh yeah. Nikki… I really like her, she's fantastic… That's your roommate?" I nodded, and unsure why, I said,

"Yeah, to be honest this is actually her suit." She smiled and then asked,

"Tell me what your favorite thing to do is? Do you have a hobby of some kind?" My initial thought was to make a joke that I obviously liked to eat as a hobby. Instead, I replied,

"Well, I use to refinish old furniture, but I don't do that very often." She slightly tilted her head to one side and curiously, she asked,

"Why is that?" I shrugged my shoulders and just said,

"Time, resources, I guess. It used to be something I did with my dad when I was a kid and then a teenager, but I hardly do it now. Just an occasional hobby." She nodded and seemed curious about my answer but changed subjects as she asked.

"I noticed you worked for the same real estate office for years, tell me about that." I was confused by her level of interest because I was not interviewing for a position in the real estate industry.

"I learned a lot. Answered a lot of calls. I worked closely with several title companies and always made sure that the agents turned in the correct forms to upload listings." I wasn't sure what else to say because my old job wasn't that complicated or difficult. She thought for a few minutes and then asked,

"Have you ever worked for a financial company?" My heart

dropped, as I knew this question was the one that was going to keep me from the job. I politely answered,

"No, I have not."

"Amy, we handle a lot of money here in this building. We have several big name clients on our roster. One of my personal favorites is Abigail Archer, the cosmetics CEO." She took a breath and then continued, "It's true I do need an assistant for a position here. However, and to be very honest with you, I asked you in for an interview because your resume had real estate experience and others did not." I still looked confused as she continued, "I am unable to offer you a position with this corporation due to the fact that you don't meet the minimal requirements." My heart sank and I put on the best smile I could force on my lips as I said,

"I really appreciate you taking the time to meet with me."

She repositioned her legs as she crossed them in the other direction that I noticed through the glass top of her desk, and then she said,

"I can't offer you a position here with this company because human resources and the main CEO really wants someone with no less than a bachelor's degree for this position. However, I personally own several properties. Real estate just happens to be my fun hobby. I am at a point where I need a personal assistant for that. I would like to offer you a job as my personal assistant for my real estate ventures."

I wasn't sure what to say or what that would even look like. Did that mean I took her clothes to the dry cleaners or her tiny dog (that I automatically assumed she had) to be washed? She noticed the curious look on my face as she continued,

"I would need assistance with my forms, keeping in contact with the realtors and making sure closings and such are taken care of with the title companies. It would be part time, but I would compensate you generously." I sat there for a long moment unsure what to say because I was not prepared to be offered any job on the spot. Vanessa stood and walked around the desk and leaned back against it while resting her hands on both sides of her hips, her body language resembling the high-level executive she was. Then she said, "You don't need to give me an answer now. Go home and think about it. Here's my personal cell phone number when you decide, or if you want to ask me questions about the position." She shifted her body and turned sideways as she slid a pen off her desk and one of her business cards that was sitting in a cardholder only a few inches from her right hip. She quickly wrote her personal number on the back of the card and handed it to me with a bright smile on her face. Then she said, "I'm a very good judge of character, Amy, and I like you. I hope the position is something you will seriously consider."

"Yes ma'am. I'll call you with an answer in two days or less, if that's okay?"

She used her hands to push herself forward from the desk. As she stood, she stuck out her hand. I quickly stood to my feet and reached forward to shake her hand as she replied,

"Sounds good. Thank you so much for coming. I'll walk you to the elevator." We shook hands and then I snatched up my briefcase, which I realized I never used but still made the outfit look good, and we walked to the office door.

"Thank you so much, Vanessa, for considering me for this opportunity."

She glanced back at me, with a pleasant smile on her face as we walked toward the elevators. I was trying hard to read her and think if she would be a good boss to work for but I was having difficulty. I knew I would need Nikki's advice because she had more experience with Vanessa Winters than I did. It would tell me a lot knowing how she treated Nikki as her server and whether or not I wanted to work for her.

The elevator door dinged as it opened and I stepped out into the main lobby and back on the marble flooring as my shoes clinked and I walked towards the front door. The receptionist with the short pixie haircut was setting down the phone receiver as she glanced up and smiled before she said,

"Have a nice day."

"Thank you."

I opened the glass doors and almost did a happy dance as a wave of excitement hit me, but I managed to contain myself. I knew if I had ever married Chad this moment in my life would have never existed, or any of my current experiences.

THIRTY-TWO

"Take it! Totally take it." Nikki exclaimed as she sat up on the couch, swinging her legs to the floor. Her eyes were big and she reached up to comb through her messy hair to put it in a loose ponytail. I could tell by her demeanor when I walked in the door that she hadn't been wake for that long, she still had on the same lipstick pajama pants from when I left for the interview.

"You really think so?" She dropped her hands to her lap and said,

"Well, duh, yeah. I don't know what it's like to work for her, but she's very pleasant to have as a customer and usually if someone is cool to wait on, then they would be cool to work for. She always tips really well. Once she got a phone call when she sat down, then she told me she was super tight on time and it was important she get out as soon as possible. So I made sure the kitchen rushed her food.

Well, she tipped me a hundred dollars! So if home girl says you gonna be well compensated, then you probably can take that to the bank, literally." I took off my heels, walked across the room and sat down on the couch next to Nikki. My feet were tired and I hadn't realized it until I sat down, I was busy telling Nikki the whole story of my interview. I turned over everything Nikki said in my head and I knew she was probably right.

"I think I will take it, but even if she compensates me well, what if I'm still not making enough money?"

"Amy, rent for me here is so cheap, I told you that already. I wouldn't stress about it. Things will work itself out. Have you called Ryan since he left?" I shook my head to indicate no. Then I answered,

"He's supposed to call me when he gets back home. He shouldn't be back home for maybe another hour I think. Is it crazy I miss him already?"

"No, it's not. I know you care about him a lot. He really seems like a good guy. One of the few I've seen in a long time."

My mind began to think of all the conversations I had with him over just the last few days. The hours and hours of talking we had done. How much I've learned about his life, especially in the service. I realized the more I got to know him, the more I respected him. I also realized my biggest setback was my fear he would finally see what an incredible loser I was and realize he could do so much better than me. I knew better than to say this out loud to Nikki so I asked,

"You working tonight? If not, you wanna go get something

to eat?" Her eyes lit up and she looked more awake than she had for the last ten minutes.

"No, I don't work tonight, and yes, let's go eat, but first you should tell your dad about this, and your brother Mike."

I agreed and stood to walk over to the phone in the kitchen, since it was much closer than my cell phone that was still in my purse by the front door. I picked up the receiver and instinctively dialed my dad's number. Three rings later, I heard the chipper voice of Della on the other end.

"Hi Della, is my dad there by chance?" Without even seeing her, I could hear the smile in her voice.

"Oh, hi darling, yes, he's around here somewhere. He's going to ask if you girls can go out to dinner tonight, just a head's up." I glanced over at Nikki and put the phone against my shirt to whisper while Della went to go look for my dad.

"Hey, Nikki, your mom said they want to go out to dinner tonight and there's something they want to talk to us about. I think they were gonna talk to us last night but you had to work. You wanna just go out to eat with them instead of us going out?" She nodded as she stood, stretching her arms above her head.

"Yeah, sure, I'm good either way." I put the phone back up to my ear and waited only a few seconds longer before I heard my dad's voice.

"Hi Amy. How did your interview go this morning?" Even though he almost always was even tempered, he sounded a little different, so that it caught me off guard for a moment.

"Really great, that's why I was calling you actually."

"You got the job, didn't you? I knew you would, sweetie." I cleared my throat and replied,

"Well no, I didn't get offered that job. I didn't meet the minimum qualifications for that position." Trying to sound hopeful and encouraging, he said,

"It's okay, honey. You'll get something, you are a very smart girl and it just wasn't meant to be for you to have that job." I laughed a little and said,

"Well, she offered me a position as her personal assistant for real estate. She's a regular of Nikki's and Nikki said she's a great tipper and always nice when she comes in. She said I should take the position, what do you think, Dad?"

"I think if Nikki says she would be good to work for you should go with that. Besides, you can always keep looking for another job if you feel that's something you need to do. Hey, can you and Nikki come out to dinner tonight? We wanna talk to you girls about something. She doesn't work tonight, does she?" I thought about his advice for a moment, and then I answered,

"Sure, where do you guys wanna meet? She doesn't work so it's good for us, and Dad, I think I'm going to take the job."

"Good honey. Tell Nikki we can meet at seven at that one Mexican restaurant on the corner by the bank; the one Della really likes, but I can never remember the name to it. She'll know." He laughed a little and I laughed along with him.

"See you at seven, Dad. I have to call Mike and tell him the news."

"Okay honey. Love you. We'll see you tonight."

I turned to Nikki as I hung up the phone. She had taken the ponytail out of her hair and she was attempting to punch it back up again as it swished around in a mess. I was a little confused as I said,

"They want to tell us something tonight, but I don't know what it is. My dad sounded different on the phone. What do you think it is?" Nikki tilted her head to the side as she thought for a moment then said sadly,

"You don't think they're splitting up, do you? I mean people that age don't do that, do they?" I shrugged my shoulders and felt just as sad as Nikki looked. Then I shook my head and replied,

"I don't think so. I mean they always seem really happy together. Maybe they're getting married!"

Nikki's eyes got wide for a moment as a smile crossed her lips, and then she put her hands on her hips before she calmly said,

"Yeah, but I don't think they would be able to wait to tell us though. They would want to call us on the phone immediately I would think." I began to think of all the crazy scenarios they might possibly tell us. My mind ranged from getting a dog to adopting a child to fostering an exchange student. Then I said with a laugh in my voice,

"It's probably nothing at all. Maybe they want to take up bingo or something and they are just looking for an excuse to have us come out to dinner." Nikki nodded in agreement before she said,

"I agree. It's probably something lame and we are stressing and thinking of the worst cases possible." We both smiled at each other and I realized looking at Nikki's face that she had also just ran a barrage of silly situations around in her mind also. Then she said,

"I'm going to jump in the shower. Let's go shopping before we head out to dinner. Are you game?"

"Are you kidding? I am always up for shopping."

Two pair of shoes, four outfits, one manicure each, and five hours later (still no call from Ryan); we pulled up in front of the Mexican restaurant.

We walked in and immediately spotted our parents at a four-chair table close to the wall. We walked over and sat down, giving each other a look as we noticed they both had slightly nervous expressions on their faces. I could tell Nikki was thinking the same thought I was as I began to wonder if they were in fact splitting up.

"Hi girls!" Della stood up, walked over to us, wrapping her arms around us, and giving us a hug at the same time.

"Hi Mom… Is everything okay?" My dad stood before Della could answer, walked over, and gave me a big hug, and then gave Nikki a little squeeze just as Della replied,

"Sure it is, honey. You girls wanna sit down so we can order something? Are you hungry?"

Nikki and I gave each other puzzled looks because something strange was going on but we just didn't know what it was yet. We all sat down with Nikki on my left as the server came up to the table. She was a short pale-skinned girl not older than twenty with red hair and freckles lining her cheeks. We quickly gave her our order as she briskly walked toward the kitchen, the swinging door flying back and forth, as she walked through it. Nikki turned to her mom and crossed her arms as she asked, almost accusingly,

"What is going on, Mom? You guys are acting strange and I know there is something you want to tell us. What is it? Just spill it please 'cause you're killing us with this suspense." Both our parents passed a knowing look at each other and gave a little half smile before my dad replied to Nikki's questions.

"Well girls, we are going to be moving."

Both Nikki and I smiled because we knew that apartment, even though a decent size, was still too small for them. Then Nikki dropped her smile, but I asked before she could,

"Where are you moving?"

Nikki had the same look I did and it was apparent we both had wondered if they were moving out of state. My dad smiled and reached his arm over and put his hand on top of mine as he smiled. Unlike my mother's icy grip, my dad's hand was warm.

"Don't worry, sweetie, we are only moving a few miles down the road into a nice ranch style home." Both Nikki and I simultaneously let out a long sigh and Nikki uncrossed her arms and let her hands fall to her lap before she said much more calmly,

"Well, that's great news, why were you guys acting so strange about it? We thought you guys were splitting up or something." Both of our parents gave nervous laughs and then glanced at each other as Nikki scrunched her eyebrows together asking.

"Wait, are you guys splitting up?" My dad cleared his throat just as Nikki's eyes got big and a smile crossed her lips as she exclaimed, “I knew it! You’re getting married, aren’t you?” I smiled to and looked over at my dad as he had a happy, but nervous smile on his face. He glanced over at Della and replied,

“Well, girls, here’s the thing. We’re not getting married because we already are married.” My eyebrows scrunched together in confusion just like Nikki’s as she asked in a baffled tone,

“What do you mean? When? How… What?” Then I looked at my dad and added to Nikki’s question,

“Yeah, when did this happen?” My mind began to wonder if it had happened when we were in Italy, but I just couldn’t imagine them not including us in it, not to mention I had just met Della for the first time only a few months ago. Then Della looked at Nikki and she put her hand on Nikki’s arm as my father had mine.

“Honey, we’ve actually been married for a little while. We got married before we moved in together in the apartment. I have not legally changed my last name yet.”

Nikki’s face continued to scrunch up with questions and confusion and I could see her mind trying to put things together before a few moments later she asked,

“Mom, I’m so confused. When did this happen and why didn’t I know about this?” I had not realized I was nodding my head in agreement with Nikki the whole time until my neck started to feel stiff. Della glanced over to my dad as she went on.

“I knew the first two weeks we were dating that I was going to marry this man.” Della gave a large happy smile and she leaned over. My dad also leaned over and they gave each other a kiss.

“Dad, why didn’t you tell me this? I mean, I really love

Della, but I just met her." My dad sighed and looked at me with his gentle father eyes that he usually had as he answered,

"Well, sweetie, I met Della when you first got engaged to Chad and I didn't want to bombard you with this new relationship I was in and have it put any tension on you or your relationship. Not to mention I knew that sometimes your mother can be a little difficult and I didn't want her to rant about anything in my life and put that kind of stress on you. I wanted to have you come out and meet Della all those months ago but it never seemed the right time." Della turned to Nikki and picked up where my dad had left off.

"And we decided we wouldn't tell any of our kids until it was the right time for all of them to know about it." Nikki nodded and smiled with a look on her face like she understood why her mother had the intentions she did.

"I take it you guys didn't have a wedding… or did you?" Della shook her head and laughed a little.

"No dear, we just went down to the justice of the peace. We're too old for those shenanigans." Nikki put her hands on her hips while sitting in her chair as she exclaimed,

"No Mom! No woman is ever too old for a nice dress." I laughed a little as her mom gave her a little smile and eye roll. Then I asked my dad,

"Why were you guys acting so nervous to tell us?"

"We thought you girls might be mad we didn't tell you beforehand, or upset we even got married in the first place." Both Nikki and I glanced at each other before Nikki said,

"I mean I wish we would have known at first, but we're not

mad. You guys are good together. It's not like you're teenagers running off to Vegas. I mean you guys are smart enough to know healthy relationships when you see them." I nodded and since there wasn't much for me to add, I just simply agreed.

"Yeah. Exactly."

Both our parents seemed so happy. Just then, we heard the swinging door swoosh open as the server carried out a large tray that was practically the same size as her to the table.

As we began to eat our food, Nikki glanced over at me and I smiled looking at her as she had a look on her face and gave a wink. At that moment, I knew she was planning something but I also knew better than to ask and foil any plan she had. I smiled back and took a bite of my enchilada as I began to ponder all the things Nikki might be planning in her head.

THIRTY-THREE

Soft melody hummed out of my cell phone as it vibrated and buzzed on the nightstand next to my bed. I yawned and coughed as I reached over and picked it up, my mind fuzzy as to if it was my alarm or my actual phone ringing. I glanced at it and realized Ryan was calling me. My heart leaped, then dropped, as I was giddy that he was calling, then upset because he had not called yesterday when he got home like he said he would. Then in fear, I quickly answered,

"Hi… Ryan? Are you okay?" He sounded fully awake and I glanced at the clock that let me know it was a few minutes before nine thirty. Then I realized he had probably already been up for hours and even gotten a morning jog in.

"Yes ma'am. I'm very sorry I didn't call you yesterday when I got home. I got home later than expected and there was an issue at the bar. I'm really sorry, Amy." I knew I probably sounded like I just woke up as I said,

"It's okay. Nikki and I ended up going out, and then we had dinner with our parents. I hadn't even noticed." I felt bad knowing that was a complete lie because I had been watching the clock all evening, trying to calculate when he would most likely call. When the hours dragged on, I had to get help from Nikki as she helped me fight the urge to call him. Nikki was a pro at playing hard to get. I was a pro at it being hard to get anything. Therefore, I had trusted her advice and refrained from calling him, waiting for him to call me instead.

I heard him pause for a second, not sure how to respond to my statement. Then he said with a smile I could hear,

"How did your interview go? I was thinking about that on the drive home last night."

I cleared my throat and realized if I was going to have a half coherent conversation with him I would need to get out of bed, drink something, and move around for a minute, as my mind was still foggy, so I asked,

"Hey Ryan, would it be okay if I called you back in about ten minutes?" He agreed and I hung up the phone and slowly slid out of bed heading to the kitchen to get a glass of water.

Minutes later, I sat on the couch and took another drink of my water as I picked up my cell phone from my lap and called Ryan back. His voice sounded just as alert as it had the first time.

"Hi Amy, so tell me about your interview."

For some reason, I gave him extraordinary detail of my interview, all the way down to her shoes and the temperature of the building. Even though it was equal to the amount of detail I had given Nikki, I hadn't even given that much information to my dad. Ryan listened closely and sounded excited for me.

"Oh, and you're never going to believe this. My dad is actually married to Della. Apparently, they got married several months ago, but just told me and Nikki about it last night." Ryan's tone sounded very intrigued by this as he said,

"Really? That's cool. Why did they wait to tell you guys?" I responded by recounting all the details of our dinner including our conversation in its entirety. Ryan said, "How do you feel about that? Are you okay with them being married?" Even though he couldn't see me, I nodded my head as I answered.

"Yeah, of course. It's a little strange that my dad got remarried before I ever got married for a first time, but they are a cute older couple. I know they are happy with each other."

Ryan and I talked for what was probably another forty minutes but only seemed like ten minutes as I remembered and quickly said,

"I have to call this lady Vanessa Winters on her cell phone and let her know I'm going to take the position. Can we talk later if that's okay?"

A few seconds later, I hung up the phone just as Nikki walked into the kitchen with her hair in the usual tangled mess I had seen it every morning since we had become roommates. She shuffled her feet over to the high-end espresso maker and I could hear her packing espresso down in the machine to make herself a cup. She typically preferred coffee over espresso, but on the rare occasion, I saw her use the espresso machine. She told me on my first day there I could use it whenever I wanted, but honestly, I felt it was too much work for me to get some caffeine. Nikki did not agree when she needed it at an expresso level.

"Hey, lady, how you feeling?" I asked Nikki as she gave me a faint smile.

"I'm good," she sleepily replied. "What do you think about my idea of throwing our parents a vow renewal ceremony?"

I got up and walked around to the edge of the counter as the hum and sharp hiss of the machine along with the fresh espresso scent filled the air. I answered,

"I think it's a good idea, but maybe it shouldn't be a surprise. Get your mom in on the whole idea. She might be excited and want to go through the whole experience with the planning and picking out a dress and everything."

"You mean, *our* mom." I smiled and agreed as Nikki thought for a few minutes, then she replied, "I think you're right. She probably would like that. I'm gonna suggest maybe they do it on the same date that they went to the justice of the peace. What do you think?" I thought for a moment as I watched Nikki warm up some milk and pour her espresso in it right before adding a scoop of sugar.

"I think that's a good idea. I'm not sure how my mother is going to react to all this, but honestly, I don't care. My dad's happy and that's what matters. Oh, I mean *our* dad." Nikki smiled at me as she took a sip out of her soft pink and black mug that she used for espresso. I held up my phone and said as I started to head to my room. "I'm calling Vanessa Winters now to tell her I'm taking the job." As I walked into my room, I heard Nikki yell,

"Great!"

A professional, but pleasant fifteen-minute conversation later, I was employed and felt great. She already had a couple of assignments for me to work on and I gave her my word I would start in three days upon her request. It was nice that she didn't seem to mind if I worked from home and even had a computer for me to use if I needed. I laid back into my bed and stared up at the ceiling with a bright smile on my lips. I looked at the phone and started to dial Ryan, but just then, I heard a tap on the door, I dropped the phone and sat up just as I heard Nikki's voice.

"How'd it go?" Nikki stepped in, looking and sounding more awake than before her espresso drink.

"Good, I'm meeting her in three days to get started. I think this will go well, but my dad is right. If I'm not content or making the money I want, I can just keep looking for another job."

"I agree. You have to do something you like and work for someone you like. Did you talk to Ryan yet?" I held up my phone and replied,

"Yeah, we talked for a pretty long time this morning and I was just getting ready to call him back, but I think I should shower first and eat something before I do."

"Hey, Amy, did Ryan explain why he never called last night when he got home? That doesn't seem like him."

"Not really, he just said there was an issue at the bar he had to deal with… he was kinda vague about it. I know I haven't been talking to him that long, but you don't think he's flaking out on me already do you, Nikki?" Nikki half shrugged her shoulders and looked to the side for a moment while pondering my question, and then she replied,

"I'm not sure, but I don't think so. I mean, you gotta think about the fact that he does own his own business and he has spent a lot of time with you in the last week. I mean I could see that something could have come up because he hasn't been there a lot lately."

"So basically I should just relax?" Nikki laughed a little, walked over to the bed, and sat next to me on the edge as she said.

"Yeah probably. I mean it's new and all, but I wouldn't start to worry that he's flaking until he stops calling for days. I don't think you need to stress about it. I can tell he cares about you."

"I know this is a dumb question, but should I call him when I'm done with my shower or just wait for him to call me?" Nikki asked in reply to my question.

"Did you tell him you'd call him back later? If you did, then yeah you should call."

I stood up and walked to the bathroom as Nikki walked out of my room.

Sitting back on my bed with a leftover bagel Ryan had bought the other day in my hand, I reached over and picked up my phone to call Ryan with a smile on my face. After several rings and leaving a short voicemail on his phone, I set the phone back on my nightstand with a frown on my face. I walked out to the living room to see Nikki sitting on the couch with her legs crossed and watching a morning talk show. She glanced over and saw the disappointed look on my face before she said,

"He didn't answer did he?"

I didn't speak but just shook my head letting her know she was right as she let out a sigh. She opened her mouth to say something just as the doorbell rang. I took a few more steps and opened the door to see a young man, no older than twenty in a navy blue hat and delivery suit.

"I have a delivery for Ms. Stanton." I looked at the large bouquet of colorful flowers and I smiled wide thinking of Ryan sending me them, not letting Dante outdo him.

"I'm Ms. Stanton." He reached out with a signature pad, barely able to balance the large bundle of flowers in one arm and let me sign with the other arm. I took the beautiful flowers out of his hands after I signed and walked in with a smile on my face and closed the door with my foot as I walked over to the table setting them down. Nikki had a bright smile on her face as she said,

"There you go, now you see he's not flaking on you. He must have been pretty jealous when he saw those other flowers. I think you throwing them away with him was a super smart move."

I nodded my head in agreement and picked up the card with my name in typed letters on the front. I opened the card when my smile dropped. They weren't from Ryan, but they were another batch of flowers from Dante. I set the card down on the table. Nikki stood up and walked over to the table as she asked,

"They're from Dante, aren't they?" I just looked at her letting her know she was right. Then she sighed and said, "I know what you're thinking, but don't do it. You're thinking that maybe you can make Dante an option, just in case Ryan flakes on you. I would say don't do it. Dante's just a smooth player. He's not genuine at all. Don't forget that… ever."

She was right, that thought had crept into my mind, but she was right on all accounts. At the same time, it was hard keeping negative feelings towards Dante with the intoxicating scent of flowers filling the air.

THIRTY-FOUR

Stacks of files and loose white papers rested near the corner of my new desk I had just purchased less than a week ago. I found that along with prepping for one closing in a few days and a few light paperwork things, most of my assistant work involved research for Vanessa for more real estate purchases. I glanced over at my glass of water, which was now empty. Picking it up, I walked out to the kitchen.

"Hey, how's work going?" Nikki asked with a smile on her face while she leaned with her back against the counter and a bowl of cereal in her hand. She had her uniform on and her hair pulled up in a high large bun with a ribbon tied in it. Her make-up was done almost to professional standards and she resembled a classic silver screen actress.

She had become really fond about asking how work was or

what my day was like in the office. She had told me more than once she was slightly envious I could work from home, I suspected because she would love nothing more than wear her pajama pants from dawn till dusk.

"Good, I came out to get more water. She gave me a list of properties to research and I'm also putting together a list of my own for the next county over. I sure tell you, I wish I had a hobby like buying up places." I raised my hands and did air quotations with the word 'hobby' as Nikki laughed a little. Then she replied,

"Yeah, I think we all do. Did she happen to say if we could use her pool next weekend?" I nodded and replied,

"She said it was not an issue if we wanted to come over and use her pool while she was out of town. She's already given me her security code and a key in case of an emergency." I was not a fan of putting on a swimsuit and taking my chubby butt to a pool where people could see me, but a large in ground pool that was private was another story all together.

I was actually surprised when I said I enjoyed swimming when Vanessa had asked me after I saw the pool. I had only spent a few minutes at Vanessa's place to pick up a couple of files, but my breath was taken away by the luxury of it all. In size it wasn't anything spectacular, maybe only twenty-four hundred square feet, but the high-class detail of everything and the amount of security spoke a different story.

"That's great, I'm gonna see if I can get off work on a day next weekend, or maybe if you are free during next week we can go over there. Hey, have you heard from Ryan?" I lightly shook my head, as I replied,

"No. Not really, I talked to him a few days ago briefly, and it was a good conversation, but he seemed almost distracted. I think that maybe he met someone else. I don't know."

I tried hard to play it off and act indifferent about it, but I could tell by the look on Nikki's face she wasn't buying my act. She put the spoon in her mouth and chewed on her cereal as she continued to lean on the counter. A few seconds later after she swallowed, she casually replied without looking up from her bowl.

"Don't worry, he'll call."

Her response was as calm and collective as anyone could imagine and for that reason it calmed me down and made me stop worrying about if he would call or not. So I smiled and said as I walked back to my room, now my office.

"Okay. Thanks sis." I didn't have to look back to know she had a smile on her face as she had been calling me sis the day after our parents told us the news, but I had not said it yet until that moment. It was natural for me to hear being called 'sis', but unnatural for me to call someone by that title. I did find it peculiar that Nikki had not referred to Mike as 'lil bro' or her 'brother' whenever I brought up his name or even in the short conversation we had with him where we talked about planning a vow renewal ceremony for our parents. I was beginning to think Nikki had become romantically drawn to Mike, but the thought of anyone being romantically attracted to my little brother seemed strange to me. I just couldn't see any woman falling for the little toddler who cried until he fell asleep when he lost his dirty and severely tattered 'blankie' in the backyard. I did know I was usually wrong about feelings of the heart, but I'd rather put the whole idea in the back of my mind and keep moving, not that I begrudged them a relationship, because I was confident they would be good to each other, but I had too much on my own plate to think about.

I sat back down at my desk and picked up the folder I had just picked up from Vanessa yesterday as I heard the doorbell ring. I flipped it open, and then set it down as I heard Nikki's voice as she yelled that the door was for me. My heart fluttered because my imagination had been running wild since the batch of flowers had arrived from Dante. I had almost imagined Dante or even Ryan to show up unannounced at the condo.

"This certified mail is for you," Nikki said as she turned around closing the door behind her. She held a white cardboard overnight envelope in her hand as she stretched out and handed it to me. My first reaction was that it must be the papers for the closing I was going to on behalf of Vanessa in a few days, but I had already arranged to pick those up personally from the title company to review them first. I took the envelope from her and turned it over in my hand as I said,

"Well it's pretty thin. Who dropped it off?" Nikki looked confused and answered,

"Just a mailman. You're not expecting anything from Vanessa?"

I shook my head and turned over the large envelope instantly recognizing the zip code of my hometown, which made me more confused. I pulled the tab as I walked over to the kitchen counter.

Nikki was at my heels with curiosity on her face. I shook the envelope as one legal sized white business envelope fell out on the counter. I looked up at Nikki as she looked back at me, both of us having puzzled looks on our faces. I opened the envelope and pulled out a single letter with a check that was paper clipped to it. With wide-eyed shock, I looked up at Nikki. Without saying a word, I handed it to her as she glanced at the check, turned it over, and then examined it again before she exclaimed completely bewildered.

"That's a lot of money! Where did it come from and why did they send it to you?"

I slowly took the paper back out of her hands and skimmed over the letter again, noticing it was written on letterhead from the Wheeler's logistics company. Still not completely sure I was speaking accurately, I answered the best I could.

"I think that's all the money I had saved and given Chad towards the down payment for a house for when we got married, and more than that… it looks like money for the honeymoon to Italy too."

Nikki was shaking her head in disbelief and I shrugged my shoulder letting her know I was feeling the same disbelief she was. Then she asked,

"How long did it take you to save that money? Are you shocked he paid you back?"

"When we first started dating, we had a conversation about getting a house and I started saving at that point. Then I started giving him everything I had saved plus some every week when we got engaged. I think he was actually spending it. It's not Chad that paid me back because he wanted to. I'm sure his father wouldn't allow his son to screw over a girl like that. His dad has a pretty good character."

Nikki continued to look confused and she slowly shook her head back and forth as she tried to processes everything I said. Then with a big smile on her face, she said,

"I'm really happy for you. You deserved to get your money back. Now that little douche is completely out of your life and you have no ties to him at all."

I smiled because I had not thought about the truth of what she had said yet. She was right, Chad was completely out of my life and I would have no need to contact him in the future for repayment. Then I said,

"I was going to wait till Ryan called me, but I have to call him and tell him this." Nikki nodded in agreement then she asked,

"What does the letter say?"

I looked at the few short sentences in typed letters that were printed on the sheet of paper as I answered, "It's very professional sounding and just says; *I'm sorry for the delay in returning your funds. Please see the check attached and do not hesitate to contact me if the amount enclosed is not the sufficient amount to be returned. Chadwick Wheeler*. That's all it says. I know that it wasn't Chad that composed that, but whatever, I'm going to take this check to the bank this afternoon." Nikki asked,

"Sounds like he didn't know how much money you had given him towards the house. What'd you think?" I agreed with her, and as I looked over the letter again, I replied,

"Yeah, I think he was actually spending it and had lost track, but he knew he had spent a lot. Part of this might not even be for the honeymoon. It might be what he just thought I had given him." My imagination switched gears from thinking about Dante or Ryan showing up to what I should do or invest the money in.

I sat the envelope on top of my desk and picked up my cell phone to call Ryan and tell him the good news. I laid on my back and looked up at the ceiling as I waited for Ryan to pick up as the phone rang. My heart sank when several rings later it went to voicemail. I clicked the phone off and dropped it to my side as my smile curled down into a frown. I began to smile again as my phone started to ring and I picked it up to look at Ryan's name. My smile faltered slightly as I saw Vanessa's name on my screen. I quickly answered.

"Hi Vanessa." I could hear the smile in her voice as she said,

"Hello Amy. How is everything going for you?" I quickly replied,

"Really good, I have most of the paperwork done that you had sent and I'm going to the title company this afternoon to pick up the documents for the one closing." I could hear the smile get even bigger in her tone as she said,

"That's fantastic. You're doing a great job, Amy. I do appreciate your help. I don't know how I went so long without an assistant to be honest. I wasn't planning on selling one of my properties, but I have since changed my mind. I know I haven't discussed this part of the job before, but would you possibly be willing to show this client the property this afternoon? I know this is not exactly your job, but the realtor is out of town until the coming closing and I don't trust anyone else. Would you please be able to do this?"

I became excited, because all the years I had worked behind the desk and watched realtors show properties, I had wondered what that was like for them. I jumped at the opportunity and replied,

"I'd love to actually. What time today? I can probably go to the title company before or after I meet with them." Vanessa's tone was appreciative and professional as she responded,

"Can you meet with them two hours from now? I can text you the address of the location and the key code for access."

"Yeah, that's perfect. The title company will have the documents ready at least an hour before then. Yes, please text me the address and code." I had never felt so professional in all my life, and the feeling was great. I started to think of which suit I would wear to meet with this client.

"Sounds perfect, Amy. Thank you so much, and you will be compensated for this."

My smile got even bigger thinking that I was not only feeling professional, but I was going to get paid like a professional. We said good-bye and I stood and rushed out to the kitchen as I saw Nikki rinsing her bowl in the sink.

"Nikki, I'm going to go show a property today. I'm kinda excited. Help me pick out something to wear, will you?" Nikki turned around with her excitement on her face as she replied,

"That's super cool, and I can't believe you even asked. Of course, I'll help you pick out something to wear!" We both laughed softly and headed toward the large master closet. I flicked on the light switch as my cell phone I still had in my hand started to ring. I quickly answered it without thinking twice to hear the sound of Ryan's voice on the other end.

"Hey, Amy, I'm so sorry I missed your call. How are you?"

I was bubbling over with excitement and joy that I had temporarily forgotten that I was upset he had not answered in the first place.

"I'm great, Ryan! This morning has been amazing. I'm going to go show a property, which doesn't sound super special, but I'm excited to do it. But you're not gonna believe this." I heard him clear his throat as he asked,

"What happened?" I couldn't stop smiling as I joyfully exclaimed,

"Chad paid me all that money back, plus a little extra cause I think he didn't know how much I had actually saved." Ryan paused for a long moment then with a smirk on his face I could actually hear in his voice, he said,

"Oh yeah? Well that's fantastic. Glad he did that."

For some unknown reason, I felt suspicious and glanced over at Nikki who was standing in the middle of the closet trying her hardest not to appear to be listening to my conversation. I pressed the mute key and looked at Nikki as I whispered,

"He sounds suspicious for some reason. I don't know why? He doesn't seem at all surprised Chad paid me back." Nikki looked at me curiously then whispered back,

"He must know something. Ask him about it."

Then I shrugged my shoulders and quickly took him off mute as I asked him,

"How come you don't sound shocked? Do you know something I don't?" In a nervous fashion and unconvincingly, he said,

"Why would you think I did something?"

"Did something? I asked if you knew something… Wait a minute… did you have something to do with me getting paid back?"

A picture of Chad lying in a hospital bed with a broken leg was the first image to flash in my mind as Ryan calmly replied,

"Maybe a little. That issue I told you I had to deal with at the bar the first night I got home… the night I forgot to call you. They had called me because Chad had shown up at the bar and I told my staff to let me know if he ever came there cause he wasn't allowed in. But he showed up with his dad, and I might have said some harsh, but truthful things to him in front of his pops." I paused for a moment then seriously asked,

"Did you hit him in front of his dad?"

"No ma'am. Not that I'm not tempted to hit him when I look at his weasely little face, but I did mention the money situation and how he wasn't a real man. By the look on his dad's face, I'm betting odds he had no clue his son was the little slime he actually is."

I felt a sudden rush of enormous endearment for Ryan. I wanted to hug him and kiss all over his face, if we didn't get interrupted of course, and just tell him how thankful I was for him doing that. I was fully aware had he not of done that, then Chad probably would never have paid me back without his father's involvement. I took a breath and said to Ryan,

"Ryan, thank you so much. I can't begin to tell you how grateful I am for you doing that. I'm not trying to cut this conversation short, but I have to get ready for this showing and swing by the title company. Can I call you later when I'm done?"

"Yes ma'am. Absolutely."

We said good-bye and I hung up the phone as I watched Nikki pluck a few more pieces off the rack. I looked at Nikki and unable to contain it, I squealed with joy before I said,

"This day is turning out to be completely awesome! Ryan said something in front of Chad's dad. That's the main reason I got paid back. Okay, now I've got to get ready."

Nikki smiled wide as she held up two suits side by side. Without any hesitation, I pointed to the sharp looking black one I had fallen in love with since the first time I saw it. It was tight that first day in the closet when I tried it on, but the day had been going so wonderful I was determined to wear that particular suit, even if it didn't fit. Nikki smiled and handed me the suit as she asked,

"You want me to do your make-up? I have a half-hour before I have to leave for work." I smiled and said,

"I can't believe you even asked."

THIRTY-FIVE

It was an unusually sunny afternoon as the smile I had on my face had not left me since I looked at the check, and got the call from Vanessa. I swung open the glass door to the title company as shards of reflective light fluttered off the glass windows adjacent to the door. I kept my smile as I heard the clinking of my heels come to a silence once I stepped from the tiles onto the gray office carpet that ran throughout the front lobby and into the rooms.

A woman in her late forties with dark brown hair looked up from the desk, she had deep dimples in her cheeks. I walked up to the desk, keeping my voice low because the whole office was quiet like a library.

"Hi. I'm Amy Stanton, I'm Ms. Winters' assistant. I'm supposed to pick up some documents." She gave me a pleasant smile and her dimples dove even deeper as she replied.

"Hi Amy, it's very nice to meet you. I'm Brenda. We are all very fond of Vanessa here and we are here to help you with anything you need. I actually was going to have two packages for you to pick up, but we are not yet complete with the second. Here are the ones that you came for today." I watched as she leaned over and picked up a large white and red legal size folder that was at least an inch thick.

Then worried I had not heard Vanessa tell me about the second group of documents, I asked concerned,

"I'm so sorry. I didn't know I was supposed to pick up two packages of documents. Did she say she needed them looked at right away?" Brenda shook her head and answered,

"No, it was a last minute thing that came up. She said if they just happened to be finished, I could give them to you, so you could give them to her when you see her next. She's already scheduled that closing so she can be present for it. That's all I know about it." She smiled and then said, "That's a very nice suit. Would you care for some water or coffee, dear?" I shook my head no and I kindly replied,

"No thank you. I better take off. I have to make another appointment." I slid the thick folder into the middle of the briefcase. I realized I would now be able to afford my own and give Nikki back the one I had been borrowing. I walked through the glass doors and out into the sunny parking lot.

A short ten minute drive later, I pulled up in front of the address that Vanessa had texted to me on my phone. I had been expecting a house, possibly a run down one at that, but instead I drove up to a brick storefront on a street that was snuggled in the middle of a coffee shop and lighting store. I double-checked the address and then decided to get out of my car once I saw the lock box on the large brass handle. I glanced down the street that was lined with pots of flowers on every block and I didn't seem to see anyone waiting to go inside. I made a mental note that should Vanessa ask me to do this again in the future, I must be smart enough to ask for the person's phone number in case something happened.

After my third attempt, due to sticky fingers, I finally was able to take the large bulky lock off the door. The heavy wooden door creaked and moaned with low groans as I opened it. The cloudy piece of oval glass in the middle was so dusty and dim even the bright sun didn't make it sparkle.

I stepped inside and the large front store windows cast enough light through that I could see the dust hovering in the air like a smoky fog. The floor was all wood with long thick planks that ran from the door all the way to the back room. Most of the space was open and empty, with the exception of a few vacant shelves that were lined with dirt and a couple pieces of trash near the edges of the wall.

A faint moldy smell lingered from the back room. The draft from the front door being opened had seemed to pull the scent towards the front. I was almost to the back as I heard the low painful creak of the door as it opened again. I turned around to see the client as he walked through the front door, shielding his eyes from the sun that was pouring in through the front window.

I stopped and stared as I asked, completely confused,

"What are you doing here? What's going on?"

Ryan stepped forward and ran his fingers through short hair as he smiled and said,

"I've come to look at a place I'm buying. I asked if you'd be able to show it to me, but I wanted it to be a surprise." I was completely confused as I asked,

"When did you get here? I just talked to you not that long ago, and I can't believe you cut your hair."

Ryan just grinned at me and ran his fingers through his hair again, obviously not used to his long hair not being there. He walked up to me and looked down with the smile still on his face. I had so many questions about what was happening that my smile faded for a moment. Then he asked,

"I look stupid with short hair, don't I?" I shook my head because he looked not only equally as handsome, but possibly even more so than he did with long hair. Then I said,

"No, you look really good with short hair, but please tell me what's going on. Why are you buying this place and why did you cut your hair?"

"Well, I liked this area when I was jogging here and I saw it was for sale. I really liked it."

I turned around looking at the space and began to imagine him putting a pub or small bar inside the space. Then I asked,

"Are you going to own two bars so far apart from each other? What about Denver's Place?"

"I sold the bar. Well, actually, I let my buddy and right hand man buy me out in installments." Then I spun around and exclaimed,

"Are you moving here?"

"I got a job offer at a base about thirty minutes outside this city. They need G.I. Joe nerdy tech guys pretty bad. It pays well and I'm coming in ranked well. So I took it, so yeah, I guess I'm moving here." I was overcome with surprise and emotion as I exclaimed like a small child,

"Are you serious?" Ryan laughed a little and my heart started pounding at such a rate that within seconds soft tears began to fill my eyes. Then with a concerned look on his face he asked,

"Are you okay? You look like you're gonna cry."

I blinked and sniffed as I quickly caught the loose drops on my fingertips so they didn't mess up the wonderful make up job Nikki had done to my eyes. Then I responded,

"I'm beyond okay. I'm just really happy." I sniffed again as I continued, "I really thought you were starting to flake on me. I had just thought we would slowly stop talking. I can't believe you're moving here."

"No ma'am. I'm not flaking on you. I was just busy getting things done so I could get out here. I need to go back tomorrow so I can finish signing things over to him for the bar. But I'll spend a day with you if you don't mind."

"Nope, don't mind at all, wanna look around at the place?"

"Yes ma'am. Absolutely."

We walked around and I quickly noticed that the wood planking on the floor was overall in good condition, and was high quality wood and would look great refinished.

"You know, Ryan, you could easily refinish this floor and it would look great. This floor is probably decades old. If you do your bar counter in wood, you could find a nice piece that would complement the floor." Ryan smiled wide and glanced at me from the side as we continued walking around and with a little half smile on his face he replied,

"Oh yeah? You think so?"

I quickly nodded and began to picture little tables, where the bar would go and even a spot for pool tables if he wanted. We walked through the large door to the back of the building. The back was a large, almost completely empty storage room with a small office to the side. The space housed a few shelves on either side of the wall and sink near the back door. It had gray cement floors and dingy looking walls. It was bleak and dismal with a few towels near the door that had patches of what appeared to be black mold on them. I pointed to the towels and said,

"Well, I'm pretty sure that's where the moldy smell is coming from."

I started to bend down to pick up the towels so I could just throw them out the back door a few feet away when Ryan reached out and grabbed my arm stopping me, he said,

"Don't touch that. Some molds are really dangerous. I'll get a specialized cleaning crew to handle stuff like that."

I quickly agreed and walked over to the little office to peer inside. Like the back part of the space, it had cement floors, but it had wood planks that lined half way up the wall with a small window looking out into the storage area. This office was the kind I could easily imagine a used car sales man in his mid-eighties to be sitting in.

"So what do you think?" I asked as I stepped out of the office while Ryan walked around the back looking at the area closely.

"It has potential, don't you think?"

"Yeah, Ryan, I really think so. It's a nice space and a good location. This back room here is really big." I continued to walk around before he paused and said,

"I think so too. If you like it, that means something."

I smiled wide and then remembered I had not yet thanked him for intervening for my money.

"Thank you so much, Ryan, you've had my back more in a week than I think anyone else ever has in my life." He looked over from across the room and with the same shy look he gave me in the bar the first night I met him, he replied,

"I was glad to help you, Amy."

I was so excited about the thought of Ryan moving near me that I had completely forgotten I had not eaten anything at all since I woke up until my stomach growled so loud that he heard it across the room.

"Well, Amy, I'm hungry, how 'bout you?" I could feel my cheeks blush, as I felt embarrassed that even my stomach betrayed me, not letting me think I was thin for even a minute. I shyly answered as I looked down at my stomach.

"Yeah… I guess I am."

He tilted his head toward the building next door and asked,

"Do you like cheesecake? The girls at the coffee shop told me that they're supposed to have some of the best cheesecake you can imagine. You game?" The thought of lemon cheesecake filled my mind and I couldn't contain the enthusiasm in my voice.

"Uh, don't I look like I like cheesecake?" I took my hand and ran it up and down my body like a model showing off a prized pig at the county fair. He looked at me and shook his head with a smile on his face as he replied.

"If it helped you get those beautiful hips, then God bless cheesecake." He looked at me from head to toe, his smile never fading.

For the first time in my entire life, I had never wanted to marry anyone as much as I wanted to marry Ryan at that exact moment.

"Yeah, I'm game. Let's get some cheesecake. Oh, and I'm paying."

He paused for a second looking almost offended that I insisted on paying. Then as he saw the seriousness in my eyes, he held up his hands as if surrendering and replied,

"It really goes against my principal, but if you insist."

"I do."

THIRTY-SIX

Unbelievably glad is what I was when I opened the front door to the condo and remembered I had put the bouquet of flowers in my room away from the front door, since Ryan followed right in behind me.

"Do you want something to drink?" I asked as we walked in and a soft lingering smell of rain floated in behind us. The sky had rapidly turned from bright to a dismal gray in a matter of an hour as a storm apparently moved in.

"Sure, may I sit?"

I gestured to the couch for him to sit down while I walked to the kitchen. I couldn't take my eyes off him with his hair short the way that it was. He was very handsome but it was a cleaner look I had to adjust to. I asked,

"We have strawberry lemonade if you want some?" He

nodded his head while I walked to the kitchen and swung open the fridge, reaching for the glass pitcher with whole strawberries floating in it. Nikki liked to make the lemonade with real strawberries and I had grown to love it. I poured his glass, then walked over to the couch and handed it to him just as my phone rang in my pocket. I quickly reached in my pocket to see the call coming in was from Vanessa.

"Hi Vanessa." I could hear her shuffling some papers in the background as she politely asked,

"Hi Amy, how did the showing go?" I smiled and replied,

"Oh, he liked it very well. That was a good surprise you gave me." I could hear her laugh a little in the phone as she replied,

"Actually, it happened to be a coincidence. I had just recently acquired that space when he called the realtor about it, only a day after you accepted the position. He was the one that put everything together when I said I would need to have my new assistant, Amy show it, and he wanted to see it immediately."

I looked at him sitting on the couch and drinking his lemonade as Vanessa was talking. He could tell she was talking about him because a little guilty smirk curled up on the corner of his mouth. I replied,

"Well, I'm glad for the surprise. I picked up all the documents for the closing but there was another packet of documents that weren't ready yet."

I heard the shuffling of papers switch on the other end to clicks on a computer as she paused and said,

"Oh, now that it's not a secret, the other package is for Mr.

Ryan's closing on that property he just saw. He wanted to close as soon as humanly possible and I believe the title company can get it done by the end of next week. It'll be tight though, so about nine business days I would estimate."

I knew from all my experience working at the front desk in the real estate office, any closing done in under a month was considered fast, but I had come to learn that Vanessa owned such a large amount of property as her 'hobby', that the title company was quick to please her.

"Okay, just let me know what I need to assist you with and I'm there." With a pleased sound in her voice, she replied before we hung up,

"Of course, Amy. Thank you for all your help. I will keep you updated on all the appropriate paperwork needed for closing. I'm going to call a little later tomorrow so we can discuss the package you picked up earlier today. Have a lovely evening."

"Thank you. You too, Vanessa." I ended the call and slid the phone back in my pocket as the devious look remained on Ryan's face. Then I said, coyly,

"So, you told my boss not to let me know it was you I was showing the property to, huh?" He shrugged his shoulders and replied,

"I thought you might like to be surprised. I didn't realize that she was the same lady you told me you had the interview with, until she mentioned your name. Then I put two and two together. That was not planned. But once I found out, the coincidence was too good not to work with." He looked up and smiled at me as he patted the seat next to him before he said, "Come sit next to me."

I dropped down on the couch next to him, sitting close enough to feel the warmth of his body. He wrapped his arm around me, and instinctively, I leaned into him and rested my head against the side of his chest. Then I reached up and wrapped my hand around his arm that was holding me. I felt so comfortable and worry free as we sat on the couch in that position for minutes, silent, absorbing each other's company. I closed my eyes just as the rushing sound of rain began to pour down and tap against the side of the building and windows. Then I heard his voice, soft and curious.

"Amy?"

"Yeah?"

I could feel his body shift as he reached up with his free hand and smoothed his hair back nervously.

"Would you want to be my girl? I mean officially and stuff." I snuggled even closer into him and teasingly said,

"Well, I'm not sure about that. I mean I'm trying to keep my options open and all." Obviously, he couldn't see that I was smiling, so he said somewhat sadly,

"Oh, I see." I laughed as I sat up and turned to the side to look him in the face before I said,

"I'm teasing you. Yes, I'm your girl, Ryan." He smiled shyly and raised his eyebrows with a look on his face as he sat up a little further on the couch too. Then he said, as he moved a piece of hair off my shoulder,

"Good."

I looked at him with his short hair and his bright blue eyes that felt comfortable and familiar to my heart. Just as I opened my mouth to ask him something, the front door only a few feet away swung open as Nikki practically jumped inside. She held a plastic grocery bag at her side as if she had tried to use it as a makeshift umbrella. As she stepped inside, she blurted out,

"It's pouring rain out there. Don't the clouds know sugar melts! I can't be out in this weather." She shut the door behind her. Her high bun now a saggy wet mess and her clothes were drenched as if she just jumped out of a shower. Then she looked up with a big frustrated sigh before she realized Ryan was sitting on the couch. She paused for a long moment, staring at him confused she said, "Uh, hi Ryan. Did I miss something?" Instantly, I thought it was us that had missed another opportunity for a first kiss. Instead, I answered,

"Ryan is buying a property here that Vanessa owns. Oh, and he's moving out here." Nikki exclaimed,

"Really? That's cool." She had a wide smile on her face as she shot me a look that said I told you so. Then Ryan responded,

"Yes, I sure am. I have to head back tomorrow to wrap up some business back home, and then I'm coming back in about a week for the closing."

Nikki looked surprised, but it still didn't remove the smile from her face. She leaned over, pulled her shoes off as she glanced up, and noticed the strawberry lemonade sitting in front of us on the coffee table. Then she said,

"Oh, that looks good. I need some in my life. Did you guys eat dinner yet?" I was confused as well and asked,

"Why are you home so soon?"

She shrugged her shoulders as she walked past the couch and replied from the kitchen as I heard her opening and shutting cabinets.

"The storm moved in and we died. We had too many servers so I offered to go home. They cut me early." I got up, walked over to the kitchen, and asked.

"Hey, how do you feel about me calling our parents to see if they would let all three of us come over for dinner? Would that be a burden on your mom?" Nikki gave me an annoyed look and answered,

"Uh, no, *our* mom always makes more than enough food, plus she would really like that. Would Ryan want to go over there seeing as the last time he got interrogated?" Nikki was still amused by that and laughed so hard her shoulders shook. I laughed a little too and said in a low voice so Ryan couldn't hear me,

"He can handle it. Besides, he needs to learn to if he can't, since I'm his girl now and all." Then I gave Nikki a wink. With wide eyes, she asked,

"Ohhhh… so you're his girl now? Seems right, good."

While she took a big drink of her lemonade, I walked back into the living room and quickly got Ryan to agree to go to dinner again at our parents' house. I motioned with hand gestures for Nikki to call her mom and ask. She pointed to her hair and said,

"I have to blow dry my hair before we go though." A thought struck me suddenly and I walked across the room, leaned into Nikki's ear, and carefully whispered,

"Take the flowers out of my room and put them in yours, just in case." She looked at me and I could see in her eyes she was on board with the plan.

Thirty minutes after Nikki changed her clothes and dried her hair, and the rain let up, we finally pulled into a parking spot outside our parents' apartment. Nikki and I had spent the entirety of the car ride recounting the conversation to Ryan where we had learned that our parents had been married for some time without us knowing. He seemed almost as amused as we did that they kept it a secret for so long.

"Don't judge me, but I think that's kinda romantic of your parents," he said in all seriousness. I wasn't sure why, but it was very attractive to see a muscular marine who was covered in tattoos say something about romance. I thought about it for a moment and realized he was right.

We knocked on the door and Della swung it open as she reached out and pulled us in for a tight hug one by one, squeezing Ryan the tightest and longest. Nikki noticed and joked,

"Are you trying to steal Amy's boyfriend, Mom?" Then before Della could say anything, we heard my dad's loud voice as he approached the door.

"Boyfriend? Who's got a boyfriend?" He walked up behind Della and locked his eyes on Ryan who tensed up immediately. I looked at my dad and said happily,

"Ryan is my boyfriend now." I could tell by my dad's face he approved but he was still trying to put some fear into Ryan. Then he said in a low voice,

"I'll be keeping my eyes on you, young man, so you better not slip up. Wait, don't you live out of state? What are you doing here?" I couldn't keep myself for answering on behalf of Ryan as I replied to my dad.

"He's moving here, bought a property and is working for a military base too." My dad glared at Ryan and asked,

"Is that true?" Ryan swallowed hard and answered,

"Yes Sir." Then Nikki spoke up.

"Can we come in now? Everything is wet out here." With Nikki's question, as quick as the interrogation started, it ended.

Dinner went smoothly and in less than twenty minutes, both my dad and Ryan warmed up to each other. After dinner, Nikki and I started to run the idea of a vow renewal ceremony past Della when Ryan and my dad snuck away to the other room. I assumed they didn't want to hear talk about wedding vows and flowers and so on. Nikki started to yawn so Della suggested,

"You girls look tired, so you probably should head home so you can get some rest." We both agreed and moments later, Ryan and my dad walked back in the room. Then we all walked to the front door to leave. As we were saying our good byes, my dad gently took my arm right before I walked out of the door while Nikki and Ryan were already several feet in front of me. I looked at him concerned and prepared myself for him to say something negative about Ryan. Then with a specific type of love that only a father can have in his eyes, he said,

"Amy, I like that boy. He's a good one." I looked a little

confused and simply replied before I headed home,

"Okay."

I quickly caught up with Nikki and Ryan as we piled in the car and took off back home while I thought about what my dad said the entire drive back.

THIRTY-SEVEN

Close all possibilities, I knew that's what I had to do. Ryan was already on his way back and I knew I had to cut all ties with Dante so he didn't somehow stay in my life and mess things up with Ryan. I tapped on Nikki's door, not afraid I would wake her up as I heard her radio start to play a few minutes earlier. She was an avid listener to the morning show of her favorite station.

"Come in." I opened the door and my eyes fell right on the large bouquet of flowers I asked her to hide in her room for me. She must have heard Ryan leave as she walked across her room to her dresser in a tank top and baby pink boy short panties. I sat on the edge of her bed and said to her,

"Ryan's gone. I need to throw away those flowers, don't I? Maybe even cut off Dante completely?" I didn't know the exact advice Nikki would give me, but a little part of me was hoping she would suggest that I keep my options open, not put all my eggs in one Ryan-basket, something along those lines. Nikki glanced up from her dresser at me with a pair of socks in her hand as she responded,

"There's no maybe about it. Matter of fact, I'm already on it for you. I put a call into Lucca this morning and he's supposed to call me back. I don't really want to talk to Lucca again, but he seems to be able to relay messages to Dante." I wasn't sure what Nikki was trying to say, which she saw in my face as she went on to explain more. "So, all I have to do is tell Lucca you have a husband now and don't live here anymore, and your husband would be very upset to find out Dante is sending you flowers. Lucca would relay that message real quick and problem solved. If you want to." I realized as she spoke it wasn't just a matter of wanting to, but needing to. I told Nikki,

"Yeah, tell Lucca that."

She walked over to the bed and sat down next to me with her socks in her hands as she looked down at her bare knees before she said,

"And this must be the last time I talk to Lucca. It still hurts a little every time I hear his voice. He made his decision when he picked that girl his family knows over me. I have to cut him loose completely, too."

I reached over and put my hand on her shoulder as we just sat there for a few minutes. I wasn't great at saying profound words of wisdom in a time of need. However, I surprised myself when I opened my mouth and said,

"Yes, we both need to cut them out, once and for all. We are just closing a chapter in this story but we have so many more coming down the road." She looked over at me with an appreciative look on her face. Then she said,

"You're right, Amy. It was all an experience, part of our story." Then she continued, "I'm so glad we're sisters. You have been the greatest friend I have ever had." I agreed with her, and for a brief moment, I felt sad thinking of Betsy, and about how I had once thought that about her. Then I realized that in all the years, and even decades I was friends with Betsy, our friendship was always lacking something, and I couldn't figure out what it was until Nikki came into my life.

"I feel the same. Nikki, you are the greatest best friend I've ever had, including Betsy." Nikki grunted and muttered,

"That little heifer. No real friend of any kind sleeps with your man."

I didn't say anything because there was no argument from my side. That philosophy was a pretty open and closed case. At a half attempt to change the conversation I said,

"What did you think of Ryan's haircut?" Nikki's eyes lit up and she responded,

"Wow, it looked hot. He's a good looking guy, Amy, and nice. Score on that for you." I shrugged my shoulders and looked down at my thick thighs as Nikki looked at my expression and asked, "What's with the face?" I shook my head and sighed as I answered,

"I just don't understand why he's into all this chub. I worry he's just playing games with me. Maybe this whole thing is just a joke to him. Maybe I'm just a joke to him." Nikki looked both angry and surprised, as she was quick to reply.

"I'm sure he's not playing with you. He seems really into you, Amy. And I don't know what you're talking about? So what, you have a figure. You tell me you wish you were my size. Well guess what, we are the same size. You have been borrowing my clothes since you've moved in, and you *still* don't think they'll fit you. Amy, you are beautiful, like model beautiful, plus a great person. Ryan sees that. You need to see what he sees."

I looked at her, knowing if I disputed any of what she said, I would get a massive eye roll and another fifteen minute lecture, so I simply replied,

"I think you're probably right."

She glared at me, not quite satisfied but dropped the lecture anyway. I glanced at the clock and stood up walking to the door. I knew Vanessa would call any minute and I wanted to be at my desk near the documents when she did.

"Vanessa is going to call soon. Are you calling Lucca now?" Nikki stood up as well and headed to her closet to get dressed as she replied,

"Yeah."

Moments later, I was sitting at my desk and putting the closing package together as my cell phone rang. I quickly answered as Vanessa's voice came through the other end.

Our conversation lasted less than ten minutes and as I ended the call with her, I realized I would have to keep myself busy so time didn't drag on before Ryan came back for his closing. It was now roughly eight business days until they would most likely be able to close on the property, but it felt like eight years until I would see him again, even though he had just left less than two hours earlier.

I sighed and picked up the phone to call Mike and see how things were going for him with our mother. I could only imagine she was driving him crazy with how demanding she was. I also wanted to make sure he was staying on top of her pain meds and doctor appointments. A few rings later, he answered.

"Hey bro. How's it going for you?" With a happy sound, he exclaimed,

"Hey Sis! Things are going good here. Mom's making a quick recovery. She's almost completely off her pain meds now. The doctors think her recovery is going well and fast too. How about you?"

"That's good, Mike. Me? I'm doing great." Then he quickly said,

"Hey, Mom is right here, and she wants to talk to you. Here she is." Before I could refuse, I heard air blowing on the phone as it was getting shuffled around.

"Amy dear, how are you?" I politely replied.

"I'm really good, Mom. Mike says you're having a quick recovery. That's great." She had slightly more energy in her voice, but overall sounded weaker than usual.

"Oh yes, dear, recovery is going well. Mike says you really like your new job. That's wonderful, Amy. I'm so happy for you." I paused for a moment, waiting for her to ask me if I would be able squeeze in dieting and exercise with this job, or if I had lost any weight. The moments dragged on and finally, she asked, "Amy? Are you still there?"

I cleared my throat, realizing she was not going to ask me about losing weight so I replied,

"Yes. I really like it so far. I get my first paycheck at the end of this week. Everything is going great here. I'm really happy." I made sure to tell her how happy I was, just in case she was set on asking me to move back home. Then to my surprise, she said,

"If you're happy, Amy, then I'm happy for you… Amy?" Once again, I paused for a long moment. This relationship was not the one I had always had with my mother, so I felt I was being tricked or on a hidden camera show.

"What Mom?" With what sounded like sincerity she said,

"I'm very proud of you, Amy. I love you, dear."

I wasn't sure what to say. I couldn't ever remember in my life where my mother told me she was proud of me, let alone combine it with I love you. My eyes filled with tears and I wasn't sure how to respond exactly. Again, I thought she must have been dying.

I love you too, Mom."

We said good-bye and I quickly asked to speak to Mike again to see if she was in fact dying. He laughed and responded,

"No, Mom's not dying. She does miss you though. She has said that every day, Sis, just so you know."

A feeling rose inside me I didn't understand and I said good-bye to Mike and got off the phone as I began to sob. So many emotions flooded me that I couldn't separate them.

It's a strange thing, with a hurricane of emotions, finally to feel loved by your mother for the first time when you're almost thirty.

THIRTY-EIGHT

I did my best to occupy myself to pass the time while I waited for Ryan to come back for his closing. It helped a great deal that we talked for several hours every night. I would spend the majority of my days watching my phone for texts from him or waiting until it got late enough I knew he probably was free to talk for a few hours so I could call. I loved our conversations. The more I learned about him the more admiration I had for him. He was not like any other man I had ever known. He was funny and smart, but most importantly, he seemed honestly to care for me. I found I could tell him absolutely anything. I could talk to him like I couldn't talk with anyone else.

"Is Ryan meeting you there?" I looked up from my dresser into the mirror as the reflection of Nikki leaning against the doorframe looked back at me. I smiled and answered,

"Yeah. How do I look?"

Nikki uncrossed her arms and sauntered over to the dresser as she looked at me with a grin on her face before she replied,

"You look hot. What are you doing after he signs the papers for the inspection? Closing tomorrow or the next day? I can't remember."

I looked at my refection in the mirror. I had a pang of guilt for giving Nikki a hard time about dragging me away from my phone, when I was waiting for Ryan to call the other night, just so she could take me to the salon, but now looking at myself in the mirror, it was worth it. My hair looked amazing and my skin was glowing and clear. I had one of my favorite dresses on in a deep crimson cherry that hugged me in all the right places. I was very slowly starting not to see the hideous fat girl every time I looked in the mirror. She still creeped into my mind every now and then when I looked at my reflection, but she was getting farther off into the distance. I began to wonder how long until she would completely go away, if ever. Nikki's mom, soon to be my mom too, always reminded me that God made us each beautiful in his eyes as his creation. I found her to be a supportive beacon of wisdom and could see more clearly why Nikki was the confident girl she was.

"Closing is tomorrow. He's going to meet me at the place to sign the final inspection papers. The title company wants the signatures today. So first, we're gonna drop them off, and then probably go out to dinner or lunch I guess." I shrugged my shoulders as if I didn't care and it didn't matter what we did. Just seeing him was all I really wanted.

Nikki gave me a funny little wink before she walked toward my bedroom door as she remarked in a playful tone.

"Well, have fun. Don't do anything I wouldn't do."

I picked up my lip-gloss and looked in the mirror with a smile as I responded with a little laugh in my voice.

"Thanks."

The late afternoon sky was cloudy when I pulled up to the front of the building. My heart was pumping with excitement as I spotted Ryan's pick-up truck a few parking spots from the door. I grabbed the file with the inspection papers, and then very slowly I got out of the car so I wouldn't fall or trip in the new strappy heels I had just bought. I had practiced wearing them for an entire day in the apartment as Nikki had suggested, but I quickly realized it was not the same as walking on cement.

I let out a breath and knocked on the door as I noticed he had removed the key code lock box off the door. I saw the shadows of a figure move toward the door through the dingy glass in the large oak doors. He unlocked and pulled open the thick heavy doors as I smiled up at him.

"Hey, Ryan, how was your drive?" He gave me a sly smile and asked,

"So, you're gonna turn into formal Amy now, huh?"

I laughed a little and stepped past him into the space. It seemed a little different with the absence of sun pouring in through the window. It appeared less lively, but also less dirty as the dirt was not as noticeable. I turned around and waved the manila folder in the air as I said in a teasing voice,

"Hot off the press. Who wants to sign some papers?"

He shook his head with a smile on his face and then paused with a little flirtatious look in his eyes. Then he said,

"Okay, so before we turn into business-formal Ryan and Amy, I just want to say you look beautiful, Amy. That's some dress you got there." I blushed a little and smiled as I walked over to one of the shelves left behind, as it was the best flat surface I could find. Then I asked,

"You want to sign so we can drop these off to the title company?"

He had a mischievous look on his face as I reached in my purse to pull out the pen I had brought. I handed it to him as he walked up to the shelf and as I opened the file, he casually remarked,

"Oh, by the way, I have a surprise for you." I snapped my head up as I turned the first page and asked,

"What is it?" He shook his head and pressed his lips tight as if he wasn't going to tell me, so I rolled my eyes and laughed a little as I found the first line for him to sign. I pointed to the empty space and said, "Just sign here above the line that says, Denver Jacob Ryan." I flipped another page, knowing I had to get three signatures total. I found the second required signature page and said as I pointed to the line, "If you agree with the inspection, sign above Denver Jacob Ryan."

He nodded and slowly signed his signature on the line. As I flipped for the next signature, I asked,

"You do agree with the inspection, right?" He laughed a little and answered,

"Yeah, I hope so. I'm signing my name to it."

I flipped to the last page and looked at the bottom where it asked for his signature. I laid it on the counter and pointed my finger to the line.

"Okay, Denver Jacob Ryan, you know what to do."

He put the pen to the paper and I smiled, knowing the big smiles that would come tomorrow and all the days following when he moved close to me.

"Well, Denver Jacob Ryan… is that your real full name?" I glanced at him sideways.

"Yes, ma'am." I continued to look at him and couldn't shake the ring that name had in my mind. Denver Jacob Ryan, Denver Jacob Ryan, Denver… Jacob… Ryan…

I looked at him curious for a moment before I asked,

"Have you always gone by Ryan or just because of the service?"

He looked at me a little confused about my questions as the name continued to ring in my mind. I looked at his eyes and for a moment, which felt like an eternity, I couldn't breathe. I was unintentionally holding my breath. Then, as if I had been hit with a ton of bricks, I blurted out,

"Wait a minute!.. Noodle arm Jake?" I stared at him like a wild woman that had just spent ten years in the wilderness and was seeing a person for the first time. He chuckled and said,

"I haven't been called that for a really long time."

I could hardly speak. I was bewildered. I managed to ramble a few words from my mouth.

"Noodle arm Jake, as in the same Jake that rode the school bus with me and Betsy? The same scrawny kid that could hardly open his own locker?" He nodded his head and asked in a confused tone.

"I thought you knew this whole time that we went to grade school together. You're telling me that you didn't know I was Jake from school this whole time we've been talking?"

I shook my head a million miles an hour and with my eyes getting wider, I exclaimed,

"Nope! I mean, let's be honest, you've changed a lot. Wow, this is a lot to process." I put my hands up to my head and with a long breath I continued, "Well, you look really good, Jake." We smiled at each other, and since hindsight is twenty-twenty, I understood why his eyes felt so comforting and familiar when I looked at them. Then in a serious voice, he said,

"I'm sorry, Amy, I really thought you knew it was me the whole time. Do you still want to be my girl?" His question was so odd to hear and I didn't understand it fully, but I answered anyway.

"Of course I do. Was that the surprise you had for me?"

He shook his head again and with a smile, he reached out and took my hand as he led me to the back room he said,

"No, I have it here in the back."

My heart began to beat for the surprise, but my mind wouldn't stop pulling up memories from school and every encounter with young Jake it could recall. I stopped in my tracks and unintendedly dropped his hand as I stared at it. Then I exclaimed, "

When did you get this?" I walked over and touched the top of it as tears of joy started slowly to swell up in my eyes. The vintage vanity looked even more beautiful than I had remembered it. I glanced around and noticed four other pieces in the back room, all pieces I had remarked that I had really liked. I had not thought he had been paying that close of attention during our visit to the store. I spun around to see a pleased look on his face. Then I asked,

"When did you get this? How did you get it here? How are you going to store stuff for your bar with these in this room?"

He laughed a little and took a few steps towards me as he also reached over and touched the top of the vanity.

"I never said I was buying this space for a bar. I'm done with that. I only bought the other bar because it was a business opportunity that fell in my lap at the time." Very confused I asked,

"What did you buy this building for?"

He glanced at me with a look on his face as if he was surprised I didn't understand. Then he said with a smile,

"This space is for you, Amy. You can put all your supplies back here and refinish whenever you want, and if you choose to sell some pieces, you can throw them in the front of the store. I'm sure you'll get buyers." I began to blink to try to prevent the tears that I felt coming up to my eyes again, but it was no use. I shook my head in disbelief. Then he pointed up quickly and said, "I'm having them install a vent fan next week for the fumes and stuff." Only one word came to my lips, one question that I couldn't shake.

"Why?"

He looked up at the ceiling and opened his mouth to explain the benefit of a ceiling vent fan when I shook my head and asked again.

"No… I mean why are you doing all this for me?" Once again, he looked confused, but he answered,

"Because, I have been crazy about you since I was fourteen, Amy. I had the biggest crush on you. I would see you walk down the halls and I'd say to myself, she's the most beautiful girl in this school. When Kara was so nasty to me on the bus and you stood up to her… well, no one has ever had my back like that, so I knew for sure you were my girl. Kara was so nasty. I had just spent that night listening to my mom cry because of my dad, so Kara got me good that day. If you hadn't said something to her, I know I would have cried like crazy, then been made fun of even more." He paused for a long second as I stared at him. Then he took a breath and finished. "We got off that bus and I knew I wanted to marry you one day. There's no one like you, Amy."

I stared at him, surprised by this revelation. I had a few little memories that came to my mind of him looking at me in the hall or during lunch, but I had never really thought anything about it. I wasn't sure how to respond to such a decoration, so I simply said,

"Really?"

He shook his head a little with a smile and then a more serious look crossed his face as he continued,

"Yeah. I only moved back close to our hometown and bought that bar because I was going to look you up to try and see if I could get the courage to ask you out. But after I signed the papers for the bar, I had newspaper on the floor for the construction work and saw your post in the paper for your engagement. It was like reading my own obituary. I thought I had lost my chance for good."

I hated all the work I went through to take that stupid picture with Chad for the engagement announcement. I looked at Ryan and said,

"Well, you haven't lost your chance. I think Chad was never supposed to be for me anyways."

He reached past me and tapped the top of the vanity before he said,

"Open the top drawer, Amy."

I turned around and slowly opened the top drawer and found a little gray box sitting in the middle of the small drawer. I picked up the box and opened it to see a titanium ring with two hearts that inter-locked with each other, diamonds along the band. My heart got stuck in my chest as I swallowed the lump in my throat and coughed. He quickly spoke up.

"It's not an engagement ring. It's a 'would you be-my-girl when-you're-ready ring'. I just want you to know I'm not going anywhere, Amy."

I looked at him hardly able to speak, before I looked down and slid the ring on my finger, feeling a hundred times happier than I did when I had gotten a ring from Chad.

I looked back up at him and just smiled as he smiled back at me before he cleared his throat and asked,

"You wanna take the papers over to the title company? Maybe go get something to eat?"

I nodded my head, still unable to speak as we headed to the front of the space. We reached the front door and he started to open the door, before he quickly shut it and locked it. Pulling me back into the room, he looked down at me and put both hands on my arms. I glanced at the door alarmed that he had acted so abrupt in shutting and locking door. I asked,

"Is there someone outside? Are we in danger?"

He shook his head no and with a serious look on his face, he said,

"No… I don't mean to sound creepy, but I've thought about this moment since I was fifteen, Amy… I can't take it anymore, we will *not* be interrupted again."

I looked up into his eyes and smiled as he reached out and slid my hair off my shoulders. Then he smiled down at me and a few moments later, my knees felt weak as I felt his soft lips against mine. A wave of warmth flooded throughout my body as my heart pounded while I tasted the sweet mint in his mouth and smelled the clean aroma of his after-shave. I let my lips linger on his for a while longer before I pulled back and looked into his eyes as I said,

"Jake."

He smiled wide hearing me call him by his childhood name. Then he said,

"I'm crazy about you Amy, I sure do love you."

I let my hand slide down his arm to find his hand as I wrapped my fingers comfortably around his, like they finally found home. I could feel the coolness of the metal ring against my skin and my lips curled up in the most genuine smile I'd had in a long while. Then I replied,

"Same here."

Made in the USA
Lexington, KY
16 September 2018